THE
BARTIMAEUS
TRILOGY
BOOK THREE

Ptolemy's Gate

THE
BARTIMAEUS
TRILOGY
BOOK THREE

Ptolemy's Gate

JONATHAN STROUD

DISNEY • HYPERION
LOS ANGELES   NEW YORK

First U.S. Paperback edition, January 2007
7 9 10 8 6
FAC-025438-18325
Printed in the United States of America
This book is set in 12-point Bembo.
Reinforced binding

Library of Congress Cataloging-in-Publication Control Number: 2005052655
ISBN-13: 978-0-7868-3868-4
ISBN-10: 0-7868-3868-X

Visit www.DisneyBooks.com

SUSTAINABLE
FORESTRY
INITIATIVE

Certified Chain of Custody
Promoting Sustainable Forestry

www.sfiprogram.org
SFI-01054

The SFI label applies to the text stock

For Isabelle, with love

The Main Characters

THE MAGICIANS

Mr. Rupert Devereaux	Prime Minister of Great Britain and the Empire, and acting Chief of Police
Mr. Carl Mortensen	Minister of War
Ms. Helen Malbindi	Foreign Minister
Ms. Jessica Whitwell	Security Minister
Mr. Bruce Collins	Home Secretary
Mr. John Mandrake	Information Minister
Ms. Jane Farrar	Deputy Police Chief
Mr. Quentin Makepeace	A playwright; author of *Petticoats and Rifles* and other works
Mr. Harold Button	Magician, scholar, and book collector
Mr. Sholto Pinn	A merchant; proprietor of Pinn's Accoutrements of Piccadilly
Mr. Clive Jenkins	Magician Second Level, Department of Internal Affairs
Ms. Rebecca Piper	Assistant to Mr. Mandrake, Information Ministry

THE COMMONERS

Ms. Kitty Jones	A student and barmaid
Mr. Clem Hopkins	An itinerant scholar
Mr. Nicholas Drew	A political agitator
Mr. George Fox	Proprietor of the Frog Inn, Chiswick
Ms. Rosanna Lutyens	A private tutor

THE SPIRITS

Bartimaeus	A djinni—in service to Mr. Mandrake
Ascobol	
Cormocodran	
Mwamba	Greater djinn—in service to Mr. Mandrake
Hodge	
Purip	
Fritang	Lesser djinn—in service to Mr. Mandrake

Part One

Alexandria: 125 B.C.

The assassins dropped into the palace grounds at midnight, four fleet shadows dark against the wall. The fall was high, the ground was hard; they made no more sound on impact than the pattering of rain. Three seconds they crouched there, low and motionless, sniffing at the air. Then away they stole, through the dark gardens, among the tamarisks and date palms, toward the quarters where the boy lay at rest. A cheetah on a chain stirred in its sleep; far away in the desert, jackals cried.

They went on pointed toe-tips, leaving no trace in the long wet grass. Their robes flittered at their backs, fragmenting their shadows into wisps and traces. What could be seen? Nothing but leaves shifting in the breeze. What could be heard? Nothing but the wind sighing among the palm fronds. No sight, no noise. A crocodile djinni, standing sentry at the sacred pool, was undisturbed though they passed within a scale's breadth of his tail. For humans, it wasn't badly done.

The heat of the day was a memory; the air was chill. Above the palace a cold round moon shone down, slathering silver across the roofs and courtyards.[1]

Away beyond the wall, the great city murmured in the night: wheels on dirt roads, distant laughter from the pleasure district along the quay, the tide lapping at its stones. Lamplight shone in windows, embers glowed on roof hearths, and from the top of the tower beside the harbor gate the great watch fire burned its message out to sea. Its image danced like imp-light on the waves.

At their posts, the guards played games of chance. In the pillared halls, the servants slept on beds of rushes. The palace gates were locked by triple bolts, each thicker than a man. No eyes were turned to the western gardens, where death came calling, secret as a scorpion, on four pairs of silent feet.

The boy's window was on the first floor of the palace. Four black shadows hunched beneath the wall. The leader made a signal. One by one they pressed against the stonework; one by one they began to climb, suspended by their fingertips and the nails of their big toes.[2] In this manner they had scaled marble

---

[1] This was one of the peculiarities of their sect: they acted only when the moon was full. It made their tasks more difficult, their challenge greater. And they had never failed. Aside from this, they wore only black, avoided meat, wine, women, and the playing of wind instruments, and curiously ate no cheese save that made from the milk of goats bred on their distant desert mountain. Before each job they fasted for a day, meditated by staring unblinking at the ground, then ate small cakes of hashish and cumin seed, without water, until their throats glowed yellow. It's a wonder they ever killed anyone.

[2] All horrid and curved they were, filed sharp like eagles' talons. The assassins took good care of their feet, because of their importance in their work. They were washed frequently, rubbed with pumice, and marinated in sesame oil until the skin was soft as eiderdown.

columns and waterfalls of ice from Massilia to Hadhramaut; the rough stone blocks were easy for them now. Up they went, like bats upon a cave wall. Moonlight glinted on bright things gripped between their teeth.

The first of the assassins reached the window ledge: he sprang tigerlike upon it and peered into the chamber.

Moonlight spilled across the room; the pallet was lit as if by day. The boy lay sleeping, motionless as one already dead. His dark hair fell loose upon the cushions, his pale lamb's throat shone against the silks.

The assassin took his dagger from between his teeth. With quiet deliberation, he surveyed the room, gauging its extent and the possibility of traps. It was large, shadowy, empty of ostentation. Three pillars supported the ceiling. In the distance stood a door of teak, barred on the inside. A chest, half filled with clothes, sat open against the wall. He saw a royal chair draped with a discarded cloak, sandals lying on the floor, an onyx basin filled with water. A faint trace of perfume hung on the air. The assassin, for whom such scents were decadent and corrupt, wrinkled his nose.[3]

His eyes narrowed; he reversed the dagger, holding it between finger and thumb by its shining, gleaming tip. It quivered once, twice. He was gauging the range here—he'd never missed a target yet, from Carthage to old Colchis. Every knife he'd thrown had found its throat.

His wrist flickered; the silver arc of the knife's flight cut the

---

[3] The sect avoided perfumes for practical reasons, preferring to coat themselves with scents appropriate to the conditions of each job: pollen in the gardens, incense in the temples, sand-dust in the deserts, dung and offal in the towns. They were dedicated fellows.

air in two. It landed with a soft noise, hilt-deep in the cushion, an inch from the child's neck.

The assassin paused in doubt, still crouched upon the sill. The back of his hands bore the crisscross scars that marked him as an adept of the dark academy. An adept never missed his target. The throw had been exact, precisely calibrated ... yet it had missed. Had the victim moved a crucial fraction? Impossible—the boy was fast asleep. From his person he pulled a second dagger.[4] Another careful aim (the assassin was conscious of his brothers behind and below him on the wall: he felt the grim weight of their impatience). A flick of the wrist, a momentary arc—

With a soft noise, the second dagger landed in the cushion, an inch to the *other* side of the prince's neck. As he slept, perhaps he dreamed—a smile twitched ghostlike at the corners of his mouth.

Behind the black gauze of the scarf that masked his face, the assassin frowned. From within his tunic he drew a strip of fabric, twined tightly into a cord. In seven years since the Hermit had ordered his first kill, his garrote had never snapped, his hands had never failed him.[5] With leopard's stealth, he slid from the sill and stole across the moonlit floor.

---

[4] I won't say *where* he pulled it from. Let's just say that the knife had hygiene issues as well as being quite sharp.

[5] The Hermit of the Mountain trained his followers in numerous methods of foolproof murder. They could use garrotes, swords, knives, batons, ropes, poisons, discs, bolas, pellets, and arrows inimitably, as well as being pretty handy with the evil eye. Death by fingertip and toe-flex was also taught, and the furtive nip was a specialty. Stomach-threads and tapeworms were available for advanced students. And the best of it was that it was all guilt-free: each assassination was justified and condoned by a powerful religious disregard for the sanctity of other people's lives.

In his bed the boy murmured something. He stirred beneath his sheet. The assassin froze rigid, a black statue in the center of the room.

Behind, at the window, two of his companions insinuated themselves upon the sill. They waited, watching.

The boy gave a little sigh and fell silent once more. He lay faceup among his cushions, a dagger's hilt protruding on either side.

Seven seconds passed. The assassin moved again. He stole around behind the cushions, looping the ends of the cord around his hands. Now he was directly above the child; he bent swiftly, set the cord upon the sleeping throat—

The boy's eyes opened. He reached up a hand, grasped the assassin's left wrist and, without exertion, swung him headfirst into the nearest wall, snapping his neck like a reed stalk. He flung off his silken sheet and, with a bound, stood free, facing the window.

Up on the sill, silhouetted against the moon, two assassins hissed like rock snakes. Their comrade's death was an affront to their collective pride. One plucked from his robe a pipe of bone; from a cavity between his teeth he sucked a pellet, eggshell thin, filled with poison. He set the pipe to his lips, blew once: the pellet shot across the room, directed at the child's heart.

The boy gave a skip; the pellet shattered against a pillar, spattering it with liquid. A plume of green vapor drizzled through the air.

The two assassins leaped into the room; one this way, the other that. Each now held a scimitar in his hand; they spun them in complex flourishes about their heads, dark eyes scanning the room.

The boy was gone. The room was still. Green poison nibbled at the pillar; the stones fizzed with it.

Never once in seven years, from Antioch to Pergamum, had these assassins lost a victim.[6] Their arms stopped moving; they slowed their pace, listening intently, tasting the air for the taint of fear.

From behind a pillar in the center of the room came the faintest scuffling, like a mouse flinching in its bed of straw. The assassins glanced at each other; they inched forward, toe-tip by toe-tip, scimitars raised. One went to the right, past the crumpled body of his fellow. One went to the left, beside the golden chair, draped with the cloak of kings. They moved like ghosts around the margins of the room, circling in upon the pillar from both sides.

Behind the pillar, a furtive movement: a boy's shape hiding in the shadows. Both assassins saw it; both raised their scimitars and darted in, from left, from right. Both struck with mantis speed.

A dual cry, gargling and ragged. From around the pillar came a stumbling, rolling mess of arms and legs: the two assassins, locked together in a tight embrace, each one skewered on the other's sword. They fell forward into the pool of moonlight in the center of the chamber, twitched gently, and lay quiet.

Silence. The windowsill hung vacant, nothing in it but the moon. A cloud passed across the bright round disc, blacking out the bodies on the floor. The signal fire in the harbor tower cast

---

[6] And they didn't intend to start now. The Hermit was known to be pretty sniffy about disciples who returned in failure. There was a wall of the institute layered with their skins—an ingenious display that encouraged vigor in his students, as well as nicely keeping out the drafts.

faint redness on the sky. All was still. The cloud drifted out to sea, the light returned. From behind the pillar walked the boy, bare feet soundless on the floor, his body stiff and wary, as if he sensed a pressure in the room. With careful steps, he neared the window. Slowly, slowly, closer, closer . . . he saw the shrouded mass of gardens, the trees and sentry towers. He noticed the texture of the sill, the way the moonlight caught its contours. Closer . . . now his hands rested on the stone itself. He leaned forward to look down into the courtyard at the bottom of the wall. His thin white throat extended out. . . .

Nothing. The courtyard was empty. The wall below was sheer and smooth, its stones picked out by moonlight. The boy listened to the quietness. He tapped his fingers on the sill, shrugged, and turned inside.

Then the fourth assassin, clinging like a thin black spider to the stones *above* the window, dropped down behind him. His feet made the noise of feathers falling into snow. The boy heard; he twisted, turned. A knife flashed, swiped, was deflected by a desperate hand—its edge clinked against stone. Iron fingers grappled at the boy's neck; his legs were knocked from under him. He fell, landing hard upon the floor. The assassin's weight was on him. His hands were pinioned. He could not move.

The knife descended. This time it met its mark.

So it had finished as it must. Crouching above the body of the boy, the assassin allowed himself a breath—his first since his colleagues had met their ends. He sat back on his sinewy haunches, loosened his grip upon the knife, and let the boy's wrist drop free. He inclined his head in the traditional mark of respect to the fallen victim.

At which point the boy reached up and plucked the knife from the center of his chest. The assassin blinked in consternation.

"Not silver, you see," the boy said. "Mistake." He raised his hand.

An explosion in the room. Green sparks cascaded from the window.

The boy rose to his feet and tossed the knife upon the pallet. He adjusted his kilt and blew some flakes of ash from his arms. Then he coughed loudly.

The faintest of scrapings. Across the room the golden chair shifted. The cloak draped over it was nudged aside. Out from between its legs scrambled another boy, identical to the first, though flushed and tousled from many hours of hiding.

He stood over the bodies of the assassins, breathing hard. Then he stared up at the ceiling. On it was the blackened outline of a man. It had a kind of startled look.

The boy lowered his gaze to the impassive doppelgänger watching him across the moonlit room. I gave a mock salute.

Ptolemy brushed the dark hair from his eyes and bowed.

"Thank you, Rekhyt," he said.

I

Times change.

Once, long ago, I was second to none. I could whirl through the air on a wisp of cloud and churn up dust storms with my passing. I could slice through mountains, raise castles on pillars of glass, fell forests with a single breath. I carved temples from the sinews of the earth and led armies against the legions of the dead, so that the harpers of a dozen lands played music in my memory and the chroniclers of a dozen centuries scribbled down my exploits. Yes! I was Bartimaeus— cheetah quick, strong as a bull elephant, deadly as a striking krait!

But that was then.

And now . . . well, *right* now I was lying in the middle of a midnight road, flat on my back and getting flatter. Why? Because on top of me was an upturned building. Its weight bore down. Muscles strained, tendons popped; try as I might, I could not push free.

In principle there's nothing shameful about struggling when a building falls upon you. I've had such problems before; it's part of the job description.[1] But it *does* help if the edifice in

---

[1] There was the time when a small section of Khufu's Great Pyramid collapsed upon me one moonless night during the fifteenth year of its construction. I was guarding the zone that my group was working on, when several limestone blocks tumbled down from the top, transfixing me painfully by one of my extremities. Exactly how it happened was never resolved, though my suspicions were directed at my old chum Faquarl, who was working with a rival group on the opposite side. I made no outward complaint, but bided my time while my essence healed. Later, when Faquarl was returning across the Western Desert with some Nubian gold, I invoked a mild sandstorm, causing him to lose the treasure and incur the pharaoh's wrath. It took him a couple of years to sift all the pieces from the dunes.

question is glamorous and large. And in this case, the fearsome construction that had been ripped from its foundations and hurled upon me from a great height was neither big nor sumptuous. It wasn't a temple wall or a granite obelisk. It wasn't the marbled roof of an emperor's palace.

No. The object that was pinning me haplessly to the ground, like a butterfly on a collector's tray, was of twentieth-century origin and of very specific function.

Oh, all right, it was a public lavatory. Quite sizable, mind, but even so. I was glad no harpers or chroniclers happened to be passing.

In mitigation, I must report that the lavatory in question had concrete walls and a very thick iron roof, the cruel aura of which helped weaken my already feeble limbs. And there were doubtless various pipes and cisterns and desperately heavy taps inside, all adding to the total mass. But it was still a pretty poor show for a djinni of my stature to be squashed by it. In fact, the abject humiliation bothered me more than the crushing weight.

All around me the water from the snapped and broken pipework trickled away mournfully into the gutters. Only my head projected free of one of the concrete walls; my body was entirely trapped.[2]

So much for the negatives. The good side was that I was unable to rejoin the battle that was taking place up and down the suburban street.

----

[2] The obvious solution would have been to change form—into a wraith, say, or a swirl of smoke, and just drift clear. But there were two problems. One: I found it hard to change shape these days, very hard, even at the best of times. Two: the considerable downward pressure would have blown my essence apart the moment I softened it to make the change.

It was a fairly low-key sort of battle, especially on the first plane. Nothing much could be seen. The house lights were all out, the electric street lamps had been tied in knots; the road was dark as an inkstone, a solid slab of black. A few stars shone coldly overhead. Once or twice indistinct blue-green lights appeared and faded, like explosions far off underwater.

Things hotted up on the second plane, where two rival flocks of birds could be seen wheeling and swooping at each other, buffeting savagely with wings, beaks, claws, and tails. Such loutish behavior would have been reprehensible among seagulls or other down-market fowl; the fact that these were eagles made it all the more shocking.

On the higher planes the bird guises were discarded altogether, and the true shapes of the fighting djinn came into focus.[3] Seen from this perspective, the night sky was veritably awash with rushing forms, contorted shapes, and sinister activity.

Fair play was entirely disregarded. I saw one spiked knee go crunching into an opponent's belly, sending him spinning away behind a chimney to recover. Disgraceful! If I'd been up there I'd have had no truck with that.[4]

But I wasn't up there. I'd been put out of action.

Now, if it had been an afrit or marid who'd done the damage, I could have lived with it. But it wasn't. In fact

---

[3] Truer, anyway. At bottom, we are all alike in our seeping formlessness, but every spirit has a "look" that suits them, and which they use to represent themselves while on Earth. Our essences are molded into these personal shapes on the higher planes, while—on the lower ones—we adopt guises that are appropriate to the given situation. Listen, I'm sure I've told you all this before.

[4] I'd have kneed him first, then stuck a wingtip in his eye, while kicking his shin for good measure. Much more effective. The techniques of these young djinn were so inefficient, it pained me.

my conqueror was none but a third-level djinni, the kind I could normally roll up in my pocket and smoke after dinner. I could still see her now from where I lay, her nimble feminine grace rather undermined by her pig's head and the long rake she clutched in her trotters. There she was, standing on a post-box, laying left and right with such brio that the government forces, of which I was nominally a part, backed off and left her well alone. She was a formidable customer, with experience in Japan if her kimono was anything to go by. In truth, I'd been misled by her rustic appearance and had ambled close without upping my Shields. Before I knew it, there was a piercing oink, a blur of movement, and—*whump!*—she'd left me pinned in the road, too weary to break free.

Little by little, however, my side was gaining the upper hand. See! Here strode Cormocodran, snapping off a lamppost and swinging it like a twig; there raced Hodge, loosing off a volley of poison darts. The enemy dwindled and began to adopt ever more fatalistic guises. I saw several large insects buzzing and dodging, one or two wisps twisting frantically, a couple of rats heading for the hills. Only the she-pig stubbornly maintained her original appearance. My colleagues surged forward. One beetle went down in a corkscrew cloud of smoke; a wisp was blown apart by a double Detonation. The enemy fled; even the pig realized the game was up. She leaped gracefully onto a porch, somersaulted up onto a roof, and vanished. The victorious djinn set off in hot pursuit.

It was quiet in the street. Water trickled past my ears. From topknot to toes, my essence was one long ache. I gave a heart-felt sigh.

"Dear me," a voice chuckled. "A damsel in distress."

I should have mentioned that in contrast to all the centaurs and ogres at my side, I'd been wearing a human guise that night. It happened to be that of a girl: slender, long dark hair, feisty expression. Not based on anybody in particular, of course.

The speaker appeared around the edge of the public convenience and paused to sharpen a nail against a snaggy bit of pipe. No delicate guise for him; as usual he was decked out as a one-eyed giant, with lumpy muscles and long blond hair braided in a complex and faintly girly way. He wore a shapeless blue-gray smock that would have been considered hideous in a medieval fishing village.

"A poor sweet damsel, too frail to pry herself free." The cyclops considered one of his nails carefully; finding it a little long, he bit at it savagely with his small sharp teeth and rounded it off against the pebbledash wall of the lavatory.

"Mind helping me up?" I inquired.

The cyclops looked up and down the empty road. "Better watch out, love," he said, leaning casually on the building so that its downward pressure increased. "There's dangerous characters abroad tonight. Djinn and foliots . . . and naughty imps, who might do you a mischief."

"Can it, Ascobol," I snarled. "You know full well it's me."

The cyclops's single eye batted becomingly under its layer of mascara. *"Bartimaeus?"* he said in wonder. "Can it possibly be . . . ? Surely the great Bartimaeus would not be so easily snared! You must be some imp or mouler cheekily adopting his voice and . . . But, no—I am wrong! It *is* you." He raised his eyebrow in an affectation of shock. "Incredible! To think the noble Bartimaeus has come to this! The master will be *sorely* disappointed."

I summoned my last reserves of dignity. "All masters are

temporary," I replied. "All humiliations likewise. I bide my time."

"Of course, of course." Ascobol swung his apelike arms and did a little pirouette. "Well spoken, Bartimaeus! You do not let your decline depress you. No matter that your great days are over, that you are now as redundant as a will-o'-the-wisp![5] No matter that your task tomorrow is as likely to be damp-dusting our master's bedroom as roaming free upon the air. You are an example to us all."

I smiled, showing my white teeth. "Ascobol," I said, "it is not *I* who have declined, but my adversaries. I have fought with Faquarl of Sparta, with Tlaloc of Tollan, with clever Tchue of the Kalahari—our conflicts split the earth, gouged rivers. I survived. Who is my enemy now? A knock-kneed cyclops in a skirt. When I get out from here, I don't see *this* new conflict lasting long."

The cyclops started back, as if stung. "Such cruel threats! You should be ashamed. We are on the same side, are we not? Doubtless you have good reasons for skulking out the fight under this restroom. Being polite, I will not trouble to inquire, though I may say that you lack your normal courtesy."

"Two years' continual service has worn it all away," I said. "I am left irritable and jaded, with a perpetual itch in my essence that I cannot scratch. And that makes me dangerous, as you will shortly learn. Now, for the last time, Ascobol, get this off."

Well, there were a few more tuts and pouts, but my postur-

---

[5] *Will-o'-the-wisps:* small spirits who struggle to keep up with the times. Visible as flickering flames on the first plane (although revealed on others to be more like capering squid), wisps were once employed by magicians to lure trespassers off remote paths into pits or quags. Cities changed all that; urban wisps have now been forced into lurking over open manhole covers, to rather less effect.

ing had its effect. With a single shrug of his hairy shoulders, the cyclops levered the lavatory up and off me, sending it clattering away onto the opposite pavement. A somewhat corrugated girl got unsteadily to her feet.

"At last," I said. "You took your own sweet time about it."

The cyclops plucked a bit of debris from his smock. "Sorry," he said, "but I was too busy winning the battle to help you out before. Still, all's well. Our master will be pleased—by *my* efforts, anyhow." He glanced at me sidelong.

Now that I was vertical I had no intention of squabbling further. I considered the damage to the houses all around. Not too bad. A few broken roofs, smashed windows . . . The skirmish had been successfully contained. "A French lot?" I asked.

The cyclops shrugged, which was some feat given that he lacked a neck. "Maybe. Possibly the Czechs or Spanish. Who can tell? They're all nibbling at us nowadays. Well, time presses, and I must check on the pursuit. I leave you to nurse your aches and pains, Bartimaeus. Why not try peppermint tea or a camomile footbath, like other geriatrics? Adieu!"

The cyclops hitched up his skirts and, with a ponderous spring, launched himself into the air. Wings appeared on his back; with great plowing strokes he drew away. He had all the grace of a filing cabinet, but at least he'd got the energy to fly. I hadn't. Not until I'd had a breather, anyhow.

The dark-haired girl crept across to a broken square of chimney in a nearby garden. Slowly, with the gasps and gingerly movements of an invalid, she slumped down into a sitting position and cupped her head in her hands. She closed her eyes.

Just a brief rest. Five minutes would do.

Time passed, dawn came. The cold stars faded in the sky.

2

As had become his custom in recent months, the great magician John Mandrake took his breakfast in his parlor, seated in the wicker chair beside the window. The heavy curtains had been carelessly drawn back; the sky beyond was gray and leaden and a sinewy mist threaded its way between the trees of the square.

The small circular table before him was carved from Lebanese cedar. When warmed by sunlight, it gave off a pleasant fragrance, but on this particular morning the wood was dark and cold. Mandrake poured coffee into his glass, removed the silver cover from his plate, and set upon his curried eggs and bacon. In a rack behind the toast and the gooseberry conserve sat a crisply folded newspaper and an envelope with a blood-red seal. Mandrake took a swig of coffee with his left hand; with his right he flicked the newspaper open on the table. He glanced at the front page, grunted dismissively, and reached for the envelope. An ivory paperknife hung from a peg upon the rack; flinging down his fork, Mandrake slit the envelope with one easy motion and drew out a folded parchment. He read this with care, brows puckering into a frown. Then he refolded it, stuffed it back into the envelope, and with a sigh returned to his meal.

A knock at the door; with mouth half full of bacon, Mandrake gave a muffled command. The door opened silently and a young, slim woman stepped diffidently through, a briefcase in her hand.

She halted. "I'm sorry, sir," she began. "Am I too early?"

"Not at all, Piper, not at all." He waved her over, indicated a chair on the other side of his breakfast table. "Have you eaten?"

"Yes, sir." She sat. She wore a dark blue skirt and jacket with a crisp white shirt. Her straight brown hair was scraped away from her forehead and clipped at the back of her head. She settled the briefcase on her lap.

Mandrake speared a forkful of curried egg. "Forgive me if I keep eating," he said. "I was up until three, responding to the latest disturbance. Kent, this time."

Ms. Piper nodded. "I heard, sir. There was a memo at the ministry. Was it contained?"

"Yes; as far as my globe could tell, at any rate. I sent a few demons down. Well, we shall see presently. What have you got for me today?"

She unclipped the briefcase and drew out some papers. "A number of proposals from the junior ministers, sir, regarding the propaganda campaigns in the outlying regions. For your approval. Some new poster ideas . . ."

"Let's see." He took a gulp of coffee, held out a hand. "Anything else?"

"The minutes of the last Council meeting—"

"I'll read that later. Posters first." He scanned the topmost page. "'Sign up to serve your country and see the world' . . . What's *that* supposed to mean? More like a holiday brochure than recruitment. Far too soft . . . Keep talking, Piper—I'm still listening."

"We've got the latest frontline reports from America, sir. I've ordered them a little. We should be able to make another story out of the Boston siege."

"Stressing the heroic attempt, not the abject failure, I trust. . . ." Balancing the papers on his knee, he smeared some gooseberry conserve upon a piece of toast. "Well, I'll try writing something later. . . . Now then, this one's okay—'Defend the mother country and make your name' . . . Good. They're suggesting a farm-boy type looking manly, which is fine, but how about putting his family group—say, parents and little sister—in the background, looking vulnerable and admiring? Play the domestic card."

Ms. Piper nodded eagerly. "Could show his wife too, sir."

"No. We're after the single ones. It's the wives who are most troublesome when they don't come back." He crunched on his toast. "Any other messages?"

"One from Mr. Makepeace, sir. Came by imp. Wonders if you'll drop by and see him this morning."

"Can't. Too busy. There'll be time later."

"His imp also dropped off this flyer. . . ." With a rueful face, Ms. Piper held up a lilac-colored paper. "It's advertising the premiere of his play later this week. *From Wapping to Westminster*, it's called. The story of our Prime Minister's rise to glory. An evening we will never forget, apparently."

Mandrake gave a groan. "If only we could. Put it in the bin. We've got better things to do than discuss theater. What else?"

"Mr. Devereaux has sent a memo around too. Owing to the 'troublesome times,' sir, he's placed the nation's most important treasures under special guard in the vaults of Whitehall. They will remain there until he says otherwise."

Mandrake looked up then, frowning. "Treasures? Such as what?"

"He doesn't say. I wonder if it'll be—"

"It'll be the Staff and the Amulet and the other grade-one items." He hissed briefly through his teeth. "That's not what he should be doing, Piper. We need them *used*."

"Yes, sir. There's also this from Mr. Devereaux." She brought out a slender packet.

The magician eyed it grimly. "Not another toga?"

"A mask, sir. For the party this evening."

With a cry, he indicated the envelope in the rack. "I've already got the invitation. It beggars belief: the war's going badly, the Empire's teetering on the brink, and all our Prime Minister can think about is plays and parties. All right. Keep it with the documents. I'll take it along. The posters seem okay." He handed back the papers. "Maybe not snappy enough. . . ." He thought for a moment, nodded. "Got a pen? Try 'Fight for Freedom and the British Way.' Doesn't mean anything, but it sounds good."

Ms. Piper considered it. "I think it's rather profound, sir."

"Excellent. Then the commoners'll snap it up." He stood, dabbed his mouth with a napkin, and tossed it down upon the tray. "Well, we'd better see how the demons have been getting on. No, no, Piper, please—after you."

If Ms. Piper regarded her employer with more than a little wide-eyed admiration, she was by no means alone among the women of the elite. John Mandrake was an attractive young man, and the scent of power hung about him, sweet and intoxicating, like honeysuckle in the evening air. He was of medium height, slender of body, and swift and confident in action. His pale, slim face presented an intriguing paradox, combining extreme youth—he was still only seventeen years old—with experience and authority. His eyes were dark and quick and serious, his forehead prematurely lined.

His intellectual self-assurance, which had once perilously outstripped his other skills, had now been bolstered by a certain social poise. To peers and inferiors alike he was courteous and charming at all times, although also somewhat remote, as if distracted by an inner melancholy. Alongside the crude appetites and eccentricities of his fellow ministers, this subdued detachment attained an elegance that only added to his mystique.

Mandrake wore his dark hair close in a military crop—a conscious innovation to honor the men and women still at war. It had been a successful gesture: spies noted that, among commoners, he was the most popular magician. His haircut had thus been mimicked by many others, while his dark suits had likewise inspired a brief vogue. He no longer bothered with a tie: the collar of his shirt was casually unbuttoned.

Mr. Mandrake was considered by his rivals to be formidably, indeed dangerously, talented, and—following his promotion to Information Minister—they responded accordingly. But each attempted assassination had been cursorily rebuffed: djinn failed to return, booby traps rebounded on the sender, hexes snapped and withered. At last, tiring of this, Mandrake made a point of publicly challenging any hidden enemy to come forward and tackle him in magical combat. No one answered his call, and his standing rose higher than ever.

He lived in an elegant Georgian town house surrounded by other elegant Georgian town houses on a broad and pleasant square. It was half a mile from Whitehall, and sufficiently far from the river to escape its smell in summer. The square was a generous expanse of beech trees and shady walkways, with an open green in the center. It was quiet and unfrequented, though never unobserved. Gray-uniformed police patrolled the perimeter by day; after dark, demons in the form of owls and nightjars flitted quietly from tree to tree.

This security was due to the inhabitants of the square. It was home to several of London's greatest magicians. On the south side Mr. Collins, the recently appointed Home Secretary, dwelt in a cream-colored house decorated with fake pillars and buxom caryatids. To the northwest sprawled the grandiose pile of the War Minister, Mr. Mortensen, with a golden dome glinting upon the roof.

John Mandrake's residence was less ostentatious. A slender four-story building, painted buttercup-yellow, it was reached by a row of white marble steps; white shutters bordered the tall windows. The rooms were soberly furnished, with delicately patterned wallpapers and Persian rugs upon the floors. The minister did not flaunt his status; he displayed few treasures in the reception rooms, and employed just two human servants to keep house. He slept on the third floor, in a plain, whitewashed room adjoining his library. These were his private chambers, which no one visited.

On the floor below, separated from the other rooms of the house by an empty, echoing corridor lined with panels of stained wood, was Mr. Mandrake's study. Here he conducted much of his daily work.

Mandrake walked along the corridor, chewing a vestige of toast. Ms. Piper tripped along behind. At the end of the corridor was a solid brass door, decorated in its center by a molded brass face of surpassing ugliness. Its bulbous brows appeared to be melting down across the eyes; the chin and nose jutted out like nutcracker handles. The magician halted and gazed at the face with deep disapproval.

"I thought I told you to stop doing that," he snapped.

A thin-lipped mouth opened; the jutting chin and nose knocked together indignantly. "Do what?"

"Taking on such a hideous appearance. I've just had my breakfast."

A section of brow lifted, allowing an eyeball to roll forward with a squelching sound. The face looked unapologetic. "Sorry, mate," it said. "It's just my job."

"*Your* job is to destroy anyone entering my study without authority. No more, no less."

The door guard considered. "True. But I seek to *preempt* entry by scaring trespassers away. To my way of thinking, deterrence is more aesthetically satisfying than punishment."

Mr. Mandrake snorted. "Trespassers apart, you'll likely frighten Ms. Piper here to death."

The face shook from side to side, a process that caused the nose to wobble alarmingly. "Not so. When she comes alone, I moderate my features. I reserve the full horror for those I consider morally vicious."

"But you just looked that way to me!"

"The contradiction being . . . ?"

Mandrake took a deep breath, passed a hand across his eyes and gestured. The face retreated into the metal to become the faintest of outlines; the door swung open. The great magician drew himself up and, ushering Ms. Piper along before him, walked into his study.

It was a functional room—high, airy and white-painted, lit by two windows looking out upon the square. It had no excess decoration. On this particular morning thick clouds covered the sun, so Mandrake switched on the ceiling lights as he entered. Bookcases ran along the entirety of one wall, while the opposite side was bare except for a giant pin board, covered in notes and diagrams. The wooden floor was smooth and dark. Five circles were inscribed upon it, each with its own pentacle, runes, candles, and incense pots. Four of these were of a conventional size, but the fifth, nearest the window, was significantly larger: it contained within it a full-size desk, filing cabinet, and several chairs. This master-circle was joined to the smaller ones by a series of precisely drawn lines and rune-chains. Mandrake and Ms. Piper crossed into the largest circle and sat behind the desk, spreading out their papers before them.

Mandrake cleared his throat. "Right then. To business. Ms. Piper, we will deal with the ordinary reports first. If you would activate the presence indicator."

Ms. Piper spoke a brief incantation. Instantly the candles around the perimeters of two of the smaller circles flickered into life; wisps of smoke rose to the ceiling. In the pots beside them, flakes of incense stirred and shifted. The other two circles remained quiet.

"Purip and Fritang," Ms. Piper said.

The magician nodded. "Purip first." He uttered a loud command. The candles in the leftmost pentacle flared; with a queasy shimmering, a form appeared in the center of the circle. It was shaped like a man and respectfully dressed in a sober suit and dark blue tie. It nodded briefly in the direction of the desk and waited.

"Remind me," Mandrake said.

Ms. Piper glanced at her notes. "Purip has been observing the response to our war pamphlets and other propaganda," she said. "Watching the commoners' mood."

"Very well. Purip—what have you seen? Speak."

The demon bowed slightly. "There is not much new to report. The people are like a herd of Ganges meadow cattle, half-starved but complacent, unused to change or independent thought. Yet the war presses on their minds, and I believe discontent is spreading. They read your pamphlets, just as they buy your newspapers, but they do so without pleasure. It does not satisfy them."

The magician scowled. "How is this discontent expressed?"

"I detect it in the careful blankness of their features when your police draw near. I see it in the hardness of their eyes as they pass the recruitment booths. I watch it pile up silently with the flowers at the doors of the bereaved. Most will not declare it openly, but their anger at the war and at their government is growing."

"These are just words," Mandrake said. "You give me nothing tangible."

The demon shrugged its shoulders and smiled. "Revolution is *not* tangible—not to begin with. The commoners barely know the concept exists, but they breathe it when they sleep and they taste it when they drink."

"That's enough riddles. Continue with your work." The magician snapped his fingers; the demon sprang out of the circle and vanished. Mandrake shook his head. "All but useless. Well, we'll see what Fritang has to offer."

Another command: the second circle flared into life. In a cloud of incense a new demon appeared—a short, fat gentleman with a round red face and plaintive eyes. It stood blinking agitatedly in the artificial light. "At last!" it cried. "I have terrible news! It cannot wait another moment!"

Mandrake knew Fritang of old. "As I understand it," he said slowly, "you have been patrolling the docks, hunting for spies. Does your news have anything to do with this?"

A pause. "Indirectly . . ." the demon said.

Mandrake sighed. "Go on, then."

"I was carrying out your orders," Fritang said, "when—oh,

how the memory appalls me!—my cover was blown. Here is my account. I had been conducting inquiries in a wine shop. As I exited, I found myself surrounded by a tribe of street urchins, some scarcely taller than my knee. I was disguised as a manservant, going about my quiet business. I had made no loud noises or extravagant gestures. Nevertheless I was singled out and hit by fifteen eggs, mostly thrown with force."

"What was your exact guise? Perhaps that was itself a provocation."

"I was as you see me. Gray-haired, sober, and straight-backed, the model of tedious virtue."

"Evidently the young scoundrels decided to waylay a man of such qualities. You were unlucky, that is all."

Fritang's eyes widened and its nostrils flared. "There was more to it than that! They knew me for what I am!"

"As a demon?" Mandrake flicked skeptically at a particle of dust upon his sleeve. "How could you tell?"

"My suspicions were aroused by their repetitive chanting: 'Get out, get out, vile demon. We hate you and your dangling yellow crest.'"

"Really? That *is* interesting. . . ." The magician appraised Fritang carefully through his lenses. "But what yellow crest is this? *I* don't see it."

The demon pointed at a space above its head. "That is because you cannot see the sixth or seventh planes. On those, my crest is self-evident, resplendent as a sunflower. I may add that it is *not* dangling, though captivity *does* make it droop a little."

"The sixth and seventh planes . . . and you're quite sure you didn't let your guise slip for a moment? Yes, yes." Mandrake held up a hasty hand as the demon began a vehement protest.

"I'm sure you're right and I am grateful for the information. You will doubtless want to rest after your egg trauma. Be gone! You are dismissed."

With a yell of delight, Fritang departed in corkscrew motion through the center of the pentacle, as if sucked noisily down a plughole. Mandrake and Ms. Piper looked at each other.

"*Another* case," Ms. Piper said. "Children again."

"Mmm." The magician leaned back in his chair and stretched his arms out behind his head. "You might just check the files, get the exact number. I must summon the demons back from Kent."

He sat forward, his elbows on the desk, and made the incantation in an undertone. Ms. Piper got up and crossed to the filing cabinet on the edge of the circle. She opened the topmost drawer and drew out a bulging manila file. Returning to her seat, she removed the elastic around the file and began sifting rapidly through the documents within. The incantation ended amid a suffusion of jasmine and sweetbriar. In the right-hand pentacle a hulking form appeared—a giant with blond, braided hair and a single glaring eye. Ms. Piper went on reading.

The giant performed a low and complex bow. "Master, I greet you with the blood of your enemies, with their cries and lamentations! Victory is ours!"

Mandrake raised an eyebrow. "So you chased them away, then."

The cyclops nodded. "They fled like mice before lions. Literally, in some cases."

"Indeed. That was to be expected. But did you capture any?"

"We killed a good many. You should have heard them

squeak! And their fleeing hooves fairly shook the earth."

"Right. So you didn't capture a single one. Which was expressly what I ordered you and the others to do." Mandrake rapped his fingers on the table. "In a matter of days they will attack again. Who sent them? Prague? Paris? America? Without captives it is impossible to say. We are no further forward."

The cyclops gave a crisp salute. "Well, my work is done. I am pleased to have given satisfaction." It paused. "You seem lost in thought, O master."

The magician nodded. "I am debating, Ascobol, whether to subject you to the Stipples or the Unfortunate Hug. Do you have a preference?"

"You could not be so cruel!" The cyclops wiggled agonizedly back and forth, toying with a braid of hair. "Blame Bartimaeus, not me! Once again, he took no useful part in the action, but was waylaid by a single blow. I was delayed from the chase by his loud requests to help him up from beneath a pebble. He is as weak as a tadpole and vicious with it: you should subject *him* to the Stipples forthwith."

"And where is Bartimaeus now?"

The cyclops gave a pout. "I know not. Possibly he has expired from exhaustion in the interim. He took no part in the chase."

The magician sighed deeply. "Ascobol—be gone from here." He made a dismissive sign. The giant's fluting cries of thanks were abruptly cut off; it vanished in a gout of flame. Mandrake turned to his assistant. "Any joy, Piper?"

She nodded. "These are the unauthorized demon sightings of the last six months. Forty-two—no, forty-*three* now in total. As far as the demons go, there's no pattern: we've had afrits, djinn, imps, and mites all spotted. But when you look at the commoners . . ." She glanced down at the open file. "Most are children, and most of those children are young. In thirty cases the witnesses were under eighteen. What's that? Seventy percent or so. And in over half of those the witnesses were under twelve." She looked up. "They're being born with it. With the power to see."

"And who knows what else." Mandrake swiveled his chair and stared out over the bare gray branches of the trees in the square. Mists still meandered around them, cloaking the ground from view. "All right," he said, "that's enough for now. It's nearly nine, and I've private work to do. Thanks for your help, Piper. I'll see you at the ministry later this morning. Don't let that door guard give you any cheek as you go out."

For some moments after his assistant's departure the magician remained motionless, tapping his fingers together aimlessly. Finally he leaned over and opened a side drawer in his desk. He pulled out a small cloth bundle and set it down in front of him. Flicking the fabric aside, he revealed a bronze disc, shiny with the use of years.

The magician stared down into the scrying glass, willing it into life. Something stirred in its depths.

"Fetch Bartimaeus," he said.

3

With dawn, the first people returned to the little town. Hesitant, fearful, groping their way like blind men up the street, they began to inspect the damage wrought to their houses, shops, and gardens. A few Night Police came with them, ostentatiously flourishing Inferno sticks and other weapons, though the threat was long since gone.

I was disinclined to move. I spun a Concealment around the chunk of chimney where I sat and removed myself from the humans' sight. I watched them passing with a baleful eye.

My few hours' rest had done me little good. How could it? It had been two whole *years* since I'd been allowed to leave this cursed Earth; two full years since I'd last escaped the brainless thronging mass of sweet humanity. I needed more than a quiet kip on a chimney stack to deal with *that*, I can tell you. I needed to go home.

And if I didn't, I was going to die.

It is technically possible for a spirit to remain indefinitely on Earth, and many of us at one time or another have endured prolonged visits, usually courtesy of being forcibly trapped inside canopic jars, sandalwood boxes, or other arbitrary spaces chosen by our cruel masters.[1] Dreadful punishment though this

---

[1] When goaded into invoking the spell of Indefinite Confinement, magicians usually compress the spirit into the first object they spy close at hand. I once cheeked a master a little too cleverly during his afternoon tea; before I knew it I was imprisoned inside a half-filled pot of strawberry jam and would have remained there, possibly for all eternity, had not his apprentice opened it by mistake at supper that same evening. Even so, my essence was infested with sticky little seeds for ages after.

is, it at least has the advantage of being safe and quiet. You aren't called upon to *do* anything, so your increasingly weakened essence is not immediately at risk. The main threat comes from the remorseless tedium, which can lead to insanity in the spirit in question.[2]

My current predicament was in stark contrast. Not for me the luxury of being hidden away in a cozy lamp or amulet. No—day in, day out, I was a djinni on the street, ducking, diving, taking risks, exposing myself to danger. And each day it became a little more difficult to survive.

For I was no longer the carefree Bartimaeus of old. My essence was raddled with Earth's corruption; my mind was bleary with the pain. I was slower, weaker, distracted from my tasks. I found it hard to change form. In battle my attacks were sputtering and weak—my Detonations had the explosive power of lemonade, my Convulsions trembled like jelly in a breeze. All my strength had gone. Where once, in the previous night's scrap, I would have sent that public convenience right back at the she-pig, adding a phone box and a bus stop for good measure, now I could do nothing to resist. I was vulnerable as a kitten. A few small buildings in the face, I could stand. But already I was practically at the mercy of second-rate fops such as Ascobol, a fool with no great history to speak of.[3] And if I met a foe with even a grain of power, my luck would surely end.

A weak djinni is a bad slave—bad twice over, since he is both ineffective *and* a laughingstock. It does a magician no favors to maintain one in the world. This is the reason why they

---

[2] The afrit Honorius was a case in point: he went mad after a hundred years' confinement in a skeleton. A rather poor show; I like to think with my engaging personality I could keep myself entertained a *little* longer than that.

usually allow us back to the Other Place on a temporary basis, to repair our essence and renew our strength. No master in his right mind would permit a djinni to deteriorate as far as I had done.

No master in his right mind . . . Well, that of course was the problem.

I was interrupted in my gloomy cogitation by a stirring in midair. The girl looked up.

Above the road appeared the faintest shimmering—a delicate tingling of pretty pink and yellow lights. It was invisible on the first plane, and thus went unnoticed by the people trudging up the street, but if any children had seen it, they'd probably have guessed it to be fairy dust.

Which shows how wrong you can be.

With an abrupt scratching noise, the lights froze and were drawn back from the middle like two curtains. Between them appeared the grinning face of a bald baby with bad acne. Its evil little eyes were red and sore, indicating an owner who kept long hours and bad habits. For a few moments they peered myopically to and fro; the baby swore under its breath and rubbed its eyes with dirty little fists.

---

[3] It is a curious fact that, despite our fury at being summoned into this world, spirits such as I derive a good deal of retrospective satisfaction from our exploits. At the time, of course, we do our darnedest to avoid them, but afterward we often display a certain weary pride in the cleverest, bravest, or most jammy events on our résumé. Philosophers might speculate this is because we are essentially *defined* by our experiences in this world, since in the Other Place we are not so easily individualized. Thus, those with long and glittering careers (e.g. me) tend to look down on those (e.g. Ascobol) whose names have been unearthed more recently, and haven't amassed so many fine achievements. In Ascobol's case, I also disliked him for his silly falsetto voice, which ill becomes an eight-foot cyclops.

All at once it noticed my Concealment and let out a dreadful oath.[4] I regarded it with cool impassivity.

"Oi, Bart!" the baby cried. "That you in there? Stir yourself! You're wanted."

I spoke casually. "By whom?"

"You know full well. And boy, are you in trouble! I reckon it's the Shriveling Fire for sure this time."

"Is that so?" The girl remained firmly seated on the broken chimney and crossed her slender arms. "Well, if Mandrake wants me, he can come and get me himself."

The baby grinned nastily. "Good. I was hoping you'd say that. No problem, Barty! I'll pass that on. Can't wait to see what he'll do."

The imp's malicious glee irritated me.[5] If I'd had a little more energy I'd have leaped up and swallowed it there and then. I contented myself with snapping off a chimney pot and throwing it with unerring aim. It struck the baby's bald fat head with a satisfactory ringing sound.

"As I thought," I said. "Hollow."

The unlovely grin converted into a scowl. "You cad! Just you wait—we'll see who's laughing when I watch you burn." Propelled by a gust of ripe language, it popped back behind its curtains of glimmering lights and drew them smartly together. Twinkling softly, the lights dissipated on the breeze. The imp was gone.

------

[4] Probably Germanic in origin—it involved nailing someone's entrails to an oak tree.

[5] We were, after all, slaves together; we had both suffered long at Mandrake's hands. A bit of empathy would not, I think, have been out of place. But the imp's long confinement had rather soured its worldview, which has happened to far better spirits than it over the years.

The girl pushed a strand of hair behind one ear, refolded her arms grimly, and settled back to wait. *Now* there would be consequences, which was exactly what I needed. It was time for a proper confrontation.

To begin with, years before, my master and I had got along well enough. I don't mean amicably, or anything ridiculous like that, but our mutual irritation was founded on something approximating respect. During a series of early incidents, from the Lovelace conspiracy to the golem affair, I'd been forced to acknowledge Mandrake's verve and daring, his energy and even (faintly) the glimmerings of his conscience. It wasn't much, admittedly, but it made his prissiness, stubbornness, pride, and ambition a little less hard to stomach. In return, I obviously had no shortage of wonderful traits for him to admire, and anyway, he could barely get up in the morning without needing me to save his sorry skin. We coexisted in a wary state of toleration.

For a year or so after the defeat of the golem and Mandrake's promotion to Head of Internal Affairs, he didn't push me around too much. He summoned me from time to time to help out with minor incidents, which I haven't got time to go into here,[6] but generally speaking he left me pretty much alone.

On the odd occasion that he did call me, we both knew where he stood. We had an agreement of sorts. I knew his birth

---

[6] If memory serves, these included the case of the Afrit, the Envelope, and the Ambassador's Wife; the affair of the Curiously Heavy Trunk; and the messy episode of the Anarchist and the Oyster. Mandrake nearly lost his life in all of those. As I say, none of them was of much interest.

name, and he knew I knew it. Though he threatened me with dire consequences if I told anyone, in practice he treated me with careful detachment in all our dealings. I kept his name to myself and he kept me away from the most dangerous tasks—which basically boiled down to the fighting in America. Dozens of djinn were dying there—the reverberations of the losses rang harshly through the Other Place—and I was happy to have no part in it.[7]

Time passed; Mandrake worked at his job with his usual zeal. An opportunity for promotion came, and he accepted it. He was now Information Minister, one of the great ones of the Empire.[8]

Officially, his duties were to do with propaganda—devising clever ways of selling the war to the British people. Unofficially, at the Prime Minister's behest, he continued much of his Internal Affairs police work, operating an unsavory net-

---

[7] To those of us abreast with human history, the cause of the latest war was drearily familiar. For years the Americans had refused to pay the taxes demanded of them by London. The British swiftly fell back on the oldest argument of all, and sent over an army to beat the colonists up. After initial easy victories, stagnation set in. The rebels retreated into thick woods, sending djinn out to ambush the advancing troops. Several prominent British magicians were killed; the Sixth and Seventh fleets were summoned from the China Seas to bolster the campaign—but still the fighting dribbled on. Months went by, the Empire's strength was frittered away in the American wastes, and the repercussions resounded around the globe.

[8] His chance came thanks to the war. The rebel guerrillas were causing the British army problems. After a year of attritional fighting the Foreign Minister, a certain Mr. Fry, visited the colonies secretly with a view to arranging a truce. Eight magicians watched him as he traveled; a host of horlas guarded his every step: the minister was invulnerable. Or so they thought. On his first night in Philadelphia he was treacherously slain by an imp concealed in his evening pie. Amid general outrage, the Prime Minister reshuffled his ministers, and Mandrake joined the ruling Council.

work of surveillance djinn and human spies, which reported directly to him. His workload, which had always been severe, now became crippling.

There followed a dismal sea change in my master's personality. Never exactly famous for his lighthearted banter, he became positively abrupt and antisocial, even less willing than before to shoot the breeze with a debonair djinni. But by cruel paradox, he also began to summon me more and more frequently, and for less and less reason.

Why did he do so? Mainly no doubt because he wished to minimize the chances of my being summoned by another magician. His old fear, now fueled by chronic fatigue and paranoia, was that I would divulge his birth name to an enemy, rendering him vulnerable to attack. Well, fair enough, that was always *possible*. I *might* have done it. Can't say for sure. But he'd managed without me in the past, and nothing had happened to him. So I thought something else was going on too.

Mandrake masked his emotions well enough, but his whole life was work—remorseless and never-ending. Moreover, he was now surrounded by a gang of vicious, hot-eyed maniacs— the other ministers—most of whom wished him harm. His only close associate, for a time, was the hack playwright Quentin Makepeace, as self-serving as all the rest. To survive in this friendless world, Mandrake cloaked his better qualities under layers of smarm and swank. All his old life—the years with the Underwoods, his vulnerable existence as the boy Nathaniel, the ideals he'd once espoused—was buried away deep down. Every link with his childhood was severed, except for me. I don't think he could bring himself to break this last connection.

I proposed this theory in my usual gentle way, but Mandrake

37

was unwilling to listen to my taunts. He was a worried man.[9] The American campaigns were vastly expensive, the British supply lines overstretched. With the magicians' attention diverted, other parts of the Empire had become troublesome. Foreign spies infested London like maggots in an apple. The commoners were volatile. To counter all this, Mandrake worked like a slave.

Well, not *literally* like a slave. That was *my* job. And a pretty thankless one it was too. Back at Internal Affairs, some of the assignments had been almost worthy of my talents. I'd intercepted enemy messages and deciphered them, given out false reports, trailed enemy spirits, duffed a few of them up, etc. It was simple, satisfying work—I got a craftsman's pleasure from it. In addition, I helped Mandrake and the police in the search for two fugitives from the golem affair. The first of these was a certain mysterious mercenary (distinguishing features: big beard, grim expression, swanky black clothes, general invulnerability to Infernos/Detonations/pretty much everything else). He'd last been seen far away in Prague, and predictably enough we never got a whiff of him. The second was an even more nebulous character, whom no one had even set eyes on. He apparently went by the name of Hopkins, and claimed to be a scholar. He was generally suspected of masterminding the golem plot, and I'd heard he'd been involved with the Resistance too. But he might as well have been a ghost or shadow for all the substance we could pin down. We found a spidery signature in an

---

[9] I'm stretching the term a bit here, I know. By now, in his mid to late teens, he might just about have passed for a man. When seen from behind. At a distance. On a very dark night.

admissions book at an old library that might have been his. That was all. The trail, such as it was, went cold.

Then Mandrake became Information Minister and I was soon engaged in more depressing work, viz. pasting up adverts on 1,000 billboards across London; distributing pamphlets to 25,000 homes across ditto; corralling selected animals for public holiday "entertainments";[10] supervising food, drink, and "hygiene" for same; flying back and forth across the capital for hours on end trailing pro-war banners. Now, call me picky, but I'd argue that when you think of a 5,000-year-old djinni, the scourge of civilizations and confidante of kings, certain things come to mind—swashbuckling espionage, perhaps, or valiant battles, thrilling escapes and general multipurpose excitement. What you *don't* readily think of is that same noble djinni being forced to prepare giant vats of chili con carne for festival days, or struggling on street corners with bill-posters and pots of glue.

Especially without being allowed to return home. Soon my periods of respite in the Other Place became so fleeting I practically got whiplash traveling there and back. Then, one day, Mandrake ceased dismissing me altogether, and that was it. I was trapped on Earth.

Over the next two years I grew steadily weaker, and just when I was hitting rock bottom, scarcely able to lift a poster brush, the wretched boy began sending me out on more dangerous

---

[10] Following the Roman tradition, the magicians sought to keep the people docile with regular holidays, in which free shows were put on in all the major parks. Lots of exotic beasts from across the Empire were displayed, as were minor imps and sprites allegedly "caught" during the war. Human prisoners were paraded along the streets, or enclosed in special glass viewing globes in the St. James's Park pavilions for the populace to jeer at.

missions again—fighting bands of enemy djinn that Britain's many enemies were using to stir up trouble.

In the past I'd have had a quiet word with Mandrake, expressing my disapproval with succinct directness. But my privileged access to him was no more. He'd taken to summoning me along with a host of other slaves, giving orders en masse and sending us off like a pack of dogs. Such multiple summoning is a difficult business, requiring great mental strength on the part of the magician, but Mandrake did it daily without apparent effort, talking quietly with his assistant or even flicking through a newspaper while we stood and sweated in our circles.

I did my best to get to him. Instead of using a monstrous guise like my fellow slaves (Ascobol's cyclops and Cormocodran's boar-headed behemoth were typical), I took to wearing the semblance of Kitty Jones, the Resistance girl Mandrake had persecuted years before. Her assumed death still weighed on his conscience: I knew this because he always reacted to my echo of her face with a reddening of his own. He'd get all angry and sheepish, assertive and embarrassed at the same time. Didn't make him treat me any better, mind.

Well, I'd had about as much as I could stand from Mandrake. It was time to have it out with him. By refusing to go back with the imp, I obliged the magician to recall me officially, which would doubtless hurt, but was at least likely to mean he gave me the benefit of his attention for five minutes.

The imp had been gone for hours. In the past I'd have got a swift response from my master, but the delay was typical of his new distractedness. I smoothed back Kitty Jones's long dark hair and cast my eye around the little rural town. Several commoners had gathered around the ruined post office and were engaged in passionate debate; they resisted the efforts of a lone policeman to make them return to their homes. No doubt about it: the people were growing restless.

Which turned my thoughts to Kitty once again. Despite appearances to the contrary, she *hadn't* died in battle with the golem three years before. Instead, after acting with unusual self-lessness and bravery to save Mandrake's worthless hide, she'd slipped quietly away. Our encounter had been brief but stimu-lating: her passionate opposition to injustice reminded me of someone else I'd known, a long time ago.

Part of me *hoped* Kitty had bought a one-way ticket to somewhere safe and distant and had set up a café on a beach or something, out of harm's way. But deep down I knew she was still close by, working against the magicians. That knowledge rather pleased me, though she'd had no love for djinn.

Whatever she was doing, I hoped she was keeping out of trouble.

4

The demon saw Kitty the moment she moved. A wide mouth opened in the stubby, featureless head; double rows of teeth descended from above and rose from the lining of the jaw. It snipped its teeth together curiously, making a noise like a thousand scissors, slicing in unison. Folds of gray-green flesh shifted on either side of the skull, revealing two golden eyes that glinted as they turned on her.

Kitty did not repeat her mistake. She stood stock-still, barely six feet from the bent and snuffling head, and held her breath.

The demon scraped a foot experimentally against the floor, scoring five thick claw gashes in the tiles. It made a curious crooning noise deep in its throat. It was sizing her up, she knew it was, appraising her strength, debating whether to attack. In the final moments of crisis her brain took in many irrelevant details of its guise: the flecks of gray hair about the joints, the bright metal scales upon the torso, the hands with too many fingers and too few bones. Her own limbs shook; her hands twitched as if to encourage her to run, but she fought against her fear and beat it down.

Then a voice came: sweet and female, curiously inquiring. "Aren't you going to run, my dear? I can only lope along on these club feet. Ah me, so slow! Try it. You never know—you might escape." So gentle was the voice it took Kitty a moment to realize it came from the dreadful mouth. It was the demon that spoke. Numbly she shook her head.

The demon flexed six fingers in an incomprehensible gesture. "Then at least step toward me," the sweet voice said. "It would save me the torture of hobbling over to you on these poor club feet of mine. Ah me, so sore! My essence flinches from the pull of your harsh, cruel earth."

Again Kitty shook her head, slower this time. The demon sighed, bowing its head as if crushed and disappointed. "My dear, you have no courtesy. I wonder whether your essence would disagree with me if I ate you. I am a martyr to indigestion. . . ." The head rose; the eyes sparkled, the teeth snipped like a thousand scissors. "I will risk it." Without pause the leg joints bent and sprang, the jaws opened, wide, wide, wide; the fingers clasped. Kitty fell back, screamed.

A wall of silver shards, thin as rapiers, rose from the floor, spearing the demon as it leaped; a flash, a shower of sparks—its body burst into lilac flames. It hovered in midair for a split second, twitched, emitted a single gout of smoke, then drifted softly to the floor, light as burning paper. A little voice whispered, sad, resentful: "Ah me . . ." Now it was nothing but a husk, which fell in upon itself and presently dwindled into ashes.

Kitty's muscles were frozen in a rictus of terror; with a grim effort, she managed to close her mouth and blink, once, twice. She ran a trembling hand through her hair.

"Great heavens," her master said from the pentacle on the opposite side of the room. "I didn't expect *that*. But the stupidity of these creatures is boundless. Sweep away the mess, dear Lizzie, and we can discuss the procedure. You must be very proud of your success."

Dumbly, eyes still staring, Kitty managed the faintest of nods. She stepped stiff-legged from the circle and went to fetch the broom.

★   ★   ★

"Well, you're a clever girl and no mistake." Her master was sitting on the sofa nearest the window, sipping from a china cup. "And you make good tea too, which is a blessing on a day like this one." Rain battered the windowpanes and gusted haphazardly across the street. The wind whined in the passages of the house. Kitty drew her feet up out of the draft skirling across the floor and took a swig of strong brown tea from her mug.

The old man wiped his mouth with the back of his hand. "Yes, a very satisfactory summons. Not bad at all. And most interesting for me—who'd have thought the true form of a succubus looked like *that*? Gracious! Now, Lizzie, did you notice that you slightly mispronounced the Restraining Syllable, right at the end? Not enough to break the safety wall, but the creature was emboldened, thought it would try its luck. Fortunately, everything else you did was perfect."

Kitty was still shaking. She sank back among the cushions of the ancient sofa. "If I'd . . . made any *other* mistakes, sir," she said haltingly, "what would have—?"

"Oh, gracious—I wouldn't worry your head about that. You didn't, and that's what counts. Have a chocolate digestive." He indicated the plate between them. "Settles the stomach, I find."

She took a biscuit, dunked it in her tea. "But *why* did it attack me?" she said, frowning. "Surely it must have been able to tell that the pentacle's defenses would come into force."

Her master chuckled. "Who can say? Perhaps it hoped you would flinch out of the circle as it leaped: that would have instantly destroyed its prison and allowed it to devour you. Notice that it had already tried two childish stratagems to persuade you to leave the pentacle. Hum, it was not a sophisticated djinni. But perhaps it had grown tired of bondage; perhaps it simply wished to die." He eyed the dregs at the bottom of his teacup musingly. "Who can tell? We understand so *little* about demons, about what makes them tick. They are hard to fathom. Is there any more in the pot?"

Kitty inspected it. "Nope. I'll make some more."

"If you would, dear Lizzie, if you would. You might pass me that copy of Trismegistus on your way out. He has some interesting notes on succubi, if I recall."

Chill air bit into her as she entered the passage and stomped down to the kitchen. There, leaning close to the blue gas flame hissing beneath the kettle, her self-control finally slackened. She began to tremble—proper heavy body-shuddering shakes that made her grasp the work surface for support.

She closed her eyes. The demon's open jaws plummeted toward her. She opened them again at speed.

A paper bag of fruit sat beside the sink. Mechanically she took an apple and ate it, gulping it down desperately in great rough chunks. She took another, and finished it more slowly, staring sightlessly at the wall.

Her trembling subsided. The kettle whistled. Jakob was right, she thought, rinsing her mug under an icy stream of water. I'm an idiot. Nobody but a fool would do this. Nobody but a fool.

But a fool could still be lucky. And so far, for three long years, her luck had held.

Since the day when her death had been reported and accepted, and the authorities had sealed their file on her with a blob of hot black wax, Kitty had never once left London. No matter that her good friend Jakob Hyrnek, safe with relatives in

Bruges and working as a jeweler, sent her imploring epistles weekly, begging her to come and live with him. No matter that his family urged her, during their secretive, irregular meetings, to leave the dangers of the city and start her life afresh. No matter that her common sense cried out to her that she could do nothing useful on her own. Kitty was undeterred. In London she remained.

Stubborn she still might be, but her old recklessness was now swathed with caution. Everything from her appearance to her daily routine was carefully judged to avoid arousing the suspicions of the authorities. This was essential, since for Kitty Jones existence was itself a crime. To conceal herself from the eyes of those few who knew her, she had cropped her dark hair short and wore it in a bob beneath her cap. She kept tight rein on her mobile features, no matter what the provocation; she did her best to be dull-eyed, stone-faced, nothing but a numeral in a crowd.

Though perhaps a little thinner in the face from overwork and lack of inessential food, though perhaps a little lined around the eyes, she still possessed the same mercurial energies that had borne her into the Resistance and out again, alive. They supported her in pursuit of a certain ambitious project, and in the maintenance of no fewer than two false identities.

She had taken lodgings on the third floor of a dilapidated West London town house, in a street near the munitions factories. Above and below her bedsit were several other rooms that had been crammed by the enterprising landlord into the shell of the old building. Each was occupied, but save for the caretaker, a diminutive man who lived in the basement, Kitty had not spoken to any of the tenants. She passed them on the stairs sometimes: men and women, old and young, all living lives of isolation and anonymity. She was satisfied with this: she both liked and needed the solitude the house afforded her.

The contents of her room were few. A small white cooker, a fridge, a cupboard, and, in a corner, behind a dangling sheet, a sink and toilet. Below the window, which looked out over a tangle of walls and unkempt yards to the house backs opposite, sat a confusion of jumbled sheets and pillows: Kitty's bed. Beside this were neatly stacked her worldly possessions: clothes, tins of food, newspapers, recent pamphlets about the war. Her most precious items were variously hidden beneath the mattress (a silver throwing disc wrapped in a handkerchief), in the cistern of her toilet (a sealed plastic bag containing the documents she needed to maintain her new identities), and at the bottom of her laundry bag (several thick books bound in leather).

Being of practical disposition, Kitty did not regard her room with great affection. It was a place to sleep and little more. She did not spend much time in it. Nevertheless, it was her home, and she had lived there for three years.

The name she had given the landlord was Clara Bell. This coincided with the documents that she carried around with her most often—the stamped identity card and the residence, health and education papers that mapped out her recent past. They had been forged for her with great skill by old Mr. Hyrnek, Jakob's father, who had also created a separate set for her under the name of Lizzie Temple. She did not have any papers with her real name. Only at night, when she lay back in the bed with curtain drawn and the single light switched off, did she become Kitty Jones once more. It was an identity swathed in darkness and dreams.

★ ★ ★

For some months following Jakob's departure, Clara Bell had worked at the Hyrneks' printing factory, delivering newly bound books and earning a basic wage. This did not last long—Kitty was reluctant to imperil her friends by too close an association, and had quickly taken on an evening job at a pub beside the river. By then, however, her humdrum errands had provided her with a most unusual opportunity.

One morning Kitty had been summoned to Mr. Hyrnek's office and handed a package to deliver. It was heavy, smelled of glue and leather, and was methodically wrapped in string. It was labeled: MR. H. BUTTON, MAGICIAN.

Kitty inspected the address. "Earls Court," she said. "Not many magicians there."

Mr. Hyrnek was attending to his pipe with a blackened penknife and piece of cloth. "Among our beloved rulers," he said, flicking out a fragment of burned soot, "this Button is regarded as an incurable eccentric. He's skilled enough, by all accounts, but has never attempted to rise through the political ranks. Used to work as a librarian at the London Library, until he had an accident. Lost a leg. Now just reads, collects books where he can, writes a bit. Told me once that he was interested in knowledge for its own sake. Hence no money. Hence Earls Court. Take it along, will you?"

Kitty had done so, and found Mr. Button's house in a region of gray-white villas, tall and heavy, with immense pillars supporting ostentatious porches above the doors. Once they had been occupied by the rich; now the district carried a melancholy aura of poverty and decay. Mr. Button lived at the end of a tree-lined cul-de-sac, in a house shrouded by dark laurels. Kitty had rung the bell and waited on a stained and dirty step.

No one answered; she noticed then that the door was hanging ajar.

She peered inside: a dilapidated hall, made narrow by stacks of books against the walls. She coughed uncertainly. "Hello?"

"Yes, yes, come in!" A muffled voice echoed faintly. "At speed, if you will. I am a little inconvenienced."

Kitty hastened forward, and in a neighboring room, rendered indistinct by dust-caked curtains drawn across the windows, discovered a twitching boot protruding from beneath a colossal pile of fallen books. Exploring further, she came upon the head and neck of an elderly gentleman, vainly struggling to wriggle free. Without preamble, Kitty made a rapid excavation; in a few minutes Mr. Button was settled in a nearby chair, a little crumpled and very out of breath.

"Thank you, my dear. Would you mind passing me my stick? I was using it to extract a book, which I fear caused all the trouble."

Kitty rescued a long ash stick from among the debris and handed it to the magician. He was a small and fragile man, bright-eyed, thin-faced, with a disordered mop of straight gray hair hanging low over his forehead. He wore a checked shirt without a tie, a patched green cardigan, and gray trousers, scuffed and stained. One trouser leg was missing; it had been folded over and sewn shut just below the torso.

Something about his appearance disconcerted her . . . It took her a moment to realize she had never seen a magician so informally dressed.

"I was simply trying to get hold of a volume of Gibbon," Mr. Button was saying, "which I spied at the bottom of a pile. I was careless and lost my balance. There was *such* a landslide! You cannot imagine how taxing it is to find anything in this place."

Kitty looked around. Across the room innumerable stacks of books rose like stalagmites from the ancient carpet. Many of these columns were as tall as her; others had half capsized against each other, forming precarious arches swathed in dust. Books rested high upon a table and filled the cupboards of a dresser; they receded in unguessed-at numbers through an open door and deep into a side room. A few narrow walkways remained clear, connecting the windows with two sofas squeezed before a fireplace and the exit to the hall.

"I think I've got some idea," she said. "Anyway, here's something to add to your problem." She picked up her package. "From Hyrnek's."

The old man's eyes sparkled. "Good! Good! That would be my edition of Ptolemy's *Apocrypha*, newly bound in calf hide. Karel Hyrnek is a marvel. My dear, you have improved my day twice over! I *insist* you stay for tea."

Within half an hour Kitty had learned three things: that the old gentleman was garrulous and affable, that he possessed a fine supply of tea and spice cake, and that his need for an assistant was greatly pressing.

"My last helper left me a fortnight ago," he said, sighing heavily. "Joined up to fight for Britain. I tried to talk him out of it, of course, but his heart was set on going. He believed what he was told—glory, good prospects, promotion, all that. He'll be dead soon, I expect. Yes, do have that last piece of cake, dear. You need feeding up. It's all very well for *him*, going off to die, but I fear my studies have been severely restricted."

"What studies are those, sir?" Kitty asked.

"Researches, dear. History of magic and other things. A fascinating area, sadly neglected. It's a crying shame that so many libraries are being closed—once again the government is acting out of fear. Well, I've saved a good many important books on the subject, and I wish to catalog and index them. It is my ambition to prepare a definitive list of all surviving djinn—existing records are *so* haphazard and contradictory . . . but as you have seen, I am not even dextrous enough to research my own collection, thanks to this impediment. . . ." He shook a fist at his nonexistent leg.

"Erm, how did it happen, sir?" Kitty ventured. "If you don't mind my asking."

"My leg?" The old gentleman lowered his brows, glanced left and right, and looked up at Kitty. He spoke in a sinister whisper. "Marid."

"A marid? But aren't they the most—?"

"The most powerful type of commonly summoned demon. Correct." Mr. Button's smile was slightly smug. "I'm no slouch, my dear. Not that any of my *colleagues*"—he spoke the word with vehement distaste—"would admit as such, blast them. I'd like to see Rupert Devereaux or Carl Mortensen do as well." He sniffed, settled back into his sofa. "The irony of it was that I just wanted to ask it a few questions. Wasn't going to enslave it at all. Anyway, I'd forgotten to add a Tertiary Fettering; the thing broke out and had my leg off before the automatic Dismissal set in." He shook his head. "That's the penalty of curiosity, my dear. Well, I get by somehow. I'll find another assistant, if the Americans don't kill our entire population of young males."

He took a tetchy bite of his spice cake. Even before he had swallowed, Kitty had made up her mind. "I'll help you out, sir."

The old magician blinked at her. "You?"

"Yes, sir. I'll be your assistant."

"I'm sorry, my dear, but I thought you worked for Hyrnek's."

"Oh, I do, sir, but only temporarily. I'm looking for other work. I'm very interested in books and magic, sir. Really I am. I've always wanted to learn about it."

"Indeed. Do you speak Hebrew?"

"No, sir."

"Or Czech? Or French? Or Arabic?"

"No, none of those, sir."

"Indeed . . ." For a moment Mr. Button's face became less amiable, less courteous. He looked at her sidelong, out of half-shut eyes. "And the fact of the matter is, of course, that you are nothing but a *commoner's* girl. . . ."

Kitty nodded brightly. "Yes, sir. But I've always believed that misfortunes of birth shouldn't stand in the way of talent. I'm energetic and quick, and nimble too." She gestured around the maze of dusty piles. "I'll be able to get hold of any book you like, fast as thinking. From the bottom of the farthest stack." She grinned, and took a sip of tea.

The old man was rubbing his chin with small, plump fingers, muttering to himself. "A commoner's child . . . unvetted . . . it is highly unorthodox . . . in fact, the authorities expressly forbid it. But well, after all—why not?" He tittered to himself. "Why shouldn't I? They've seen fit to neglect *me* all these years. It would be an interesting experiment . . . and they'd never know, blast them." He looked at Kitty again, eyes narrowed. "You know I couldn't pay you anything."

"That's all right, sir. I'm, erm, interested in knowledge for its own sake. I'll get other work. I could help you out whenever you needed it, part-time."

"Very well, then, very well." Mr. Button extended a small

pink hand. "We shall see how it works out. Neither of us has any contractual obligation to the other, you understand, and we are free to terminate the relationship at any time. Mind—if you are lazy or dishonest I shall raise a horla to shrivel you. But goodness, where are my manners? I've not yet asked your name."

Kitty selected an identity. "Lizzie Temple, sir."

"Well, Lizzie, very glad to have met you. I hope we shall get along well."

And so they had. From the beginning Kitty made herself indispensable to Mr. Button. To start with, her chores were entirely concerned with navigating her way about his dark and cluttered house, accessing obscure books in distant stacks, and bringing them out to him unscathed. This was easier said than done. She frequently emerged into the lamplight of the magician's study wheezing and covered in dust, or bruised by a nasty book-fall, only to be told she had the wrong volume, or an incorrect edition, and be sent back to begin again. But Kitty stuck with it. Gradually she became adept at locating the volumes Mr. Button required; she began to recognize the names, the covers, the methods of binding employed by different printers in different cities across the centuries. For his part, the magician was highly satisfied: his helper spared him much inconvenience. So the months passed.

Kitty took to asking brief questions about some of the works she helped locate. Sometimes Mr. Button gave succinct and breezy answers; more often he suggested she look up the solution herself. When the book was written in English, this Kitty was able to do. She borrowed some of the easier, more general volumes and took them home to her bedsit. Her nocturnal readings prompted further questions to Mr. Button, who directed her to other texts. In this way, directed by caprice and whimsical inclination, Kitty began to learn.

After a year of such progress Kitty began going on errands for the magician. She procured official passes and visited libraries across the capital; she made occasional forays to herbalists and to suppliers of magical goods. Mr. Button had no imps at his service, and did not practice much actual magic. His interest lay in the cultures of the past, and the history of contact with demons. Occasionally he summoned a minor entity to question it on a particular historical point.

"But it's a difficult business with one leg," he told Kitty. "Summoning's bad enough with two of 'em, but when you're trying to draw the circle straight and your stick's slipping and you keep dropping the chalk, it's hellish tricky. I don't risk it often anymore."

"I could give you a hand, sir," Kitty suggested. "You'd have to teach me the basics, of course."

"Oh, that would be impossible. Far too dangerous for us both."

Kitty found Mr. Button quite adamant on this, and it took her several months of pestering to win him over. Finally, to gain a moment's peace, he allowed her to fill the bowls with incense, hold the pin in position while he inscribed the circles' arcs, and light the pig's-fat candles. She stood behind his chair when the demon appeared and was questioned. Afterward she helped douse the scorch marks left behind. Her calm demeanor impressed the magician; soon she was actively assisting in all his summonings. As in all things, Kitty learned swiftly. She began to memorize some of the common Latin formulae, although she remained ignorant of the language. Mr. Button, who found active work taxing on his health, and who was also inclined to laziness, began to entrust his assistant with more and more procedures. In his cursory way, he helped fill in some of the gaps in her knowledge, although he refused to instruct her formally.

"The actual craft," he would say, "is simplicity itself, but it has infinite variations. We shall always keep to basics: summon the creature, keep it constrained, send it off again. I have neither the time nor the inclination to teach you all the subtleties."

"That's fine, sir," Kitty said. She had neither the time nor the inclination to learn them. A basic practical knowledge of summoning was all that she required.

The years passed. The war dragged on. Mr. Button's books were neatly sorted, cataloged, and stacked by author. His assistant was invaluable to him. Now he could direct her to summon foliots and even minor djinn while he sat in comfort watching. It was a highly satisfactory arrangement.

And—barring the odd fright—Kitty found it satisfactory too.

With the kettle boiled at last, Kitty made the tea and returned to the magician, who was sitting as before in the sofa's depths, studying his book. Mr. Button gave a grunt of thanks as she set the teapot down.

"Trismegistus notes," he said, "that succubi tend to recklessness when summoned, and are often impelled to self-destruction. They can be placated by placing citrus fruits among the incense, or by the soft playing of panpipes. Hum, they are sensual beasts evidently." He scratched his stump absently through his trousers. "Oh, I found something else too,

Lizzie. What was that demon you were asking about the other day?"

"Bartimaeus, sir."

"Yes, that's it. Trismegistus has a reference to him, in one of his tables of Antique Djinn. Somewhere in the appendices, you'll find."

"Oh, really, sir? That's great. Thank you."

"Gives a little of his summoning history. Brief. You won't find it terribly interesting."

"No, sir. I very much doubt it." She held out a hand. "Do you mind if I take a look?"

Part Two

Alexandria: 126 B.C.

On a hot morning in midsummer, a sacred bull broke free of its compound beside the river; it rampaged up among the fields, biting at flies and swinging its horns at anything that moved. Three men who tried to secure it were badly injured; the bull plunged on among the reeds and broke out onto a path where children played. As they screamed and scattered, it paused as if in doubt. But the sun upon the water and the whiteness of the children's clothes enraged it. Head down, it charged upon the nearest girl, and would have gored or trampled her to death had not Ptolemy and I been strolling down that way.

The prince raised a hand. I acted. The bull stopped, mid-charge, as if it had collided with a wall. Head reeling, eyes crossed, it capsized into the dust, where it remained until attendants secured it with ropes and led it back into its field.

Ptolemy waited while his aides calmed the children, then resumed his constitutional. He did not refer to the incident again. Even so, by the time we returned to the palace a flock of rumors had taken flight and was swooping and swirling about his head. By nightfall everyone in the city, from the lowest beggar to the snootiest priest of Ra, had heard or misheard something of it.

As was my wont, I had wandered late among the evening markets, listening to the rhythms of the city, to the ebb and flow of information carried on its human tide. My master was sitting cross-legged on the roof of his quarters, intermittently scratching at his papyrus strip and gazing out toward the darkened sea. I landed on the ledge in lapwing's form and fixed him with a beady eye.

"It's all over the bazaars," I said. "You and the bull."

He dipped his stylus into the ink. "What matter?"

"Perhaps no matter; perhaps much. But the people whisper."

"What do they whisper?"

"That you are a sorcerer who consorts with demons."

He laughed and completed a neat numeral. "Factually, they are correct."

The lapwing drummed its claws upon the stone. "I protest! The term 'demon' is fallacious and abusive in the extreme!"[1]

Ptolemy put down his stylus. "It is a mistake to be too concerned with names and titles, my dear Rekhyt. Such things are never more than rough approximations, matters of conven-

---

[1] Note my restraint here. My standard of conversation was pretty high in those days, on account of conversing with Ptolemy. Something about him made you disinclined to be too vulgar, blasphemous, or impudent, and even made me rein in my use of estuary Egyptian slang. It wasn't that he forbade any of it, more that you ended up feeling a bit guilty, as if you'd let yourself down. Harsh invective was a no-no, too. It's surprising I had anything left to say.

ience. The people speak thus out of ignorance. It's when they understand your nature and are *still* abusive that you will have to worry." He grinned at me sidelong. "Which is always possible, let's face it."

I raised my wings a little, allowing the sea wind to ruffle through my feathers. "Generally you come off well in the accounts so far. But mark my words, they'll be saying you let the bull loose soon."

He sighed. "In all honesty, reputation—for good or ill—doesn't much bother me."

"It may not bother *you*," I said darkly, "but there are those in the palace for whom the issue is life and death."

"Only those who drown in the stew of politics," he said. "And I am nothing to them."

"May it be so," I said darkly. "May it be so. What are you writing now?"

"Your description of the elemental walls at the margins of the world. So take that scowl off your beak and tell me more of it."

Well, I let it go at that. Arguing with Ptolemy never did much good.

From the beginning he was a master of curious enthusiasms. The accumulation of wealth, wives, and bijou Nile-front properties—those time-honored preoccupations of most Egyptian magicians—did not enthrall him. Knowledge, of a kind, was what he was after, but it was not the sort that turns city walls to dust and tramples on the necks of the defeated foe. It had a more otherworldly cast.

In our first encounter he threw me with it.

I was a pillar of whirling sand, a fashionable getup in those days. My voice boomed like rock-falls echoing up a gully. "Name your desire, mortal."

"Djinni," he said, "answer me a question."

The sand whirled faster. "I know the secrets of the earth and the mysteries of the air; I know the key to the minds of women.[2] What do you wish? Speak."

"What is essence?"

The sand halted in midair. "Eh?"

"Your substance. What exactly is it? How does it work?"

"Well, um . . ."

"And the Other Place. Tell me of it. Is time there synchronous with ours? What form do its denizens take? Have they a king or leader? Is it a dimension of solid substance, or a whirling inferno, or otherwise? What are the boundaries between your realm and this Earth, and to what degree are they permeable?"

"Um . . ."

In short, Ptolemy was interested in us. Djinn. His slaves. Our *inner* nature, that is, not the usual surface guff. The most hideous shapes and provocations made him yawn, while my attempts to mock his youth and girlish looks merely elicited hearty chuckles. He would sit in the center of his pentacle, stylus on his knee, listening with rapt attention, ticking me off when I introduced a more than usually obvious fib, and frequently interrupting to clarify some ambiguity. He used no Stipples, no Lances, no other instruments of correction. His summonings rarely lasted more than a few hours. To a hardened djinni like me, who had a fairly accurate idea of the vicious ways of humans, it was all a bit disconcerting.

---

[2] Patently all lies. Especially the last bit.

I was one of a number of djinn and lesser spirits regularly summoned. The normal routine never deviated: summons, chat, frenzied scribbling by the magician, dismissal.

In time, my curiosity was aroused. "Why do you do this?" I asked him curtly. "Why all these questions? All this writing?"

"I have read most of the manuscripts in the Great Library," the boy said. "They have much about summoning, chastisement, and other practicalities, but almost nothing about the nature of demons themselves. Your personality, your own desires. It seems to me that this is of the first importance. I intend to write the definitive work on the subject, a book that will be read and admired forever. To do this, I must ask many questions. Does my ambition surprise you?"

"Yes, in truth. Since when has any magician cared about our sufferings? There's no reason why you should. It's not in your interests."

"Oh, but it is. If we remain ignorant, and continue to enslave you rather than understand you, trouble will come from it sooner or later. That's my feeling."

"There is no alternative to this slavery. Each summons wraps us in chains."

"You are too pessimistic, djinni. Traders tell me of shamans far off among the northern wastes who leave their own bodies to converse with spirits in another world. To my mind, that is a much more courteous proceeding. Perhaps we too should learn this technique."

I laughed harshly. "It will never happen. That route is far too perilous for the corn-fed priests of Egypt. Save your energy, boy. Forget your futile questions. Dismiss me and have done."

Despite my skepticism, he could not be dissuaded. A year

went by; little by little my lies dried up. I began to tell him truth. In turn, he told me something of himself.

He was the nephew of the king. At birth, twelve years before, he had been a frail and delicate runtling, coughing at the nipple, squealing like a kitten. His discomfort cast a pall over the ceremony of naming: the guests departed hurriedly, the silent officials exchanged somber looks. At midnight his wet nurse summoned a priest of Hathor,[3] who pronounced the infant close to death; nevertheless, he completed the necessary rituals and gave the child into the protection of the goddess. The night passed fitfully. Dawn came; the first rays of sun glimmered through the acacia trees and fell upon the infant's head. His squalling subsided, his body grew calm. Without noise or hesitation, he nuzzled at the breast and drank.

The nature of this reprieve did not go unnoticed, and the child was swiftly dedicated to the sun god, Ra. He grew steadily in strength and years. Quick-eyed and intelligent, he was never as strapping as his cousin, the king's son,[4] eight years older and burly with it. Ptolemy remained a peripheral figure in the court, happier with the priests and women than with the sun-browned boys brawling in the yard.

In those days the king was frequently on campaign, struggling to protect the frontiers against the incursions of the Bedouin. A series of advisers ruled the city, growing rich on

---

[3] *Hathor*: divine mother and protector of the newborn; djinn in her temples wore female guises with the heads of cattle.

[4] He was a Ptolemy, too. As they all were, these kings of Egypt, for 200 years and more, one after the other until Cleopatra spoiled the run. Originality was not the family's strong suit. Easy to see, perhaps, why *my* Ptolemy regarded names so casually. They meant little. He told me his the first time I asked him.

bribes and port taxes, and listening ever closer to the soft words of foreign agents—particularly those of the emerging power across the water: Rome. Swathed in luxury in his marbled palace, the king's son fell into precocious dissipation. By his late teens he was a grotesque, loose-lipped youth, already potbellied with drink; his eyes glittered with paranoia and the fear of assassination. Impatient for power, he dawdled in the shadow of his father, seeking rivals in his blood-kin while waiting for the old man to die.

Ptolemy, by contrast, was a scholarly boy, slim and handsome, with features more nearly Egyptian than Greek.[5] Although distantly in line for the throne, he was clearly not a warrior or a statesman and was generally ignored by the royal household. He spent most of his time in the Library of Alexandria, close to the waterfront, studying with his tutor. This man, an elderly priest from Luxor, was learned in many languages and in the history of the kingdom. He was also a magician. Finding an exceptional student, he imparted his knowledge to the child. It was quietly begun and quietly completed, and only much later, with the incident of the bull, did rumor of it seep out into the wider world.

Two days afterward, while we were in discussion, a servant knocked upon my master's door. "Pardon me, Highness, but a woman waits without."

"Without what?" I wore the guise of a scholar, in case of just such an interruption.

---

[5] They came from his mother's side, I guess. She was a native girl from upriver somewhere, a concubine in the royal apartments. I never saw her. She and his father died of plague before my time.

Ptolemy silenced me with a gesture. "What does she want?"

"A plague of locusts threatens her husband's crops, sir. She seeks your aid."

My master frowned. "Ridiculous! What can *I* do?"

"Sir, she speaks of . . ." The servant hesitated; he had been with us in the field. "Of your power over the bull."

"This is too much! I am hard at work here. I cannot be disturbed. Send her away."

"As you wish." The servant sighed, made to close the door.

My master stirred. "Is she *very* miserable?"

"Mightily, sir. She has been here since dawn."

Ptolemy gave a gasp of impatience. "Oh, this is rank foolishness!" He turned to me. "Rekhyt—go with him. See what can be done."

In due course I returned, looking plump. "Locusts gone."

"Very well." He scowled at his tablets. "I have altogether lost the thread. We were talking about the fluidity of the Other Place, I believe. . . ."

"You realize," I said, as I sat delicately on the straw matting, "that you've done it now. Got yourself a reputation. Someone who can solve the common ills. Now you'll *never* get any peace. Same thing happened to Solomon with the wisdom thing. Couldn't step outdoors without someone thrusting a baby in his face. Mind you, that was often for a different reason."

The boy shook his head. "I am a scholar, a researcher, nothing else. I shall aid mankind by the fruits of my writing, *not* by my success with bulls or locusts. Besides, it's *you* who's doing the work, Rekhyt. Do you mind removing that wing-case from the corner of your mouth? Thank you. Now, to begin . . ."

He was wise about some things, Ptolemy was, but not about

others. The next day saw two more women standing outside his chambers; one had problems with hippos on her land, the other carried a sick child. Once again I was sent to deal with them as best I could. On the morning after that, a little line of people stretched out into the street. My master tore his hair and lamented his ill fortune; nevertheless I was dispatched again, along with Affa and Penrenutet, two of his other djinn. So it went. Progress on his research slowed to a snail's pace, while his reputation among the ordinary people of Alexandria grew fast as summer's flowering. Ptolemy suffered the interruptions with good, if exasperated, grace. He contented himself with completing a book on the mechanics of summoning and put his other inquiries aside.

The year aged, and in due time came the Nile's annual inundation. The floods went down, the dark earth shone fertile and wet, crops were planted, a new season began. Sometimes the queue of supplicants at Ptolemy's door was lengthy, at other times less so, but it never went away entirely. And it was not long before this daily ritual became known to the black-robed priests of the greater temples, and to the blackhearted prince sitting brooding on his wine-soused throne.

5

A disrespectful sound alerted Mandrake to the return of the scrying-glass imp. He put aside the pen with which he was scribbling notes for the latest war pamphlets, and stared into the polished disc. The baby's distorted features pressed up against the surface of the bronze as if it were frantically trying to push free. Mandrake ignored its writhing. "Well?" he asked.

"Well what?" The imp groaned and strained.

"Where's Bartimaeus?"

"Sitting on a lump of masonry twenty-six miles southeast of here in the shape of a long-haired girl. Very pretty she is, and all. But she ain't coming."

"What? She—he refused?"

"Yep. Ooh, it's dreadful tight in here. Six years I've been inside this disc with never a glimpse of home. You might let me out, you really might. I've served you heart and soul."

"You *have* no soul," Mandrake said. "What did Bartimaeus say?"

"I can't tell you, you're that young. It was rude, mind. Made my ears wax up. Well, he ain't coming voluntarily and that's all there is to it. Burn him and have done, I say. Can't think why you ain't snuffed him already. Oh, not back in that drawer *again*—can't you have mercy, you hateful boy?"

With the disc wrapped and the drawer shut fast, Mandrake rubbed his eyes. The Bartimaeus problem was growing intractable. The djinni was weaker and more cantankerous than ever; almost useless as a servant. In all logic he should let him go, but—as always—he found the thought distasteful. Quite *why* was hard to say, since alone of all his slaves the djinni never treated him with anything approaching respect. His abuse was tiring, exasperating beyond measure . . . and also oddly refreshing. Mandrake lived in a world where true emotions skulked forever behind politely smiling masks. But Bartimaeus made no pretense of his dislike. Where Ascobol and company were emollient and fawning, Bartimaeus was as impertinent now as the day he had first met him, back when he was just a child, owner of an entirely different name. . . .

Mandrake's mind had drifted. He coughed and drew himself up. *That* was the basic point, of course. The djinni knew his birth name. A risky thing for a man in his position! If another magician summoned him and learned what the demon knew. . . .

He sighed; his mind trundled from one well-worn track to another. *A dark-haired girl. Pretty.* No prizes for guessing the djinni's guise. Ever since Kitty Jones had died, Bartimaeus had used her shape to mock him. Not without success, either. Even three years on, visualizing her face gave Mandrake a sharp pang in his side. He shook his head in weary self-reproach. Forget her! She was a traitor, dead and gone.

Well, the wretched demon was of no importance. The pressing issue was the growing disruption caused by the war. That—and the dangerous new abilities appearing among the commoners. Fritang's tale of the egg-throwing urchins was just the latest in a long line of troublesome accounts.

Since Gladstone, magicians had observed a basic rule. The less commoners knew about magic and its tools, the better. Thus, every slave, from the scrawniest imp to the most arrogant afrit, was ordered to avoid unnecessary exposure when out on his master's business. Some utilized the power of invisibility; most went in disguise. So it was that the myriad demons thronging the streets of the capital or rushing above its rooftops went, as a rule, unnoticed.

But now this was no longer the case.

Each week brought new accounts of demonic exposure. A flock of messenger imps was spotted above Whitehall by a squealing group of schoolchildren; magicians reported that the imps had been correctly disguised as pigeons—they should not have aroused suspicion. Days later a jeweler's apprentice, newly arrived in London, ran wild-eyed down Horseferry Road and leaped over the river wall into the Thames. Witnesses claimed he had screamed warnings of ghosts among the crowds. Close inquiry revealed that spy demons *were* at work in Horseferry Road that day.

If commoners were being born with the power to see demons, the disruption that had lately plagued London could only get worse. . . . Mandrake shook his head irritably. He needed to visit a library, look for historical precedent. Such an outbreak might have happened before. . . . But he had no time—the present was difficult enough. The past would have to wait.

A knock at the door; his servant entered unobtrusively, keeping well away from the pentacles on the floor.

"The Deputy Police Chief is here to see you, sir."

Mandrake's forehead runkled in surprise. "Oh. Really? Very well. Show her up."

It took three minutes for the servant to descend to the reception room two floors below and return with the visitor, giving Mr. Mandrake ample time to draw out a small pocket mirror and inspect himself carefully. He smoothed down his shorn hair where it stuck up in a tuft; he brushed a few motes of dust from off his shoulders. Satisfied at last, he immersed himself in the papers on his desk—a model of zealous, well-kempt industry.

He recognized that such preening was laughable, but he did it anyway. He was always self-conscious when the Deputy Police Chief came to see him.

A brusque knock; with light feet and deft, decisive movements, Jane Farrar entered and crossed the room, carrying an orb-case in one hand. Mr. Mandrake half stood courteously, but she waved him back down.

"You don't need to tell me what an honor this is, John. I'll take it as read. I've got something important to show you."

"Please . . ." He indicated a leather chair beside the desk. She sat, laying the orb-case heavily on the table, and grinned at him. Mandrake grinned back. They grinned like two cats facing each other over an injured mouse, sleek and strong and confident in their mutual distrust.

The golem affair three years earlier had ended with the death and disgrace of the Police Chief, Henry Duvall, and since then the Prime Minister had not seen fit to appoint a successor. In fact, in a mark of his increasing distrust of the magicians around him, he had awarded *himself* the title, and relied upon the Deputy Police Chief to do most of the work. For two years Jane Farrar had fulfilled this role. Her aptitude was well known: it had allowed her to survive a close association with Mr. Duvall and work her way back into Mr. Devereaux's favor. She and Mandrake were now two of his closest allies. For that reason, between themselves they were achingly cordial; nevertheless, their old rivalry bristled beneath the surface.

Mandrake found her disconcerting for another reason. She was still very beautiful: her hair long and darkly gleaming, her eyes wry and green beneath long lashes. Her looks distracted him; it took all the confidence of his maturity to keep pace with her in conversation.

He slouched casually in his seat. "I've got something to tell you too," he said. "Who's first?"

"Oh, go on. After you. But hurry up."

"Okay. We *must* get the PM interested in these new abilities some commoners are getting. Another of my demons was spotted yesterday. It was kids again. I don't need to tell you the trouble this brings."

Ms. Farrar's elegant brows furrowed. "No," she said, "you don't. This morning we've got new reports of strikes by dock workers and machinists. Walkouts. Demonstrations. Not just in London, but the provinces too. It's being organized by men and women with these unusual powers. We're going to have to round them up."

"Mmm, but the *cause*, Jane. What is it?"

"We can find out when they're safely in the Tower. We've spies working through the pubs now, getting information. We'll come down hard. Anything more?"

"We need to discuss the latest attack in Kent too, but that can wait till Council."

Ms. Farrar reached out two slender fingers and unzipped her case, pulling back the cloth to expose a small crystal orb, blue-white and perfect, with a flattened base. She pushed it toward the center of the desk. "My turn," she said.

The magician sat up a little. "One of your spies?"

"Yes. Now pay attention, John—this is important. You know that Mr. Devereaux has asked me to keep close watch on our magicians, in case anyone tries to follow in the footsteps of Duvall and Lovelace?"

Mr. Mandrake nodded. More than the American rebels, more than their enemies in Europe, more than the angry commoners demonstrating on the streets, the Prime Minister feared his ministers, the men and women who sat at his table and drank his wine. It was a justified anxiety—his colleagues had ambitions; nevertheless it distracted him from other pressing business. "What have you found?" he asked.

"Something." She passed a hand across the orb, leaning forward so that her long black hair fell down around her face. Clearing his throat, Mandrake leaned forward too, enjoying (as always) her scent, her shape, their shared proximity. Dangerous and feline as she was, Ms. Farrar's company had its charms.

She spoke a few words: grains of blue ran away across the surface of the orb to collect in a pool near the bottom. The upper surface was left clear. Here an image formed—a face of shadows. It flickered, moved, but did not draw near.

Ms. Farrar looked up. "This is Yole," she said. "Yole has been keeping watch on a certain junior magician who has aroused my interest. Name of Palmer, second level, works in the Home Office. He has been passed over for promotion several times and is a frustrated man. Yesterday Palmer reported in sick; he did not go to work. Instead he left his apartment on foot and made his way to an inn near Whitechapel. He wore common workman's clothes. Yole here followed him and can relay what occurred. I think it will interest you."

Mandrake made a noncommittal gesture. "Please proceed."

Jane Farrar snapped her fingers and spoke into the orb. "Show me the inn, with sound."

The shadowy face retreated, vanished. An image formed inside the orb—rafters, whitewashed walls, a trestle table beneath a hanging brass light. Smoke drifted against grimy pebble-glass windows. The viewpoint was low down; it was as if they were lying on the floor. Dowdy women passed above, and men in rough-cut suits. Faintly, as if from far away, came laughter, coughing, and the chink of glasses.

A man sat at the trestle table, a burly gentleman in middle age, somewhat pink about the face, with gray flecks in his hair. He wore a shabby overcoat and a soft cap. His eyes ranged ceaselessly back and forth, evidently scanning the people in the inn.

Mandrake leaned closer, taking in a gentle breath: Farrar's perfume was especially strong that day. There was something pomegranaty about it. "That's Palmer, is it?" he asked. "This is an odd angle we've got. Too low."

She nodded. "Yole was a mouse by the skirting board. He wished to be unobtrusive, but it was a costly error, wasn't it, Yole?" She stroked the surface of the orb.

A voice from within, whimpering and meek. "Yes, mistress."

"Mmm. Yes, that's Palmer. Ordinarily a very dapper fellow. Now—this is important. It's hard to see from down here, but he has a pint of beer in his hand."

"Remarkable," Mandrake murmured. "This being a pub and all." *Definitely* pomegranates . . . and possibly a hint of lemon . . .

"Just wait. He's watching for someone."

Mandrake considered the figure in the orb. As was to be expected in a magician among commoners, Mr. Palmer seemed ill at ease. His eyes moved constantly; sweat glistened on his neck and shiny forehead. Twice he lifted his glass as if to drink his ale; twice he halted with it at his lips and replaced it slowly on the table out of sight.

"Nervous," Mandrake said.

"Yes. Poor, poor Palmer."

She spoke softly, but something in her tone carried the

sharpness of a knife. Mandrake breathed in again. That hint of tartness was just right. Set off the sweeter scent quite nicely.

Ms. Farrar coughed. "Something wrong with your chair, Mandrake?" she inquired. "Any farther forward and you'll be in my lap."

He looked up hurriedly from the orb, narrowly avoiding crashing his forehead into hers. "Sorry, Farrar, sorry." He cleared his throat, spoke in a deep voice. "It's just the tension—can't pull myself away. I wonder what this Palmer's game is. A most suspicious character." He pulled absently at a cuff.

Ms. Farrar regarded him for a moment, then gestured at the orb. "Well, observe."

Into view from the side of the orb came a newcomer, carrying a pint of beer. He went bareheaded, his ginger hair slicked back, dirty worker's boots and trousers shuffling beneath a long black raincoat. With casual but deliberate steps, he drew near to Mr. Palmer, who had shuffled over on his bench to make room for him.

The newcomer sat. He placed his beer upon the table and pushed his glasses higher on his little nose.

Mr. Mandrake was transfixed. "Wait!" he hissed. "I *know* him!"

"Yole," Farrar ordered. "Halt the scene."

The two men in the orb were half turning their heads to greet one another. At her command, the image froze.

"That's good," Farrar said. "You recognize him?"

"Yes. That's *Jenkins*. Clive Jenkins. Worked in Internal Affairs with me. Still may do for all I know. Secretary level. Going nowhere. Well, now. This *is* interesting."

"You wait." Her fingers snapped; Mandrake noted their pale pink nail polish, the soft color of her cuticles. The image in the orb restarted: the heads of the two men turned, nodded at each other, looked away. The newcomer, Clive Jenkins, took a sip of beer. His lips moved; half a second later, his voice, tinny and distorted, was audible in the orb.

"Now then, Palmer. Things are moving fast and it's decision time. We need to know if you're in, or if you're out."

Mr. Palmer took a long drink from his glass. His face gleamed with perspiration, his eyes were never still. He mumbled rather than spoke. "I need more information."

Jenkins laughed, adjusted his spectacles. "Relax, relax. I'm not going to bite you, Palmer. Information you'll get. But first we need proof of your good intentions."

The other man made an odd champing motion with his lips and teeth. "When have I ever given you reason to doubt me?"

"You haven't. But you haven't given us much reason to *believe* in you either. We need proof."

"How? You mean a test?"

"Of sorts. Mr. Hopkins needs to see your commitment for himself. You could be police for all we know. Working for Devereaux, or that bitch Farrar." He took another sip of beer. "Can't be too careful."

Outside the orb, in another time and another place, John Mandrake looked up at Jane Farrar and raised an eyebrow. She smiled lazily, showing a pointed canine.

"*Hopkins* . . ." he began. "You think that's the same one—"

"The scholar who showed Duvall how to work the golems," Farrar said. "The missing link of the last conspiracy. Yes, I do. But listen."

Mr. Palmer was in the middle of a red-faced expostulation, working himself up into an agony of wounded reproach. Clive Jenkins said nothing. Finally Palmer's tirade finished; he subsided like a limp balloon. "Well, what do you want me to do?" he said. "I'm warning you, Jenkins, you'd better not be setting me up—"

He raised his glass to refresh himself. As he did so, Jenkins seemed to flinch; his patched elbow knocked the other's arm. The pint glass jerked, beer dashed against the table. Palmer gave a little mew of anger. "You clumsy fool—"

Jenkins offered no apology. "If you do what's required," he said, "you'll reap the rewards along with me and the rest. You're to meet him . . . *here*."

"When?"

"*Then*. That's all. I'm going now."

Without another word, the slight, ginger-haired man slipped out from behind the trestle table and disappeared from view. For a few minutes Mr. Palmer remained sitting, his red face blank and desperate. Then he too departed.

Ms. Farrar snapped her fingers. The image faded; far in the distance the face of shadows reluctantly returned. Farrar sat back in her chair. "Needless to say," she said, "Yole failed us. From his vantage point as a mouse he could not see the surface of the table. He did not think that Jenkins had spilled the beer on purpose, nor that he had written the hour and place of meeting in the liquid on the table. Well, Yole followed Palmer for the remainder of the day and saw nothing. That night he reported back to me. While he was so doing, Palmer left his flat and did not come back. Evidently he went to keep his appointment with the mysterious Hopkins."

John Mandrake tapped his fingers together eagerly. "We shall have to interrogate Mr. Palmer when he returns."

"Therein lies a problem. At dawn this morning engineers working at the Rotherhithe Sewage Works saw something lying on a midden. They thought at first it was a pile of rags."

Mandrake hesitated. "Not . . ."

"I fear so. It was the body of Mr. Palmer. He had been stabbed through the heart."

"Oh," Mandrake said. "Ah. That's awkward."

"It is indeed. But it is promising too." Jane Farrar passed a hand across the orb; it darkened, became a cold, dull blue. "It means that this Clive Jenkins of yours—and this Hopkins—are planning something big. Big enough to involve quite casual murder. And *we're* onto it." Her eyes gleamed with excitement. Her long black hair was a little disheveled; several wisps fell down across her brow. Her face was flushed, and she was breathing quickly.

Mandrake adjusted his collar slightly. "Why are you telling *me* this now, outside Council?"

"Because I *trust* you, John. And I don't trust any of the others." She pushed the wisps away from her eye. "Whitwell and Mortensen are both intriguing against us. You know that. We've no friends in Council, apart from the PM. If we can flush out these traitors ourselves, our position will be admirably strengthened."

He nodded. "True. Well, it's clear what to do. Send a demon to tail Clive Jenkins and see if he can lead us to the truth."

Ms. Farrar zipped the crystal orb into its bag and stood. "I'll leave that to you, if I may. Yole's hopeless and my others are all on assignment. It's observation only at this stage. You won't need anything powerful. Or are all your djinn tied up?"

Mandrake looked toward the silent pentacles. "No, no," he said slowly, "I'm sure I'll be able to find someone."

6

I ask you. You fluff a mission, you harass a messenger, and you flatly refuse an order to return. Then you sit back waiting for the magician to respond. And nothing happens. For hours. No summons, no attempted punishment, nothing.

What kind of master do you call that?

If there's one thing that *really* annoys me, it's being ignored. Harsh treatment I can stand, insulting gestures likewise. At least they show you're having some kind of effect. But just being left to fester as if I were no better than that tuppenny imp in the scrying glass . . . that makes me more than a little annoyed.

The day was half done by the time I felt the first tweaking in my essence: firm, insistent, like razor wire passing through my vitals. The summons at last! Good—time to go! Not for me any fearful reluctance or holding back. I stood up from the broken chimney, stretched, removed the Concealment upon myself, scared a passing dog, made a rude noise to an old lady in the next garden, and lobbed the chimney as far as I could into the street.[1]

No more messing about. I was still Bartimaeus of Uruk, al-Arish, and Alexandria. This time I meant business.

I allowed the summons to pull my essence up and away. The street fast disintegrated in a welter of lights and colored

---

[1] Owing to my weakness it didn't make it across the pavement. But, boy, the gesture was savage.

bands. A second later these coalesced once more into the shape of a typical summoning hall: striplights on the ceilings, multiple pentacles on the floor. The Information Ministry, as usual. I allowed my body to reform in Kitty Jones's guise. It was simpler than trying to think of something else.

Right. The cursed Mandrake: where was he?

There! Sitting behind a desk, pen in hand, staring at a wodge of papers laid before him. He wasn't even glancing in my direction! I cleared my throat, put dainty hands on hips, prepared to speak—

"Bartimaeus!" A gentle voice. Too low to be Mandrake's. I turned, saw a delicate young woman with vole-brown hair sitting at another desk in a neighboring pentacle. It was Piper, my master's assistant, today doing her best to be severe. Her forehead was puckered in something resembling a frown; her fingertips were steepled sternly. She eyed me like a cross schoolmistress in a kindergarten. "Where *have* you been, Bartimaeus?" she began. "You should have returned this morning when requested. Mr. Mandrake has had to exert himself to draw you back, when he is so desperately busy. It isn't good enough, you know. Your behavior is really becoming *most* tiresome."

This wasn't what I'd had in mind at all. I drew myself up. "Tiresome?" I cried. "Tiresome? Have you forgotten whom you are addressing? This is Bartimaeus here—Sakhr al-Jinni, N'gorso the Mighty, builder of walls, destroyer of empires. I have twenty names and titles in as many tongues and my exploits reverberate in every syllable! Do not attempt to degrade me, woman! If you wish to live, I advise you to pick up your skirts and depart at speed. I intend to speak to Mr. Mandrake alone."

She clicked her tongue. "You simply are being quite impossible today, Bartimaeus. I think you should know better. Now, we have a little job here for you—"

"What? Not so fast!" In the pentacle I gave a half step forward; sparks snapped from my eyes and a nimbus of coral fire trembled upon my skin. "I'll have things out with Mandrake first!"

"I'm afraid the minister is currently indisposed."

"Indisposed? Baloney! I can see him right there!"

"He is busy working on today's news pamphlet. A deadline approaches."

"Well, he can leave off inventing his lies for a few minutes.[2] I want a word."

Ms. Piper wrinkled her nose. "You can have nothing worthwhile to say to him. Now please attend to your mission."

I turned away from her; addressed the figure at the desk. "Hoi, Mandrake!" No answer. I repeated myself, only louder. The papers flapped and fluttered on his desk.

The magician ran his hand through his short, cropped hair and looked up with a vaguely pained expression. It was as though he were being called upon to remember an old injury in a sensitive spot. He turned to his assistant. "Ms. Piper, please

---

[2] As part of his attempt to appease the commoners, Mandrake had initiated a series of penny-dreadful pamphlets, which told heroic tales of British soldiers fighting in the American wilderness. A typical title was *Real War Stories.* They were illustrated by bad woodcuts and purported to be true accounts of recent events. Needless to say, the American magicians were savage and cruel, using the blackest magic and the most hideous demons. Conversely, the square-jawed Brits always insisted on good manners and fair play and invariably got out of scrapes by improvising homemade weapons from fence posts, tin cans, and pieces of string. The war was depicted as being both necessary and virtuous. It was the old, old story—I've seen imps carve similar claims on official stelae up and down the Nile delta, defending pharaohic wars. The people tended to ignore those too.

inform Bartimaeus that I'm not remotely interested in his complaints. Remind him that most masters would have punished him severely for his incompetence in battle and that he is lucky to be alive. That's all." He picked up his pen once more.

Ms. Piper opened her mouth to speak, but I was faster. "Please inform that stubble-headed pipsqueak," I snapped, "that it is imperative he dismiss me on the instant. My powers, while still awesome, are somewhat reduced and need reviving. If he does not agree to this reasonable and just demand, I shall be forced to act, in desperation, *against my interests and his own*."

She frowned. "What's that last bit mean?"

I raised an eyebrow. "*He* knows." I turned to Mandrake. "You do know, don't you?"

He glanced at me. "Yes, obviously."[3] With portentous deliberation, he set down his pen once more. "Ms. Piper," he said, "please point out to that pernicious demon that should a certain thought of betrayal even flicker across his mind, I will relocate him to the Boston marshes, where every day a dozen djinn are seen to perish."

"Tell him that this breaks no ice now, buddy. My defenses are so low that I'm liable to perish doing his shopping. What do I lose where it happens?"

"Tell him that he surely exaggerates his weakness. This doesn't sound like the Bartimaeus who rubbed shoulders with Solomon."

"*And* Faustus and Zarbustibal."

"Faustus, Zarbustibal, whoever. I'm not giving a full list. However, tell him, Ms. Piper, that if he successfully completes the following mission I shall agree to his temporary

---

[3] Too right he did. His birth name hung over his head like a naked sword.

dismissal for purposes of recuperation, and let him be satisfied with that."

I sniffed disparagingly. "Tell him that this offer will only be acceptable if the mission is simple, swift, and utterly without danger."

"Tell him—oh, for heaven's sake, just tell him what the mission is and have done!" With a flurry of papers and a squeaking of his leather chair, the magician returned to his work. Ms. Piper's head came to a standstill; it had been swiveling from side to side like a worried owl's. She rubbed her neck gingerly.

"So get on with it, then," I said.

She looked a bit hurt by my curt tone, but I was in no mood for niceties. Once again Mandrake had treated me with contempt and derision. Once again he'd ignored my threats and entreaties. For the thousandth time I vowed revenge. Perhaps I *should* just risk America, go out there and chance my arm in battle. I'd survived such things before. But not when I was anything like as weak as this . . . No, I'd have to recharge my strength first, and that meant agreeing to this "final" mission. I waited grimly. On the other side of the room I heard Mandrake's pen go traveling across the paper, scratching out more lies.

Ms. Piper was evidently relieved that the confrontation was over. "Well," she said, smiling breezily, "I'm sure you'll find this *very* simple, Bartimaeus. We wish you to trail a minor magician named Clive Jenkins, keeping track of his every act and movement. Do not allow yourself to be seen or sensed. He is engaged in some kind of conspiracy against the government, and has been involved in murder. Furthermore, we know he is working for the fugitive scholar Hopkins."

That aroused my interest in a vague sort of way. It had been years since we'd had a lead on him. But I kept Kitty's face in sullen teenage mode.

"Jenkins: is he strong?"

She frowned. "I don't think so."

My master looked up, snorted. "Jenkins? Hardly."

"He works in Internal Affairs," Ms. Piper said. "Second level. Has an imp named Truklet. We know that he has been trying to corrupt other low-level magicians; it is not clear why. He is certainly in communication with Clem Hopkins."

"*That's* the priority," Mandrake said. "Find Hopkins. Don't act or attack: we know you're as weak as a weevil, Bartimaeus. Just find out where he is. Also, discover what they're up to. If you succeed, I'll—oh, *blast* it." The telephone on his desk had rung. He picked up the receiver. "*Yes?* Oh—hello, Makepeace." He rolled his eyes to the ceiling. "Yes, yes, I'd love to drop by, love to, but I can't right now. I'm off to Council shortly—in fact I'm late already. . . . What's it about? Hmm, hmm, *very* mysterious. Maybe later this—All right, I'll try. See you then." He thumped the phone down. "Got to go, Piper. I'll finish the Boston siege story over lunch. Send it to you by imp later, all right? We can get it printed for the evening fairs." He was standing up now, stuffing papers into a briefcase. "Anything else you need to know, Bartimaeus? I don't mean excuses or whinges; haven't time for them."

My version of Kitty gritted her teeth. "What about back-up? If I get to this Hopkins, there'll be more than an imp guarding him."

"He's just a *scholar*, Bartimaeus. But even if he's got defenses, we don't want you to wade in. I can send Cormocodran and the others to deal with him presently, and Ms. Farrar's got a lot of police on standby. Just report in to me when you've got the information. I'll give you an open-door injunction: you can return to me whenever you're ready."

"Where will you be?"

"Westminster Hall this afternoon; Devereaux's mansion at Richmond through the evening. Tonight, my house." His brief-case clipped shut; he was eager to depart.

"Where is Jenkins to be found now?"

"Internal Affairs building, sixteen Whitehall. Office at the back. He's a diminutive, ginger-haired little twerp. Anything else on your mind?"

"You wouldn't want to hear it."

"No doubt. One last point, Bartimaeus," he said. "I've given you my word, but you might encourage me to keep it if you drop that particular guise." He looked at me then, head-on—almost for the first time. "Think about it." He made a complex sign: the bonds that kept me imprisoned in the circle wrapped themselves about me, spun in opposite directions, and sent me spiraling out into the world.

7

Bartimaeus: By-name of the demon Sakhr al-Jinni, mentioned in Procopius and Michelot. A middle-ranking djinni of ancient standing, great ingenuity, and no little power. First recorded in Uruk; later in Jerusalem. Fought at the battle of al-Arish against the Assyrians. Known masters have included: Gilgamesh, Solomon, Zarbustibal, Heraclius, Hauser.

Bartimaeus's other names of power include: N'gorso, Necho, Rekhyt.

Linnaean ranking: 6, dangerous. Still extant.

Kitty lowered the book into her lap and stared out of the bus window. From her place on the upper deck she could see the sinews and tendons of the magicians' rule running up and down the London streets. Night Police strolled among pedestrians, vigilance spheres drifted on every corner, small swift points of light passed far above in the afternoon sky. Ordinary people went about their business, keeping their eyes carefully averted from the watchers all around. Kitty sighed. Even with its armies in action far away, the government's power was too complete, too obvious to allow dissent. Commoners alone could do nothing, that much was clear. They needed assistance of a different kind.

She glanced back down at Trismegistus's *Manual*, screwed up her eyes at the small crabbed typeface and reread the passage for the umpteenth time. The names Necho and Rekhyt were new to her, but the rest was drearily familiar. The meager list of masters, for instance. Though nothing much was known about the faces of Gilgamesh or Solomon, they were certainly adult kings. Heraclius was a magician-emperor—a warrior, not a child. As for Zarbustibal, she'd located a description of him months ago in an old inventory of Arabian masters: he was renowned about the Red Sea for his hook nose and protruding warts. Hauser *had* been youthful, right enough, but he was north European, fair and freckled—an engraving in one of Mr. Button's books had told her so. Not one of them could have been the dark-haired, dark-skinned boy whose guise Bartimaeus was fond of using.

Kitty shook her head, shut the book, and dropped it into her bag. She was probably just wasting time. She should forget her hunch and make the summons anyway.

Lunchtime had come and gone, and the bus was crowded with men and women returning to work. Some spoke together in hushed tones; others, worn-out already, dozed and nodded. A man sitting across the aisle from Kitty was reading the latest installment of *Real War Stories*, the Information Ministry's regular account of the war's progress. The front cover of the pamphlet was decorated by a woodcut; it showed a British soldier running up a hillside, bayonet at the ready. He was noble, determined, a classical statue in motion. At the top of the hill an American rebel cowered, his face contorted with anger, terror, and other unpleasant emotions. He wore an old-style magician's robe, drawn to seem ludicrous, effeminate. His arms were raised defensively; beside him sat his ally—a minor demon in similar pose. Its face was wizened and wicked; it wore, in miniature, the same clothes as the magician. The British soldier had no demon. A caption below the woodcut read: "Another Boston Triumph."

Kitty curled her lip contemptuously at the blatant

propaganda of the woodcut. That was Mandrake's work: he was head of Information now. And to think she'd let him live.

But it had been the djinni Bartimaeus who had encouraged her to do it, to act to spare the magician's life, and three years later, this still puzzled and intrigued her. Nothing that she had known about demons had quite prepared her for Bartimaeus's personality. Their conversations, framed against a backdrop of fear and danger, remained fresh in her mind—full of vitality, insight, and, above all, an unexpected rapport. He had opened a door for her, giving her a glimpse of a historical process she had never guessed at: thousands of years of magicians enslaving demons, forcing them to lend their power. Thousands of years, during which time a dozen empires had risen to glory, waned, then crumbled. The pattern recurred again and again. Demons were summoned, magicians fought their way to wealth and fame. Stagnation set in. Commoners discovered inherent abilities they didn't know they had—magical resilience built up through the generations that allowed them to rebel against their rulers. The magicians fell; new ones appeared elsewhere and began the process once more. So it went on: an endless cycle of strife. The question was—could it be broken?

A horn blared; with a jerk, the bus came to a sudden stop. Kitty lurched back into her seat and craned her neck against the window in an effort to see the cause.

From somewhere beyond the front of the bus a young man came flailing through the air. He landed heavily on the pavement, lay there an instant, and began to rise. Two Night Police, gray-uniformed, shiny of boot and cap, hurried into view. They flung themselves upon the youth, but he fought and kicked, punched his way free. He struggled to his feet. One officer produced a stick from her belt: she spoke a word—a glimmering blue current crackled at its end. The crowd that had gathered drew back in alarm. The young man retreated slowly. Kitty saw that his head was bloodied, his eyes wild.

The policewoman advanced, waving her jolt-stick. A sudden lunge, a jab. The current caught the young man in the chest. He jerked and twitched a moment; smoke billowed from his burning clothes. Then he laughed—a harsh and mirthless sound, like the calling of a crow. His hand reached out and grasped the stick at its active end. Blue energies juddered on his skin, but he seemed impervious: in two quick movements he had seized the stick, reversed it—and sent the policewoman jerking back upon the pavement in a flash of light. Her limbs twitched, her body arched, subsided. She lay quite still.

The young man threw the jolt-stick aside, turned upon his heel and, without a backward glance, disappeared down a side alley. The silent crowd parted for him.

With a grinding shudder and a rumble of gears, the bus set off. A woman sitting in front of Kitty shook her head at nobody in particular. "The war," she said. "It's causing all this trouble."

Kitty looked at her watch. Fifteen minutes to the library. She closed her eyes.

It was half true: the war *was* causing most of the trouble, both at home and abroad. But the spreading resilience of the commoners was helping to fan the flames.

Six months previously the War Minister, Mr. Mortensen, had implemented a new policy. In a bid to bludgeon the American rebels into submission, he determined to dramatically increase the size of the government force. To this end he enacted the

Mortensen Doctrine—a policy of mobilization across the country. Recruitment offices were opened, and commoners were encouraged to sign up to the armed forces. Lured by the prospect of preferential jobs on their return, many men did so. After a few days of training they sailed for America on special troopships.

Months passed; the expected return of the conquering heroes did not materialize. Everything went quiet. Information from the colonies was hard to come by; government statements became elusive. At length rumors began, perhaps spread by traders operating across the Atlantic: the army was bogged down deep in enemy territory; two battalions had been massacred; many men were dead, some had fled into the trackless forests and had never been seen again. There was talk of starvation and other horrors. The recruitment office queues dwindled and died away; a sullenness stole imperceptibly across the faces of people in the London streets.

In due course passive resentment turned to action. It began with a few disjointed episodes, far-flung and brief, each of which could be ascribed to random local causes. In one town a mother conducted a solitary protest, hurling a rock through the window of a recruitment office; in another, a group of laborers set down their tools and refused to toil for their daily pittance. Three merchants tipped a truckload of precious goods— golden oats, fine flour, sun-cured hams—upon the Whitehall road and, dousing it with oil, ignited it, sending a fragile ribbon of smoke into the sky. A minor magician from the eastern colonies, perhaps maddened by years of foreign diet, ran screaming into the War Ministry with an elemental sphere in his hand; in seconds he had activated the sphere, destroying himself and two young receptionists in a maelstrom of raging air.

While none of the incidents was as dramatic as the attacks

once carried out by the traitor Duvall, or even by the moribund Resistance, they had greater staying power in the public mind. Despite the best efforts of Mr. Mandrake at the Information Ministry, they were discussed repeatedly in markets, at workplaces, in pubs and cafés, until by the strange alchemy of gossip and rumor they were joined together into one big story, becoming the symptoms of a collective protest against the magicians' rule.

But it was a protest without teeth, and Kitty, who had tried active rebellion in her time, was under no illusions about how it was going to end. Each evening, at work in the Frog Inn, she heard proposals of strikes and demonstrations, but no suggestion of how to prevent the magicians' demons from cracking down. Yes, a few scattered individuals had resilience, as she had, but that alone was not enough. *Allies* were needed too.

The bus set her down in a peaceful, leafy road south of Oxford Street. Shouldering her bag, she walked the last two blocks to the London Library.

The guard had seen her often, both singly and in the company of Mr. Button. Nevertheless, he ignored her greeting, held out his hand for her pass, and scanned it sourly from his perch on a high stool behind a desk. Without comment, he ushered her on. Kitty smiled sweetly and strolled into the library foyer.

The library filled five labyrinthine floors, extending across the width of three town houses in the corner of a quiet square. Although out of bounds to commoners, it was not primarily concerned with magical texts, but instead with works that the authorities considered dangerous or subversive in the wrong hands. These included books on history, on mathematics, astronomy and other stagnant sciences, as well as literature that had been forbidden since Gladstone's day. Few of the leading magicians had the time or inclination to visit it, but Mr. Button, from whose attentions few historical texts were safe, sent Kitty to browse there frequently.

As usual, the library was almost deserted. Looking into the alcoves stretching away from the marbled stairs, Kitty made out one or two elderly gentlemen, sitting crumpled below the windows in the apricot afternoon light. One held a newspaper loosely in his hands; another definitely slept. Along a distant aisle a young woman was sweeping the floor; *shht, shht, shht* went the broom, and faint clouds of dust seeped through the shelving to the aisles on either side.

Kitty had a list of titles to borrow on Mr. Button's behalf, but she also had an agenda of her own. After two years' regular visits, she knew her way around; before long she was in a secluded corridor on the second floor, standing in front of the Demonology section.

Necho, Rekhyt . . . Her knowledge of ancient languages was nonexistent: these names might belong in almost any culture. Babylonian? Assyrian? On a hunch, she tried Egyptian. She consulted several general demon listings, all bound in cracked black leather, yellowed pages covered in tight, faint columns of script. Half an hour passed; she found nothing. A brief consultation with the library index led her to a remote alcove beside a window. A window seat with purple cushions waited invitingly. She hauled down several specialist Egyptian almanacs and began to search.

Almost immediately, in a portly dictionary, she found something.

Rekhyt: Engl. transl.: *lapwing*. This bird symbolized slavery to the Egyptians; occurs commonly in tomb art and in hieroglyphs on magicians' papyri. Demons with this by-name recur in the Old, New, and Late Periods.

Demons *plural* . . . That was frustrating. But she'd pinned the epoch down, for sure. Bartimaeus *had* been employed in Egypt; for some of that time, at least, he had been known as Rekhyt. . . . In her mind's eye Kitty saw the djinni as she remembered him: dark, slight, wearing a simple wraparound kilt. From what she knew of the appearance of the Egyptians, Kitty felt she might be onto something.

For another hour she sat there, flipping contentedly through the dusty pages. Some books were useless, written in foreign tongues, or in phrases so abstruse that the sentences seemed to coil up on themselves before her eyes. The rest were dense and forbidding. They gave her lists of pharaohs, of civil servants, of the warrior-priests of Ra; they provided tables of known summonings, of surviving records, of obscure demons sent on mundane tasks. It was a daunting search, and more than once, Kitty's head nodded. She was startled back into life by police sirens in the distance, by shouts and chanting from a nearby street, once by an elderly magician blowing his nose loudly as he shuffled down the passage.

The autumn sun was lowering level with the library window; its rays warmed the seat with a golden light. She glanced at her watch. Four-fifteen! Not long before the library closed, and she hadn't even found Mr. Button's books. In three hours she must be at work too. It was an important night and George Fox of the Frog Inn was a stickler for punctuality. Wearily she pulled another volume across the window seat and flipped it open. Just another five minutes, then—

Kitty blinked. There it was. A list, eight pages long, of selected demons, tabulated alphabetically. Now then . . . Kitty scanned down it with practiced speed. Paimose, Pairi, Penrenutet, Ramose . . . Aha—Rekhyt. Three of them.

> *Rekhyt* (I): Afrit. Slave of Sneferu (4th Dynasty) and others; of legendarily vicious temperament. Killed at Khartoum.
>
> *Rekhyt* (II): Djinni. By-name of Quishog. Guardian of the Necropolis of Thebes (18th Dynasty). Morbid tendencies.
>
> *Rekhyt* (III): Djinni. Also named Nectanebo or Necho. Energetic, but unreliable. Slave of Ptolemaeus of Alexandria (fl. 120s B.C.).

It was the third one, it *had* to be. . . . The entry was shortness itself, but Kitty felt a surge of excitement in her veins. A new master, a new possibility. Ptolemaeus . . . the name was quite familiar. She was sure she'd heard Mr. Button mention it; sure even that he owned books with it in the title . . . *Ptolemaeus*. She racked her brains—well, it would be easy enough to track down the reference, when she got back.

With fevered haste, Kitty noted down her findings in her jotter, snapped the elastic band around it, and shoved it into her tattered satchel. She gathered the books into an untidy pile, hoisted them into her arms, and returned them to the shelves. As she did so, the distant buzzer sounded in the foyer. The library was closing! And she'd *still* not got her master's books!

Time to move. But it was with a definite sense of triumph that Kitty sprinted down the corridor. Better look out, Bartimaeus, she thought as she ran. Better look out . . . I'm closing in on you.

8

The afternoon's Council meeting was even less satisfactory than John Mandrake had feared. It took place in the Hall of Statues at Westminster, a rectangular room built of pink-gray stone, with soaring medieval vaulting high above, and thickly layered Persian rugs covering the flagstones. In a dozen niches along the walls stood life-size statues of the great magicians of the past. There at the end, austere and forbidding, was Gladstone; opposite him, flamboyant in a frock coat, his deadly rival Disraeli. All the succeeding Prime Ministers were featured, together with other notables. Not every alcove yet contained a statue, but Mr. Devereaux, the current premier, had ordered the empty ones to be filled with sumptuous floral displays. It was guessed the vacant spaces reminded him of his own mortality.

Globes of imp-light drifted against the ceiling, illuminating—in the center of the room—a circular table of English oak, broad in diameter and polished to perfection by laboring imps. Around this sat the Council, the great ones of the Empire, toying with their pens and bottles of mineral water.

Mr. Devereaux had chosen a round table for reasons of diplomacy. Technically no one person took precedence over another—an admirable policy which had been undermined by his insistence on using a gigantic golden chair, ornately carved with swollen cherubs. Mr. Mortensen, the War Minister, had followed suit with an ostentatious seat of burnished redwood. Not to be outdone, Mr. Collins of the Home Office had

95

responded with a monumental throne of emerald brocade, complete with perfumed tassels. So it went. Only John Mandrake and his erstwhile master Ms. Jessica Whitwell had resisted the temptation to somehow modify their seating.

The placing of each magician's chair was likewise subtly fought over, until the situation had stabilized to reflect the factions that were opening up in Council. Mr. Devereaux's two favorites sat beside him: John Mandrake, the Information Minister, and Jane Farrar of the police. Beyond Farrar sat Ms. Whitwell and Mr. Collins, who were known to be skeptical about the direction of the war. Beyond Mandrake were Mr. Mortensen and Ms. Malbindi of the Foreign Office: it was their policies that the government was currently following.

The meeting began inauspiciously with an advertisement. From a side room a giant crystal orb came rumbling on a wheeled platform. It was pulled by a slave-gang of implets, led by a foliot overseer wielding a horsehair whip. As they drew near the table, the foliot uttered a cry, the implets sprang to attention, and with the cracking of the whip vanished one after the other in clouds of colored steam. The crystal orb glowed pink, then orange; in its center appeared a broad and beaming face, which winked and spoke.

"Esteemed ladies and gentlemen of the Council! Let me remind you that we are only two days from the theatrical event of the decade, the society event of the year! Reserve your tickets now for the premiere of my latest work, based on the life of our beloved friend and leader, Mr. Rupert Devereaux! Get ready to laugh, cry, tap your feet, and sing along to the choruses of *From Wapping to Westminster: A Political Odyssey*. Bring your partners, bring your friends, and don't forget your handkerchiefs. I, Quentin Makepeace, promise you all a sensational night!"

The face faded; the orb went dark. The assembled ministers coughed and shuffled in their seats. "Dear God," someone whispered. "It's a *musical.*"

Mr. Devereaux beamed around at them. "Quentin's sweet gesture is a *mite* unnecessary," he said. "I'm sure you all already have your tickets."

So they had. There was little option.

The day's business commenced. Mr. Mortensen gave a report of the latest news from America, brought by djinn across the ocean. It was sour fare: deadlock in the wilderness, minor skirmishes, nothing decisive gained. It had been so for weeks.

John Mandrake barely listened. The account was predictable and depressing; it only increased the frustration that boiled within him. *Everything* was out of control—the war, the commoners, the situation across the Empire. Something decisive needed to be done, and soon, if the nation was to be saved. And he knew what that something was. The Staff of Gladstone—a weapon of incredible power—lay useless in the vaults below that very chamber, begging to be brought out by anyone with the talent to use it. If wielded effectively, it would destroy the rebels, cow Britain's enemies, send the commoners scampering back to work. But it needed a magician of the strongest level to command it, and Devereaux was not that man. Hence—out of fear for his own position—he kept it safely locked away.

Would Mandrake have been able to use the Staff, given the opportunity? In all honesty, he didn't know. Perhaps. He was the strongest magician in the room, with the possible exception of Whitwell. Then again, three years before, when he had acquired the Staff on the government's behalf, he had tried to get it working, and had failed.

That knowledge, that frustrated ambition mixed with self-doubt, contributed to the listlessness which had lately come over him. Day to day, his job was futile—he was surrounded by squabbling fools, unable to improve the situation. The only glimmer of hope came from the hunt for the traitor Hopkins. Perhaps *there* he could make a breakthrough, achieve something tangible for once. Well, he would have to see what Bartimaeus found.

Mortensen droned on. Overcome by boredom, Mandrake made desultory notes on his pad. He sipped his water. He appraised his fellow Council members, one by one.

First: the Prime Minister, his hair streaked with gray, his face puffy and blotched with the strain of war. A heaviness hung about him; he seemed tentative and quavering in speech. Only when discussing theater would a trace of his old animation return, the infectious charisma that had so inspired Mandrake as a boy. At other times he was dangerously vindictive. Not long before, Mr. Collins's predecessor in the Home Office, a woman named Harknett, had spoken out against his policies. Six horlas had come for her that evening. Such events troubled Mandrake—it did not suggest the clear thinking worthy of a leader. Besides, it was morally unsound.

Beyond Devereaux sat Jane Farrar. Sensing his appraisal, she looked up and smiled; her eyes were conspiratorial. As he watched, she scribbled something on a piece of paper and pushed it across to him. It read: HOPKINS. ANY NEWS? He shook his head, mouthed, "Too soon," made a rueful face, and turned his eyes to her neighbor.

The Security Minister, Jessica Whitwell, had endured

several years out of favor; now she was steadily clawing it back. The reason was simple—she was too powerful to be ignored. She lived frugally, did not attempt to accumulate great wealth, and devoted her energies to enhancing the Security services. A number of recent raids had been annihilated thanks to her efforts. She was still bone-thin, her hair ghost-white and spiky. She and Mandrake regarded each other with respectful loathing.

To her left: Mr. Collins, the newest member of the Council. He was a fiery little man, swarthy, round-faced, eyes habitually bright with indignation. He had repeatedly emphasized the damage the wars were doing to the economy; prudently, however, he had stopped short of overtly demanding an end to hostilities.

On Mandrake's right was the war faction: first, Helen Malbindi, Foreign Minster. She was by nature meek and malleable, but the pressure of her current post had made her prone to outbursts of shrieking rage among her staff. Her nose was a good indicator of her mood: at times of stress it went white and bloodless. Mandrake held her in low esteem.

Carl Mortensen, the War Minister, stood beyond Malbindi, rounding up his report. For years his star had been in the ascendant; it had been he who most strongly advocated war upon America, he whose strategies had been most closely followed. His lank blond hair remained long (he had not deigned to crop it into military style) and he still spoke confidently of success. Nevertheless, his nails were bitten to the quick, and the other Council members watched him with the steady eyes of vultures.

"I remind you all that we must remain committed," he said. "It is a crucial time. The rebels are running ragged. By contrast, we have barely tested our resources. We could maintain our presence there for at least another year."

In his golden chair Mr. Devereaux ran a finger across a cherub's rump; he spoke softly. "A further year would not see you in this room, Carl." He smiled up under hooded lids. "Unless you were incorporated into some kind of ornament."

Mr. Collins tittered; Ms. Farrar smiled icily. Mandrake inspected his pen top.

Mr. Mortensen had blanched, but held the Prime Minister's gaze. "We will not need a year, of course. I used the term for illustration only."

"A year, six months, six weeks—it is all one." Ms. Whitwell was speaking angrily. "In the meantime our enemies across the world are taking advantage of us. There is talk of rebellion everywhere! The Empire is in ferment."

Mortensen made a face. "You overstate this."

Devereaux sighed. "What is *your* report, Jessica?"

She bowed stiffly. "Thank you, Rupert. Only last night three separate attacks occurred on our own soil! My men destroyed a Dutch raiding party off the Norfolk coast, while Collins's djinn had to repel an air attack over Southampton: we assume they were Spanish demons, do we not, Bruce?"

Mr. Collins nodded. "They wore yellow and orange tabards, decorated with the arms of Aragon. They sent Infernos raining down upon the city center."

"Meanwhile *another* band of demons savaged a section of Kent," Ms. Whitwell continued. "I believe Mr. Mandrake dealt with that." She sniffed.

"I did," John Mandrake said blandly. "The enemy force was destroyed, but we have no evidence where they came from."

"A pity." Whitwell's thin white fingers tapped a rhythm on

the table. "Even so, the problem is clear: this is a European-wide phenomenon, and our main forces are not on hand to crush it."

Mr. Devereaux nodded wearily. "Indeed, indeed. Does anyone else fancy a sweetmeat at this moment?" He looked around. "No? Then I shall venture one alone." He coughed. A tall, gray shadow stepped from nowhere around his chair, and with spectral fingers laid a golden tray before him; it was piled high with yellow pies and pastries. The shadow withdrew. Devereaux selected a glazed doughnut. "Ah, excellent. Jane— pray give us the police's perspective on the domestic situation."

Ms. Farrar adopted a languid pose that nevertheless displayed her figure to fine advantage. "Frankly, it is troubling. Not only do we have these raids, which are hard to deal with, but there is the matter of commoner disruption. More and more people are seemingly resistant to magical attacks. They see through illusions, observe our spies. . . . Inspired by their example, strikes and demonstrations have been held. I regard this as potentially more important even than the war."

The Prime Minister wiped fragments of sugar from his mouth. "Jane, Jane, we must not get distracted. Commoners can be dealt with in due time. They are restless *because* of the war." He looked meaningfully at Mr. Mortensen.

Ms. Farrar inclined her head; a strand of hair fell attractively across her face. "It is your decision, of course, sir."

Mr. Devereaux slapped a hand against his thigh. "It certainly is! And I decide that we shall now have a little break. Coffee and sweetmeats all round!"

The shadow returned; with varying degrees of reluctance, the ministers accepted their refreshments. Mandrake slouched over his cup, looking at Jane Farrar again. It was true that they were allies in Council: distrusted by the others, favored by Devereaux, they had long been thrown together. But that meant little. Such allegiances could change at the drop of a hat. As always, he found it hard to resolve her strong personal allure with the cool flintiness of her personality. He frowned; it was a curious fact that, despite his self-control, despite his belief in the virtues of magicians' rule, viewing someone like Farrar close up made him feel, deep down, uncertain, hesitant, clouded by unease. Still, she was very beautiful.

When it came down to it, of course, *all* the Council made him feel uneasy. It had taken all his inner steel to maintain his status in their company. They each radiated ambition, strength, cleverness, and guile; none of them ever acted against their own interests. To survive, he had done the same.

Well, perhaps this was the natural way. Had he ever met anyone who *had* acted otherwise? Unbidden, the face of Kitty Jones came into his mind. Ridiculous! A traitor, violent, tempestuous, untamed. . . . He made a doodle in his pad: a face with long dark hair. . . . Ridiculous! Anyway, the girl was dead. He crossed it out hurriedly.

And further back—long, long ago now—there had been his art tutor too. Ms. Lutyens. Funny, he could no longer clearly recall her face—

"Didn't you hear me, John?" That was Devereaux, speaking almost in his ear. He felt little flakes of sugar doughnut being blown against his cheek. "We are discussing our position in Europe. I was requesting your opinion."

Mandrake sat up. "Sorry, sir. Um, my agents tell me there is discontent as far afield as Italy. There have been riots in Rome, I understand. But it is not my area."

Gaunt, severe, stick-thin, the Security Minister, Jessica

Whitwell spoke. "But it *is* mine. Italy, France, Spain, the Low Countries. Everywhere it is the same. Our troops are at an all-time low. What is the result? Dissent, riot, rebellion. All Europe is erupting. Every last malcontent under the sun is preparing to strike at us; we will be fighting in a dozen countries before the month is out."

"This is no time for exaggeration, Jessica." Mr. Mortensen's eyes were steely.

"Exaggeration?" A bony hand slammed against the table; Ms. Whitwell stood. "This will be the worst uprising since 1914! And where are our forces? Thousands of miles away! I am telling you, we will lose Europe if we are not careful!"

Now Mortensen was raising his voice too. He half rose from his chair. "Oh, and perhaps *you* have a solution, do you?"

"Certainly I do. We pull out from America and bring our forces home!"

"What?" Mortensen turned to the Prime Minister, face dark with fury. "Do you hear that, Rupert? That is nothing but rank appeasement! It borders on treachery!"

A blue-gray glow erupted around Jessica Whitwell's clenched fist; the air hummed with a surge of unearthly force. Her voice was suddenly quiet. "Would you be so good as to repeat that, Carl?"

The War Minster remained rigid, fingers locked around the armrests of his redwood chair, eyes flicking to and fro. At last he sank back into a position of furious repose. The glow upon Ms. Whitwell's fist flickered and went out. She waited a few seconds more, then sat with victorious care.

According to their allegiance, the other ministers smirked or scowled. Mr. Devereaux studied his cuticles; he looked a little bored.

John Mandrake stood up. Affiliated to neither Mortensen nor Whitwell, he felt a sudden urge to wrest back the initiative, to take a gamble, throw off his inertia. "I'm sure neither of our excellent ministers intended to give offense, nor was so childish as to receive it," he said. "Clearly both are in the right: Jessica's anxiety is prudent, since the situation in Europe is becoming unfortunate; Carl's refusal to admit defeat is also laudable. We cannot leave America in the hands of criminals. I would like to suggest a solution to the problem."

"Which is?" Ms. Whitwell was unimpressed.

"Withdrawing troops is not the answer," Mandrake went on coldly. "That sends out quite the wrong message to our enemies worldwide. But we *must* bring this conflict to an end. Our demons are not enough and nor—saving Mr. Mortensen's pardon—are the common soldiers. We need a decisive weapon that the Americans do not have. Something with which they cannot contend. Simple. We use Gladstone's Staff."

He had expected the barrage of noise that greeted his proposal; he did not attempt to speak further, but with a thin smile, sat himself down. Jane Farrar met his gaze and raised a quizzical eyebrow; the faces of the others were variously indignant.

"Impossible!"

"A foolish fancy!"

"Quite out of the question!"

The noise subsided. Mandrake stirred. "I'm sorry," he said, "but I don't quite understand your objections."

Carl Mortensen made a dismissive gesture. "The Staff is untried, untested."

"It is hard to control," Helen Malbindi said.

"A highly dangerous artefact," Jessica Whitwell added.

"But that's the *point*," Mandrake said. "With the Staff, Gladstone conquered Europe. It will do the same to Boston easily enough. Our friends in Paris and Rome will hear about it and duck down behind their parapets again. Problem solved. Once it has crossed the ocean, the whole thing would take no more than a week. Why keep the Staff under lock and key when it's the solution to our difficulties?"

"Because," a cold voice said, "*I* do not choose to use it. And *my* word goes."

Mandrake turned to face the Prime Minister, who had swiveled in his chair and drawn himself upright. Devereaux's face had become hard and lined, the flabbiness less obvious. The eyes were dull, opaque. "You may perhaps have received a memo this morning, Mandrake," he said. "The Staff, and other items, have been removed to the Room of Treasures in this very building. They are surrounded by a range of high-level magical safeguards. They will not be used. Do you understand?"

Mandrake hesitated; he thought of standing his ground. Then he remembered the fate of Ms. Harknett. "Of course, sir," he began. "But I must ask why—"

"*Must?* You must do nothing!" The face was suddenly twisted, contorted, the eyes wild and staring. "You will know your place and not seek to destabilize this Council with your inane theories. Now be silent and think before you speak again! And be careful lest I suspect you of having an agenda of your own." The Prime Minister turned away. "Mortensen—bring out the maps. Give us a firmer update on our position. I understand we have pinned the rebels in an area of marshland. . . ."

"That was a little rash," Jane Farrar whispered, as she walked with Mandrake in the corridor an hour later. "Whoever has the

Staff holds true power. Devereaux's frightened of what that person'll do to *him*."

Mandrake nodded sullenly. The depression he had briefly shaken off had speedily returned. "I know. But someone's got to make the case openly and clearly. The country's falling into chaos. I wouldn't be surprised if half the Council aren't planning something."

"Concentrate on the plot we *do* know about. Anything yet on Jenkins?"

"Not yet. But it won't be long. My best djinni's on the case."

9

Since the days of old Egypt, when I took the form of a silver hawk and shadowed Kushite raiders far out across the sand hills, I've always been a dab hand at trailing unobserved. Take those raiders, now: they left djinn in the form of jackals and scorpions to guard the desert in their wake. But the hawk flew high against the sun and easily evaded them. I found the raiders' base hidden among the blue-green gum trees of the Kharga oasis and drew the pharaoh's army down upon them. So they perished to a man.

I was employing similar discreet but deadly skills now, although it has to be said that the circumstances were a mite less glamorous. Instead of a ferocious horde of puma-pelted raiders you had a scrawny, ginger secretary; in place of the aching vistas of the Sahara you had a smelly Whitehall backstreet. Apart from that, the parallel was exact. Oh, and I wasn't a hawk this time—a woebegone sparrow was more the job in London.

I was sitting on a sill watching a grubby window opposite. Whoever owned the sill wasn't very keen on birds: he'd laced it with bird lime, metal spikes, and scraps of poisoned bread. A typical English welcome. I kicked the bread into the street, used a small Inferno to incinerate the lime, bent a couple of spikes out of true, and wedged my frail little carcass between them. I was so weak by now that this Herculean effort pretty much finished me off. Head spinning, I settled in to watch my quarry.

It wasn't exactly unmissable viewing. Through the accumulated grime on the windowpane I could see Clive Jenkins
sitting at a desk. He was thin, stooped, and rather puny; if it had
been a straight fight between him and the sparrow, I'd have put
my money on the bird. An expensive suit hung uneasily on his
frame, as if reluctant to get too close; his shirt was a disturbing
mauve. He was pale-faced and a bit freckly, with small eyes
peering myopically from behind thick glasses and reddish hair
plastered back in a kind of oily pelt, reminiscent of a fox who'd
been caught out in the rain. Small bony hands tapped unen-
thusiastically at a typewriter.

Mandrake had not been wrong in his assessment of Jenkins's
powers. As soon as I took up my perch, I checked the seven
planes for sensor webs, watch prisms, gimlet eyes, shadow-
stalkers, orbs, matrices, heat traps, trigger-plumes, sprites,
weirds, and other means the magician might have employed for
magical protection. Not a sausage. He had a cup of tea on his
desk and that was about it. I watched closely for any sign of
supernatural communication with Hopkins or another, but the
secretary spoke no words and made no untoward signs. Pitter-
patter, pitter-patter went his fingers on the keys; occasionally
they rubbed his nose, adjusted his glasses or scratched an itchy
spot on the end of his chin. So the afternoon passed. It was
simply riveting.

Although I did my best to keep focused on the job in hand,
I did find my mind wandering at intervals, (a) because it was so
damn dull, and (b) because the ache in my essence made me
clothy-headed and distracted. It was like suffering chronic lack
of sleep: I kept drifting off and thinking of unrelated topics—
the girl, Kitty Jones; my old enemy Faquarl sharpening his
cleaver; far off in the distance, Ptolemy—before he changed.

Each time I had to force myself back into the present with a start; but Jenkins was always as before, so no harm done.

Five-thirty came, and with it an almost imperceptible change in Jenkins. A new and stealthy life seemed to flicker in his veins; his lethargy receded. With quick movements, he drew a cover over the typewriter, tidied his desk, gathered up a few bundles of paper, and slung a coat over his arm. He departed his office out of view.

The sparrow stretched a painful wing, shook its head to relieve the numbing ache behind its eyes, and took off. I drifted down the side road and out above the bustle of Whitehall, where buses nudged slowly through the heavy traffic and armored vans disgorged Night Police at intervals among the crowds. The war had brought disturbance to the streets, and the authorities were taking no chances in the center of the capital. Imps and foliots watched from recesses in the eaves of nearby buildings.

I alighted in a walnut tree in the little courtyard that separated the Internal Affairs building from the road, and waited. A policeman stood below me at the gate. Presently the door opened and Jenkins emerged; he wore a long leather coat and carried a crumpled hat in one hand. At the gate he nodded to the guard, showed a pass, and exited. He turned north into Whitehall, set his hat on his head at a jaunty angle, and with suddenly eager steps plunged into the crowd.

It's not easy following an individual amid a milling throng, but when you're an expert tracker like me, you take it in your stride. The secret is not to get distracted. I kept my eyes fixed upon the crown of Jenkins's hat and fluttered high above, keeping a little behind him, just in case he looked around. There wasn't much chance that he would guess he was being followed, but you know me, I do things properly. You have to get up pretty early to catch *me* out in the art of trailing.[1]

Beyond the roofs the autumn sun was dropping down behind the trees of Hyde Park; a pretty red haze hung in the sky. The sparrow watched it approvingly. It reminded me of evening at the pyramids, when the djinn flitted like swallows above the tombs of the kings, and—

A bus horn honked; the sparrow snapped back to the present. *Careful*—almost caught daydreaming there. . . . Now then: Jenkins . . .

Ah.

I scanned frantically to and fro. Where was the distinctive hat? Nowhere to be seen. Perhaps he'd taken it off . . . Nope: no fox's coiffure in the vicinity. Men, women, children, yes. All the flotsam and jetsam of humanity. But no Jenkins.

The sparrow snapped its beak together in irritation. This was *Mandrake's* fault. If he'd given me a few months' rest, my head would be clearer. I wouldn't keep getting distracted. It was like the time when—

Concentrate. Perhaps Jenkins was on a bus. I did a quick fly-past the nearest few, but the secretary was not aboard. Which meant he'd either dematerialized or gone inside a building. . . . I noticed a pub now, the Cheddar Cheese, squeezed between two government offices, roughly at the point where Jenkins

---

[1] Once, when I was employed by the Algonquin shamans, an enemy afrit came to our tribe by night and abducted a chief's child. When the discovery was made, the afrit was far away; it had disguised itself as a buffalo cow, and spun a Glamour on the child, so it seemed a lowing calf. But afrits have fiery hooves: I followed the singed grass stalks for a hundred miles across the rolling prairie and slew the abductor with a silver spear. The child was returned alive, if a little green from eating so much grass.

had vanished. Since voluntary dematerializing in humans is rare,[2] I figured the pub was the likely option.

No time to waste. The sparrow dropped like a stone to the pavement and crept, unnoticed by the hurrying throng, to the open door. In the act of passing through, I gritted my teeth and changed: the sparrow became a fly, a bluebottle with a furry rump. The flash of pain from the alteration made my flight pattern erratic; I lost track of where I was, meandered for a moment through the smoky air and landed, with a soft plop, in the wineglass of a lady who was just setting it to her lips.

She looked down, sensing movement, and saw me floating on my back an inch below her nose. I waved a hairy leg; she emitted a scream like a baboon and dashed the glass away. Wine spattered into the face of a man standing at the bar; he careered back in shock, knocking two other ladies from their stools. Cries, yells, much flailing of limbs. All around was tumult. Soused with wine, the bluebottle landed on the surface of the bar, bumped, skidded, righted itself, and hid behind a bowl of peanuts.

Well, if I hadn't been *quite* as unobtrusive as I'd wished, there was at least enough distraction for me to make a quick survey of the room. I wiped a couple of eye-facets clean and did a quickstep off the bar and up a nearby pillar, sashaying between the crisps and bags of pork scratchings. From a vantage point aloft I looked about.

There, standing in the center of the room, talking avidly with two others, was Jenkins.

The fly flitted closer among the shadows, checking the planes. None of the men had active magical defenses, though

---

[2] It tends to be *in*voluntary: i.e. when you hit them with a Detonation.

the stench of incense clung to their clothes and their skin had the pallor of the typical working magician. They were a shabby trio to be sure—like Jenkins, the others wore suits too big and too good for them; their shoes were pointed, their shoulder pads a little high. All three were in their twenties, or so I judged. Apprentices, secretaries: none gave off the aura of power. But they spoke avidly; their eyes glittered in the dusk of the Cheddar Cheese with fanatics' fervor.

Upside down on the ceiling, the fly craned its head to listen to their words. No luck—the squawking at the bar blocked out the sound. I dropped into midair, circled stealthily down toward them, cursing the lack of walls nearby. Jenkins was speaking; I flitted nearer, close enough now to smell the lacquer on his scalp, see the pores in his little red nose.

". . . thing is to make sure you're ready for the night. Have you both chosen yours?"

"Burke has. I've not." It was the weediest of the trio who spoke: rheumy of eye, concave of chest—compared to him, Jenkins looked like Atlas.[3] The third man, Burke, was scarcely better, a bandy-legged individual, shoulders flecked with scurf.

Jenkins grunted. "Get on with it then. Try using Trismegistus or Porter—they've both got a lot of choice."

The weedy fellow let out a melancholy bleat. "It's not *choice* that's the problem, Jenkins. It's just—how powerful should I go for? I wouldn't want—"

---

[3] *Atlas*: a marid of unusual strength and muscular definition, employed by the Greek magician Phidias to construct the Parthenon, circa 440 B.C. Atlas shirked the work and bodged the foundations. When cracks appeared, Phidias confined Atlas below ground, charging him to hold the building up indefinitely. He may still be there, for all I know.

"Not *scared*, are you, Withers?" Jenkins's smile was scathing, hostile. "Palmer was scared; and you know what happened to *him*. It's not too late to find someone else."

"No, no, no." Withers was aflurry with reassurance. "I'll be ready. I'll be ready. Whenever you want."

"Are there many of us?" Burke asked. If Withers bleated like a sheep, Burke's voice was more bovine, that of a ruminative dullard.

"No," Jenkins said. "You know not. Just seven in total. One for each chair."

Burke gave a low hiccupping laugh. Withers sniggered in a higher key. The idea seemed to entertain them.

Withers's caution resurfaced. "And you're sure we're safe till then?"

"Devereaux's distracted with the war, Farrar and Mandrake with the restless commoners. Far too much going on for anyone to take any notice of *us*." Jenkins's eyes gleamed. "Who, after all, has *ever* taken any notice of us?" He paused to allow a bit of mutual glowering, then popped his hat back on his head. "Right, I have to go," he said. "I've a few more visits to make. Don't forget the imps, either."

"But the experiment"—Burke had leaned in close— "Withers had a point. We'll need to see *proof* that it's been successful, before we . . . you understand?"

Jenkins laughed. "You'll *get* that proof. Hopkins himself will show you there are no side effects. But I assure you it's most impressive. For a start—"

Whup. With that unusual sound, my eavesdropping came to an abrupt halt. One moment I was buzzing discreetly by Jenkins's ear, the next a rolled-up newspaper descended like a thunderbolt from the skies and walloped me from behind. It was a treacherous attack.[4] I was knocked plumb out of the air and onto the floor, head reeling, six legs akimbo. Jenkins and company looked down at me in vague surprise. My assailant, a brawny bartender, flourished the paper cheerfully at them.

"Got it," he smiled. "Buzzing right by your ear, sir. Horrible big 'un too, very out of season."

"Yes," said Jenkins. "Isn't it?" His eyes narrowed, no doubt studying me through his lenses, but I was a fly on planes one to four, so it told him nothing. He moved suddenly, stretching out a foot to crush me. With perhaps more nimbleness than a wounded fly *ought* to have, I dodged and drifted off unsteadily toward the nearest window.

Out in the street I kept the pub door in view, while inspecting my tender essence. It's a sorry state of affairs when a djinni who _____[5] is laid low by a rolled-up piece of paper, but that was the sad fact of the matter. All this changing and being batted about was not doing me any good. *Mandrake* . . . It was Mandrake's doing. He'd *pay* for this, first chance I got.[6]

I was worried that Jenkins might have suspected I was no ordinary insect, and have taken evasive steps, but to my relief he

---

[4] What made it worse was that it was a copy of *Real War Stories* that did the deed. Mandrake's paper! Another injury to add to my list of his endless crimes.

[5] Insert achievement of your choice from the following selection: (a) fought the utukku single-handed at the battle of Qadesh, (b) carved the great walls of Uruk from the living ground, (c) destroyed three consecutive masters by use of the Hermetic Quibble, (d) spoke with Solomon, or (e) other.

[6] Not that I could do anything against him in my current state. At least, not alone. Certain djinn, Faquarl among them, had long espoused collective rebellion against the magicians. I'd always dismissed this as so much hogwash, impossible to achieve, but if Faquarl had come up to me with some boneheaded scheme right then, I'd have joined him with much high-fiving and inane whoops of joy.

appeared at the door a few minutes later and set off back up Whitehall. I knew the fly guise would no longer wash with him, so—groaning with the pain—I became a sparrow once more, and set off in pursuit.

As dusk settled on the city, the magician Jenkins made his way, on foot, along the lanes of central London. He had three further assignations. The first was in a hostelry not far from Trafalgar Square. I didn't attempt to enter this time, but watched him through a window, speaking to a narrow-eyed woman in dowdy dress. Next he crossed Covent Garden up to Holborn, where he entered a small coffee shop. Again I deemed it sensible to keep my distance, but I got a clear view of the person he spoke to, a middle-aged man with an oddly fishlike face. His lips looked as if they'd been loaned him by a cod. Like my essence, my memory was full of holes; even so, something about him was a bit familiar. . . . No—I gave up. I couldn't place him.

It was a curious business all round. From what I'd overheard, some kind of plot was certainly on the boil. But these people seemed oddly unsuited for dangerous machinations. None of them was powerful or dynamic. In fact, the reverse was true. If you'd lined every magician in London up against a playground wall and picked sides for soccer, they'd have been the ones left standing at the end, next to the fat kid and the one with the plaster cast. Their general rubbishness was evidently part of a pattern, but I couldn't for the life of me tell what it was.

We came at last to a dilapidated café in Clerkenwell and here, for the first time, I noticed a slight alteration in Jenkins. Hitherto he had been breezy, abrupt, casual in his dealings; now, before entering, he paused as if to steady himself. He slicked back his hair, adjusted his tie, and went so far as to inspect the pimple on his chin with a small mirror he had in his pocket. Then he entered the café.

Now *this* was interesting. He wasn't talking to equals or inferiors any more. Perhaps the mysterious Mr. Hopkins himself waited inside. I needed to find out.

Which meant I had to gird my diminutive sparrow's loins and make another change.

The café door was shut, the windows likewise. A small gap beneath the door let out a slit of yellow light. With a groan of despair, I shifted and became a wisp of coiling smoke, which issued its weary way through the crack.

A warm fug of coffee, cigarettes, and frying bacon. The smoke's tip peeped under the door, reared up, and looked left and right. Everything was a little blurred—following my transformation my eyes were misting worse than ever—but I could make out Jenkins settling himself at a distant table. A dark shape sat there too.

The smoke slithered across the room, keeping low against the floor, winding cautiously around chair legs and the shoes of customers. An uneasy thought occurred to me; halting beneath a table, I sent forth a Pulse to search for hostile magic.[7] While waiting, I looked toward Jenkins's companion, but his back was to me: I could see no details.

The Pulse returned—virulent orange, streaked with red.

---

[7] The Pulse had the form of a small green-blue sphere, about the size of a marble, visible only on the seventh plane. It would meander at speed around the locale before returning to its sender. On its return its appearance indicated the level of magic it had discovered: green-blue meant the area was clear; yellow that a trace of magic existed; orange suggested strong enchantments, while red and indigo were my cue to make my excuses and head for the exit.

Grimly I watched it fade. So there *was* magic here, and it wasn't weak.

What should I do? Leaving the café in a funk wouldn't help me learn Jenkins's plans, which was the only way I could secure my dismissal. Besides, if the dark figure *was* Hopkins, I could then trail him, return to Mandrake, and be free by dawn. All in all—whatever the risks—I had to stay.

Well, Prague's walls weren't built without danger or effort.[8] With a couple of silent undulations, the coil of smoke drifted between tables, closer and closer to where Jenkins sat. At the penultimate table I gathered my energies in the overhang of the plastic cloth, then peered tentatively out.

I could see the dark figure more clearly now, though he still faced away from me. He wore a heavy greatcoat, and also a broad-brimmed hat, which obscured his face.

Jenkins's skin was waxy with tension: ". . . and Lime arrived from France this morning," he said.[9] "All of them are ready. They await their moment eagerly."

He cleared his throat unnecessarily. The other did not speak. A faintly familiar magical aura exuded from him. I racked my bleary brains. Where had I seen it before?

A sudden movement across my table. The smoke recoiled like an anemone—but all was well. A waiter passed me, carrying two mugs of coffee. He plonked them down in front of Jenkins and the other. Whistling tunelessly, he departed.

---

[8] Or indeed by me. The battalions of imps I'd foced into my service had a frightful time, while I reclined in my hammock at a safe distance, gazing at the stars.

[9] Lime! *That's* the name I was searching for. The fish-faced man in the coffee shop had been one of the conspirators in the Lovelace affair five years before. If he was coming out of hiding suddenly, things were definitely hotting up.

I watched the next table. Jenkins took a sip of coffee. He did not speak.

A hand stretched out for the second mug—a big hand; its back was laced with an odd crisscrossing of thin white scars.

I watched the hand take the mug, raise it delicately from the table. The head turned a little as it bent to drink; I saw the heavy brow, the hooked nose, the bristles of the trim black beard. And then, too late, I felt the surge of recognition.

The mercenary drank his coffee. I shrank back into the shadows.

IO

Thing was, I knew this mercenary. Both times we'd met we'd had a difference of views, and we'd done our best to resolve it in a civilized fashion. But whether I squished him under a statue, blew him up with a Detonation, or (as in our last encounter) simply set him on fire and hurled him down a mountainside, he never seemed to suffer the slightest injury. For his part, he'd come annoyingly close to killing me with various silver weapons. And now, just when I was at my weakest, here he was again. It gave me pause. I wasn't *scared* of him, of course; dear me, no. Let's call it judiciously nervous.

As always, he was wearing a pair of ancient leather boots, scratched and worn, which positively stank of magic.[1] Presumably it was these that had triggered my Pulse. Seven-league boots, which can cover great distances in the blink of an eye, are rare indeed; combined with the fellow's extreme resilience and his assassin's training, he was a formidable foe. I was rather glad I was well concealed behind the tablecloth.

The mercenary finished his coffee in a single gulp,[2] and rested his scarred hand on the table once again. He spoke. "So they have all chosen?" It was the old familiar voice, calm, deliberate, and ocean-deep.

Jenkins nodded. "Yes, sir. And their imps too. I hope it will be enough."

---

[1] In contrast to most of my master's shoes, which just positively stank.

[2] It must have been piping hot, too. Boy, he was tough.

"Our leader will provide the rest."

Aha! Now we were getting down to business! A leader! Was this Hopkins, or someone else? Thanks to my pain, there was a buzzing in my head—I found it hard to listen. Better get closer. The smoke wriggled a little way out from under the table.

Jenkins sipped his drink. "Is there anything further you wish me to do, sir?"

"Not for now. I shall organize the vans."

"What about the chains and ropes?"

"I will deal with them too. I have . . . experience in that department."

Chains! Ropes! Vans! Put them together and what do you get? No, I hadn't a clue either. But it sounded like dirty work to me. In my excitement I wriggled a little nearer.

"Go home," the mercenary said. "You have done well. I shall report to Mr. Hopkins now. Things gather pace."

"What if I need to contact him? Is he still at the Ambassador?"

"For the moment, yes. But do so only as a last resort. We must not attract attention."

Under the nearby table the coil of smoke would have been hugging itself with glee, had its essence not been quite so stiff. The Ambassador was bound to be a hotel or something. Which meant I had Hopkins's address, exactly as Mandrake had required. Freedom was almost mine! Like I said, I might be a little below par, but I don't make mistakes when it comes to stealthy trailing.

Jenkins was looking a little pensive. "Speaking of that, sir . . . I have only just recalled . . . well, earlier this evening there was a fly hovering near while I spoke to Burke and Withers. It was probably innocent enough, but—"

The mercenary's voice was like distant thunder. "Is that so? And you did what?"

Jenkins pushed his little round glasses up his nose—an anxious gesture, which I could well understand. The mercenary was a full foot taller than he, and almost twice as wide. He could have snapped Jenkins's spine with a single blow. "I kept careful watch as I continued," he stammered, "but I saw nothing."

Naturally. Beneath the table the coil of smoke grinned to itself.

"Also I asked Truklet, my imp, to follow at a distance and report back here."

Ah. Not so good. I ducked back out of sight and twisted to and fro, staring between the chair legs, looking on all the planes. At first—nothing. Then what should I see but a little spider come creeping, creeping along the floor. It was looking under every table, eyes brightly questing this way and that. I rose up out of view, hung undulating in the shadows. Waiting.

The little spider came creeping, creeping to my table. It passed below . . . caught sight of me in an instant, and reared up on its back legs to sound an alarm. The coil of smoke swept down, engulfed the spider. There was a moment's struggle, a desperate squeak.

Presently the coil of smoke moved again. It went slowly at first, in cumbrous rolls, like a python after a heavy feed, but soon began to gather pace.[3]

I looked back. The conspirators were parting company; the

---

[3] Poor Truklet's essence was meager fare. Ordinarily I'd have turned my nose up at it. But these were desperate times, and I needed all the energy I could get. Besides, the little swine was going to snitch me up.

mercenary standing, Jenkins staying put, presumably until his imp turned up.[4] It was decision time.

Mandrake had told me to locate Hopkins and uncover his plot, and I'd gone a fair way toward fulfilling the first request. I *could* have simply headed back to my master there and then, since by rights I'd done enough to justify my dismissal. But "rights," particularly mine, weren't things Mandrake understood very well. He'd disappointed me before. So it was better to make absolutely certain; to hit him with so much information that all he could do was thank me humbly and show me to a pentacle.

And right now the mercenary was going to Hopkins.

The coil of smoke curled up like a spring beneath the table. I watched the floor nearby. Nothing . . . nothing . . . Two boots came into view; old brown leather, scratched and worn.

Just as they passed, I uncoiled, sprang—and in so doing, made another change.

The mercenary crossed to the door with stately steps. His coat rustled, weapons clinked about his person. A small long-clawed lizard clung to the leather of his right boot.

Outside, night had fallen. A few cars droned on a distant road. Passersby were few and far between. The mercenary let the café door bang shut behind him, walked a couple of paces, then stopped. The lizard dug its claws in deeper. I knew what was coming.

A throb of magic, a vibration that shook my essence to its core. The boot I was on rose, tipped, fell to earth again—it was a single step, but all around me the street, the night and the

---

[4] It was going to be quite a wait. I should have bought him another coffee.

lights of the café had blurred into a liquid stream. Another step, and yet another. The stream of light flickered; dimly I sensed buildings, people, and broken shards of noise, but I was too busy hanging on for dear life as the seven-league boots moved without regard for normal space and time. It was like being back in the Other Place again; I would have quite enjoyed the ride had I not felt little grains of essence breaking loose from my extremities, flicking away behind us like dead embers from a fire. Even warmed as I was by my recent feed, it was beginning to be hard to maintain a viable form.

At the third step the boot rested. Instantly the blurring lights congealed, became a new set of surroundings, another part of London, some miles from the café. I waited for my eyes to stop revolving, then took a bleary look around.

We were in one of the parks, close to Trafalgar Square. With the onset of evening the city's commoners had straggled here to lose themselves in relaxation. In this aim they were aided by the kind authorities, who—in the months since the war turned sour—provided daily festivities of the most gaudy kind, designed to stimulate the senses and discourage contemplation.

Away over in the center of the park gleamed the great Glass Palace, a marvelous confusion of domes and minarets, all shimmering with light. Made of twenty thousand curved glass sheets set upon an iron frame, it had been built in the first year of the war, and afterward stuffed full of snack bars and carousels, bear pits and freak shows. It was popular among commoners; less so among djinn. We didn't like all that iron.

Other pavilions were dotted about the park, which was sporadically illuminated by colored imp-lanterns hanging among the trees. Here, train cars looped and plummeted, whirligigs bucked and spun; over at the Sultan's Castle sultry beauties danced before a horde of drunken commoners.[5] Along the central pathway vats of wine and ale were broached, and melancholy oxen turned on spits. The mercenary set off among them now, going at a human pace.

We passed Traitors' Corner, where several captive rebels dangled above the baying crowd in a cage of glass. Alongside, in another prism, a hideous black demon was visible on the first plane. It growled and pranced, shaking its fist at the awestruck throng. Beyond this, a stage had been set up. A banner proclaimed the title of the piece: *Colonial Treachery Overcome*; actors ran about, telling the official story of the war with the aid of rubber swords and papier-mâché demons. Everywhere you looked smiling ladies thrust free supplements of *Real War Stories* into outstretched hands. Such was the ceaseless noise and color and confusion that it was impossible for anyone present to think straight, let alone frame a coherent argument against the war.[6]

I had seen it all before, many times. I concentrated now on clinging to the mercenary, who had left the central path and was striding off across the darkened lawns toward an ornamental lake among the trees.

This lake was scarcely a large affair—during the day waterfowl no doubt sat drably upon it, while children splashed

---

[5] Some of the beauties were real people, though on the higher planes I spotted two who weren't all they should have been: one an empty shell, solid at the front, hollow at the back; another a grinning foliot with spiny limbs concealed beneath its Glamour.

[6] I saw Mandrake's hand behind much of this—it had all his attention to detail, together with the theatricality he had learned off his mate, the playwright Makepeace. A perfect combination of the crude and the subtle. The captive "American" demon was particularly good, I thought, doubtless summoned by someone in the government specially for the occasion.

about in little hired boats—but by night it held a certain quiet mystery. Its margins were lost in shadows and a maze of reed beds; Oriental-style bridges spanned it, linking silent islands. A Chinese pagoda rose from one such. In front of the pagoda was a wooden veranda, extending above the water.

The mercenary made for this in haste. He set off across an ornamental bridge, boots pattering on the planking. Beyond, on the darkness of the veranda, I glimpsed a figure waiting. About his head, on the higher planes, sinister shapes drifted watchfully.

Time for caution. Attached to the boot, I would soon be spotted by even the most half-witted imp. But I could still get close enough to watch and listen. Below the walkway a reed bed stretched, thick and black. A perfect place for lurking. The lizard disengaged itself, gave a leap, fell in among the reeds. Seconds later, after yet another painful transformation, a small green snake was swimming toward the island between the decaying stalks.

I heard the mercenary's voice up above, quiet, respectful. "Mr. Hopkins."

A gap in the reeds. The snake wound itself about a rotten branch protruding from the water and reared up, gazing toward the veranda. There stood the mercenary, and with him another man, slight, stoop-shouldered, who clapped a hand to his arm in a gesture of comradely support. I strained my weary eyes. For a brief instant I caught sight of his face: bland, even-featured, utterly unmemorable. So why was it that something in it aroused a deep sense of recognition and made me shudder?

The men moved away from the veranda, out of view. Cursing fluently, the snake plowed onward, looping through the reeds with elegant undulations. A little farther . . . if I could just hear Hopkins speak, get the slightest clue—

Ten reed stalks moved; five tall gray shadows isolated themselves from the mass of reeds. Ten stick legs bent and sprang. It all happened without a sound: one moment I was alone upon the lake; the next five herons plunged upon me like gray-white ghosts, sword-beaks snapping, red eyes blazing. Flailing wings cracked upon the water, blocking avenues of escape, claws slashed at the desperate snake, beaks stabbed. I coiled myself up and, fast as thinking, dived below the surface. But the herons were swifter still: one beak snared my tail; another snapped fast upon my body, just below the head. They flapped their wings and rose into the air, taking me between them, dangling like a worm.

I scanned my adversaries on the seven planes: they were foliots, all five of them. In normal circumstances I'd have decorated the city with their feathers, but in my current state to fight a single one was pushing it. I felt my essence beginning to tear.

I struggled, thrashed, and twisted. I spat venom left and right. Anger filled me, supplied a little strength. I changed, downsizing further into a small and slimy eel, which slipped free of their hold and fell toward the welcoming water.

A beak lunged.

Snap! Blackness all around.

Now this *was* deeply embarrassing. After my recent treatment of the imp, *I'd* been swallowed too. Alien essence swirled around me. I could feel it beginning to corrode my own.[7]

I had no choice. I summoned all my energies and used a Detonation.

Well, it was loud and it was messy, but it had the desired

---

[7] In such circumstances you have to act quickly before you are simply absorbed by the other. Weak entities have no chance if swallowed by a greater power, and this was going to be a close-run thing.

effect. Small pieces of foliot rained down through the air, and I rained down with them, in the semblance of a small, black pearl.

The pearl dropped into the water. Instantly the four remaining herons were at the spot, hot eyes glinting, spearing their beaks in and out in feverish pursuit.

I allowed myself to sink swiftly into the murk, deep down out of range, to where the mud and ooze and rotten tangle of dead reeds concealed me on every plane.

My mind flickered; I nearly lost consciousness. No, they would find me if I slept. I must escape, return to my master. I needed to make one final effort and get away.

Giant legs stalked the gloom around me; spear-beaks fizzed, cutting the water like bullets. Muffled echoes of the herons' swearing boomed among the weeds. A small, injured tadpole wormed its way toward the shore, leaving specks of dying essence drifting in its wake. Reaching the lakeside, it broke all aging records and became an ill-favored frog, with a clubfoot and a downcast mouth. The frog skittered away into the grass as fast as it could go.

I was halfway to the road before the foliots saw me. One of them must have flown high, glimpsed my limping progress; with raucous cries they erupted from the lake, came hurtling over the dark grass.

One dived; the frog gave a frantic leap. The beak plunged into the ground.

Out onto the path, among the crowds. The frog hopped hither, thither, between legs, under awnings, leaping from heads to shoulders, baskets to prams, all the while emitting croaks and gargles, staring with its mad pop-eyes. Men shouted, women screamed, children gasped in wonder. Behind came the herons, feathers flashing, wings buffeting, blind with bloodlust. They crashed through stalls, upturned wine vats, sent dogs howling into the dark. People were tossed aside like ninepins; piles of *Real War Stories* went flying—some landing in the wine, others in the roasting pits.

Up onto the outdoor stage hopped the fugitive amphibian, under the bright imp-lights, sending one actor leaping into the arms of a second, causing a third to swan dive into the crowd. It sprang down a trapdoor, closely followed by a heron; reappeared an instant later through another, riding the head of a cardboard goblin. It leaped onto the banner above, clung there with two webbed feet. A heron reared up from below, snapped its beak, and tore the banner asunder—the strip of fabric fell, swung like a jungle vine, and catapulted the frog over the path to land beside the crystal prism where the captive demon sat.

By this point I was losing track of where I was and what I was doing. In fact, my essence was fast disintegrating: I could scarcely see; the world was awash with discordant sound. I hopped unthinkingly, changing direction with every hop, seeking to avoid the attack I knew would come.

Sure enough, one of my pursuers lost patience with the chase. It must have tried a Convulsion, I think; I'd leaped aside anyway—I didn't see it hit the prism, didn't hear the crystal crack. Not my fault. Nothing to do with me. I didn't see the big black demon give a grimace of surprise and set its long curved fingernails to the break. I didn't hear the ominous shattering when the entire globe gave way, nor the screams and wailing of the people as the demon leaped into their midst.

I knew nothing of it. I knew only the endless pounding rhythms of the chase, felt only my essence softening and seeping into liquid with every desperate hop and spring. I was dying now, but I could not rest. A swifter death flew close behind.

11

Kitty's master looked up from his sofa—a lonely island amid a sea of scattered paper, all scrawled upon with his tight, close script. He was chewing the end of a ballpoint pen, which had left little blue ink stains on his lips. He blinked in mild surprise.

"Didn't think to see you back this evening, Lizzie. Thought you had to get off to your work."

"I do, sir. Very shortly. Now, sir—"

"Tell me, did you get hold of that original copy of Peck's *Desiderata Curiosa?* And what about *The Anatomy of Melancholy?* I wanted volume four, mind."

Kitty's lie was smoothly practiced. "Sir, I'm sorry, I didn't, either of them. The library closed early today. There was a disturbance outside—a commoners' protest—and they shut the gates for safety. I was asked to leave before I found your books."

Mr. Button gave a petulant exclamation and bit harder at his pen. "Such inconvenience! Commoners protesting, you say? What next? Horses throwing off the bridle? Cows refusing to be milked? Those wretched people need to *know their place*." He emphasized this statement with neat little stabbing motions of his pen, then looked up guiltily. "No offense meant, Lizzie."

"None taken, sir. Sir, who was Ptolemaeus?"

The old man stretched his arms wearily behind his head. "Ptolemaeus is Ptolemy. A most remarkable magician." He flashed her a plaintive look. "Do you have time to put the kettle on, Lizzie, before you go?"

Kitty persisted: "Was he Egyptian?"

"Indeed he was, though the name is Greek, of course. He came of Macedonian stock originally. Well done, Lizzie. Not many protesting commoners would know *that*!"

"I was hoping to read something by him, sir."

"You'd find that tricky, since he wrote in Greek. I have his main work in my collection: *The Eye of Ptolemy*. It is required reading for all magicians, since it is very perceptive on the mechanics of drawing demons from the Other Place. Mind you, the style is tepid. His other writings are known as the *Apocrypha*. I seem to remember you brought me them from Hyrnek's, on your first visit here. . . . They are an odd collection, full of whimsical notions. About that tea . . ."

"I'll put the kettle on," Kitty said. "Is there something I could read about Ptolemy, sir, while I do that?"

"Goodness, you *do* have your little fancies. Yes, *The Book of Names* will have an entry. Doubtless you know which stack it's in."

Kitty read the passage swiftly with the kettle popping and bubbling behind her.

Ptolemaeus of Alexandria (fl. *c*.120 B.C.)

Child-magician, born into the ruling Ptolemaic Dynasty, nephew of Ptolemy VIII and cousin of the crown prince (later Ptolemy IX). He spent most of his short life in Alexandria, working at the Library, but details remain obscure. A notable prodigy, he acquired a considerable reputation for magic while very young; his cousin is said to have felt threatened by his popularity among the common people, and attempted his assassination.

The circumstances of his death are unknown, but it is certain he did not live to a great age. He may have died by violence, or succumbed to bodily frailty. Mention is made in an Alexandrine manuscript of a sudden deterioration in his health following a "difficult journey," though this is at odds with other records that state he never left the precincts of the city. He is definitely recorded as dead by the time of his uncle's funeral and his cousin's accession to the throne (116 B.C.), so is unlikely to have reached his twenties.

His papers remained at the Library for over three hundred years, during which time they were studied by Tertullian and other Roman magicians. Part of his writing was published, in Rome, as the famous *Eye of Ptolemy*. The original archive was destroyed in the great earthquake and fire of the third century; surviving fragments have been collected as his *Apocrypha*. Ptolemy is a figure of historical interest, since he is credited with the invention of several techniques, including the Stoic Incision and the Mouler Shield (both used during summonings until the days of Loew) as well as unusual speculative fantasies, such as the "Gate of Ptolemy." All this despite his extreme youth; if he had survived to maturity, he would surely have ranked among the great. His demons, with whom he is said to have had an unusual bond, included: Affa,† Rekhyt or Necho,‡ Methys,† Penrenutet.†

† demise recorded
‡ fate unknown

Mr. Button smiled absently when Kitty brought in the tea. "Did you find what you wanted?"

"I don't really know, sir, but I do have a question. Is it

common for demons to take on the appearance of their masters?"

The magician put down his pen. "You mean to taunt, or befuddle them? Certainly! It is an ancient trick, one of the oldest in the book, and one guaranteed to unman the inexperienced. Nothing is more unsettling than facing a phantom of oneself, particularly when the creature uses it to perform provocative contortions. Rosenbauer of Munich was so distressed, I believe, by an accurate depiction of his many affectations that he threw down his pomade and rushed sobbing from his circle, with melancholy results. I myself have been forced to witness my own body decaying slowly to a rotting corpse, complete with hideous sound effects, while I tried to question it on the principles of Cretan architecture. It is to my credit that my notes made any sense at all. Is that what you mean?"

"Well, actually . . . no, sir." Kitty took a deep breath. "I wanted to know whether a djinni ever took on its master's appearance out of . . . respect, or even affection. Because they were comfortable with it." She made a face; on hearing it, the idea sounded quite ridiculous.

The old man wrinkled his nose. "I hardly think so."

"I mean, after the magician was dead."

"My dear Lizzie! Perhaps, if the magician in question was unusually hideous or deformed, the demon might employ his shape to startle others. I believe Zarbustibal of Yemen did reappear for a time following his demise. But out of respect? Goodness! The notion presupposes a relationship between master and slave that would be quite unprecedented. Only a comm— forgive me—only someone as inexperienced as you would come up with such a quaint conceit! Dear me, dear me . . ." He tittered to himself as he stretched a hand toward the tea tray.

Kitty had set off for the door. "Thank you, sir; you've been very helpful. By the way," she added, "what was the Gate of Ptolemy?"

From the middle of his sofa, among his mess of papers, the old magician groaned. "What is it? A ridiculous notion! A myth, a figment, a barrel of moonshine! Save your questions for subjects of value. Now I must work. I have no need for the witterings of foolish assistants. Be off with you! The Gate of Ptolemy, indeed . . ." He winced, waved her pettishly away.

"But—"

"Don't you have a job to go to, Lizzie?"

Forty minutes later Kitty alighted from a bus upon the Embankment road. She wore a thick black duffel coat and chewed intently at a sandwich. In her pocket were the documents confirming her second false identity—Clara Bell.

The sky was blackening, though a few low clouds still glimmered a dirty yellow with the city's reflected glow. Below the tide wall the Thames lay distant, shrunk and withered. Kitty passed above a great gray mud-bank, where herons stalked amid the stones and flotsam. The air was cold; a strong breeze blew toward the sea.

At a bend in the river the pavement took a sudden ninety-degree turn away from the Thames, its route blocked by an extensive building with steep roofs and sharply pointed dormers. Heavy black beams laced its walls; lit windows gleamed at random heights, casting a rich light upon the street and the dark waters of the river. The upper story projected out above the lower on all sides, here vigorously, here sagging as if about to fall. A faded green sign swung from a pole above the path, so weather-beaten that its words could not be read. This was of small account, since The Frog was a notable local landmark. It was famous for its beer, its beef and for its weekly domino tournaments. It was also Kitty's workplace in the evenings.

She ducked under a low arch and walked down the pitchblack side alley into the pub's yard. As she entered it, she glanced up. A faint red light hovered by the gables. If you looked directly at it, its shape was blurred and indistinct; if you looked away, you saw its outline clearly—a small, neat vigilance sphere, watching.

Kitty ignored the spy. She crossed the yard to the main door, which was sheltered from the weather by an ancient blackened porch, and entered the Frog Inn.

The bright lights of the taproom made her blink. The curtains had been drawn against the night and a fire lit in the grate. Its colors flickered in rows of glasses assembled on the bar; George Fox, the manager, was industriously polishing them one by one. He nodded at Kitty as she passed to hang her satchel on the coat-rail.

"In your own time, Clara. In your own time."

She glanced at her watch. "Still twenty minutes before they get here, George."

"Not long enough for what I've got planned for you."

Kitty flipped her hat onto a peg. "No problem." She motioned with her head back toward the door. "How long's it been there?"

"Couple of hours. Usual sort. Just trying to spook us. Can't hear. Won't interfere."

"Okay. Chuck me a cloth."

In fifteen brisk and efficient minutes the taproom was clean and ready, the glasses polished, the tabletops spic and span. Kitty had placed ten pitchers on the counter above the tap, and Sam, The Frog's barman, began filling them with light-brown frothing drafts of beer. Kitty distributed the last of the domino boxes, wiped her hands on her trousers, plucked an apron from a hook, and took up position behind the bar. George Fox opened the main door and allowed the customers in.

As usual, The Frog's reputation ensured an ever-changing clientele, and tonight Kitty noticed several people she hadn't seen before: a tall military gentleman, an old lady smiling and shuffling to a seat, a young blond man with beard and mustache. The familiar click of the dominoes began; conviviality filled the air. Smoothing down her apron, Kitty hastened between tables and took orders for the evening meal.

An hour passed; the remains of thick-slabbed hot beef sandwiches lay on plates at the players' elbows. With the food finished, interest in dominoes quickly paled. The pieces were kept in position on every table, in case the police should raid, but the players now sat up in their seats, suddenly alert and sober. Kitty filled a last few empty glasses, then returned to stand behind the counter as a man sitting near the fireplace slowly got to his feet.

He was old and frail, bent with years. The whole room quietened to a hush.

"Friends," he began, "little of note has happened since last week, so I shall shortly open our meeting to the floor. As always, I would like to thank our patron, Mr. Fox, for his hospitality. Perhaps we could hear from Mary first, for news of the American situation?"

He sat. At an adjacent table a woman stood, thin-faced and weary. Kitty judged her to be not yet forty, though her hair was flecked with gray. "A merchant ship came in late last night," she began. "Its last berth was Boston, in the war zone. The crew breakfasted at our café this morning. They told us that the most recent British offensive has failed—Boston is still in American hands. Our army withdrew to the fields, searching for supplies, and has since been attacked. Losses are high."

A low muttering filled the room. The old gentleman half stood. "Thank you, Mary. Who cares to speak next?"

"If I may?" The young bearded man spoke up; he was stocky, self-confident; he carried an assertive air. "I represent a new organization, the Commoners' Alliance. Perhaps you've heard of it."

There was a general shuffling, a sense of unease. From behind the bar Kitty frowned. Something about the speaker's voice . . . it bothered her.

"We're trying to gather support," the man went on, "for a new round of strikes and public demonstrations. We've got to show the magicians what's what. The only way to make them sit up is concerted action by us all. I'm talking mass protests here."

"May I speak?" The elderly lady, immaculately presented in a dark blue dress and crimson shawl, sought to rise; a chorus of amiable protest ensued, and she remained seated. "I am fearful of what is happening in London," she said. "These strikes, this unrest . . . Surely it is not the answer. What will they achieve? Only sting our leaders to harsh reprisals. The Tower will echo with the laments of honest men."

The young man thumped the table with a thick pink fist. "What is the alternative, madam? Sit quiet? The magicians won't thank us if we do! They'll grind us further into the dirt. We must act now! Remember—they can't imprison every-one!"

There was a round of ragged clapping. The old lady stubbornly shook her head. "You're quite wrong," she said. "Your argument only works if the magicians can be destroyed. They cannot!"

Another man spoke out. "Steady on, Grandma. That's defeatist talk."

She jutted her chin. "Well? Can they? How?"

"They're obviously losing control, or they'd have beaten the rebels easily."

"We can get help from the Europeans too," the young blond man added. "Don't forget that. The Czechs will fund us. And the French."

George Fox nodded. "French spies have given me a couple of magical items," he said. "Just in case of trouble. Never had to use them, mind."

"Excuse me," the old lady said, "but you've not explained how a few strikes will actually bring the magicians down." She raised her bony chin and looked defiantly around at the company. "Well?" Several of the men made noises of disapproval, but were too busy sipping drinks to voice an exact reply.

From behind the bar Kitty spoke. "You are right, madam, that defeating them will be difficult," she said in a quiet voice, "but it is not impossible. Revolutions have succeeded dozens of times. What happened to Egypt, Rome, or Prague? All were invincible—for a time. All fell when the people stirred themselves."

"But my dear," the old lady said, "in each case there were enemy armies. . . ."

"In each case," Kitty went on determinedly, "foreign leaders took advantage of the kingdom's internal weaknesses. The people were already rebelling. They didn't have strong magic or vast armies—they were commoners just like us."

The old lady pursed her lips into a humorless smile. "Perhaps. But how many of us want an invasion by *foreigners*? Our rulers may not be perfect, but at least they're British."

The young bearded man snorted. "Let's get back to *now*. Tonight the Battersea steelworkers are going on strike—just down the river from here. Come and join us! So what if the magicians send their demons? They will get no more cannon from us!"

"And where will your steelworkers be?" the old lady said harshly. "Some in the Tower, some at the bottom of the Thames. And others will take their place."

"The demons won't get it all their own way," the young man said. "Some people have *resilience*. You must have heard of it. They can withstand attacks, see through illusions—"

As he spoke, Kitty's eyes suddenly cleared. She saw beyond his thick mustache, his scruffy blond beard: she knew him, clear as day. Nick Drew, last surviving companion in the Resistance. Nick Drew, who had fled Westminster Abbey in their darkest hour, leaving his friends behind. He was older, stouter, but full of the same old bluster. You still *talk* a good fight, she thought viciously. You always were good at *talking*. I bet you'll keep well away when the strike gets nasty. . . . A sudden fear took hold of her; she stepped back out of his line of sight. Useless though Nick was, if he recognized her, her cover would be blown.

The group was busy discussing the phenomenon of resilience. "They can see magic. Clear as day," a middle-aged woman said. "That's what I've heard."

The old lady shook her head again. "Rumors, cruel rumors," she said sadly. "This is all secondhand tittle-tattle. It would not surprise me if it wasn't started by the magicians themselves, to tempt you into rashness. Tell me," she went on, "has anyone here ever actually *seen* any of this resilience in action?"

A silence in The Frog. Kitty shifted impatiently from one foot to another, longing to speak. But Clara Bell was no one special—she'd decided that long ago. Besides, wariness of Nick prevented her. She looked around the taproom. The company, most of which had met there in secret for many years, was generally middle-aged or older. Resilience was not something they knew much of, firsthand. Except Nick Drew, who possessed as least as much resilience as Kitty. But he sat quiet, saying nothing.

The mood in the room had been soured by the argument. After a few minutes' glum reflection the old gentleman got slowly to his feet again. "Friends," he began, "let us not be downcast! Perhaps the magicians are too dangerous to fight, but we can at least resist their propaganda. A new issue of *Real War Stories* is out today. Spurn it! Tell your friends about its lies!"

At this George Fox spoke up. "I think you're being a bit harsh there." He raised his voice against the general murmur of disbelief. "Yes. I've made it my business to collect as many editions of *Real War Stories* as I can."

"Oh, shame on you, Mr. Fox," said the elderly lady, in a quivery voice.

"No, I'm proud to admit it," he went on. "And if any of you choose to pay a visit to the restrooms later on, you shall find ample proof of those pamphlets' worth. They are most absorbent." There was a general laugh. Keeping her back to the young blond man, Kitty stepped forward with a pitcher to refill a few glasses.

"Well, time is moving on," the old gentleman said, "and we must part. But first, as is traditional, we will take our usual oath." He sat down.

George Fox reached under the bar and drew out a large cup,

aged and battered, with a pair of crossed dominoes rampant on the lid. It was made of solid silver. He took a dark bottle from a shelf and, removing the lid, poured a generous measure of port into the cup. Kitty took the cup in both hands and carried it to the old gentleman.

"We shall all drink in turn," he said. "May we live to see the day when a Commoners' Parliament is established once again. May it uphold the ancient rights of every man and woman—to discuss, debate, and dissent from the policies of our leaders, and hold them accountable for their actions." With due reverence, he lifted the cup and took a sip, before passing it clockwise to his neighbor.

This ritual was a high point of such meetings at The Frog: after the debates, which never reached any conclusion, it offered the solace of something fixed and familiar. The silver cup was slowly passed from person to person, from table to table. Everyone awaited its arrival, old hands and newcomers alike, except for the elderly lady, who was readying herself for departure. George moved around to the front of the bar and—together with Sam, the bartender—began clearing glasses from tables near the door. Kitty accompanied the cup, moving it between tables when required. She kept her face turned from Nick Drew as best she could.

"Do we need more port, Clara?" George called. "Mary there had a great big gulp, I saw her."

Kitty took the cup, inspected it. "No. We've plenty left."

"Good enough. My dear lady, surely you're not leaving us?"

The old woman smiled. "I must go, dear. With all these disturbances on the street, I'll not stay out too late."

"Yes, of course. Clara, bring this lady the cup so she can drink before she goes."

"Right you are, George."

"Oh, it's not necessary, dear. I'll take a double drink next time." This roused laughter and a few cheers; one or two men got up to allow the old woman to squeeze by.

Kitty followed her. "Here you are, madam, there's plenty left."

"No, no, I really must be going, thank you. It's *so* late."

"Madam, you've dropped your shawl."

"No, no. I can't wait. Excuse me, please . . ."

"Steady on, love! Watch where you're pushing—"

"Excuse me, excuse me . . ."

Stony-faced, her eyes dark and blank like the cutout holes on an empty mask, the old woman moved rapidly across the room, turning her head repeatedly to look back at Kitty, who was advancing fast behind her. Kitty held the silver cup outstretched—first reverently, as if offering up a gift; then suddenly jerking it back and forth like a feinting blade. The proximity of the silver seemed to give the lady discomfort—she flinched away. George placed his stack of glasses carefully on a side table and put a hand into a pocket. Sam opened a cupboard on the wall, reached in. The rest of the company remained seated, expressions caught between amusement and uncertainty.

"The door, Sam," George Fox said.

The old woman darted forward. Sam turned to face her, blocking the door; he held a short, dark rod in his hand. "Hold on, lady," he said reasonably. "Rules are rules. You've got to take a drink from the cup before you go. It's a sort of test." He made an embarrassed gesture and looked ruefully at her. "I'm sorry."

The old lady stopped, shrugged. "Don't be." She raised a hand. A blue light stabbed from her palm, engulfing Sam in a crackling network of bright blue force. He leaped, shuddered, danced oddly like a puppet, then fell smoking to the floor. Someone in the taproom screamed.

A whistle sounded, shrill and impertinent. The old woman turned, her cupped hand raised and steaming. "Now then, my dear—"

Kitty threw the silver cup into the old woman's face.

A flash of bright green light, a hiss of scalding. The old lady snarled like a dog, clutched at her face with clawing fingers. Kitty turned her head: "George—!"

From his pocket the landlord drew a small box, delicate and oblong. He threw it to Kitty, hard and fast, over the shouting, rising heads of the nearest men and women. She caught it in one hand, spun in a single movement to toss it at the writhing figure—

The old lady removed her fingers from her face, which had largely disappeared. Between the neat white hair and the necklace of pearls at her throat a misshapen mass was glistening. It had no regular shape, no features. Kitty was taken aback; she hesitated. The faceless woman lifted her hand and another bright stream of sapphired light shot out, striking Kitty head-on, engulfing her in a vortex of shimmering energy. She groaned. Her teeth rattled in her skull; every bone seemed to be shaking free of its neighbors; dazzling lights blinded her. She sensed her clothes singeing on her body.

The attack ceased; the lines of blue energy vanished; from where she had been suspended, about a meter up, Kitty fell limply to the ground.

The old lady flexed her fingers, grunted in satisfaction, and looked around the taproom. In all directions people were fleeing, knocking over tables, sending chairs flying, colliding with each other, squealing in mortal fear; the young blond-haired man had hidden behind a barrel. Across the room she spied George Fox edging toward a chest beside the bar. Another blast—but he had launched himself desperately to the side: a section of the counter disintegrated in a heap of glass and matchwood; George Fox rolled away behind a table out of view.

Ignoring the laments and scurryings around her, the old lady turned to leave once more. She adjusted her twinset, brushed a stray coil of gray hair from her ruined face, stepped across Sam's body, and reached for the door.

Another whistle, shrill and impertinent, sounded above the clamor. The old lady froze with her fingers on the handle. She cocked her head and turned.

Then Kitty, whose eyes were slightly crossed, whose clothes were streaked and torn, whose hair frizzed all about her like a mane of cotton wool, but who had struggled to her feet again regardless, tossed over the small box. As it landed at the old lady's feet, Kitty spoke a single word.

A burst of light, searing in its intensity; a column of flame, two meters in diameter, rose from floor to ceiling. It was utterly smooth-sided, more like a pillar than a moving thing. It surrounded the old lady on all sides—she could be seen transfixed within it, like an insect within amber: gray hair, pearl necklace, blue dress, all. The pillar became solid, suddenly opaque, and the old woman was hidden within it.

The light faded, the pillar became faint and nebulous. It vanished, leaving a perfectly circular burn mark on the floor. The old lady with the molten face was gone.

At first the taproom of The Frog was very still: a wasteland of upturned tables, smashed chairs, wood fragments, prone bodies, and scattered dominoes. Only Kitty stood, arms poised, breathing hard, staring at the space before the door.

Then, one by one, the members began to express their shock and fear; they moved upon the floor, they stirred, they slowly rose, they began to moan and babble. Kitty remained silent; she looked toward the ruined bar. From a distant point along it George's face emerged. He stared at Kitty wordlessly.

She raised an eyebrow. "Well?"

"Let them get their breath back. Then they can go. The sphere mustn't notice anything."

With slow, stiff moments, Kitty clambered over the nearest pile of shattered wood and stepped around the body of the bartender. Pushing aside a teary gentleman who was blundering toward the exit, she locked the door. She stood there for five minutes while the frightened customers recovered, then she let them out, one by one.

Last to leave was Nicholas Drew, who had emerged from behind his barrel. Their eyes met; he paused at the door.

"Hello, Kitty," he said. "Still as energetic as ever, I see."

Kitty's expression did not change. "Nick."

The young man smoothed back his hair and began buttoning his coat. "Don't worry," he said. "I'll forget I've seen you. New life, and all that." He looked around the debris of the room. "Unless you want to join up with the Commoners' Alliance, of course. We could do with someone like you."

She shook her head. "No, thanks. I'm happy as I am."

He nodded. "Right. Well, then. Good-bye. And . . . good luck."

"Good-bye, Nick." She closed the door behind him.

George Fox was hunched over Sam's body; white, terrified faces peeped in from the kitchen. Kitty leaned back against the door and closed her eyes. Just one demon—one spy—had done this. In London there were hundreds of them. At the same time, next week the people would return to The Frog to talk, debate, and do nothing. Meanwhile, every day, across London, voices of protest were briefly heard—and swiftly, ruthlessly, cut off. Demonstrations were useless. Talk was useless. There *had* to be another way.

Perhaps there was. It was time to carry out her plan.

12

Night had fallen upon the Prime Minister's mansion at Richmond. Upon the western lawns a number of tall columns had been built; from their tops burned colored imp-fires, illuminating the scene with weird radiance. Servants in the vibrant garb of firebirds and salamanders drifted here and there, offering refreshment. From the black wall of trees beyond the lake, invisible musicians played a sweet pavane; the sounds carried gently above the voices of the guests.

The great ones of the Empire meandered about the garden, talking quietly, listlessly, looking at their watches. They wore formal gowns and dress suits; their features were concealed behind ornate masks depicting animals, birds, and demons. Such parties were among Mr. Devereaux's many extravagances, and had become quite common during the period of the war.

John Mandrake leaned against a pillar, watching the guests drift by. His mask was made of flakes of moonstone, sewn cleverly together to resemble an albino lizard's head. Doubtless it was skillful, an object of wonder, but it still didn't fit. He found it difficult to see and had twice stepped into the flower beds. He sighed. No word yet from Bartimaeus . . . He would have expected *something* by now.

A small group passed him, a peacock surrounded by two attentive she-lynxes and a fawning dryad. In the peacock's paunch and self-important strut he recognized Mr. Collins; the women were probably lower magicians from his department, eager for advancement. Mandrake scowled. Collins and the rest had not been slow to criticize him when he'd brought up the Staff in Council. He'd spent the rest of the meeting enduring a dozen sly insinuations, as well as Devereaux's frosty glances. No question about it, his proposal had been ill advised, a foolish blunder for a politician.

To hell with politics! Its conventions smothered him—he felt like a fly caught up in a choking web. His whole *life* was spent appeasing Devereaux, fighting off his rivals. An utter waste of time. *Someone* was needed to steady the Empire before it was too late. *Someone* had to defy the others, and use the Staff.

Before he'd left Whitehall, Mandrake had descended to the vaults below the Hall of Statues. He had not been there for years; now, as he stood at the foot of the stairs, he was surprised to see a line of red tiles embedded in the floor at the far end of the chamber. A portly clerk, who had leaped up from a desk, approached.

Mandrake nodded to him. "I wish to inspect the treasure vaults, if possible."

"Certainly, Mr. Mandrake. Would you follow me?"

They crossed the chamber. Beside the red tiles the clerk halted. "At this juncture, sir, I must ask you to remove any magical objects about your person, and to dismiss any invisible presence. The line marks a boundary. Beyond the tiles nothing magical is permitted, not even a Charm. The merest trace will invoke a terrible sanction."

Mandrake scanned the dim, bare corridor ahead. "Really? Of what kind?"

"I am not permitted to say, sir. You have nothing eerie to declare? Then we can proceed."

They entered a maze of blank stone passages, more ancient than the Parliament buildings above. Here and there were wooden doors, dark openings. Electric bulbs lit the central corridor. Mandrake looked hard, but saw no clue to the hidden trap. The clerk looked only straight ahead; as he walked, he hummed quietly to himself.

At length they arrived at a great steel door. The clerk pointed. "The Room of Treasures."

"May we go in?"

"That would not be advisable, sir. There is a viewing grille, if you desire."

Mandrake stepped forward, flipped back a tiny hatch in the center of the door. He squinted through. Beyond was a brightly lit room of considerable size. Far off, in its center, stood a plinth of pink-white marble. On the plinth, in open view, were the most precious treasures of the government—a little pile of ornaments, glinting with a dozen colors. Mandrake's eyes instantly picked out the long wooden Staff, rough and unadorned, with a plainly carved knobble at its head. Beside it he glimpsed a short gold necklace, with a small gold oval suspended from it; in the center of that oval came the deep, dark flash of jade.

Gladstone's Staff and the Amulet of Samarkand . . . Mandrake felt the sharp internal pain of dispossession. He scanned the first three planes: there was no evidence of hexes, wires, webs, or other guards. Even so, the tiles around the plinth were an odd green color; they had an unhealthy look.

He stepped from the grille. "What guards the room, if I am permitted to be told?"

"A Pestilence, sir. A particularly voracious one. Would strip you to the bone in seconds, sir, should you decide to enter unadvisedly."

Mandrake looked at the clerk. "Quite. Very well. Let's go."

★ ★ ★

A gust of laughter drifted from the house. Mandrake stared down at the blue cocktail in his glass. If his visit to the vaults had proved one thing, it was that Devereaux fully intended to cling to power. The Staff was out of reach. Not that he actually intended to . . . well, he didn't know *what* he intended. A sour mood was on him; the party and all its fripperies left him cold. He lifted the glass and gulped the liquid down. He tried to remember when he had last been happy.

"John, you old lizard! I see you skulking on that wall!" Across the lawns came a short, round gentleman, splendidly attired in turquoise evening dress. His mask depicted a ferociously laughing imp. On his arm was a tall, slender youth wearing a mask like a dying swan. The youth giggled uncontrollably.

"John, John," the imp said. "Are you or are you not having the devil of a time?" He slapped Mandrake playfully on the shoulder. The youth guffawed.

"Hello, Quentin," Mandrake murmured. "Having fun?"

"Almost as much as dear Rupert." The imp pointed toward the house, where a capering figure with a bull's head was illuminated against the windows. "It *does* take his mind off things, you know. Poor dear."

Mandrake adjusted his lizard mask. "And who is this young gentleman?"

"This," the imp said, hugging the swan's head to him, "is young Bobby Watts, star of my next extravaganza! A boy of meteoric talent! Do not forget, do not forget"—the imp seemed a little unsteady on his feet—"that the premiere of *From Wapping to Westminster* is almost upon us. I am reminding everyone. Two days, Mandrake, two days! It is guaranteed to change the lives of all who see it! Eh, Bobby?" He pushed the youth away from him roughly. "Now, go and get us another drink! I have something to say to my scaly friend here."

The swan's head departed, stumbling across the grass. Mandrake watched him silently.

"Now, John." The imp drew close. "I've been sending you messages for *days*. I believe you've been ignoring me. I want you to come visit me. Tomorrow. You won't forget, will you? It's important."

Beneath his mask Mandrake wrinkled his nose at the smell of drink wafting from the other man. "I'm sorry, Quentin. Council dragged on and on. I couldn't get away. Tomorrow it shall be."

"Good, good. You always were the brightest one, Mandrake. Keep it that way. Good evening, Sholto! I believe I recognize you in there!" A hulking figure with the incongruous mask of a baby lamb was passing; the imp detached itself from Mandrake, playfully jabbed the newcomer in the belly with a finger, and waltzed away.

The lizard and the lamb regarded each other.

"That Quentin Makepeace," the lamb said in deep, heartfelt tones. "I do not like him. He is impudent, and I believe mentally unsound."

"He has high spirits, certainly." Privately Mandrake shared the sentiments. "Well, well. I have not seen you for some time, Sholto."

"No indeed. I have been in Asia." The big man sighed, leaned heavily upon his stick. "I am reduced to scouting for my own goods now. Times are hard."

Mandrake nodded. The fortunes of Sholto Pinn had never

fully recovered after the destruction of his flagship store during the golem's reign of terror. Although he had laboriously rebuilt his shop, his finances became parlous. This coincided with the war and the disruption of trade; fewer artifacts were finding their way to London, and fewer magicians were willing to buy them. Like many in the last few years, Pinn had aged noticeably. His massive frame seemed slightly shrunken; his white suit hung listlessly about his shoulders. Mandrake felt a certain pity for him.

"What news from Asia?" he asked. "How goes the Empire?"

"These *foolish* costumes—I swear they have given me the most ridiculous one of all." Pinn lifted the lamb's mask and dabbed a handkerchief at his sweating face. "The Empire, Mandrake, is floundering. There is talk of rebellion in India. Hill-magicians from the north are busily summoning demons for the attack, or so word has it. Our garrisons in Delhi have asked our Japanese allies for assistance defending the town. Imagine that! I fear for us, I really do." The old man sighed, replaced his mask. "How do I look, Mandrake? Like a sprightly lamb?"

Inside his mask Mandrake grinned. "I *have* seen nimbler."

"I guessed as much. Well, if I'm to make an idiot of myself, I'll do it on a full belly. You, girl!" He raised his stick in an ironic salute and departed in the direction of a serving maid. Mandrake watched him go, his momentary good humor evaporating rapidly on the chill night air. He looked up at the blank night sky.

Sitting in a garden long ago, a pencil in his hand.

He tossed his glass behind the column and set off in the direction of the house.

★　★　★

In the hallway of the mansion, a little apart from the nearest knot of revelers, Mandrake saw Jane Farrar. Her mask—a bird-of-paradise with slender apricot plumes—dangled from her wrist. She was stepping into her traveling coat, held out for her by an impassive servant. At Mandrake's approach he drifted away.

"Going so soon?"

"Yes. I'm tired. And if Quentin Makepeace buttonholes me about that wretched play of his once more, I shall strike him." She pouted prettily.

Mandrake came close. "I'll escort you back, if you like. I'm just about finished here too." With a careless motion, he removed his mask.

She smiled. "I have three djinn and five foliots to escort me, should I require them. What can you offer me that they cannot?"

The melancholy detachment that had been growing in Mandrake all evening now ignited into sudden recklessness. He cared nothing for implications or consequences; Jane Farrar's proximity emboldened him. He lightly touched her hand. "Let us take my car back to London. I will address your question as we go."

She laughed. "It is a long journey, Mr. Mandrake."

"Perhaps I have many answers."

Jane Farrar slipped her arm through his; together they progressed along the hall. Several pairs of eyes watched them as they went.

The mansion's vestibule was unoccupied, save for two menservants standing ready at the door. A log fire crackled beneath a wall of stags' heads and faded coats of arms, stolen long ago from foreign hearths. A great stained-glass window on the opposite wall depicted in flat perspective the buildings of central London: the abbey, the palace of Westminster, the main government offices standing beside the Thames. The streets were filled with adoring crowds; at the center of the palace courtyard sat the radiant figure of the Prime Minister, hands raised in a gesture of benediction. The glass glinted dully in the hall lights; behind rose the dark slab of night.

Below the window sat a low green couch, laden with silken cushions.

Mandrake stopped. "It is warm here. Wait while I find my chauffeur."

Jane Farrar did not disengage her arm, but looked toward the couch. "Or we could *both* stay here a while . . ."

"True."

He turned to face her, his body tingling. She gave a little shudder.

"Did you feel that too?" she asked.

"Yes," he said softly, "but don't talk."

She pushed him away. "It was our sensor webs, you fool. Something's triggered them."

"Oh. Yes." They stood listening to the wood snapping in the fire, to the noise of muted revelry from the garden beyond the passage. Distantly above it all came a high, shrill whine.

"That's Devereaux's nexus alarm," Mandrake said. "Something's broken into the gardens from outside."

She frowned. "His demons will intercept it."

"Sounds like they're attacking the intruder . . ." From somewhere beyond the stained-glass window strange cries echoed in inhuman throats, together with great noises, like rolls of thunder rebounding off distant mountains. The two magicians stood quite still. Faintly they heard shouting in the garden.

The sounds grew in volume. A man with dark glasses and a dinner jacket ran past, muttering an incantation as he did so. Dark orange plasms flared in his cupped hand; with his other hand he flung open the main door and disappeared outside.

Mandrake made as if to follow. "We should go and see—"

"Wait, John!" Jane Farrar's eyes were fixed upward, on the window. "It's coming this way. . . ."

He looked up, transfixed, at the panes of glass, which were suddenly illuminated into brief glories of varied color by a flash of light beyond. The noises escalated further. Now it was as if a hurricane bore down upon them—a screaming, whistling blast of madness and ferocity. Louder and louder it grew. They shrank back. Explosions sounded, and hideous yells. Another flash: and for an instant they saw outlined the silhouette of a giant, monstrous shape, all tentacles, wings, and scything claws, hurling itself toward the window.

Mandrake gasped. Farrar screamed. They fell back, pawing at each other.

A flash: the black shape filled the window. It collided with the glass—

Plink! A small pane in the middle of the window, the one depicting the Prime Minister, burst into a thousand pieces. Through it came a tiny object, flashing emerald in the hall light, arcing through the air. It fell on the tiles before them with a soft, sad sound, bounced once limply and lay still.

The two magicians stood dumbly looking at it. A lifeless frog.

Outside the window, noises continued to be heard, but more faintly now, receding with each second. One or two flashes briefly lit the window, then the night was dark once more.

Mandrake bent down to the crumpled frog. Its legs were bent and splayed, its mouth half open, its eyes tight shut. An odd colorless fluid spread slowly out upon the tiles around it. Heart pounding, he used his lenses: on all three planes the frog looked exactly the same. Nevertheless . . .

"What *is* this hideous creature?" Jane Farrar's pale face was contorted with distaste. "I shall summon my djinni to view it on the higher planes, then we can dispose—"

Mandrake held up a hand. "Wait." He bent closer, addressed the frog: "Bartimaeus?"

Ms. Farrar frowned. "You mean this thing is—?"

"I don't know. Be silent." He spoke again, louder this time, nearer the poor bent head. "Bartimaeus—is that you? It is I . . ." He paused, moistened his lips. "Your master."

One of the forelegs twitched. Mandrake sat back on his haunches and looked up excitedly at his companion. "He's still alive! Did you see—?"

Ms. Farrar's lips were a hard line. She stood a little apart, as if subtly detaching herself from the scene. One or two wide-eyed footmen appeared at the margins of the hall; with angry motions, she waved them away. "It will not be alive for long. Look at the essence draining off. Did you request it to come here?"

Mandrake was not looking at her; he anxiously surveyed the body on the floor. "Yes, yes, I gave him an open-door injunction. He was to return when he had information on Hopkins." He tried again. "Bartimaeus!"

Sudden interest flared in Farrar's voice. "Really? And from the sounds we heard, it seems he was pursued. Interesting! John, we have little time for the interrogation. Somewhere nearby Devereaux will have his pentacle chamber. It will be a close-run thing, but if we use sufficient force before the creature loses *all* its essence, we can—"

"Silence! He is waking!"

The back of the frog's head had become blurred and indistinct. The foreleg had not moved again. Nevertheless, one of the eyelids suddenly flickered; by minute increments it opened. A bulging eye looked forth, misty and unfocused.

"Bartimaeus . . ."

A tiny voice, as if from far away: "Who's asking?"

"Mandrake."

"Oh. Thought it was . . . worth waking up for a minute there." The head sagged, the eyelid drooped.

Ms. Farrar stepped close and nudged the frog's leg with the toe of a pointed shoe. "Fulfill your mission!" she said. "Tell us about Hopkins!"

The frog's eye opened a little. It swiveled painfully and focused for an instant on Ms. Farrar. The tiny voice sounded again. "Is this your bird? Tell me she's not. Oh *dear.*"

The eye closed, and despite all Mandrake's pleas and Farrar's commands, did not reopen. Mandrake sat back on his heels and ran a hand distractedly through his hair.

Farrar laid an impatient hand on his shoulder. "Pull yourself together, John. It's only a demon. Look at the spilled essence! If we don't take steps right now, we'll lose the information!"

He stood then, and looked at her wearily. "You think we can wake it?"

"Yes, with the right techniques. The Shimmering Coil or the Essence Rack perhaps. But I'd say we've got less than five minutes. It can no longer maintain its form."

"Those techniques would destroy it."

"Yes. But we'd have the information. Come *on*, John. You!"

She snapped her fingers at a manservant hovering at the fringes of a small knot of watching guests. "Over here! Bring a dust-pan or some kind of shovel—we need to scrape this mess up fast."

"No . . . there is another way." Mandrake spoke quietly, too quietly for Ms. Farrar to hear. As she issued orders to the men around her, he crouched once more beside the frog and uttered a long and complex incantation under his breath. The frog's limbs shivered; a faint gray mist dribbled off its body, as of cold air meeting warm. With great speed, the body of the frog melted into the mist; the mist coiled about Mandrake's shoes and ebbed away.

Ms. Farrar turned around in time to see Mandrake rising. The frog was gone.

For a few seconds she gazed at him dumbfounded. "What have you done?"

"Dismissed my servant." His eyes were fixed elsewhere. The fingers of one hand fiddled with his collar.

"But—the information! About Hopkins!" She was gen-uinely bewildered.

"Can be acquired from my servant in a couple of days. By which time his essence will have healed sufficiently in the Other Place for him to be able to talk to me."

"Two days!" Ms. Farrar uttered a little squeal of anger. "That might be far too late! We have no idea what Hopkins—"

"He was a valuable servant," Mandrake said. He looked at her, and his eyes were dull and distant, though his face had flushed at her words. "It will not be too late. I will talk to him when his essence has healed."

Ms. Farrar's eyes flashed darkly. She stepped close, and Mandrake caught a sudden wave of pomegranates, with a hint of lemon. "I would have thought," she said, "that you valued my regard rather higher than the spilled slime of a fading demon. That creature failed you! It was charged to bring you information, and it could not do so. Important intelligence was there for us to take . . . and you released it!"

"Only temporarily." Mandrake had waved a hand, spoken a breathless syllable: a Bulb of Silence surrounded them, blocking their words from the sizable crowd now jostling at the garden entrance of the hall. They all still wore their masks: he glimpsed the sparkling, vibrant colors, the strange, exotic shapes, the blank eye-slits. He and Farrar were the only magicians who were maskless—it made him feel exposed and naked. Furthermore he knew that he had no real answer to her anger, for his actions had taken even himself by surprise. This made him furious in his turn. "Please control yourself," he said coldly. "I deal with my slaves in the manner of my choosing."

Ms. Farrar gave a short, wild laugh. "Indeed you do. Your slaves . . . or perhaps you mean your little *friends*?"

"Oh, come now—"

"Enough!" She turned from him. "People have been hunting for your weakness for some time now, Mr. Mandrake," she said over her shoulder, "and I, inadvertently, have found it. Extraordinary! I never would have guessed that you were such a sentimental fool." Her coat swirled around her; with imperious steps she passed through the membrane of the Bulb; without any further backward glance, she stalked from the hall.

Mandrake watched her go. He took a deep breath. Then, with a single word, he dismissed the Bulb of Silence and was received eagerly by an ocean of noise, kerfuffle, and excited speculation.

Part Three

Alexandria: 125 B.C.

That morning, as on every morning, a little group of supplicants gathered outside the apartments of my master Ptolemy. They were there long before dawn, wrapped in their shawls, blue-legged and shivering, waiting patiently for the sun. As light spilled over the river, the magician's servants opened the doors and let them in, one by one.

That morning, as on every morning, the list of complaints, wrongs, and outright woes was recited and considered. To some, advice was given. To a few (the more obviously covetous or deluded), help was refused. To the rest, action of one sort or another was promised and delivered. Imps and foliots departed through the windows and flitted out across the city on a variety of errands. A certain noble djinni was seen to leave and, in due course, return. For several hours a steady stream of spirits came and went. It was a very busy household.

At half-past eleven the doors were shut and locked for the day. Thereafter, by a back route (to avoid lingering petitioners, who would have delayed him), the magician Ptolemy departed for the Library of Alexandria to resume his studies.

We were walking across the courtyard outside the library building. It was lunchtime and Ptolemy wished to get anchovy bread in the markets on the quay. I strolled beside him as an Egyptian scribe, bald-headed, hairy of leg, busily arguing with him on the philosophy of worlds.[1] One or two scholars passed us as we went: disputatious Greeks; lean Romans, hot of eye and scrubbed of skin; dark Nabataeans and courteous diplomats from Meroe and far Parthia, all here to drink knowledge from the deep Egyptian wells. As we were about to leave the library compound, a clash of horns sounded in the street below. Up came a little knot of soldiers, the Ptolemaic colors aflutter on their pikes. They drew apart to reveal Ptolemy's cousin, the king's son and heir to the throne of Egypt, slowly swaggering up the steps. In his train came an adoring cluster of favorites— toadies and fawners to a man.[2] My master and I stopped; we inclined our heads in the traditional manner of respect.

"Cousin!" The king's son lolled to a stop; his tunic was tight about his stomach, wet where the brief walk had drawn sweat from his flesh. His face was blurry with wine, his aura sagged

---

[1] He claimed that any connection between the two must be for a purpose: it was the job of magicians and spirits to work toward a closer understanding of what this purpose was. I regarded this (politely) as utter balderdash. What little interaction there was between our worlds was nothing but a cruel aberration (the enslavement of us djinn), which should be terminated as soon as possible. Our argument had become heated, and earthy vulgarities were avoided only by my concern for rhetorical purity.

[2] They included senior priests, nobles of the realm, flophouse drinking partners, professional wrestlers, a bearded lady, and a midget. The king's son had a jaded appetite and broad tastes; his social circle was wide.

with it. His eyes were dull coins under their heavy lids. "Cousin," he said again. "Thought I'd pay you a little visit."

Ptolemy bowed again. "My lord. It is an honor, of course."

"Thought I'd see where you skulk away your days instead of staying at my side"—he took a breath—"like a loyal cousin should." The toadies tittered. "Philip and Alexander and all my other cousins are accounted for," he went on, tumbling over the words. "They fight for us in the desert, they work as ambassadors in principalities east and west. They prove their loyalty to our dynasty. But you . . ." A pause; he picked at the wet cloth of his tunic. "*Well.* Can we rely on *you*?"

"In whatever way you wish me to serve."

"But *can* we, Ptolemaeus? You cannot hold a sword or draw a bow with those girlish arms of yours; so where's your strength, eh? Up *here*"—he tapped his head with an unsteady finger—"that's what I've heard. Up here. What do you do in this dismal place then, out of the sun?"

Ptolemy bowed his head modestly. "I study, my lord. The papyri and books of record that the worthy priests have compiled, time out of mind. Works of history and religion—"

"And magic too, by all accounts. Forbidden works." That was a tall priest, black-robed, head shaven, and with white clay daubed faintly around his eyes. He spat the words out softly like a cobra shooting venom. He was probably a magician himself.

"Ha! Yes. All manner of wickednesses." The king's son lurched a little closer; sour fumes hung about his clothes and issued from his mouth. "The people celebrate you for it, cousin. You use your magic to beguile them, to win them over to you. I hear they come daily to your house to witness your devilry. I hear all *kinds* of stories."

Ptolemy pursed his lips. "Do you, my lord? That is beyond my understanding. It is true that I am pestered by some of those who have fallen low in fortune. I offer them advice, nothing more. I am just a boy—weak, as you say, and unworldly. I prefer to remain alone, seeking nothing but a little knowledge."

The affectation of humility (for it *was* affectation—Ptolemy's hunger for knowledge was just as ravenous as the king's son's lust for power, and far more virile) seemed to enrage the prince into a passion. His face grew dark as uncooked meat; little snakes of spittle swayed at the corner of his mouth. "Knowledge, eh?" he cried. "Yes, but of what kind? And to what end? Scrolls and styluses are nothing to a proper man, but in the hands of white-skinned necromancers they can be deadlier than the strongest iron. In old Egypt, they say, eunuchs mustered armies with the stamp of a foot and swept the rightful pharaohs into the sea! I don't intend that to happen to *me*. What are *you* smirking about, slave?"

I hadn't meant to smile. It's just I enjoyed his account, having been in the vanguard of the army that did the sweeping, a thousand years before. It's good when you make an impression. I bowed and scraped. "Nothing, master. Nothing."

"You smirked, I saw you! You *dare* laugh at me—the king-in-waiting!"

His voice quivered; the soldiers knew the signs. Their pikes made small adjustments. Ptolemy uttered placatory noises: "He did not intend offense, my lord. My scribe was born with an unfortunate facial tic, a grimace that in harsh light can seem a baleful smirk. It is a sad affliction—"

"I will have his head stuck above the Crocodile Gate! Guards—"

The soldiers lowered their pikes, each keener than the rest

to drench the stones with my blood. I waited meekly for the inevitable.[3]

Ptolemy stepped forward. "Please, cousin. This is ridiculous. I beg you—"

"No! I will hear no argument. The slave will die."

"Then I must *tell* you." My master was suddenly very close to his brutish cousin; he seemed somehow taller, his equivalent in height. His dark eyes gazed directly into the other's watery ones, which squirmed in their sockets like a fish upon a spear. The king's son quailed and shrank from him; his soldiers and attendants shifted uneasily. The sun's warmth dimmed; the courtyard grew cloudy. One or two of the soldiers had goose pimples on their legs. "You will leave him alone," Ptolemy said, his voice slow and clear. "He is *my* slave, and *I* say he deserves no punishment. Leave with your lackeys and return to your wine vats. Your presence here disturbs the scholars and brings no credit on our family. Your insinuations likewise. *Do you understand?*"

The king's son had bent so far back to avoid the piercing stare that half his cape dragged on the ground. He made a noise like a marsh toad mating. "Yes," he croaked. "Yes."

Ptolemy stepped away. Instantly he seemed to dwindle; the darkness that had gathered around the little group like a winter cloud lifted and was gone. The onlookers relaxed. Priests rubbed the backs of their necks; nobles exhaled noisily. A midget peeped out from behind a wrestler.

"Come, Rekhyt." Ptolemy repositioned the scrolls under his arm and glanced at the king's son with studious disinterest. "Good-bye, cousin. I am late for lunch."

He made to step past. The king's son, white-faced and

---

[3] i.e. a whirlwind of slaughter. Carried out by me.

tottering, uttered an incoherent word. He lurched forward; from beneath his cloak a knife was drawn. With a snarl, he lunged at Ptolemy's side. I raised a hand and gestured: there was a muffled impact, as of a masonry block landing on a bag of suet pudding. The king's son doubled over, clutching his solar plexus, mouth bubbling, eyes popping. He sank to his knees. The knife dropped impotently on the stones.

Ptolemy kept walking. Four of the soldiers sprang to uncertain life; their pikes went low, they made aggressive sounds. I swept my hands in a semicircle; away they flew, one after the other—head first, toes last, out across the courtyard cobbles. One hit a Roman, another a Greek; a third skidded a yard upon his nose. The fourth crashed into a trader's stand and was half buried by an avalanche of sweetmeats. They lay outstretched like points upon a sundial.

The others in the group were chicken. They cowered together and made no move. I kept close watch upon the old bald priest, though—I could see he was tempted to do something. But he met my eyes and decided it was best to live.

Ptolemy kept walking. I followed after. We went in search of anchovy bread. When we returned, our quest fulfilled, the library precinct was quiet and still.

My master knew the incident was inauspicious, but his studies were his consuming interest, and he chose to ignore the implications. But *I* did not, and nor did the people of Alexandria. Rumors of the matter circulated swiftly, some more creative than accurate.[4] The king's son was unpopular; his humiliation

---

[4] One account, daubed upon the harbor walls and illustrated by a lively sketch, described the king's son being bent bare-bottomed over a library table and spanked with a royal flail by demon or demons unknown.

was regarded with general hilarity and Ptolemy's celebrity grew.

By night I floated on the winds above the palace, conversing with the djinn.

"What news?"

"News, Bartimaeus, of the king's son. His brow is heavy with wrath and fear. He mutters daily that Ptolemy might send a demon to destroy him and seize the throne. The danger pulses in his temple like a beating drum."

"But my master lives only for his writing. He has no interest in the crown."

"Even so. The king's son chews on the problem late at night and over wine. He sends emissaries out in search of men that might aid him quash this threat."

"Affa, I thank you. Fly well."

"Fly well, Bartimaeus."

Ptolemy's cousin was a fool and a sot, but I understood his fears. He himself was not a magician. The magicians of Alexandria were ineffectual shadows of the great ones of the past, under whom I'd toiled.[5] The army was weaker than for generations, and mostly far away. In comparison, Ptolemy was powerful indeed. No question, the king's son would be vulnerable should my master decide to overthrow him.

Time passed. I watched and waited.

The king's son found his men. Money was paid. One moonlit night four assassins stole into the palace gardens and paid a

---

[5] The ancient pharaohs had traditionally relied upon their priests for such services, and the Greek dynasty had seen no reason to alter this policy. But whereas in the past talented individuals had made their way to Egypt to ply their trade, allowing the Empire to grow strong on the backs of weeping djinn, that time had long since gone.

call upon my master. As I may have mentioned, their visit was of short duration.

The king's son had taken the precaution of being away from Alexandria that night; he was out in the desert hunting. When he returned, he was greeted first by a flock of carrion birds wheeling in the skies about the Crocodile Gate, then by the hanging corpses of three assassins. Their feet brushed against the plumes of his chariot as he passed into the city. Face mottled white and crimson, the prince retired to his chambers and was not seen for days.

"Master," I said. "Your life remains at risk. You must leave Alexandria."

"Quite impossible, Rekhyt, as you know. The Library is here."

"Your cousin is your implacable foe. He will try again."

"And you will be here to foil him, Rekhyt. I have every confidence in you."

"The assassins were but men. The next who come will not be human."

"I am sure you will cope. Do you have to squat so? It distresses me."

"I'm an imp today. Imps squat. Listen," I said, "your confidence in me is gratifying, but frankly I can do without it. Just as I can do without being in the firing line when a marid comes knocking on your door."

He chuckled into his goblet. "A marid! I think you overestimate the ability of our court magicians. A one-legged mouler I can believe."

"Your cousin casts his net wider. He drinks long with ambassadors from Rome—and Rome, from what I hear, is where the action is right now. Every hedge-magician from here to the Tigris is hastening there in search of glory."

Ptolemy shrugged. "So my cousin puts himself in Rome's pocket. Why should they attack me?"

"So that he will be forever in their debt. And meanwhile *I'll* be dead." I let off a gust of sulphur in annoyance—my master's blithe absorption in his studies could be rather galling. "It's all right for *you*," I cried. "You can summon up any number of us to protect your skin. What *we* suffer doesn't matter a fig." I folded my wings over my snout in the manner of a huffy bat and hung from the bedroom rafter.

"Rekhyt—you have saved my life twice over. You *know* how grateful I am to you."

"Words, words, words. Don't mean nowt."[6]

"That's hardly fair. You know the direction of my work. I wish to understand the mechanisms that divide us, human and djinni; I seek to redress the balance, build trust between us . . ."

"Yeah, yeah. And while you do, I'm guarding your back and emptying out your privy pot."

"*Now* you're making it up. Anhotep does that. I've never—"

"I'm speaking figuratively. My point is—whenever I'm in your world, I'm trapped. You call the shots. Trust doesn't enter into it." The imp glared out through the membrane of its wing and let out another sulphurous eruption.

"Will you stop doing that? I've got to sleep in this room tonight. So you doubt my sincerity, do you?"

"If you want my opinion, master, all your talk of reconciliation between our peoples is nothing but hot air."

"Is that so?" My master's tone of voice hardened. "Very well,

---

[6] Bit of Egyptian street argot crept in here. Well, I was riled.

Rekhyt, I take that as a challenge. I believe my studies are coming to the point when I can perhaps *act* as well as talk. As you know, I have studied accounts of the northern tribes. The practice there is for magicians and spirits to meet halfway. From what you and the others have told me, I think I can go one better than that." He threw his goblet aside, got up, and began pacing around the chamber.

The imp lowered its wings uneasily. "What do you mean? I don't follow you."

"Oh, you won't have to follow *me*," the boy said. "Quite the reverse. When I'm ready, I'll be following *you*."

13

The untoward incidents that took place during the Prime Minister's party at Richmond were swift and confusing, and it took some time to discover what had happened. Witnesses among the party guests were few, since when the carnage had erupted in the skies above, most had taken shelter headfirst in the rose beds and ornamental ponds. However, after Mr. Devereaux had gathered the magicians responsible for estate security, and they in their turn had summoned the demons guarding the perimeter, a picture of sorts emerged.

It appeared that the alarm had been set off when a djinni in the form of a limping frog broke through the estate nexus. It was closely pursued by a large pack of demons, which harried their prey remorselessly as it fled across the lawns. The estate demons had quickly joined the melee, valiantly attacking anything that moved, so that one or two of the invaders were soon destroyed, together with three guests, an under-butler, and much of the antique statuary on the south lawns, behind which the frog took shelter for a time. In the chaos, the frog escaped by breaking into the house itself, at which the other invaders turned about and fled the scene. Their identity, and that of their masters, remained obscure.

By contrast, the identity of the *frog's* master was soon established. Too many people had observed the events in the mansion's vestibule for John Mandrake to escape detection. Shortly after midnight he was hauled up before Mr. Devereaux, Mr. Mortensen, and Mr. Collins (the three most senior ministers remaining at the house), and admitted having given the djinni in question the freedom to return to him at any time. Under harsh questioning, Mr. Mandrake was then forced to give some details of the operation in which his demon had been engaged. The name of Mr. Clive Jenkins was mentioned, and five horlas were promptly dispatched to his London flat. In due course they returned. Mr. Jenkins was not at home. His whereabouts was unknown.

Since Mandrake knew nothing about what his djinni had discovered, and since summoning the injured Bartimaeus immediately might well destroy its essence—without any answer being forthcoming—the matter was abandoned for the present. Mandrake was ordered to appear before the Council three days later, to summon his slave for interrogation.

In the meantime the young magician bore the weight of general displeasure. The Prime Minister was beside himself with fury at the loss of his Grecian statuary, while Mr. Collins—who at the outset of the alarm had been the first to leap into the duck pond, only to be half drowned beneath one of the heavier lady guests—regarded him balefully from beneath his wad of toweling. The third minister, Mr. Mortensen, had suffered no particular injury, but had disliked Mandrake for years. Together they condemned him for his irresponsible and secretive conduct, and hinted at a broad range of punishments, though the details were left until the forthcoming Council meeting.

Mr. Mandrake made no response to the accusations. Pale-faced, he departed the mansion and was driven back to London.

The following day Mr. Mandrake breakfasted alone. Ms. Piper, reporting as usual for the early morning briefing, found the door barred by a manservant. The minister was indisposed; he would see her in the office later. Disconcerted, she took her leave.

With leaden steps the magician proceeded to his study. The door guard, attempting a mild jocularity, found itself blasted by a Spasm. Mandrake sat for a long while at his desk, staring at the wall.

Presently he picked up his telephone and dialed a number.

"Hello. Jane Farrar's office? Could I speak with her, please? Yes, it's Mandrake . . . Oh . . . I see. Very well." The receiver was slowly returned to its cradle.

Well, he had tried to warn her. That she had refused to speak to him was hardly his fault. The night before, he had done his best to keep her name out of it, but to no avail. Their altercation had been seen. No doubt she would now be reprimanded too. He felt only mild regret at this; all thought of the beautiful Ms. Farrar filled him with a strange repulsion.

The real stupidity of it was that this trouble might have been prevented if he'd just done what Farrar said. Almost certainly Bartimaeus would have had information on the Jenkins plot that would have helped placate Devereaux. He should have squeezed it out of his slave without a second thought. But instead . . . he had let him go. It was absurd! The djinni was nothing but a thorn in his flesh—abusive, argumentative, feeble . . . and, because of his birth name, potentially a fatal threat. He should have destroyed him while he was unable to fight back. How simple it should have been!

Blank-eyed, he stared at the papers on his desk. *Sentimental and weak* . . . Perhaps Farrar was right. John Mandrake, minister of the government, had acted against his own interests. Now he was vulnerable to his enemies. Even so, no matter how much cold fury he tried to muster—against Bartimaeus, against Farrar, and most of all against himself—he knew he could not have done otherwise. The sight of the djinni's small, broken body had shocked him too much: it had prompted an impulsive decision.

And *this* was the shattering event, far more significant than the threats and spite of his colleagues. For years his life had been a fabric of calculations. It was by remorseless dedication to work that Mandrake derived his identity; spontaneity had become alien to him. But now, in the shadow of his single unconsidered action, the prospect of work suddenly did not appeal. Elsewhere this morning, armies were clashing, the ministries were humming: there was much to be done. John Mandrake felt listless, floating, suddenly detached from the demands of his name and office.

A train of thought from the previous night recurred in his mind. An image: sitting with his tutor, Ms. Lutyens, long ago, happily sketching in the garden on a summer's day . . . she sat beside him, laughing, hair gleaming in the light. The vision flickered like a mirage. It vanished. The room was bare and cold.

In due course the magician left his study. In its circle of blackened wood, the door guard flinched from him as he passed.

The day did not go well for Mandrake. At the Information Ministry a tartly worded memo from Ms. Farrar's office awaited him. She had decided to raise an official complaint regarding his refusal to interrogate his demon, an act which was likely to prove detrimental to the police investigation. No sooner had Mandrake finished reading this than a somber deputation from the Home Office arrived, bearing an envelope with a black ribbon. Mr. Collins wished to question him about a serious disturbance in St. James's Park the previous evening. The details were ominous for Mandrake: a fleeing frog, a savage demon set free from its prism, a number of fatalities in the crowd. A minor riot had ensued, with commoners destroying a portion of the fair. Tension on the streets was still high. Mandrake was asked to prepare a defense in time for the Council meeting in two days' time. He agreed without discussion; he knew the thread supporting his career was fraying fast.

During meetings, the eyes of his deputies were amused and scathing. One or two went so far as to suggest he summon his djinni immediately to limit the political damage. Mandrake, stony-faced and stubborn, refused. All day he was irritable and distracted; even Ms. Piper gave him a wide berth.

By late afternoon, when Mr. Makepeace rang to remind him of their appointment, Mandrake had had enough. He departed his office for the day.

For some years, ever since the affair of Gladstone's Staff, Mandrake had been a close associate of the playwright Mr. Quentin Makepeace. There was good reason to be so—above all things, the Prime Minister loved theater, and Mr. Makepeace consequently exerted great influence upon him. By pretending to share his leader's joy, Mandrake had managed to maintain a bond with Devereaux that other, more intolerant, members of the Council could only envy. But it came at a price: more than once Mandrake had found himself cajoled into appearing in dreadful amateur productions at Richmond, prancing about the stage in chiffon leggings or bulbous pantaloons, and—on one terrible never-to-be-forgotten occasion—swinging from a harness wearing wings of sparkly gauze. Mandrake had borne his colleagues' merriment stoically: Devereaux's goodwill mattered more.

In return for his support, Quentin Makepeace had frequently offered Mandrake counsel, and Mandrake had found him surprisingly astute, quick to pick up on interesting rumors, accurate in his predictions of the Prime Minister's fluctuating moods. Many times he had gained advantage by following the playwright's advice.

But in recent months, as his work commitments escalated, Mandrake had become weary of his companion and resentful of the time wasted nurturing Devereaux's enthusiasms. He had no time for trivialities. For weeks he had avoided accepting Makepeace's invitation to call. Now, dead-eyed and rudderless, he resisted no longer.

A servant let him into the quiet house. Mandrake crossed the hall, passing beneath pink-tinged chandeliers and a monumental oil of the playwright leaning in his satin dressing gown against a pile of self-penned works. Keeping his eyes averted (he always considered the gown a little short), Mandrake descended the central staircase. His shoes padded soundlessly on the thick pile carpet. The walls were hung with framed posters from theaters across the world. FIRST NIGHT! WORLD PREMIERE! MR. MAKEPEACE'S PLEASURE TO PRESENT! Silently a dozen adverts screamed their message down.

At the foot of the stairs a studded iron door led to the playwright's workroom.

Even as he knocked, the door was flung open. A broad and beaming face looked out. "John, my boy! Excellent! I am *so* pleased. Lock the door behind you. We shall have tea, with a twist of peppermint. You look as though you need reviving."

Mr. Makepeace was a whirl of little movements, precise, defined, balletic. His diminutive frame spun and bobbed, pouring the tea, sprinkling the peppermint, restless as a little bird. His face sparkled with vigor, his red hair shone; his smile twitched repeatedly as if reflecting on a secretive delight.

As usual, his clothes expressed his buoyant personality: tan shoes, a pair of pea-green trousers with maroon check, a bright yellow waistcoat, a pink cravat, a loose-fitting linen shirt with pleats upon the sleeves. Today, however, the sleeves were rolled up above the elbows, and cravat and waistcoat were concealed behind a stained white apron. Evidently Mr. Makepeace was hard at work.

With a tiny spoon he stirred the tea, tapped it twice upon the glass, and handed the result to Mandrake. "There!" he cried. "Get that down you. Now, John"—his smile was tender, solicitous—"little birds tell me all is not well."

Briefly, without elaboration, Mandrake mentioned the events of the past few hours. The smaller man tutted and cooed with sympathy. "Disgraceful!" he cried at last. "And you were only doing your duty! But fools like Farrar are all too ready to tear you to pieces, first chance they get. You know what their problem is, John?" He gave a significant pause. "Envy. We are surrounded by envious minnows, who resent our talents. I get this reaction all the time in the theater, critics carping at my efforts."

Mandrake grunted. "Well, you'll put them in their place again tomorrow," he said. "With the premiere."

"Indeed I shall, John, indeed I shall. But you know, sometimes government is so, so friendless. I expect you feel that, don't you? You feel as if you're on your own. But *I* am your friend, John. *I* respect you, even if no one else does."

"Thanks, Quentin. I'm not sure it's quite as bad as—"

"You see, you've got something they haven't. Know what it is? Vision. I've always seen that in you. You're clear-sighted. And ambitious too. I read that in you, yes I do."

Mandrake looked down at his tea, which he disliked. "Well, I don't know—"

"I want to show you something, John. A little magical experiment. I want to get your opinion. See if you can see— well, come on. No time like the present. Could you take along that iron imp-spike beside you? Thanks. Yes, you can bring your tea."

With short, swift steps, Mr. Makepeace led the way toward an inner arch. In some perplexity, Mandrake trailed after. A magical experiment? He had never observed Makepeace do more than the most basic spells; he had always assumed him to be a fairly minor conjuror. . . . This was *everyone's* opinion. What then was he—?

He turned the corner and halted. With difficulty, he prevented his tea glass tumbling from his fingers. His eyes widened in the half light. His mouth hung open.

"What do you think? What do you think, my boy?" Mr. Makepeace was grinning at his shoulder.

For a long moment Mandrake could not speak, but simply cast his eyes around the chamber. Previously it had been home to the playwright's homage to himself: a collection of trophies, awards, newspaper cuttings, photographs, and curios. Now this shrine had gone. A single electric bulb cast dim radiance. The room contained two pentacles, carefully drawn on the concrete floor. The first, the magician's, was of standard size, but the other was much larger. And it was occupied.

A metal chair sat in the center of the summoning pentacle, fixed to the floor with four great bolts. The chair was made of iron, its limbs thick and heavily soldered; it gleamed faintly in the half light. Sitting upon it, with canvas straps constraining wrists and ankles, was a man.

"Quite a picture, is it not?" Mr. Makepeace could scarcely contain his excitement. He practically skipped and danced at Mandrake's side.

The prisoner was conscious; panicked eyes gazed at them. A rough gag covered his mouth and part of a mustache and beard; his blond hair was disordered, a faint bruise glistened on one cheek. He wore commoner's clothes, ripped about the collar.

"Who—who is he?" Mandrake could scarcely speak.

"This beauty?" Mr. Makepeace chuckled. He pranced to the small pentacle and began lighting the candles. "Of course you know there's been trouble with the Battersea steelworkers? They've 'gone on strike,' apparently, spend their time having parties in the street outside the factory. Well, late last night my agents found this fine fellow holding forth to the protestors from the back of a truck. In good voice, he was. A real orator. Harangued the crowd for twenty minutes about how they've got to revolt, how the time was fast approaching when the magicians would pack their bags. Got a nice round of applause at the end. Well, despite his pretty words he wouldn't stay out all night with the workers in the cold, and presently he set off home. So my boys followed him and knocked him on the head when no one was looking. Brought him down here. I'm going to need that imp-spike, if you don't mind. No, on second thoughts, *you* have it. I'll have my hands full with the summoning."

Mandrake's head spun. "What summoning? What—?"

Astonishment gave way to agitation. "Quentin—do you mind telling me exactly what you're doing?"

"I'll do better than that. I'll show you." Mr. Makepeace finished lighting the candles, scanned the runes and incense bowls, and hopped across to the captive's chair. With delicate fingers, he manipulated the gag. "Don't like to use this, but I had to keep him quiet. The chap became *quite* hysterical. Now, *you*"—the smile vanished from his face—"answer my questions precisely, or you know what'll happen." The gag was whisked away; color returned to constricted lips. "What's your name?"

A cough, a gasp. "Nic—Nicholas Drew, sir."

"Occupation?"

"Sh-shopworker."

"So you're a commoner?"

"Yes."

"And you're a political activist in your spare time."

"Y-yes, sir."

"Very well. What is the Shriveling Fire and when is it applied?"

The question came arrow-quick; the prisoner flinched, incomprehension filled his face. "I—I—don't know. . . ."

"Come on, come on. Answer me! Or my friend here will goad you with his stick!"

Mandrake frowned in anger. "Makepeace! Stop this non—"

"A moment, my boy." The magician loomed close to his captive. "So, even with the threat of pain, you persist with your lie?"

"It is not a lie! I swear it! I have never heard of that fire! Please—"

A broad grin. "Good. That'll do." With swift motions, the gag was replaced. Makepeace hopped back to the other pentacle. "You heard all that, John?"

Mandrake's face was white with shock and rising disgust. "Makepeace—what is the purpose of this exhibition? We cannot pluck men off the streets and subject them to torture—"

The playwright snorted. "Torture? *He's* all right. He's barely been touched. Besides, you heard him—he's an agitator, a threat to the nation. But I intend him no malice. He's just helping me with a little experiment. Observe. . . ." He adopted a dramatic pose; his fingers twitched, as if about to conduct an orchestra.

Mandrake started forward. "I insist that—"

"Careful, John. You know better than to fool about when a summoning's in progress." With this, the playwright began a rapid incantation. The light dimmed; from nowhere a gentle breeze stirred the candle flames. Two rooms away the iron door jolted in its sockets. Mandrake stepped back, instinctively raising the spike he carried. Subconsciously he listened to the words: Latin . . . a fairly typical summons, the usual clauses . . . the demon's name—Borello . . . but wait, what was that bit—? "*In corpus viri*" . . . "into the vessel that you find there . . ." "obedient to the vessel's will" . . . This was odd and unfamiliar. . . .

The incantation finished. Mandrake's gaze swiveled to the chair, where a dark shadow flickered. Now it was gone. The man's body jerked, as if all its muscles had tensed, then relaxed. Mandrake waited. The breeze subsided, the lightbulb flared once more. The young man sat inert and passive. His eyes were closed.

Mr. Makepeace lowered his hands. He winked at Mandrake. "Now then . . ."

He took a step forward. Mandrake gasped, cried out a warning. "Wait, you fool! The demon's there! It's suicide to—"

Calm and slow as a noonday cat, Makepeace stepped out of

his circle and into the other. Nothing happened. Grinning, he once more removed the gag and patted the captive gently on one cheek. "Mr. Drew! Wake up! This is no time for sleeping!"

Languorously the young man stirred. Hands and feet stretched against their bonds. His eyes opened and stared about them dreamily. He seemed to have difficulty recollecting his situation. Fascinated despite himself, Mandrake moved a little closer.

"Hold that stick ready," Makepeace said. "Things may go wrong." He bent near, spoke sweetly. "What is your name, friend?"

"Nicholas Drew."

"Is that your *only* name? Think deeply. Do you have another?"

A pause. The man's face furrowed. "Yes . . . I do."

"And what is it?"

"Borello . . ."

"Ah, good. Tell me, Nicholas, what is your occupation?"

"Shopworker."

"And what is the Shriveling Fire? When is it applied?"

A brief frown of puzzlement gave way to bland assurance. "It is the penalty for disobedience, should we purposefully fail in our charge. Our master puts our essence to the torch. Ah, we fear it!"

"Very good. Thank you." Mr. Makepeace turned away, leaped carefully over the nearest chalk marks, and approached John Mandrake, whose face had been robbed of expression. "What do you think, my boy? Is it not a fascinating situation?"

"I don't know. . . . It is a clever trick—"

"It is more than a trick! The demon has lodged itself within the man. It is trapped inside as if he were the pentacle!

Did you not hear? And the demon's knowledge is at the man's command. Suddenly he knew the meaning of the Shriveling Fire. He had knowledge, where before had just been blankness! Now, consider the implications. . . ."

Mandrake frowned. "The feat is morally dubious. This fellow is an unwilling victim. Besides, he is a commoner. He cannot properly use the demon's information."

"Aha! Perceptive as ever! Forget the moral dimension for a moment. Imagine if—"

"What is he doing?" Mandrake was studying the captive, who seemed to have newly recognized his surroundings. Agitation had returned to the face; he struggled with his bonds. Once or twice he turned his head violently from side to side, like a dog worrying at a flea.

Makepeace shrugged. "Perhaps he senses the demon inside. Perhaps it talks within him. Hard to tell. I have not tried it with a commoner before."

"You have used others?"

"A single one only. A volunteer. That union has worked extremely well."

Mandrake rubbed his chin. The sight of the writhing captive unsettled him, disrupting his intellectual interest. He could not think what to say.

Mr. Makepeace had no such problems. "The implications, as I say, are immense. Notice how I entered the pentacle unharmed? The demon was powerless to stop me, since it was within an altogether *different* prison! Now, I wanted you to see this, John, with the utmost urgency, because I trust you, just as you, I hope, trust me. And if—"

"Please!" A plaintive cry from the figure in the chair. "I can't bear it! Oh, it whispers! It drives me mad!"

Mandrake flinched. "He is suffering. The demon must be dismissed."

"Shortly, shortly. Probably he lacks the mental ability to constrain its voice—"

The captive wriggled anew. "I'll tell you all I know! About the commoners, about our plans! I can give you information. . . ."

Makepeace made a face. "Tush, you can give us nothing that our spies don't already know. Cease your hollering. I have a headache."

"No! I can tell you of the Commoners' Alliance! Of their ringleaders!"

"We know them all—their names, their wives, their families. They are ants to be stepped on when we choose. Now—I have vital matters to discuss here—"

"But—but you do not know *this*: a fighter from the old Resistance lives! She hides in London! I have seen her, hours ago! I can take you to the place—"

"That is all ancient history." Mr. Makepeace took the iron spike from Mandrake's fingers and weighed it casually in his palm. "I am a patient man, Mr. Drew, but you begin to irk me. If you do not cease—"

"Wait a moment." John Mandrake's voice had altered; its tone halted the playwright in his tracks. "What Resistance fighter is this? A woman?"

"Yes! Yes, a girl! Her name is Kitty Jones, although she goes now by another name—Ah, will you *stop* your whispering!" He groaned and thrashed beneath his bonds.

A faint rushing sounded in Mandrake's head. For a moment, he felt dizzy, as if he were about to fall. His mouth was dry. "Kitty Jones? You lie."

"No! I swear it! Release me and I will take you to her."

"Is this line of questioning *really* necessary?" Mr. Makepeace wore a petulant frown. "The Resistance is long defunct. Please concentrate on what *I* say, John. It is extremely important, especially in your current situation. John? *John?*"

Mandrake did not hear him. He saw Bartimaeus, wearing the apparel of a dark-skinned boy. He saw him standing in a cobbled courtyard years before. He heard the boy speak. "*The golem seized her . . . incinerated her in seconds.*" Kitty Jones was dead. The djinni had told him so. Mandrake had believed him. And now, out of the past, the boy's sober expression suddenly shifted horribly into a leer of contempt.

Mandrake leaned over the captive. "Where did you see her? Tell me, and you shall go free."

"The Frog Inn, Chiswick! She works there! She has the name of Clara Bell. Now please—"

"Quentin, be so good as to dismiss the demon and release this man immediately. I must depart."

The playwright had become quiet, suddenly withdrawn. "Certainly, John . . . if you wish it. But will you not wait? I strongly advise you to listen to what I have to say. Forget the girl. There are more important things. I want to discuss this experiment—"

"Later, Quentin, later." Mandrake was white-faced; he was already at the arch.

"But where are you going? Not back to work?"

Mandrake spoke through gritted teeth. "Hardly. I have a summoning of my own that I have to perform."

14

Time, as I may have mentioned once or twice, does not really exist in the Other Place. Even so, you know full well when you're being shortchanged. And I had scarcely been reabsorbed by the nourishing energies of the maelstrom when I felt the cruel tug of a summons once again, sucking me out like yolk drawn from an egg, plunging me back upon the hard and bitter earth.

Already. And my essence had hardly begun to heal.

My last activities upon the material world had been so painful, so perilous to my essence, that I could barely remember them. But one thing was clear enough: my numbing, cursed weakness! How I—whose power scattered the magicians of Nimrud, who set the Barbary Coast aflame, who sent cruel Ammet, Koh, and Jabor spinning to their doom—how I, that same Bartimaeus, had been reduced to fleeing as a miserable, no-good frog, unable to trade the smallest Detonation with a gang of hireling herons.

During the whole debacle I'd been too near death to truly feel the righteous anger that was my due. But I felt it now. My very being frothed with it.

I could dimly recall my master dismissing me. Probably he disliked the mess I was making on his floor. Perhaps my decrepitude had embarrassed him at last. Well, whatever the reason, it hadn't taken him long to change his mind.

Fine. I was through with him. We would both go to our deaths. I'd use his name against him now, come what may. My last desire was to see him squirm.

And I wasn't going to go out as a paltry amphibian, either.

In the few short hours I'd been away from Earth, the Other Place had worked its magic. I'd managed to absorb a little energy. It wouldn't last long, but I was going to put it to good use.

As I materialized, I drew what was left of my essence into a form that reflected my emotions with simple purity, e.g. a big-horned demon with muscles like melons and lots of teeth. It was the full works. You name it, I'd got it. Brimstone, spear-tail, wings, hooves, claws, even a couple of whips thrown in. My eyes were burning fishhooks, my skin glowed like cooling lava. Not particularly original, but as a statement of intent it did the job nicely. I erupted into the room with a roll of thunder fit to send the living dead scuttling to their coffins. This was followed by a howl of famished rage, the kind uttered by Anubis's jackals as they prowled about the Memphis tombs—only a bit louder and longer, a vile noise unnaturally prolonged.

In fact I was still in the middle of my ululation when I caught sight of the figure in the pentacle opposite, and was completely put off my stroke. The barnstorming roar con-tracted into a wobbling gargle that shot up a couple of octaves and ended in a falsetto squeak with a question mark on the end. The demon—which had been busily rearing up, leather wings akimbo, whips a-cracking—froze in an unstable posture with its backside protruding. The wings slumped; the whips drooped limply. The billowing brimstone cloud petered away into a timorous dribble that drifted discreetly out of view behind my hooves.

I stopped and stared.

"All right," the girl said tartly. "Quit the silly faces. Have you never been summoned by a woman before?"

The demon lifted a brawny finger and pushed its jaw back into position. "Yes, but—"

"But nothing. Stop making such a fuss."

A forked tongue identical to the tail below issued from the demon's mouth and moistened its dry lips. "But—but—hold on a minute—"

"And what horrible kind of manifestation do you call this, anyhow?" she went on. "That noise! That stench! All those folds and knobbly warts and things! What are you trying to prove?" Her eyes narrowed. "I think you're compensating for something."

"Listen," I began, "this is an established, traditional form that—"

"Traditional nothing. Where are your clothes?"

"Clothes?" I said weakly. "I don't normally bother with them in this guise."

"Well, you could put on a pair of shorts, at least. You're not decent."

"I'm not sure they'd go with the wings. . . ." The demon frowned, blinked. "Hold on, enough of this!"

"Lederhosen would. They'd compliment the leather."

With difficulty, I gathered my thoughts. "Stop! Forget the clothes! The point is . . . the point *is*—what are *you* doing here? Summoning *me*! I don't understand! This is all wrong!" In my perplexity, all attempts at established, traditional terrors ceased. Much to the relief of my wounded essence, the towering demon shrank and shimmered and adjusted itself down to fit the pentacle more snugly. My leather wings became two shoulder nubs and my tail retracted out of sight.

"*Why* is it wrong?" the girl asked. "It's just another one of those master/servant things you were telling me about when last we met. You know: *I'm* the master, *you're* the slave. *I* give the orders, *you* obey without question. Remember how it works now?"

"Sarcasm doesn't go with a pretty face," I said. "So feel free to make lots more comments along those lines. You know perfectly well what I mean. *You're not a magician.*"

She smiled sweetly and gestured about us. "Really? In what way do I not fit the bill?"

The snug-fit demon looked left. The snug-fit demon looked right. Unnervingly, she had a point. There was I, imprisoned in a pentacle. There was she, standing in another. And all around sat the usual paraphernalia: candelabra, incense bowls, chalk sticks, big book lying on a table. It was an otherwise empty room, without curtains on the window. A big round moon shone high above, splashing a silver light across our faces. Except for the smooth, raised section in the middle where the runes and circle had been painted, the floor was of warped, irregular boards. Behind the taint of rosemary the whole place smelled of damp, disuse, and assorted rodents. So far, so *ordinaire*. I'd seen this dismal view a thousand times—all that ever changed was the view out of the window.

No, what was preoccupying me was the summoner herself, the so-called magician.

Kitty Jones.

There she was. Large as life and twice as confident, standing hands on hips with a grin as wide as the Nile estuary. Exactly as I'd portrayed her all those times while annoying Mandrake.[1] Her long dark hair had been chopped back level with her ears; perhaps her face was a little thinner than I remembered. But

---

[1] Or almost so. I sometimes exaggerated the curves.

she looked in far better shape than when I'd last seen her, hobbling down the street after her triumph with the golem. How long had it been since then? Three years—no more. But time seemed to have passed differently for her, somehow: her eyes held the calmness of earned knowledge.[2]

All very well. But still, she couldn't have summoned me. I *knew* this.

The pocket demon shook its head. "It's a trick," I said slowly. I glanced about, my gaze probing the corners of the room with rapier-keen precision. "The real magician's here somewhere . . . hiding. . . ."

She grinned. "What, you think I'm concealing him up my sleeve?" She shook her arm somewhat unnecessarily. "Nope. Not there. Perhaps in your great age you're growing forgetful, Bartimaeus. *You're* the one who does the magic."

I rewarded her with a suitably demonic scowl. "Say what you like, there's another pentacle close by . . . must be . . . I've seen this kind of stunt pulled before . . . Yes, behind that door, for instance." I pointed at the only exit.

"There isn't."

I folded my arms. All four of them. "That's where he is."

She shook her head, almost laughing. "I assure you he's not!"

"Prove it! Go open it and show me."

She laughed aloud. "Step out of my pentacle? So you can tear me limb from limb? Get real, Bartimaeus!"

I masked my disappointment with a huffy face. "Tsk.

---

[2] Her outfit wasn't the issue for me right then, but for the completists among you this was her attire: she wore a black tunic and trouser combo, very fetching, if you were that way inclined. Her tunic was open at the throat; she wore no jewelry. Her feet were encased in big white trainers. How old was she now? Around eighteen, at a guess. I never thought to ask her, and now it's too late.

That's a poor excuse. He's behind there for sure. Can't fool me."

Her expressions had always been mercurial. Now they switched to one of boredom. "We're wasting time. Maybe *this* will convince you." She uttered a quick five-syllable word. A lilac-colored flame rose from the center of my pentacle and administered a swift jab in a private area. My ceiling-high leap distracted her from my whoop of pain—at least, that was my intention. By the time I landed again, the flame had vanished.

She raised an eyebrow. "*Now* don't you think you should have worn a pair of trousers?"

I looked at her long and deeply. "You're lucky," I said, with as much dignity as I could muster, "that I decided not to reverse that Punitive Jab against you. I know your *name*, Ms. Jones. That gives me protection, or have your studies not taken you that far?"

She shrugged. "I've heard something about that. I'm not interested in the details."

"Again I say it: you're not a magician. Magicians are obsessed with details. That's what keeps them alive. I really don't know how you've survived all your other summonings."

"What others? This is my first one solo."

Despite its singed bottom, from which the odor of burned toast was gently wafting, the demon had been doing its best to appear in belated command of the situation. But this new information felled it once again.[3] Yet another plaintive question formed on my lips, but I let it drift away unspoken. There was

---

[3] We fourth-level djinn are not the easiest of spirits to summon correctly, since we are fastidious and proper and keep a sharp ear out for any small errors in the incantations. For this reason, and because of our formidable intellect and overpowering presence (generally *not* involving the smell of burned toast), magicians avoid us until they have had a good deal of practice.

little point. Whichever way I looked at it, nothing here made sense. So I tried a new and unfamiliar strategy, and stayed silent.

The girl seemed taken aback by this cunning approach. After a few seconds of waiting she realized that continuing our conversation was up to her. She drew a deep breath to settle her nerves and began to speak. "Well, you're quite right, Bartimaeus," she said. "I am *not* a magician, thank goodness. And this is the one and only summoning that I ever intend to do. I've been planning it for the last three years."

She took another breath and waited. . . . A dozen more questions occurred to me.[4] But I said nothing.

"This is just a means to an end," she went on. "I'm not interested in the things that the magicians want. You don't have to worry about that."

Another pause. Did I speak? No. I just kept shtoom.

"I don't want any of that," the girl said. "I don't want to acquire vast power or wealth. I think that's all despicable."

My strategy was working, albeit with the pace of a tortoise in lead boots. I was getting an explanation.

"And I *certainly* don't want to subjugate enslaved spirits," she added brightly. "If *that's* what you're thinking."

"Not interested in subjugation?!" Bang went my strategy— but hey, I'd managed more than a minute's silence, which was itself some kind of record. The diminished demon fingered its burned region gingerly, letting off little oohs and aahs of discomfort. "You've got a funny way of going about it then. I'm in pain here, you know."

---

[4] Not to mention twenty-two possible solutions to each one, sixteen resulting hypotheses and counter-theorems, eight abstract speculations, a quadrilateral equation, two axioms, and a limerick. That's raw intelligence for you.

"I was just proving a point, that's all," she said. "Look, would you mind *not* doing that? You're putting me off my stride."

"Doing what? I was only feeling—"

"I saw quite well what you were feeling. Just stop it. And while you're about it, can't you change into something else? That really is the most hideous incarnation. I thought you had more class."

"*This*—hideous?" I whistled. "You really *haven't* done many summonings, have you? All right then, seeing as you're so sensitive. I shall cover my modesty." I changed into my favorite guise. Ptolemy suited me, as I felt comfortable in his form, and he suited the girl too, as his burned bits were hidden under his loincloth.

As soon as I altered, her eyes lit up. "*Yes*," she whispered under her breath. "*That's it!*"

I looked at her, eyes narrowed. "Sorry, can I help you with something?"

"No, it's nothing. Um, that's . . . that's a much better shape." But she was all breathless and excited and it took her a few moments to regain her poise. I sat down cross-legged on the floor and waited.

The girl sat too. For some reason she was suddenly more relaxed. Where a minute earlier her words had been slow and cumbersome, now they burst from her in a veritable flood.

"Well, I want you to listen to me very carefully, Bartimaeus," she said, leaning forward with her fingers jabbing against the floor. I watched them closely, just in case they chanced to jab a chalk line, maybe *smudging* it a little. I was interested in what she had to say, for sure, but I wasn't going to miss an opportunity of escape.

Ptolemy rested his chin upon the back on one hand. "Go ahead. I'm listening."

"Good. Oh, I'm so *pleased* it's worked out so well." She rocked back and forth on her haunches, almost hugging herself with delight. "I hardly dared to hope that I'd succeed. I had so much to learn—you have no *idea*. Well . . . maybe you do," she conceded, "but from a standing start I can tell you it was not much fun."

My dark eyes frowned at her. "You've learned all this in three years?" I was impressed, and more than a little doubtful.

"I started not long after I saw you. When I got my new identity papers through. I was able to visit libraries, get books of magic out—"

"But you *hate* magicians!" I burst out. "You hate what they do. And you hate us spirits too! You told me so to my face— which, I might add, rather hurt my feelings. What's changed that makes you want to call one up?"

"Oh, I wasn't after *any* old demon," she said. "The whole purpose of my studying all this time, of my mastering these . . . these wicked skills, was to summon *you*."

"Me?"

"You seem surprised."

I drew myself up. "Not at all, not at all. What was it that drew you back? My marvelous personality, I suppose? Or my sparkling conversation?"

She chuckled. "Well, not the personality, of course. But yes—the conversation *was* what did it for me, what caught my imagination when we spoke before."

In truth, I remembered this conversation too. Three years had passed, but it seemed longer now, back in the days when my perennial master Nathaniel was still a glum outsider, panting for recognition. It had been during the middle of the golem crisis, when London was being beset by the clay monster *and* Honorius the afrit, that my path crossed Kitty Jones's for the second time. She had impressed me then both with the force of her personality and with her fierce idealism, qualities rarely mingled in magicians. She was a commoner—scarcely educated, ignorant of everything that had conspired to create her world, but nonetheless defiant and hopeful of change. And more than that too: she had risked her life to save that of her enemy, a despicable lowlife, someone unfit to so much as lick her boots.[5]

Yep, she'd made an impression on me. And on my master too, come to think of it.

I grinned. "So you liked what you heard, eh?"

"You set me thinking, Bartimaeus, with all your talk of civilizations come and gone. Above all, you said there were *patterns* to look out for, and I knew I had to find them." One finger jabbed down as she made the point, *almost* touching the red chalk line. It was close, very close. "So," she said simply, "I went looking."

Ptolemy adjusted the corner of his loincloth. "All very well, but that's a different thing from cruelly ripping an innocent djinni from his place of rest. My essence is in sore need of respite. Mandrake's kept me in service"—I made a rapid finger-and-toe calculation—"for six hundred and eighty-three days out of the last seven hundred. And *that* has its effects. I'm like an apple at the bottom of a barrel—sweet and fair to look at, but bruised to a pulp beneath the skin. And you've taken me from my place of healing."

---

[5] My master, this was. Did you guess?

Her head was tilted; she looked up at me from under her brows. "The Other Place, you mean."

"That is one of its names."

"Well, I'm sorry to have disturbed you." She spoke as if all she'd done was rouse me from a little nap. "But I didn't know I could even do it. I feared my technique might be faulty."

"Your technique's fine," I said. "In fact it's good. And that leads me to my biggest question. *How* have you learned to summon me?"

She shrugged modestly. "Oh, it wasn't so hard. You know what I think? The magicians have been exaggerating the difficulty for years, just to put the commoners off. What does it take, after all? A few careful lines drawn with rulers, string, and compass. A few runes, some spoken words. Popping down the market to get some herbs . . . a bit of peace and quiet, a little memorizing . . . do all that and you're sorted."

"No," I said. "A commoner's never done this before, as far as I know. It's unheard of. You must have had help. With the languages, the runes and circles, that noxious plant mix—all of it. A magician. Who?"

The girl twizzled a strand of hair beside her ear. "Well, I'm hardly going to give you his *name*. But you're right. I have been helped. Not to do *this*, exactly—that goes without saying. He thinks I'm more of an amateur enthusiast. If he knew what I was doing he'd blow his top." She smiled. "Right now he's fast asleep two floors down. He's rather sweet, really. Anyway, it's taken time, but it's not been too bad. I'm surprised more people haven't given it a go."

Ptolemy gazed at her from under hooded lids. "*Most* people," I said meaningfully, "are a little nervous of what they might summon."

The girl nodded. "True. But it's not so bad if you're not scared of the demon in question."

I started. "What?"

"Well, I know that terrible things can happen if you get the incantation wrong, or misdraw the pentacle or something, but those terrible things are more or less up to the demon—sorry, I meant *djinni*, of course—the djinni in question. Aren't they? If it was some old afrit that I'd never met, I'd obviously be a bit worried, in case we got off on the wrong foot. But *we* know each other already, don't we, you and I?" She gave me a winning smile. "And I knew you wouldn't harm me if I made any little mistake."

I was watching her hands, which once again were gesticulating in the vicinity of the red chalk line. . . . "Is that so?"

"Yes. I mean, we more or less teamed up last time, didn't we? You know, with that golem. You told me what to do. I did it. Good partnership, that was."

Ptolemy rubbed the corners of his eyes. "There was a small difference then," I sighed, "which it seems that I must spell out for you. Three years ago we were both under the heel of Mandrake's boot. I was his slave, you were his quarry. We had a shared interest in foiling him and ensuring our own survival."

"Exactly!" she cried, "and we—"

"We had nothing more in common than that," I went on imperturbably. "True, we had a bit of a chin-wag. True, I did give you a few clues about the golem's weaknesses—but that was merely in a scientific spirit, to see how perversely your odd little conscience would behave. And mighty perverse it was too."

"I don't accept—"

"If I might be allowed to get a word in edgeways," I said, "I will just point out the salient difference between then and now. Then, we were both victims of the magicians. Agreed? Right. But *now*, one of us—i.e. *moi*"—I tapped my bare brown chest—"is still a victim, still a slave. As for the other one . . . she's changed sides."

She shook her head. "No."

"She's a turncoat—"

"I'm not—"

"A two-timing backstabber—"

"Bartim—"

"A conniving, treacherous, opportunistic, false-faced traitor, who's taken it upon herself to add to my endless years of slavery! Who's set out to learn the cursed arts, without prompting and without coercion! You can say this much for Nathaniel and the rest—they didn't have any choice in the matter. Most of them were molded into magicians before they were old enough to know better! But *you*—you could have taken a dozen different paths. And instead you decided to enslave Bartimaeus, Sakhr-al-Jinni, the Serpent of Silver Plumes, the wolf-jawed guardian of the Iroquois. And in your arrogance you consider I'll do you no harm! Well, let me tell you, young madam, you underestimate me at your peril! I am master of a thousand tricks, a hundred weapons! I can—ouch!!"

In rather heated fashion I had been ornamenting my argument with a series of brisk finger-jabs, one of which overshot the mark and touched the red chalk of my pentacle. With a small explosion of yellow sparks, my essence was rebuffed: I was tossed up and backward, head over heels, frantically pedaling in midair to avoid crossing the line on the other side. With the agility born of desperation, I managed it, and sank down to earth with blackened face and my loincloth torn asunder.

The girl considered the latter with a disapproving twist of the mouth. "Tsk," she said. "We're back to square one."

I delicately rearranged the fragments of cloth. "The point remains. By summoning me, you've redefined our roles. There can be nothing but hatred between us."

"Oh, rubbish," she said. "How else was I to get hold of you? I'm not enslaving you, you idiot. I wanted to discuss something with you, as equals."

I raised what remained of my eyebrows. "Hardly feasible. Do dust mites confer with lions?"

"Oh, stop being so sniffy. Who's Nathaniel, anyway?"

I blinked at her uncertainly. "Who? Never heard of him."

"You just referred to someone called Nathaniel."

"No, no, you must have misheard." I changed the subject swiftly: "The whole idea is ridiculous, anyway. Equality is impossible between humans and djinn. You are young and foolish, so perhaps I shouldn't be too hard on you, but the notion is misguided. *I* have known a hundred masters over five thousand years, and whether their pentacles have been drawn on the desert sand or on the turf-moss of the steppe, the enmity between me and my summoners has been great and everlasting. So it has always been. So it shall always be."

I finished in resounding, plangent tones that brooked no argument. They echoed dramatically back and forth across the empty room. The girl smoothed back her hair.

"Absolute tripe," she said. "What about you and Ptolemy?"

15

Kitty knew immediately that her theory had been correct. The djinni's response told her so. Since his accident at the margins of the pentacle, the young Egyptian boy had been facing her, chest and chin thrust out, hands sweeping this way and that to illustrate his expansive statements and occasionally return his loincloth to position. As soon as she spoke, however, all his blustering and bravado instantly ceased. A great stillness came over him: the face became quite frozen, the body utterly transfixed, as if somehow caught in time. Only the eyes moved: slowly, very slowly, the pupils shifted to fix their gaze on her. The boy's eyes had always seemed dark—but now they had become quite black. Without wishing it, Kitty found herself staring into them: it was like looking at a clear night sky—all black and cold and infinite, with tiny lights glinting, unreachable and far away. . . . It was terrible, yet beautiful; she was drawn to it as a child to a window. She had been sitting safely in the center of her pentacle. Now she half uncrossed her legs and leaned forward, supporting herself on one arm, stretching out the other, reaching up slowly toward the eyes, toward their solitude and emptiness. Her fingertips trembled above the fringes of her circle; she sighed, hesitated, reached out. . . .

The boy blinked, his eyelids flicking like a lizard's. The spell was broken. Kitty's skin crawled; her hand jerked back. She shrank into the center of the circle, fresh sweat beading on her brow. Still the boy did not move.

"What do you presume," a voice said, "to know about me?"

It had sounded all around her—not loudly, but very near at hand—a voice different from any that she had heard before. It spoke in English, but the inflection was odd, as if the tongue found the language alien and strange; it sounded close, but also not so, as if dredged up from some incalculable distance.

"What do you know?" the voice said again, quieter than before. The djinni's lips were still, the black eyes locked on her. Kitty hunched herself against the floor, trembling, teeth clenched together. Something in the voice unmanned her, but what? It did not speak violently or with anger, quite. But it was a voice of power from a far-off place, a voice of terrible command, and it was a child's voice too.

She lowered her head and shook it dumbly, gazing at the floor.

"TELL ME!" *Now* there was anger in the voice; as it spoke, a great noise sounded in the room—a thunderclap that shook the window and rippled out across the floorboards, sending chips of rotten plaster dropping from the walls. The door slammed shut (but she had not opened it, nor seen it open); the window shattered and fell away. At the same time a great wind rose up around the chamber, whirling all about her, faster and faster, sending the bowls of rosemary and rowan wood flying, slamming them out against the walls, seizing the book and the candlesticks, her satchel and her coat, carrying them high and low around the room, whistling and wailing, around and around and around until they blurred. And now the very walls were moving too, tearing from their sockets in the floor and joining in the frenzied dance, spitting bricks loose as they spun, spiraling around and around beneath the ceiling. And finally the ceiling was gone, and the awful immensity of the night sky stretched above, with stars and moon spinning and the clouds being drawn out into pale white threads that shot in all directions, until the only still points in all the universe were Kitty and the boy inside their circles.

Kitty clapped her fingers across her eyes and buried her head between her knees.

"Please stop," she cried. "Please!"

And the tumult ceased.

She opened her eyes; saw nothing. Her hands were still clamped to her face.

With stiff and painful care, she raised her head and lowered her hands. The room was exactly as before, as it had always been: door, book, candlesticks and window, walls, ceiling, floor; beyond the window, a placid sky. All was quiet, except . . . the boy in the opposing pentacle was moving now, bending his legs slowly, slowly—then sitting with abrupt finality, as if all the energy had gone out of him. His eyes were closed. He passed a hand wearily in front of his face.

He looked at her then, and the eyes, though dark, had nothing of their former emptiness. When he spoke, his voice was back to normal, but it sounded tired and sad. "If you're going to summon djinn," he said, "you summon their history with them. It's wise to keep matters firmly in the present, for fear of what you might awaken."

With great difficulty, Kitty forced herself to sit upright and face him. Her hair was wet with perspiration; she ran a hand through it and wiped her forehead. "There was no need for that. I merely mentioned—"

"A name. You ought to know what names can do."

Kitty cleared her throat. The first surge of fright was wearing off, to be fast replaced with a teary feeling. She fought it down. "If you're so keen to keep matters in the present," she gulped furiously, "why do you persist in wearing . . . *his* form?"

The boy frowned. "You're a little too clever today, Kitty. What makes you think I'm wearing *anyone*'s guise? Even in my weakened state I can look how I please." Without stirring, he changed shape once, twice, half a dozen times, each form more startling than the last, each one sitting in exactly the same position in the circle. He finished as a giant rodent of some kind, plump and fluffy, with hind legs crossed and forelegs folded irritably.

Kitty did not blink. "Yes, but you don't generally go around as a king-size hamster," she snapped. "You always revert to the same dark kid in a loincloth. Why? Because it means something to you. That's obvious. It's someone important from your past. All I had to do was work out who."

The hamster licked a pink paw and smoothed a tuft of fur behind one ear. "I don't acknowledge there's any truth in those far-fetched statements," it said. "But I'm curious. Where did you go from there? The boy could have been anyone."

Kitty nodded. "True. It happened this way. After our last meeting I was keen to speak with you again. All I knew about you was your name—or one of them—Bartimaeus. Which was tough enough, since I didn't even know how to spell it. But I knew that if I looked hard, you'd turn up in the historical records somewhere. So when I began to study, I kept my eyes peeled for mention of you."

The hamster nodded modestly. "I imagine that it didn't take long. There must be countless references to my exploits."

"In fact it took almost a year to find the slightest mention. I got the names of plenty of other demons of all sorts here and there among the library books. Nouda the Terrible kept coming up, as did an afrit named Tchue, and something called Faquarl was notable too in a dozen cultures. And then at last you appeared—a fleeting mention in a footnote."

The hamster bristled. "*What?* Which books did you look in? All the best ones must have been taken out. A footnote indeed!" It continued muttering indignantly into its fur.

"My problem," Kitty said hastily, "was that you weren't always known as Bartimaeus, so even when you had long, long, *very* important mentions, I couldn't pick up on it. But the footnote helped me out, you see, because it linked the name I knew—Bartimaeus of Uruk—to two others—Sakhr al-Jinni (wasn't that your Persian one?) and Wakonda of the Algonquin. After that I was able to get more references to you here and th—I mean, everywhere I looked. And so I proceeded. I learned a bit about some of your tasks and ventures, and discovered the names of several of your masters, which was interesting too."

"Well, I hope you were impressed," the hamster said. It still sounded rather put out.

"Of course," Kitty went on. "*Very.* Did you *really* speak with Solomon?"

The hamster grunted. "Yeah, yeah, only a brief chat." All the same, it seemed a little mollified.

"All the while," Kitty said, "I was learning the art of summoning. My master was rather slow, and I was slower, I'm afraid, but I was gradually getting to the stage when I felt I might call you. But I still had no clue to the identity of this boy, which was a pity, because I knew he was important to you. And then I suddenly found the vital clue! I discovered your Egyptian name—Rekhyt—and linked *that* to the magician Ptolemaeus." She broke off, grinning with triumph.

"Even so," the hamster said, "what did that tell you? I have had a hundred masters, and whether their pentacles have been drawn on the sand or the steppe, the enmity—"

"Yes, yes." Kitty waved the hamster into silence. "That was exactly the point. One account mentioned a close bond between this Ptolemaeus and his slaves. It also mentioned that he was only a boy when he died. That's when it became clear to me. That's when I realized the identity of your favorite guise."

The hamster was busy cleaning one of its toenails. "And what details," it asked lightly, "might the account have given about the relationship between the djinni and the boy? Just out of interest, you understand."

"Not a lot," Kitty admitted. "In fact, nothing. I don't think anything much is known about Ptolemaeus as a person any more. Some of his writing's survived, I believe. They mentioned a thing called 'Ptolemy's Gate,' whatever that is—"

She broke off. The hamster was staring out of the window at the midnight moon. At last it turned its head to her, and as it did so reverted back to the familiar shape of the boy-magician, Ptolemy of Alexandria.

"Enough," the boy said. "What is it you want from me?"

Now that her guess had been confirmed, Kitty found her perception of the djinni's guise had completely changed. It was a curious and disconcerting thing to realize that she was look-ing into the face of a real boy, two thousand years dead. Previously she had viewed the guise merely as a mask, a cos-tume, one illusion among many. Now, while acknowledging that still to be true, she could not help but sense the ancient presence. That the demon was reproducing the boy accurately she had no doubt: for the first time she noticed two moles on the thin brown neck, a little pale scar running beneath the chin, a particular boniness of the elbows on the slender arms. There was a devotion to detail here that could only come with genuine affection, or perhaps even with love.

This knowledge gave her confidence to proceed.

"Okay," she said, "I'll tell you. But first I want to repeat—I am not going to enslave you. Whatever your response, I'll set you free."

"That's mighty big of you," the boy said.

"All I want is for you to listen fairly to what I have to say."

"Well, if you actually get on with it, I might give it a try." The djinni folded its arms. "I'll tell you one thing that's in your favor, though," it went on ruminatively. "In all the centuries of my burden, not one *single* magician has been interested enough even to *ask* about this guise. Why should they? I'm a 'demon,' and therefore willfully perverse. I have no motives but wickedness and temptation. Through general fear and a desire for self-preservation, they never ask me anything about myself. But *you* have done so. You've found things out. I wouldn't say it was clever, because you're human, but it wasn't a bad effort, all in all. So, then"—it waved a regal hand—"fire away."

"Right." Kitty settled herself comfortably. "I don't know whether you've noticed, but things have been going from bad to worse in London. The magicians are starting to lose control. Commoners are being sent off to fight, trade's being disrupted. There's a lot more poverty and that's led to disruption—there've even been riots in some towns. And there's a lot of resentment about . . . demons."

"It's as I predicted when we last spoke," the djinni said. "People are starting to notice spirits and uncover their own resilience too. They'll explore the possibilities, then begin fighting back."

Kitty nodded. "But the magicians are responding—the police are cracking down, there's violence, people being arrested and spirited away, worse things even than that."

"It happens," the boy said.

"I think that the magicians will be prepared to carry out terrible deeds," Kitty went on, "in order to remain in power. There are many secret commoners' groups, but they are weak, divided. No one has the strength to oppose the government."

"That will come," the djinni said. "In time."

"But how *much* time? That's the issue."

"You want a rough guess?" The boy tilted his head, thinking. "I reckon another couple of generations will do it. Say fifty years. That'll allow resilience to build up to the required levels for a successful revolt. Fifty years isn't too bad. With luck you might see it happen when you're a sweet, old granny, dandling big fat babies on your knee. Actually"—he held up a hand, interrupting Kitty's cry of protest—"no, that's wrong. My projection is incorrect."

"Good."

"You'll never be a sweet old granny. Let's say, 'sad, lonely old biddy' instead."

Kitty banged her fist against the floor. "Fifty years isn't good enough! Who knows what the magicians will have done by then? My whole life will have gone by! I'll probably be dead when the revolution comes."

"True," the boy said. "But *I'll* still be here to watch it. I'll be exactly the same."

"Yes," Kitty snarled. "Aren't you lucky?"

"You think so?" The boy looked down at his cross-legged form. He was sitting straight-backed, legs folded neatly in the manner of an Egyptian scribe. "It's two thousand, one hundred and twenty-nine years since Ptolemy died," he said. "He was fourteen. Eight world empires have risen up and fallen away since that day, and I still carry his face. Who do *you* think's the lucky one?"

Kitty made no answer. At length she asked, "Why do you do it? Take on his shape, I mean."

"Because I promised myself," the djinni said. "I'm showing him how he was. Before he changed."

"But I thought he never grew up," Kitty said.

"No. That's right. He didn't."

Kitty opened her mouth to ask a question, but shook her head instead. "We're getting off the point," she said firmly. "I can't afford to wait and watch while the magicians do more wicked things; life's too short. Action is needed *now*. But we—the people, the commoners—can't unseat the government on our own. We need help."

The boy shrugged. "That may well be."

"So, my idea, or my proposal, really," Kitty said, "is that the djinn and other spirits give us that help." She sat back.

The boy looked at her. "Say again."

"You help us out. After all, like you said just now—we're *all* victims here, both djinn and commoners. The magicians subjugate us the same whether we're human or spirit. So. We can team up and defeat them."

The boy's face was expressionless. "Just like that?"

"Well, it's not going to be easy, of course. But there's bound to be a way. For instance, if commoners like me can summon important djinn like you, why can't we take on the government together? It needs a bit of thought, and a lot more de—spirits to get involved, but we'd have the advantage of surprise, wouldn't we? And it would be so much more effective for us to fight as an *equal* force: no slaves, no masters. No scrapping among ourselves or undermining each other. Just smooth cooperation. We'd be unstoppable!"

She was leaning forward in the pentacle now; eyes bright

and shining with her vision. The boy seemed transfixed too; for a long while he did not answer. At last he spoke. "Insane," he said. "Nice hair, nice outfit, but quite, quite mad."

Kitty squirmed with frustration. "You just have to *listen*—"

"Quite a few of my masters over the years have been mad," the boy continued. "I've had religious zealots beating their bottoms with brambles, dead-eyed emperors joylessly committing mass murder, misers lusting after hoards of gold. I've had countless abusers of themselves and others. . . . You are a perverse and unappetizing species. I'll go as far as to say that *your* particular madness, Kitty, is less harmful than most, but it will lead to your death, and to mine also if I'm not careful, so I'll be frank with you. What you have just suggested is ridiculous in a thousand ways, and if I went through them all, we'd still be here when the British Empire finally *does* fall. So let me single out two reasons. No djinni, no afrit, no city-trampling marid or skin-tickling mite, will ever, ever team up (as you put it) with any kind of human. *Team up* . . . I ask you! Do you see us all wearing the same jersey or something, going into battle hand in hand?" The boy laughed—a harsh, unpleasant sound. "No! We've suffered too much pain for us *ever* to view a human as an ally."

"That's a lie!" Kitty shouted. "I say again—what about Ptolemy?"

"*He* was unique!" The boy clenched his fists. "He was the exception. Don't bring him into this!"

"He disproves everything you've said!" Kitty shouted. "Sure, it would be difficult to persuade most demons, but—"

"Difficult? It could never be done!"

"That's what you said about me learning enough to summon you. But I did it!"

"Utterly irrelevant. Let me tell you something. I've been

sitting here, talking nicely, keeping pretty manners as a djinni will, but all the time I've been watching you like a hawk, waiting to see if you stuck so much as a toe outside the circle. If you had, I'd have been onto you faster than blinking, and you'd have learned something about humans and demons then, I can tell you."

"Yeah?" Kitty sneered. "Instead of which you stuck your own stupid toe out and blew your skirt off. Which more or less sums up your last few thousand years. You're going nowhere on your own, pal."

"Is that so?" The boy's face was livid with fury. "Well, let me get on to the second reason why your plan's a dud, shall I? Even if I wanted to help you, even if a hundred other djinn almost as potent as me shared that sentiment and wanted nothing better than to cast their lot in with some oat-brained humans, we couldn't. Because the only way we can come to Earth is through summoning. And that means losing free will. It means pain. It means obeying your master. And there's no equality in that equation."

"Rubbish," Kitty said. "It doesn't have to be that way."

"Of course it does. What's the alternative? Every summons binds us. That's what they do. Would you seek some way to let us off the leash? With our power? Would you be happy to give us control?"

"Of course," Kitty said stoutly. "If that was what it took."

"You wouldn't! Not in a million years."

"I would. If the trust was there, I'd do it."

"Is that so? Well, why not prove it right now? Step out of your pentacle."

"What?"

"You heard me well enough. Step out, across those lines. Yes,

210

those ones right there. Let's see this trust of yours in action, shall we? Give *me* power for a moment. Let's see you put your money where your mouth is."

As he spoke this, the boy sprang up, and after a moment Kitty did so too. They stood in the opposing pentacles, staring at each other. Kitty bit her lip. She felt hot and cold at the same time. This wasn't how she'd intended it to go—rejection of her proposal followed by an immediate challenge; she hadn't imagined it this way at all. What to do now? If she broke the summons by stepping from the pentacle, Bartimaeus would be able to destroy her before vanishing. Her resilience would not prevent him from tearing her apart. The idea of this set her flesh trembling beneath her clothes.

She looked into the face of the long-dead boy. He smiled at her in what was evidently intended to be an amiable fashion, but the eyes were hard and mocking.

"Well?" he said. "How about it?"

"You've just told me," she said huskily, "about what you would do to me if I broke the protections. You said you'd fall upon me faster than blinking."

The smile flickered. "Oh, don't pay any attention to *that*. I was only bluffing. You don't need to believe everything old Bartimaeus says, now *do* you? I'm always joking, you know that." Kitty said nothing. "Go *on*," the boy continued, "I won't do anything to you. Put yourself in my power for a moment. You might be surprised. Put your trust in me."

Kitty ran the tip of a dry tongue against her lower lip. The boy smiled harder than ever; he put such effort into it that the surface of his face was taut and straining. She looked down at the chalk marks on the floor, then at her foot, then at the chalk again.

"That's the ticket," the boy said.

Kitty suddenly realized that she had forgotten to breathe. She exhaled violently. "No," she gasped. "No. That won't achieve anything."

The dark eyes watched her, the mouth a sudden line. "Well," the djinni said sourly, "I admit my hopes weren't high."

"It's not about the trust," she said, lying. "It's that you'd simply dematerialize. You can't stay on Earth without the power of the summons, and I haven't got the energy to summon you again right now. The point is," she went on desperately, "that if you and other djinn joined forces with me, we could defeat the magicians and stop them summoning you. After we'd defeated them, you'd never be called on again."

The djinni snorted. "I've no time for fantasies, Kitty. Listen to yourself—even you don't believe a word you're saying. Well, if that's all, you might as well dismiss me." The boy turned his back on her.

At this, a great rage surged through Kitty. Memories of the last three years swam before her eyes; she felt again the enormous effort it had taken to get this far. And now this proud and blinkered spirit was rejecting her ideas out of hand. It hadn't even given them a moment's fair and considered thought. True, the details had to be worked out; there were many issues to be resolved, but clearly some kind of cooperation was both possible and necessary. She felt close to tears, but furiously drove the sensation away. She stamped her foot, making the floor reverberate. "So," she snarled, "that stupid Egyptian boy was good enough for you, was he? You put your faith in *him* happily enough. Then why not me? What did *he* do for you that I couldn't? Well? Or am I too lowly to hear about his great deeds?" She spoke bitterly, savagely, contempt for the demon rising like gall inside her.

He did not turn to look at her. Moonlight spilled over his bare back and stick-thin limbs. "For one thing, he followed me to the Other Place."

Kitty found her voice at last. "But that's—"

"It's not impossible. It's just not done."

"I don't believe it."

"*You* don't have to. But Ptolemaeus did. I challenged *him* to prove his trust in me too. And that was the way he did it: by devising the Gate of Ptolemy. He went through the four elements to find me. And he paid the price, as he guessed he would. After that—well, if *he'd* proposed a harebrained union of commoners and djinn, perhaps then I'd have gone along with it. There was no limit to our bond. But for you, well-intentioned as you are . . . ? Sorry, Kitty. I think not."

She stared at his back, saying nothing. Finally the boy turned, his face hidden in shadow. "What Ptolemy did was unique," he said softly. "I wouldn't ask it of anyone else, not even you."

"Did it kill him?" she asked.

He sighed. "No . . ."

"Then what price—?"

"My essence is a *little* vulnerable today," Bartimaeus said. "I'd be grateful if you would keep your word and let me go."

"I'm going to. But I do think you might stay and talk a little more. What Ptolemy did doesn't have to be unique. Maybe it's just that no one since knows much about this Gate thing."

The boy laughed shortly. "Oh, they know, all right. Ptolemy wrote about his journey; some of his notes survived. Like you, he talked a lot of nonsense about a truce between magicians and djinn. He hoped others would follow his example, take the same risk he did. And over the years a few *did* try, more out of greed and the lust for power than with his idealism. It didn't go well for them."

"Why not?"

No answer came; the boy looked away.

"All right, *say* nothing," she cried. "I don't care. I'll read Ptolemy's notes for myself."

"Oh, you understand ancient Greek, do you?" He laughed at the expression on her face. "Just don't worry about it, Kitty. Ptolemy's long gone, and the modern world is dark and complicated. You can't make a difference. Look after yourself and survive. That's what *I* do." He prodded at his flesh. "Or try to. Mandrake very nearly had me killed just now."

Kitty took a deep breath. Downstairs, in some book-filled corner of his decaying villa, Mr. Button slept; next morning he would expect her bright and early to begin the collation of new papers. In the evening she would be at The Frog once more, helping to repair the bar, serving out drinks to passive commoners. . . . Without her secret plan to drive her, these prospects seemed wearisome indeed.

"I don't need your advice," she said harshly. "I don't need anything from you."

The boy looked up. "Well, I'm sorry if I've deflated you a bit," he said, "but those things needed saying. I suggest—"

Kitty closed her eyes and spoke the command. It was tentative at first, then very quick—she felt a sudden violence in her: she wanted to get rid of him, be done with it.

Air moved around her face, candle smoke filled her nostrils, the demon's voice receded into nothing. She did not need to look to know that he had vanished, and with him three whole years of her hopes and dreams.

16

Halfway home from the house of Quentin Makepeace John Mandrake gave an abrupt command. His chauffeur listened, saluted, and did a U-turn in heavy traffic. They drove to Chiswick at top speed.

Night had fallen. The windows of the Frog Inn were dark and shuttered, the door was barred. A rough, handwritten sign had been posted in the porch.

SAM WEBBER'S FUNERAL TAKES PLACE TODAY
WE ARE CLOSED
REOPENING TOMORROW

Mandrake knocked repeatedly, but drew no response. The wind gusted along the drab, gray Thames; on the shingle seagulls fought over scraps deposited by the tide. A red vigilance sphere in the courtyard pulsed as he departed. Mandrake scowled at it, and returned to central London.

The matter of Kitty Jones could wait. That of Bartimaeus, however, could not.

All demons lied: this was an incontrovertible fact. So, in truth, Mandrake should not have been *particularly* startled that his slave conformed to type. But when he learned that Bartimaeus had concealed the survival of Kitty Jones, the shock affected him profoundly.

Why? In part because of the image he had built up of the

long-dead Kitty. For years her face had drifted in his memory, spotlit by a guilty fascination. She had been his mortal enemy, yet she had sacrificed herself for him; it was a gesture that Mandrake could scarcely comprehend, but its strangeness, together with her youth, her vigor, and the fierce defiance in her eyes, had taken on a bittersweet allure that never failed to pierce him. The dangerous Resistance fighter he had hunted down so long before had, in the quiet, secret places of his mind, become something pure and personal, a beautiful rebuke, a symbol, a regret. . . . Many things, in fact—all far removed from the original living, breathing girl.

But if she lived . . . ? Mandrake felt a surge of pain. It was the sensation caused by the destruction of this peaceful inner shrine, by a sudden rush of confusion and renewed memories of the actual, messy past; by waves of anger and disbelief. Kitty Jones was no longer a private image in his head—the world had reclaimed her. He felt almost bereaved.

And Bartimaeus had lied to him. *Why* had he done so? To spite him, certainly—but this did not seem quite enough. Well then—to protect Kitty. But that presupposed a closeness between girl and djinni, some kind of bond. Could this be so? Mandrake felt a jealous knowledge in the pit of his stomach that it *was* so; the notion coiled and slithered deep inside him.

If the motive for the djinni's lie was hard to fathom, the timing of the revelation could not have been more bitter, coming so soon after Mandrake had jeopardized his career to save his servant's life. His eyes burned as he recalled the act; his folly rose up to choke him.

In the midnight solitude of his study he made the summons. Twenty-four hours had passed since he had dismissed the frog;

whether Bartimaeus's essence would have healed by now he did not know. He no longer cared. He stood ramrod-stiff, hands drumming incessantly on the desk before him. And waited.

The pentacle remained cold and quiet. The incantation echoed in his head.

Mandrake moistened his lips. He tried again.

He did not make a third attempt, but sat down heavily in his leather chair, seeking to suppress the panic that rose within him. There could be no doubt: the demon was already in the world. Someone *else* had summoned him.

Mandrake's eyes burned hot into the darkness. He should have predicted this. One of the other magicians had disregarded the risk to the djinni's essence and had sought to find out what he knew about the Jenkins plot. It hardly mattered who it was. Whether Farrar, Mortensen, Collins, or another, the outlook for Mandrake was grim indeed. If Bartimaeus survived, he would doubtless tell them Mandrake's birth name. Of course he would! He had already betrayed his master once. Then his enemies would send their demons, and he would die, alone.

He had no allies. He had no friends. He had lost the support of the Prime Minister. In two days, if he survived, he would be on trial before the Council. He was on his own. True, Quentin Makepeace had offered his support, but Makepeace was quite probably deranged. That *experiment* of his, that writhing captive . . . the memory of it repelled John Mandrake. If he managed to salvage his career, he would take steps to stop such grotesque activities. But that was hardly the priority now.

The night progressed. Mandrake sat at his desk, thinking. He did not sleep.

With time and weariness, the troubles that beset him began to lose their clarity. Bartimaeus, Farrar, Devereaux, and Kitty Jones, the Council, the trial, the war, his endless resposibilities—everything merged and flickered before his eyes. A great yearning rose in him to cast it all off, remove it like a wet and fetid set of clothes, and step away, if only for a moment.

A thought occurred to him, wild, impulsive. He brought out his scrying glass, and ordered the imp to locate a certain person. It did so swiftly.

Mandrake rose from his chair, conscious of the strangest feeling. Something dredged from the past—almost a sorrow. It discomforted him, but was pleasant too. He welcomed it, though it made him uneasy. Above all, it was not *of* his current life—it had nothing to do with efficiency or effectiveness, with reputation or with power. He could not rid himself of the desire to see her face again.

First light: the skies were leaden gray and the pavements dark and sloughed with leaves. The wind skittered through the branches of the trees and around the stark spire of the war memorial in the center of the park. The woman's coat was turned up against her face. As she approached, striding swiftly along beside the road, head down, hand up against her scarf, Mandrake failed to recognize her at first. She was smaller than he recalled, her hair longer and a little flecked with gray. But then from nowhere, a familiar detail: the bag she carried her pens in—old, battered, recognizably the same. The same bag! He shook his head in wonder. He could buy her a new one— a dozen of them—should she wish it.

He waited in the car until she drew almost level, uncertain until the last moment whether he would actually step out. Her boots scattered the leaves, tripped carefully around the deeper puddles, walking speedily thanks to the cold and the moisture in the air. Soon she would be past him. . . .

He despised himself for his hesitation. He opened the road-side door, got out, and stepped across to intercept her.

"Ms. Lutyens."

He saw her give a sudden start and her eyes dart around to appraise him and the sleek, black car parked behind. She walked another two hesitant steps, came to an uncertain halt. She stood looking at him, one arm hanging limply at her side, the other clutching at her throat. Her voice, when it came, was small—and, he noted, rather scared. "Yes?"

"Might I have a word?" He had chosen to wear a more offi-cial suit than was his wont. He hadn't *needed* to do this exactly, but he'd found he wanted to make the best impression. Last time she'd seen him, he'd been nothing but a humiliated boy.

"What do you want?"

He smiled. She was *very* defensive. Goodness knows what she thought he was. Some official, come to inquire about her taxes . . . "Just a chat," he said. "I recognized you . . . and I won-dered if . . . if you recognized me."

Her face was pale, still etched with worry; frowning, her eyes scanned his. "I'm sorry," she began, "I don't— Oh. Yes, I do. Nathaniel . . ." She hesitated. "But I don't suppose I can use that name."

He made an elegant gesture. "It is best forgotten, yes."

"Yes . . ." She stood looking at him—at his suit, his shoes, his silver ring, but mostly at his face. Her scrutiny was deeper than he had expected, serious and intense. Rather to his surprise, she did not smile, or display any immediate elation. But of course his appearance *had* been sudden.

He cleared his throat. "I was passing. I saw you and—well, it's been a long time."

She nodded slowly. "Yes."

"I thought it would . . . So how *are* you, Ms. Lutyens? How are you keeping?"

"I'm well," she said, and then, almost sharply: "Do you have a name I *am* allowed to use?"

He adjusted a cuff, smiled vaguely. "John Mandrake is my name now. You may perhaps have heard of me."

She nodded again, expressionless. "Yes. Of course. So, you're doing . . . well."

"Yes. I'm Information Minister now. Have been for the last two years. It was quite a surprise, as I was rather young. But Mr. Devereaux decided to take a gamble on me and"—he gave a little shrug—"here I am."

He had expected this to elicit more than yet another brief nod, but Ms. Lutyens remained uneffusive. With slight annoyance in his voice, he said, "I thought you'd be pleased to see how well it's all turned out, after—after the last time we saw each other. That was all very . . . unfortunate."

He was using the wrong words, that much he could tell— slipping into the studied understatement of his ministerial life rather than saying exactly what was in his mind. Perhaps that was why she seemed so stiff and unresponsive. He tried again: "I was grateful to you, that's what I wanted to tell you. Grateful then. And I still am now."

She shook her head, frowning. "Grateful for what? I didn't do anything."

"You know—when Lovelace attacked me. That time he beat me, and you tried to stop him . . . I never got a chance to—"

"As you say, it was unfortunate. But it was also a long time ago." She flicked a wisp of hair from her face. "So, you're the Information Minister? You're the one responsible for those pamphlet things they're giving out at the stations?"

He smiled modestly. "Yes. That's me."

"The ones that tell us what a fine war we're waging and how only the best young men are signing up for it, that it's a man's job to sail off to America and fight for freedom and security? The ones that say that death is a fit price to pay for the survival of the Empire?"

"A trifle too succinct, but that's the thrust of it, I suppose."

"Well, well. You've come a long way, Mr. Mandrake." She was looking at him almost sadly.

The air was cold; the magician stuffed his hands in his trouser pockets and glanced up and down the road, searching for something to say. "I don't suppose you *usually* see your pupils again," he said. "When they've grown up, I mean. See how they've got on . . ."

"No," she agreed. "My job is with the children. Not with the adults they become."

"Indeed." He looked at her battered old bag, remembering its dull satin interior, with the little cases of pencils, chalks, ink pens, and Chinese brushes. "Are you happy in your job, Ms. Lutyens?" he asked suddenly. "I mean, happy with your money, and your status and all that? I ask you because I could, you know, find you other employment if you chose. I have influence, and could find you something better than this. There are strategists in the War Ministry, for example, who need people with your expertise to design mass-produced pentacles for the American campaign. Or even in my ministry—we've created an advertising department to better put across our message to the people. Technicians like you would be welcomed. It's good work, dealing with confidential information. You'd get a rise in status."

"By 'the people,' I take it you mean 'commoners'?" she asked.

"That's what we're calling them now in public," he agreed. "They seem to prefer it. Doesn't *mean* anything, of course."

"I see," she said crisply. "Well, no—thank you, but I am quite all right as I am. I'm sure none of the departments would want an old commoner like me thrust into their midst, and anyway, I still rather enjoy my job. But it is very kind of you, all the same." She pushed up her coat sleeve and glanced at her watch.

The magician clapped his hands together. "You have to get on!" he said. "Listen, why don't I give you a lift? My chauffeur can take you anywhere. Save you being crammed in like a sardine on a bus or train—"

"No, thank you. You are very kind." Her face was stony.

"Very well, if that's the way you feel about it." Despite the chilly air, he felt hot and irritable. Fervently he wished he had remained within the car. "Well, it has been a pleasure seeing you again. Of course, I must ask you to treat what you know in the strictest confidence. . . . Not that I need to mention that, I'm sure," he added, somewhat foolishly.

At this, Ms. Lutyens looked at him in such a way that he was suddenly transported back half his lifetime, to the days when her rare displeasure cast his schoolroom into desperate shadow. He found himself looking at his shoes. "Do you really think," she said tartly, "that I'll want to tell the world that I once saw you, the great John Mandrake, our beloved Information Minister, hanging upside down with your bottom in the air? That I heard your yelps and wails of pain as cruel men beat you? You think I'd tell this? That's really what you think?"

"No! Not that. I meant about my name—"

"Oh, *that*." She gave a short, dry laugh. "It may surprise you to know," she went on, "that I've got better things to do with my time. Yes, even I, with my silly little unimportant job, don't have a great desire to betray the children I once worked with, no matter *what* they've become. Your birth name, Mr. Mandrake, is safe with me. Now I must go. I'm late for my work."

She turned, began to stride off along the pavement. He bit his lip, his anger mixed with distress. "You're misinterpreting what I'm saying," he cried. "I didn't come here to crow over you. I just didn't get a chance, back then, to thank you. . . ."

Ms. Lutyens paused, and looked back over her shoulder. Her face had lost its anger. "No, I think I *do* understand," she said. "And I am pleased to know it. But you mistake yourself. It was the boy who was grateful to me, and you are no longer that boy. You do not speak for him. We have nothing in common, you and I."

"I wanted to say that I know you were trying to save me, and—"

"Yes," she said, "and I'm sorry I didn't. Good-bye, Mr. Mandrake." Then she was off, walking swiftly away from him among the damp leaves.

17

Another few hours, another summons—hey, that's the way I like it. A day without enslavement is a day that's wasted, as far as I'm concerned.

Let me see . . . I'd had Mandrake. I'd had the girl. Who would it be *this* time? After Kitty's surprise appearance in the pentacle I half expected this one to be the postman.

No such luck. It was my dear old master again, face like thunder. With a silver-tipped spear held ready in his hand.

His evident intent stimulated a swift response. I forced my poor old essence into an imposing shape: a lion-headed warrior, of the kind that fought in Egypt's wars.[1] Leather breastplate, looped bronze skirt, eyes that shone like crystal, fanged teeth glaring from black gums. Nice. I held out a warning paw.

"Don't even *think* about it, squirt."

"I want answers, Bartimaeus! Answers! And if not—see this spear? I'll make you *eat* it before I'm done." The words came tumbling from his twisted mouth. His eyes were wide and staring like a fish. He seemed a little upset.

"*You?* You'd only recognize the sharp end if you sat on it." My voice was velvet-smooth. "Be careful, though. I'm not exactly defenseless myself." From my paddy-paw a talon popped, curved like a sickle moon. I turned it idly, so it caught the light.

---

[1] Technically, I suppose I was *lioness*-headed, since I lacked a mane. Manes are very overrated; okay, they're good for posing, but they block out all your side vision in battle, and get terribly claggy with accumulated blood.

He grinned nastily. "Ah, but that's all show, isn't it? Two days ago you weren't even able to *talk*, let alone resist attack. I'm betting if I prod you with this silver here, you'll know about it. And you won't be able to reverse it on me either."[2]

"You reckon?" The lioness drew herself up to her full height. Her tufty ears scraped the ceiling. "Them's mighty big words, stranger. Go ahead and prove 'em."

He snarled, lunged weakly with the spear. The lioness flinched sideways and sliced down at the spear shaft with her claw. It was a pathetic display all round: we both missed by miles.

"What sort of thrust d'you call that?" the lion scoffed, hopping from one foot to another. "You're like a blind sparrow pecking for a worm."

"You were no better." The magician was shuffling from side to side within his pentacle, ducking down, jerking up, feinting with his spear in every direction known to man. He wheezed, he gasped; he displayed all the skill of someone whose servants normally lift his knife and fork.

"Hey," I said. "I'm this way. To the front."

"*Answers*, Bartimaeus!" he cried again. "Tell me the truth! No delays, no evasions. Who summoned you?"

I'd expected this. But I couldn't tell him that Kitty was still alive, of course. However misguided she was, she'd treated me with honor. The lioness looked sheepish.[3] "Who says *anyone* summoned me?"

---

[2] He was right, unfortunately. If he'd zapped me with a punishment spell, I could have turned it back on him (a major benefit of knowing his birth name), but I had no such defense against an actual spear-thrust, especially in my current debilitated state.

[3] A confusing analogy, but you get the idea.

"*I* do and don't deny it! I tried last night and you were gone. Who was it? Which magician were you seeing?"

"Don't get so worked up. It was a brief encounter. Nothing serious. It's over."

"*Nothing serious?*" Another jab with the spear, this time pronging the floorboards. "Think I'm going to believe that?"

"Calm down, Mr. Jealous. You're making a scene."

"Who was it? Man or woman?"

I tried to be reassuring. "Look, I know what you're thinking, and I *didn't*. Is that good enough for you?"

"No! You expect me to trust a word you say?"

So much for reassurance. The lioness reverted to barefaced cheek.[4] "All right, then—trust this: Get lost. It's none of your business. I owe you nothing."

The boy was so angry I thought he was going to burst out of his suit. It was the fear in him, of course; the fear of me passing on his name.

"Listen, sonny," I said. "I never pass information from one master to another unless it's firmly in my interests, so don't expect me to say anything to you about last night. By the same token I've not told anyone your pathetic little birth name. Why should I? It means nothing to me. But if you're so worried about me revealing your childhood secrets, there's a simple solution. Dismiss me for good! But no—you can't bring yourself to do that, can you? In fact, I don't think you actually *want* to break away from your past. That's why you keep me around, no matter how weak I get. It's so you can hang on to the Nathaniel you once were, as well as the big, bad John Mandrake you've become."

---

[4] Confusing again. Sorry.

The magician said nothing, but looked at me blankly with his hot and hollow eyes. I couldn't blame him. I was a bit surprised myself in actual fact. Don't know where those piercing insights came from. All the same, I wondered if they rather went over his head. He wasn't looking well.

We were in his study; it was, I guessed, late afternoon. Papers were strewn about the place; there was an uneaten plate of food upon his desk. The air had a sour, stale smell that suggested prolonged occupation by an unwashed youth. And sure enough, the youth in question was *not* his usual dapper self. His face was puffy, his eyes red and wild; his shirt (distressingly unbuttoned) hung over his trousers in sloppy fashion. All very out of character: Mandrake was normally defined by his rigid self-control. Something seemed to have stripped all that away.

Well, the poor lad was emotionally brittle. He needed sympathetic handling.

"You're a *mess*," I sneered. "You've lost it big-time. What's happened? All your guilt and self-loathing suddenly get to you? It can't *just* be that someone else called me, surely?"

The boy looked up into the lioness's crystal eyes. "No . . ." he said slowly. "I've other cause for complaint too. And *you're* at the heart of it all."

"*Me?*" And there was I, lamenting my decline! Looked like there was life in the old djinni yet. I perked up. "How so?"

"Well"—he set the spear against the ground, narrowly avoiding impaling his toe—"I'll just run through it for you, shall I? Firstly—in the last twenty-four hours there have been a number of serious riots in London. The commoners have caused much damage. There has been fighting and some casualties. Even now there is disorder on the streets. This morning Devereaux declared a state of emergency. Troops have blockaded Whitehall. The machinery of Empire has been seriously disrupted."

"Sounds like a bad day at the office for you," I said. "But nothing to do with me."

He coughed. "A certain frog," he said, "began it all two nights ago by causing chaos in St. James's Park. Thanks to his actions, a dangerous djinni was set loose among the crowd. It was *this* incident that triggered the riots."

The lioness uttered a roar of protest. "That was hardly *my* fault! I was trying to carry out *your* orders in a thoroughly weakened state. I succeeded in difficult circumstances. Stop— don't laugh like that. It's creepy."

The youth had thrown his head back and uttered a hollow, barking laugh not dissimilar to a hyena's. "Succeeded?" he cried. "Is that what you call it? Nearly expiring at my feet, unable to give me one word of the report I'd asked for, making me look a fool in public? If that's success, give me failure any time."

"*I* made a fool of *you?*" The lioness could barely contain her mirth. "Get real. You don't need any help on that score, chum. What did I do? Draw attention to your cruelty, perhaps, on account of being nearly dead. What magician keeps a djinni in this world till it's too weak to survive? I'm surprised you didn't finish me off."

Mandrake's eyes blazed. "They wanted to!" he cried. "They wanted to wrest the information from you and let you die! Fool that I am, I saved you. I let you go. Which left me with no defense against all the destruction you caused. As a result, my career's almost certainly finished. Maybe even my life too. My enemies are gathering. I'm due for trial tomorrow, thanks to you."

His voice quavered, his eyes were moist; you could practically hear the sound of wistful violins. The warrior lioness stuck out her tongue and made a disrespectful noise. "That could all have been avoided," I said savagely, "if you'd trusted me enough to dismiss me more. I'd have been in better nick then and could have easily avoided Hopkins's demons."

He looked up quickly. "Ah. So you found Hopkins?"

"Don't change the subject. I was saying: it's all *your* fault. You should have had faith in me. But even after all these years, after what I did for you with Lovelace, with Duvall, with the Anarchist and the Oyster—"

He winced. "Don't mention that last one."

"—even after all *that*," I continued remorselessly, "you reverted to type, became a typical magician, treated me like an enemy. I'm a nasty demon, therefore I can't be trusted to—" I broke off. "*What?* Listen, that laugh of yours is *really* getting to me."

"But that's just it!" he cried. "You *can't* be trusted. You *do* lie to me."

"Name one occasion."

His eyes glittered. "Kitty Jones."

"I don't know what you mean."

"You told me she was dead. I know she's alive."

"Ah." My whiskers drooped a tad. "Have you seen her?"

"No."

"Then you're mistaken." I rallied as best I could. "She's as dead as they come. I've never seen deader. That golem swallowed her down whole. Gulp! Smack of the lips! Gone. Sad, but still, nothing to be worrying yourself about all these years later. . . ." I petered out here. I didn't like the look in his eyes.

Mandrake nodded slowly. Red swathes of anger competed

with white blotches for possession of his face. It was a tie, a fifty/fifty split. "Swallowed whole, was it?" he said. "Funny, I seem to remember you said the golem burned her to a crisp."

"Oh, did I? Yes, well, he did that too. First. Before the swallowing bit—ouch!"

Without warning, the magician had raised the spear and jabbed. I was too slow, too weak to react—the spear caught me firmly in my midriff. I gasped in shock, looked down . . . and relaxed again.

"Wrong end," I said. "That's the blunt bit."

Mandrake had noticed this too. With a curse of frustration, he hurled the spear away from him, out of the circle. He stood staring at me, breathing hard, attempting to master his emotions. A minute or so passed. His heart rate slowed.

"Do you know where she is?" I asked.

He said nothing.

I spoke quietly. "Leave her alone. She's doing you no harm. And she saved your life, remember—I *didn't* lie about that."

He seemed about to speak, then gave his head a little shake, as if forcibly flinging the subject from his mind. "Bartimaeus," he said, "I stated to you the other day that I would dismiss you if you completed your mission, and—despite the endless provocation—I stand by my word. Tell me what happened when you followed Jenkins, and I will let you go."

The lioness's brawny arms were folded. She looked down on him from a great height. "Permanently?"

His eyes flicked to the side. "I never said that."

"But *I* am. Unless I'm much mistaken, my information's the only thing that might prevent you from going to the Tower. Correct?"

He gritted his teeth. "I believe that Hopkins is engaged in

some conspiracy. If I can foil it, my position will probably be safe, yes."

"So then, how about it? It's good info I've got here. You won't be disappointed."

His voice was practically inaudible. "All right . . . If it's good enough."

"It is. Good, that's more like it. A sensible agreement, just like the old days. You know, Mandrake," the lioness said musingly. "Things were better when you were little. You had more sense then."

He glowered at his feet. "So I'm told. Well, get on with it."

"All right." The lioness linked her paws together, cracked her knuckles and began. "I followed Jenkins all across London. He's got a network of magicians involved in his schemes; seven in total, all a bit like him: low-level, embittered, weak in strength—nothing to be afraid of, on the face of it, for someone tough like you."

"Any names?" The magician was listening intently, absorbing it all.

"Withers and Burke. Nope, didn't mean anything to me either. But you'll know this one: Lime."

Mandrake's eyes opened wide. "Rufus Lime? Lovelace's friend? *That's* more like it. Is he still—?"

"Yep. As fish-faced as ever. Just got in from Paris, apparently."

"And their plans—what details did you get?"

"Nothing concrete, to be frank. They're all busy choosing demons for it, whatever it is. But they're magicians—that's what you'd expect them to do. There was much talk about ropes and chains. Oh, and vans."

He wrinkled his nose. "Vans?"

"Go figure. They mentioned something about an experiment too. They wanted proof it had been successful. No idea what though." I scratched an ear. "What else . . . ? Oh, Jenkins said there were seven of them because it was 'one for each chair.'"

Mandrake grunted. "The Council. There are seven of us. They plan rebellion."

"As usual."

"Well, it's interesting, but rather short on specifics." Mandrake looked quizzically at me. "For *this* you expect dismissal?"

"There's more. Jenkins didn't just visit some downbeat friends; he met someone else. I'll give you three guesses."

"Who?"

"Go on, guess. Oh, you're no fun. I'll give you a clue. Beard. Oh, well done."

"I didn't give an answer."

"No, but I can tell you've got it right from the color you've gone.[5] Yep, the mercenary's back in town, and his brows are even more beetling than you remember. With utmost bravery and cunning, I attached myself to his seven-league boots and followed him to the park, where he met a man I can only assume to be the elusive Hopkins. No, I didn't hear a word they said. That's when their djinn spotted me. You know the rest. I left half my essence between there and Richmond."

"All very well," Mandrake snapped, "but what good is this to me? I can't act on any of it! I need something if I'm to survive the trial tomorrow . . . Hopkins: he's the key. Can you describe him?"

---

[5] For the record, it was an interesting yellow-white. Sort of custardy.

The lioness scratched her nose. "Funny. It's hard. . . . He's sort of undistinguished looking. A bit stoop-shouldered, maybe; plain face, unshaven . . . mousy hair, I think . . . um . . . Why are you holding your head in your hands?"

He cast his face to the ceiling. "Ahh! It's hopeless! I might have known not to give this task to you. *Ascobol* could have done a better job."

That needled me. "Oh, really? So he'd have found out where Hopkins lived, would he?"

"What?"

"He'd have got the exact address, would he? I can see it now, a big fat cyclops in a raincoat and trilby, sidling up to Jenkins and the mercenary in the café, ordering a coffee, trying to listen in. . . . Oh yes, very inconspicuous."

"Never mind all that. You know where Hopkins is? Tell me!"

"He's staying at the Ambassador Hotel," I said. "There. Just a little something I picked up, when I wasn't being chased to within a spoonful[6] of my life. Now, I—Wait, what are you doing?"

The magician had sprung into sudden action. Turning to face the other pentacles laid out on the floor, he cleared his throat and rubbed at his tired, red eyes. "I've got one chance, Bartimaeus," he said. "One chance and I'm going to take it. Tomorrow, my enemies will strike me down, unless I've something tangible to show them. And there will be few things more tangible than Mr. Hopkins, trussed and tied."

He flexed his fingers, began an incantation. A cold wind

---

[6] Technical term: a measurement of essence.

whipped around my ankles. A melancholy howling filled the air. Honestly, effects like this were frowned upon in *Uruk* for being hackneyed and out of date.[7] You wouldn't see any modern magician leave the pentacle on account of that racket, unless they'd collapsed laughing. I shook my head grimly. No prizes for guessing who was coming.

Sure enough, with a noise like a cracked dinner gong, the blond-haired giant materialized in the next pentacle along. Instantly he set up a feeble torrent of pleading and complaint, which his master sensibly ignored. He hadn't seen me. I waited till he was on his knees, wringing his hands and begging for dismissal, then kind of coughed suavely. "Need a handkerchief, Ascobol? My feet are getting wet."

The cyclops stood hurriedly, his face a flaming mask of shame and disapproval. "What's *he* doing here, sir?" he bleated. "I really don't think I can work with *him*."

"Don't worry," I said. "I'm just watching you get your orders. After that I'm out of here. Aren't I, 'sir'?"

Mandrake ignored us both. He had continued with his incantations, directing his energy at the remaining pentacles in the room. Further cheap effects ensued—pops and bursting, squeaks and sounds of running feet, smells of egg, gunpowder, and methane. It was like a kids' birthday party. All we lacked were the silly hats.

Within seconds the usual suspects had joined us, the rest of Mandrake's crowd. It was a mixed bag. First, and least, we had

---

[7] The last time *I* used that strong wind/disembodied howling gag was to distract the giant Humbaba up in the pine forests so that my master Gilgamesh could creep up from behind and slay him. We're talking 2600 B.C. here. And it only worked *then* because Humbaba was a few pinecones short of a fir tree.

Ascobol, glowering at me between his braids; next up Cormocodran, a humorless cove, third level, who'd done time in Ireland during the Celtic twilight—he favored the guise of a man-boar, with tusks and trotters daubed with bright blue woad. Beyond him was Mwamba, a djinni who'd worked with the Abaluyia tribes of eastern Africa. I had a bit of time for her; she didn't indulge in the tedious comments of the others. Today, for reasons best known to herself, she appeared as a giant spiny lizard wearing leather thigh boots. At the far end, barely squeezing himself into his pentacle, was Hodge, all prickles, odors, and bad personality. The five of us had worked together frequently over the preceding months, but sadly none of the others shared my upbeat temperament.[8] We'd had friction, harsh words. Our relationship now could best be described as strained.

Mandrake wiped sweat from his forehead. "I have summoned you," he said, "for what I hope will be the final time." This stirred a bit of interest; there was shuffling, coughing, rasping of spines. "If you complete today's mission," he continued, "I will not call on any of you again. I hope this vow will be sufficient for you to carry out this charge to the letter."

Cormocodran spoke; his voice rumbled between his tusks. "What is the charge?"

"Staying at the Ambassador Hotel is a human named Hopkins. I wish you to arrest him and bring him here to this room. If I am absent, wait within the pentacles until I return. Hopkins is probably a magician—certainly he has allies who can raise low-level djinn, although from what we have seen

---

[8] Mwamba was as flighty as a butterfly, Cormocodran taciturn and brutish, while Ascobol and Hodge were just insufferable, being regrettably prone to sarcasm.

they are unlikely to be powerful enough to trouble you. More dangerous than Hopkins is a tall, black-bearded man—not a magician, though he possesses the ability to withstand magical attack. This individual may or may not be present at the hotel. If he is, and you can capture or kill him, all well and good. But it is Hopkins that I need."

"We shall want a description," Mwamba hissed. "And a good one. All you humans look alike to me."

Ascobol nodded. "Don't they just? They're all the same basic shape, got the same number of limbs and heads . . . Mind you, there's a few bits that vary. If you look at—"

Mandrake held up his hands hurriedly. "Indeed. Fortunately, Bartimaeus has encountered Hopkins and will be able to guide you."

I gave a start. "Wait a minute! That's not on. You said I was to go free when I told you what happened."

"Agreed. But your description of Hopkins was rudimentary, incomplete. I cannot act on it. Go with the others, point out Hopkins. That's all. I don't expect you to tackle him in your condition. When you get back, you will be dismissed."

He turned to the others and began giving additional instructions, but the lioness heard nothing. My tufted ears were buzzing with rage; I was so furious I could barely stand. The arrogance of it! He was happy to renege on a vow so recent its echoes were still resounding through the room! Very well, I'd go. I had little choice. But if he ever got within my power, Mandrake would rue the times he'd cheated me.

The magician finished. "Any further questions?"

"Are *you* not coming with us?" Hodge inquired. He was shifting and adjusting his great stickleback-skin coat.

"No." Mandrake scowled. "Regrettably, I must attend the

theater. What remains of my career depends upon it. Also"—he glanced at me; I couldn't read the meaning in his eyes—"perhaps I have *another* appointment too."

The lioness regarded him implacably. "You'll be making a big mistake." I looked away. "Come on then," I said to the others. "Follow me."

18

Throughout the day Kitty had been out of humor. She was surly, withdrawn, and prickly, even short-tempered, when challenged by her master. She completed her tasks dutifully but without enthusiasm, slamming doors, stomping about the villa's rooms, and once, thanks to a hasty maneuver in a tight space, knocking over two high columns of carefully ordered books. Her master grew quite irritable in his turn.

"Have a care, Lizzie," he cried. "My patience is wearing thin!"

Kitty halted opposite the sofa. Her forehead was creased with the blackest frown. "Am I not giving satisfaction, Mr. Button?"

"Indeed not! All day you have been out of sorts, galumphing like a rogue elephant around my house, face as ugly as an afrit! When I address you, you answer rudely, without respect. I am shocked by your insolent vulgarity! And that tea you brewed me was as insipid as gnat's piss. This cannot go on. What is the matter with you, girl?"

"Nothing."

"Sullen again! I warn you, if it continues, you shall be out on your ear."

"Yes, sir." Kitty sighed. It was, after all, not Mr. Button's fault that Bartimaeus had failed her. "I'm sorry, sir. I've had . . . a spot of trouble."

"Trouble?" The lines of vexation on the old man's face softened. "My dear, you should have said. Tell me. Perhaps I can help."

A flicker of anxiety crossed his brow. "It is nothing financial?"

"No, sir. Nothing like that." Kitty hesitated. She could hardly tell him the truth, that her whole purpose in assisting him had, in the early hours of the morning, been rendered futile. After almost three years Mr. Button relied upon her; despite his brisk manner, she knew he valued her highly. But he was still a magician. "It's my evening job, sir," she said. "You know I work at an inn. We had a demon raid two days ago. One of my colleagues was killed."

"A raid?" Mr. Button frowned. "What for?"

"The usual stuff, sir—trying to uncover dissent, people prepared to act against our leaders." She took a spice cake from the plate in front of him and bit into it listlessly.

"Well, Lizzie, you must understand that it is the right of any government to protect itself. I am not sure you should be frequenting that inn, if it is such a hotbed of subversion."

"But it isn't really, sir. That's the point. All the commoners ever do is talk—about the war, the police, restrictions on their freedom. Just talk. They're powerless to do anything *about* it, as you must know."

"Mmm." Mr. Button gazed out of the grimy window at the blank October sky. "I can hardly blame the commoners for their unhappiness. The war has gone on far too long. I fear Mr. Devereaux is not acting as he should. But what can we do? Even I, a magician myself, am helpless! Power is concentrated with the Council, Lizzie. The rest of us must watch and hope for better times. Well, well, I can understand your distemper if a friend of yours was killed. I am sorry for your loss. Have another cake."

"That's very kind. Thank you, sir." Kitty sat on the sofa arm and did.

"Perhaps you should take the afternoon off, Lizzie," Mr. Button said. "I shall be working on my demonic index and that will keep me busy. So many demons! You'd think the Other Place could scarcely cram them in!"

Kitty's mouth was full of cake crumbs. She swallowed them. "Pardon me, sir, but what exactly *is* the Other Place? I mean, what's it like?"

The old man grunted. "A region of chaos, a whirl of endless abominations. Dulac, if I remember rightly, called it 'a sump of madness.' We cannot begin to imagine the horror of such a realm." He shuddered. "It's enough to make a man want a third spiced bun."

"So magicians *have* visited it?" Kitty asked. "I mean, they'd have to have done, to know what it was like."

"Ah. Well." Mr. Button shrugged. "Not exactly. In general, the authorities used reports from reliable slaves. To venture there in person is another matter. It risks both body and soul."

"So it hasn't been done?"

"Oh, it's been *tried*. Dulac's master Ficino, for example. He hoped to gain demonic power. Instead he lost his mind—literally so: it did not come back. As for his body . . . No. The details are too revolting."

"Oh, go on, sir."

"Certainly not. There has been a smattering of others, but all were left insane or worse. The only magician who claimed to have succeeded in the journey was Ptolemaeus. He left details in his *Apocrypha*, but they are of dubious value. In effect, he implies that the procedure can only be achieved with the help of a benign demon, whose name is invoked to create the Gate." He snorted. "Palpably, the notion is ridiculous—who would seriously trust a demon with their life? And it is likely that Ptolemaeus himself suffered as a result of his experiment. By most accounts he didn't live long afterward."

Trust. Bartimaeus had emphasized exactly that. Ptolemy had been willing to put his trust in him. As a result, there was no limit to their bond. Kitty gazed up at the ceiling, remembering the djinni's challenge to step out of the circle. She hadn't done it, for the obvious reason that he'd have probably torn her limb from limb. No trust there. On either side.

A great anger flared inside her once again: anger for wasting so many years in pursuit of a hopeless dream. She slipped off the sofa arm. "Do you mind if I *do* take the afternoon off, sir?" she said. "I think I need a little air."

As she retrieved her coat from the hallway, she passed a pile of books that she had lately sorted, ready for stacking on some newly purchased shelves. Among them were works from the ancient Near East, within which . . . She halted, checked. Yes. There it was, three from the top: a slim volume. Ptolemaeus's *Apocrypha.*

Kitty curled her lip. What was the point? Bartimaeus had said it was written in Greek, claimed it would be useless to her. She moved away, only to stop again halfway down the hall. She looked back. Well, why not? It couldn't do any harm.

Old investigative habits died hard. She departed the house with the book in her pocket.

That evening, with time on her hands, Kitty walked to the Frog Inn. She had hoped the exercise would burn off a little of the frustration swelling uncontrollably inside her, but if anything it only made it worse. The faces of the people she passed were pinched and sullen, their shoulders hunched; they gazed at their boots as they trudged along the road. Vigilance spheres whirled above the streets; Night Police loitered arrogantly at major intersections. One or two roads were barricaded off. There had been disorder in central London; now the authorities were cracking down. White police vans passed her more than once. Faintly she heard sirens in the distance.

Her pace grew slower, her gaze dulled and unseeing. She felt weighed down by the utter futility of things. Three years she had been shut up in libraries and dusty rooms, playing at being a magician. And all for what? Nothing had changed. Nothing *would* change. A cloak of injustice lay upon London, and she, like everyone else, was smothered by it. The Council did what they pleased, oblivious to the suffering they caused. And she was unable to do anything about it.

At The Frog a similarly somber mood prevailed. The taproom had been tidied, the devastation of two nights previously cleared away. At the end of the counter a shiny new piece of wood filled the hole made by the demon's attack; it did not quite match the rest of the bar, but George Fox had disguised it with a display of postcards and horse brasses. All the broken chairs and tables had been replaced; the circular burn mark near the door was covered with a rug.

Mr. Fox gave Kitty a subdued welcome. "Extra work for us tonight, Clara," he said. "Haven't found anyone yet to . . . you know, replace Sam."

"No, no. Of course not." Kitty's voice was mild, but impotent fury sloshed inside her. She felt she might scream. Grasping a cloth as if it were the neck of a magician, she went about her business.

Two hours passed; the taproom filled. Men and women huddled at the tables or stood talking quietly by the counter.

An unenthusiastic darts match began. Kitty pulled drinks behind the bar, lost in her thoughts. She hardly looked up when the door opened, bringing with it a gust of autumn chill.

As if a switch had just been pushed, or a battery pulled out, all conversation in The Frog suddenly wound down. Sentences were left unfinished, glasses paused en route to open mouths; eyes swiveled, a few heads turned. A dart embedded itself in the plaster wall beside the board. George Fox, who had been bent beside a table chatting, slowly drew himself erect.

A young man stood there. He shook the rain off his long black coat.

Kitty saw the newcomer between the heads of nearby customers. Her hand jerked, splashing gin upon the surface of the counter. Her mouth made a little noise.

The young man removed his gloves. He ran a slender hand through his hair—short, cropped, and flecked with rain—and looked around at the silent room. "Good evening," he said. "Who is the proprietor here?"

Silence. Shuffling. Then George Fox cleared his throat. "That would be me."

"Oh, good. A word, please." The request was quietly spoken, but it held the assumption of authority. Everything about the young man did: his coat, his smart black jacket, the ruched white shirt, his patent leather shoes. In his own way he was as alien a figure in the taproom of The Frog as the demon without a face.

Animosity and fear rippled out around the room in waves. The young man smiled. "*If* you don't mind."

George Fox stepped forward. "What can I do for you?"

The young man was shorter than Mr. Fox by half a head,

slim as he was burly. "I believe you have a girl working here," he said. "What is her name?"

One or two of the customers standing at the counter flicked their eyes at Kitty, who had shrunk back against the cabinet behind the bar. The door to the passage was close: she could slip out, through the kitchens and away.

Mr. Fox blinked. "Um, Clara Bell. She's the only girl, since Peggy left. . . ." His voice trailed off, was replaced with guarded hostility. "Why? Why do you ask?"

"Is Clara Bell working here tonight?"

George Fox hesitated—precisely the answer the young man was expecting. "Good," he said. "Fetch her out." He looked about him. Kitty was concealed behind the patrons standing at the bar. She inched toward the backroom door.

"Fetch her out," the young man said again.

Still George Fox did not move; his face was set in stone, his eyes bulging. "Why do you want her?" he repeated stolidly. "Who are you? What do you want with her?"

"I am not accustomed," the young man said; his voice was tired, "to explaining myself, nor to asking more than once. I am from the government. That should be good enough for any of you here—Oh, sorry! I don't think so—"

A man sitting near the entrance had slipped from his seat and hurried to the door. He opened it, made to depart. The magician spoke a word and gestured. The man was flung backward bodily into the room, landing hard beside the fireplace. The door slammed shut so hard the brasses rattled on the walls.

"Not one of you leaves this room until Clara Bell is found." The young man looked testily toward the commoner lying on the floor. "Stop that groaning! You're not injured." He turned back to George Fox. "Well?"

Kitty was by the backroom door. One of the customers at the bar nodded his head almost imperceptibly. "Go on," he hissed. "Get out."

The young man tapped a shoe upon the tiles. "It won't surprise you to learn that I have not come to this hovel alone. Unless the girl is brought before me in thirty seconds, I shall issue orders that you will presently regret." He glanced at his watch.

George Fox looked at the floor. He looked at the ceiling. His hands clenched and unclenched. He tried not to meet the beseeching gazes of the people all around. Lines of weariness and age were etched upon his cheeks. He opened his mouth, closed it—

"It's all right, George." Kitty pushed her way around the end of the bar; she carried her coat across one arm. "You don't have to. Thanks." She walked slowly between the tables. "Well, Mr. Mandrake? Shall we go?"

For a moment the magician did not answer. He was staring at her, his pale face a little flushed, perhaps affected by the heat of the room. Collecting himself, he gave a slight bow. "Ms. Jones! I am honored. Would you mind coming with me?" He stood aside. Stiff-backed, staring straight ahead, Kitty passed him. He followed her to the door.

The young man looked back at the silent room. "My apologies for disrupting your evening." He went out; the door closed. For almost a minute no one moved or spoke.

"You'll be needing a new barmaid, George," someone said.

In the yard the vigilance sphere had gone. A few car lights moved on the road beyond the passageway. A light rain fell. Kitty heard it tapping against the river in the darkness below the parapet. Cool air brushed her face, and specks of dampness; their sudden touch made her feel alive.

Behind her, a voice: "Ms. Jones. My car is close by. I suggest we walk to it."

At the sound, a fierce exultation suddenly flowered in Kitty. Far from the fear she *should* have felt, she knew only defiance and a kind of joy. Since the first numb shock of Mandrake's appearance she had been quite calm—calm and curiously revived. For three long years she had led a solitary, cautious life. Now, with all its prospects shattered, she knew she could not have endured that life a moment longer. She wanted action, regardless of the consequences. Her old recklessness came flooding back to her upon a tide of frustrated rage.

She turned. Mandrake stood before her—*Mandrake*, one of the Council. It was like the answer to her prayers.

"So what are you going to do?" she snapped. "Kill me?"

The young man blinked. His face was dimly lit by lights from the old inn's windows; it gave him a sickly, yellow cast. He cleared his throat. "No. I—"

"Why not? Isn't that what you do to traitors?" Kitty spat the last word out. "Or to *anyone* who crosses you? One of your demons was here two nights ago. It killed a man. He had a family. He'd never done anything against the government. But it killed him even so."

The magician made an irritable noise behind his teeth. "That is unfortunate. But it is nothing to do with me."

"No, except you control the demons." Kitty's voice was hard and shrill. "They're just the slaves. *You* direct them."

"I *meant* it wasn't me personally. That's not my department. Now, Ms. Jones—"

"Sorry," she said, laughing, "that is just the most lamentable excuse I've ever heard. *Not my department*. Ooh, that makes it all right then. And I suppose the war isn't your department either, or the Night Police, or the prisons in the Tower. None of them are anything to do with you."

"As a matter of fact, they're not." His voice grew stern. "Now can you manage to be silent on your own, Ms. Jones? Or perhaps you wish my help?" He clicked a finger; a shadow detached itself from the darkest corner of the yard. "That is Fritang," Mandrake said. "Most savage of my slaves. He will do whatever I comm—"

Kitty gave a cry of derision. "That's right, threaten me! Just like you threatened the people in the inn. Can't manage to do *anything* without force to back you up, can you? I don't know how you sleep at night."

"That's rich coming from *you*," Mandrake snapped. "I don't remember the Resistance being afraid to use force when it suited them. Let's see now, what were the casualty figures? Several people killed, others maimed and—"

"*That* was different. We were fighting for *ideals*—"

"Well, so am I. However . . ." He took a deep breath. "I admit to being discourteous in the present instance." The magician waved a hand, spoke a word of dismissal; the menacing shadow faded into nothing. "There. Now you can talk without fear."

Kitty looked directly at him. "I was not afraid."

Mandrake shrugged. He glanced back over his shoulder at the closed inn door, then out toward the road. In contrast to his imperious efficiency inside The Frog, he seemed suddenly hesitant, unsure what to do.

"Well?" Kitty said. "What normally happens next when you arrest someone? Spot of torture? A beating? What's it to be?"

A sigh. "I've not arrested you. At least, not necessarily."

"Then I'm free to go?"

"Ms. Jones," he snarled, "I am here as a private individual, *not* as a member of the government, though if you don't stop your histrionics, that may change. Officially you are dead. Yesterday I received word that you were alive. I wanted confirmation."

Kitty's eyes narrowed. "Who told you I was here? A demon?"

"No. It is not important."

Clarity came. "Ah, it was Nick Drew."

"I said it is not important. You cannot be *surprised* that I would want to find you—a fugitive from justice, a member of the Resistance."

"No," she said. "I'm just surprised you haven't cut my throat already."

The magician gave a cry of genuine annoyance. "I am a minister, not a murderer! I help protect our people against . . . against terrorists like you and your friends."

"Yeah, because the people are *so* safe in your care," Kitty sneered. "Half our young men are dying in America, and we've got the police mauling others in the street, and demons attacking anyone who protests, and enemies and spies at large in our suburbs. We're all having a great time!"

"If it wasn't for us, it would be much, much worse!" Mandrake's voice was high and tight; with evident effort he lowered it to a purr. "We use our power to rule for the good of all. The commoners need guidance. Admittedly, we're going through a ropey patch, but—"

"Your power is based on slavery! How can it be for *anyone's* good?"

The magician seemed genuinely shocked. "Not human slavery," he said. "Just demons."

"That makes it better, does it? I think not. Everything you do is tainted with that corruption."

His answer was faint. "That's not so."

"It *is* so, and I think you know it." Kitty frowned at him. "What are you here for? What do you want? The Resistance was a long time ago."

Mandrake cleared his throat. "I was told . . ." He drew his coat around him, looked out across the river. "I was told you saved me from the golem. That you risked your life to save mine." He glanced at her; Kitty kept her face impassive. "I was also told you died doing it. Now that I find you alive, I am . . . naturally curious as to the truth."

Kitty scowled. "What do you want: the details? Yes, I did, and I must have been mad. I stopped the golem from crushing your sorry head into a pulp. Then I ran away. That's all there is to it."

She stared at him fixedly; he gazed back, face pale and stark in the artificial light. The rain pattered down between them.

Mandrake coughed. "Well, the details are fine. Thanks. In fact, that wasn't exactly it so much as—as I kind of wondered *why*." He shoved his hands in his pockets.

"I don't know," Kitty said. "I really don't know."

"Put your coat on," he said. "You're getting soaked."

"Like you care." Even so, she put it on.

He watched her as she wrestled with the sleeves. When she had finished doing up the buttons he cleared his throat again. "Well, whatever your reasons might have been," he began, "I suppose I need to th—"

"Don't," she said. "Don't. I don't want to hear it. Not from you."

He frowned. "But—"

"I did it without thinking and if you want to know the truth, I've regretted it ever since, whenever I've seen your hideous, lying leaflets on the streets, or passed those stages where your actors do your lying for you. So don't thank me, Mr. Mandrake." She shivered; the rain had steadily intensified. "If you *must* thank someone, make it Bartimaeus. He's the one who prompted me to save your life."

Even in the dark she could see it startled him. His posture stiffened, his voice grew brittle. "*He* prompted you? I find that hard to credit."

"Why? Because he's a demon? Yeah, I know. Doesn't make much sense. But he told me how to stop the golem, he called me back when I would have run. Without him you'd be dead. But don't let that bother you. He's just a slave."

The magician was silent for a time. Then he said, "I had been meaning to ask you about Bartimaeus. For some reason he regards you with affection. Why is that?"

Kitty's laugh was genuine. "There is *no* affection between us."

"No? Why then did he tell me you were dead? He said the golem killed you. That is why I have not searched for you in all these years."

"He said that? I didn't know. . . ." Kitty looked out over the black river. "Well," she said, "perhaps it was because I treated him with some respect! Perhaps because I didn't enslave him, perhaps because I didn't seek to keep him in service for year after year without a break till his essence wore away!" She bit her lip, and looked quickly at the magician.

His eyes were hidden in a strip of darkness. "And *what*," he said very quietly, "can you possibly know about *that*? You haven't seen Bartimaeus for years. *Have* you?"

Kitty edged back toward the river wall. The magician stepped toward her—

A sudden hissing in midair; raindrops fizzed and steamed on something materializing above the water. A small orb, pink and shiny. Music sounded as of an orchestra far way. Mandrake drew back; he uttered a quiet curse.

A faint round face, disrupted by crackles of static, appeared in the orb. A voice issued forth, similarly disrupted. "John! I've found you! You are late! Even now the musicians are warming up! Come quickly!"

The magician gave a little bow. "Quentin. My apologies. I have been delayed."

"No time to waste!" The face seemed to fix on Kitty for a moment. "Bring your girlfriend too. I shall save a seat. Ten minutes, John. Ten minutes!"

The orb fizzed, blurred, vanished. Dark rain fell uninterrupted into the Thames.

Kitty and Mandrake stared at each other. "It seems," the magician said slowly, "that we shall have to continue this conversation later. Do you like the theater, Ms. Jones?"

Kitty pursed her lips. "Not much."

"Nor me." He made an elegant gesture up toward the road. "We shall have to suffer together."

19

Our raid on the Ambassador Hotel was planned with military precision and the utmost care. Just ten minutes' bickering in a phone box and we had the plan set straight.

After leaving our master we'd flown speedily across London in the guise of starlings, crossing above the park where so recently I'd had my misadventure. The Glass Palace, the pagoda, the ill-omened lake—all glinted dourly in the last light of evening. Most of the illuminations were off; the normal crowds were absent, though small pockets of commoners moved here and there with unknown purpose across the grass. I saw police cordons, hurrying imps, an unusual amount of activity . . . then we were over the streets of St. James, and circling down to the hotel.

It was an upmarket affair, a slender gray-stone house set among the embassies and gentlemen's clubs; a place both sophisticated and discreet, where foreign diplomats and princelings might rest their wallets while in town. It did not look the kind of hotel to welcome an invasion of five ragtag djinn, particularly ones as unsavory as Hodge. We saw hexes shimmering in the windows and a lattice of thin nodes upon the fire escape. The doorman, resplendent in lime-green livery, had the sharp-eyed look of someone wearing lenses. Caution was required. We couldn't just stroll in.

The phone box was right opposite. One by one, five starlings flew down behind it. One by one, five rats hopped through a hole inside. Mwamba used her tail to brush away the worst of the cigarette butts, and we began our solemn conclave.

"Right, troops," I said brightly. "Here's what I suggest——"

A one-eyed rat held up a paw of protest. "Just a moment, Bartimaeus," it said. "What makes *you* the leader all of a sudden?"

"You want the full inventory of my talents? Remember we have to capture Hopkins sometime this evening."

"If hot air counted for anything, Bartimaeus, we'd follow you with pleasure." This was Cormocodran. His basalt-thick voice boomed about the phone box; the vibrations made my whiskers ripple. "Unfortunately, you're old and tired and useless."

"We heard about your adventures as a mighty *frog*," Hodge added, chuckling. "Relying on the master to save you, scattering your essence like rain across the city."

"It's hardly his *fault*, though, is it?" Mwamba put in sympathetically. Of all the rats, she was the most elegant and convincing. Ascobol had one eye, Hodge had a row of poison spines amongst his bristles, and Cormocodran, as always, looked more like a small, brick outhouse than anything else. As for me, my essence was playing me up again; there were some hazy patches around my extremities, although I hoped they were too small for anyone to notice.

"Maybe not, but he's a liability on a job like this," Ascobol said. "Look at his outline now. All fuzzy."

"He'll slow us up. He was lagging when we flew."

"Yeah, and he'd be terrible in a fight."

"Probably subside into a custard."[1]

---

[1] *A custard*: another technical term. Denotes a total collapse of essence while on the mortal plane. In the Other Place, of course, our essence is freewheeling at all times and does not have to be bound in any particular shape.

"Well, you won't catch *me* scooping him up."

"Nor me. We're not on babysitting duty here."

"Your high opinion of my powers notwithstanding," I growled, "I'm the only one who's actually *seen* Hopkins. Go on without me if you want. See how far you get."

"He's getting huffy now," Hodge said in contemplative tones. "Ego like a balloon. Watch out! It's going to pop!"

Mwamba batted her tail irritably against the floor. "We're wasting time. Bartimaeus may be decrepit, but we need his advice before we start." She smiled as sweetly as a sewer rat can smile. "*Please* go on, Bartimaeus. Tell us what you saw."

You know me. I'm not one to hold grudges.[2] I gave a careless shrug. "In truth, it isn't much. I saw Hopkins, but only briefly. Whether he's a magician or not, I can't say. I assume so. Certainly *someone* used a gang of foliots and djinn to chase me off."

"Just a thought, this," Mwamba said. "You're sure he's human?"

"Hopkins? Yep, I checked him out on all seven planes. Human on each one. If we can catch him by surprise, we should be able to hold him."

"Oh, I'll hold him," Hodge said in a dark, exulting voice. "Don't you worry about that. I've got a snug place waiting for him, a place where ropes and shackles won't be needed. A place right here . . . *under my skin*." He sniggered lovingly; the sound faded.

---

[2] At least not when I can't do anything about them. But sooner or later, when I was back at full vigor, I'd meet Hodge, Ascobol, and Cormocodran again. Then I'd apply delayed retribution with all the savage ferocity of a wounded bear. Successful vengeance is all about timing.

The other four rats looked at each other.

Ascobol said, "I think we'll stick to plain old ropes, Hodge. Thanks for the offer. Right, to continue, we know Hopkins stays here. Any idea which room?"

I shrugged. "Not a clue."

"We'll have to check the book at reception. What then?"

Cormocodran shifted his hairy bulk. "We rampage upstairs, break down the door, beat Hopkins to a pulp, and spirit him away. Simple, efficient, satisfying. Next question."

I shook my head. "Tactically brilliant, but Hopkins might be alerted as we stomp upon the stairs. We must be subtle here."

Cormocodran frowned. "I'm not sure I do subtle."

"Besides," Mwamba said, "Hopkins may not yet have returned. We need to get to his room quietly and see. If he's away, we lurk within."

I nodded. "Disguises are necessary, and in Hodge's case an additional bath and fumigation. Humans have a sense of smell, you know."

The rat in question stirred indignantly, rattling his poison spines. "Step this way, Bartimaeus. I wish to taste your essence."

"Oh, yes? Think you can take me?"

"Nothing would be easier or more welcome."

For some while the argument proceeded, scintillating in its wit, verve, and skillful repartee,[3] but before I could rout my opponent with a final devastating proof, a bloke came in to use the phone box, and the rats turned tail and scattered.

---

[3] Sample dialogue: "Oh, so you reckon you can, eh?" "Yeah, no problem, pal!" "Yeah?" "Yeah!" All to a backdrop of the others whooping and slapping their hairy haunches. For intellectual reach and vigor, it was midway between the debates of ancient Athens and those of more recent English parliaments.

★ ★ ★

Twenty minutes passed. At the entrance to the Ambassador Hotel the doorman paced rhythmically from side to side and clapped his hands together to keep warm. A group of guests approached, a woman and three men, all beautifully attired in suits of Silk Road cloth. They spoke quietly* together in an Arabic tongue; the woman wore jewels of moonstone at her throat. Each gave off reassuring emanations of wealth, dignity, and social poise.[4] The doorman stepped back, saluted. The four acknowledged him with nods and gracious smiles. They passed up the steps and into the hotel foyer.

A young woman sat smiling behind a mahogany desk. "Can I help you?"

The most handsome of the men approached. "Good evening. We are from the Embassy of the Kingdom of Sheba. We have a royal party arriving in a few weeks, and wish to inspect your premises with a view to hiring rooms."

"Certainly, sir. Would you care to follow me? I will find the manager."

The receptionist rose from her desk and padded on light feet down a corridor. The four Sheban diplomats followed; as they did so, one opened a clenched fist. A small but unpleasant insect rose out, all legs, spines, and sulphurous odors, and flew on whirring wings to the vacated desk, where it proceeded to scan the register.

The hotel manager was a small, amply padded lady of middle age. Her bone-gray hair was swept back and fixed in place by a piece of polished whalebone. She received her visitors

---

[4] With the possible exception of Cormocodran, who still contrived to resemble a heifer shoehorned into a suit.

with polite reserve. "You are from the Sheban Embassy?"

I made a courteous bow. "That is correct, madam. Your perspicacity is beyond compare."

"Well, the girl just told me. But I was not aware that Sheba was an independent state. I thought it was part of the Arabian Confederacy."

I hesitated. "Erm, all that is about to change, madam. We are shortly to become self-governing. It is to celebrate this that our royal guests are coming."

"I see . . . Dear me, self-government is a dangerous trend. I hope Sheba does not set an example to *our* empire. . . . Well, I can certainly show you a typical room. This is a very prestigious hotel, as I'm sure you know—private and *extremely* exclusive. Its security systems have been authorized by government magicians. We have state-of-the-art door-guard demons for every room."

"Is that so? Every single one?"

"Yes. Excuse me—let me just get the appropriate key. I won't be a minute."

The manager bustled swiftly away. At this the female diplomat turned to me. "You *idiot*, Bartimaeus," she hissed. "You swore Sheba still existed."

"Well, it did last time I was out there."

"Which was when, exactly?"

"Five hundred years or so ago. . . . Yes, all right. You needn't get all snippy."

The hulking diplomat spoke in rumbling tones. "Hodge is taking his time."

"Can he actually read?" I said. "That may have been the flaw in our plan."

"Of course he can. Hush. She's coming back."

"I have the key now, sirs, madam. If you would be so good . . ."

The manager trotted along a dimly lit corridor, all oak panels, gilded mirrors, and unnecessary pots on stands, pointing out assorted arches. "That is the dining room in there . . . decorated in the Rococo style, with an original painting by Boucher; beyond are the kitchens. To our left is the grand lounge, the only room where one is permitted to use demons. Elsewhere we forbid their presence, since they are in general unhygienic, noisy, and a repellent nuisance. Particularly djinn. Did you speak, sir?"

Cormocodran had uttered a croak of rage. He swallowed it down. "No, no."

"Tell me," the manager continued, "is Sheba a magical society? I'm afraid I *should* know, but I have learned so little of other lands. One has so much to do to occupy oneself in one's *own* country, don't you think? It is hard to have much time for foreigners, particularly when so many of them are savages and anthropophagi. Here is the lift. We ascend to the second floor."

Manager and diplomats entered the lift and turned to face the front. As the doors eased shut, a whirring sound was heard. Unnoticed by the manager, a noisome insect, all spines and strange emissions, slipped through the closing crack, flitted onto the sleeve of the Sheban woman and crawled up to her ear. It whispered briefly.

She turned to me, mouthed the message: "Room twenty-three."

I nodded. We had the information we required. The four Sheban diplomats glanced at each other. As one, they turned their heads slowly to look down at the diminutive manager, who was wittering away complacently about the delights of the hotel sauna, oblivious to the sudden change in atmosphere in the crowded lift.

"We don't *have* to," I said in Arabic. "We could tie her up."

"She might squeak," said the female diplomat. "And where would we put her?"

"True."

"Well, then."

The old lift trundled on. It came to the second floor. The doors opened. Four Sheban diplomats stepped out, accompanied by a whirring insect. The biggest of the four was picking his teeth with a polished whalebone hair grip. He finished presently, stuck the whalebone in the soil of a voluminous pot plant outside the lift, and padded after the others down the silent hall.

With the door to room twenty-three in sight, we halted once again.

"What do we do?" Mwamba whispered.

Ascobol made an impatient noise. "We knock. If he's there, we break down the door and get him. If not . . ." His flood of inspiration had wearied him; he ceased.

"We get inside and wait." That was Hodge, buzzing around our heads.

"The woman mentioned a door guard," I cautioned. "We'll have to deal with it."

"How hard can that be?"

The group of diplomats approached the door. Mwamba knocked. We waited, looking up and down the corridor. All was still.

Mwamba knocked again. There was movement within a circular panel in the center of the door. The wood grains shifted, rippling and contorting to form the faint outline of a face. It blinked sleepily and spoke in a squeaky, nasal voice. "The occupant of this room is out. Please return later."

I stepped back and considered the base of the door. "It's pretty tight fitting. Think we could slip under there?"

"Doubtful," Mwamba said. "Keyhole might be okay, if we changed to smoke."

There was a titter from Ascobol. "Bartimaeus won't *need* to change. Look at his lower half—it's gaseous already."[5]

Cormocodran was frowning down at his hulking torso. "I'm not sure I *do* smoke."

The door guard had listened in with some concern. "The occupant of the room is out," it squeaked again. "Please do not attempt entrance. I will be forced to act."

Ascobol stepped close. "What manner of spirit are you? An imp?"

"Yes, sir. Indeed I am." The door guard seemed unfeasibly proud.

"How many planes can you observe? Five? Very well—take a look at us on the fifth. What do you see? Well? Do you not tremble?"

The face on the door had swallowed audibly. "A little, sir . . . But, if I may ask, what is that nebulous blot hovering on the right?"

"That is Bartimaeus. Pay no attention to him. We others are ruthless and strong and demand to enter the room. What do you say?"

A pause, a heavy sigh. "I am bound by a bond, sir. I must prevent you."

---

[5] Hurtful, coarse, but there *was* a grain of truth in it. I hadn't quite deteriorated as far as my condition with the frog, but with every passing minute my strength, and essence control, became a little less. I *was* a little fluid about the trousers.

Ascobol cursed. "Then you sign your death warrant. We are powerful djinn. You are a smudge of insignificance. What can you hope to do?"

"I can sound the alarm, sir. Which is what I have just done."

A faint popping, as of bubbles bursting in hot mud. The diplomats glanced left and right: along the corridor on either side a number of heads were rising from the carpet. Each head was oval like a rugby ball, smooth and shiny, beetle-black, with two pale eyes set closely near the base. Each popped free and rose into the air, trailing a writhing strip of tentacles.

"We need to deal with this quickly, quietly, and neatly," Mwamba said. "Hopkins can't know anything has happened."

"Right."

In a somewhat menacing silence the heads drifted in our direction.

We didn't hang around to see what they planned to do. We acted, each one according to their specialty. Mwamba sprang at the wall, scrambled up it and onto the ceiling, from where she clung like a lizard, discharging Spasms at the nearest head. Hodge swelled from insect size in the blink of an eye, turned, and shook his skin, hurling innumerable poison darts toward the enemy. From Ascobol's shoulders feathered wings protruded; he rose into the air and fired a Detonation. Cormocodran became a man-boar. He lowered his tusks, rotated his massive shoulders, and charged into the fray. As for me, I nipped behind the nearest ornamental pot plant, erected what Shield I could and tried to look inconspicuous.[6]

---

[6] I'd have *loved* to take part in the fight. Loved to. Ordinarily I'd have been first in line to fight the squidy head things. But that wasn't my brief just then. I had precious little essence left to spill.

I'd vaguely wondered, as I rearranged the biggest leaves, what sort of threat the floating heads might pose. I soon discovered. As soon as one or two drew close, the heads tipped back, the tentacles drew apart, and tubes within squirted forth black sprays that deluged everything before them. Cormocodran was caught mid-charge; he let forth a bellow of pain—where it hit, the liquid burned his essence; it bubbled, spat, ate into his form. Even so, he was not done. He lunged with his tusks and sent a head crashing down the hall. Ascobol's Detonation caught another, exploded it in midair; black spray splashed against the walls, further coating the writhing Cormocodran and even pattering onto the topmost leaves of my trusty pot plant.

Up on the ceiling, Mwamba sprang and dodged, avoiding all but the slightest smears of black. Her Spasms found their mark: here and there heads whirled and shook themselves apart. Hodge's poison darts had likewise speared a couple: they swelled, turned yellow, and sank to the carpet, where they became ichorous and faded.

The heads put on a surprising turn of speed. They darted this way and that, seeking to evade the darts, Spasms and Detonations, and to get around behind the djinn for further attacks. In this they were hampered by the confines of the corridor, and by a madness that seemed to have infected Cormocodran. With molten tusks and a face that blurred and steamed, he roared and charged, swiping with his fists, grasping tentacles, trampling with his hooves, seemingly insensible to the gouting spray. With such a foe, the heads were up against it. In less than a minute the last one gloopily subsided. The battle was over.

Mwamba dropped down from the ceiling, Ascobol floated •

to the floor. I stepped nimbly out from behind the plant. We regarded the corridor. It was going to give next morning's cleaners quite a surprise, whatever plane they operated on. Half the walls were coated with the spray; it hissed and foamed and ran in rivulets to the floor. The corridor was a kaleidoscope of stains, scorches, and congealing slime. Even the front half of my pot plant had been badly burned; I rotated it carefully to present its good side to the world.

"There!" I said brightly. "Think Hopkins is going to notice anything?"

Cormocodran was in poor shape, the boar's head scarcely recognizable, his tusks blackened, his nice tattoos quite gone. With limping steps, he approached the door of room twenty-three, where the imp watched blinking in its circle.

"Now, my friend," he said, "we must decide upon the nature of your death."

"One moment!" the door guard cried. "There is no need for such unpleasantness! Our difference of opinion is at an end!"

Cormocodran narrowed his eyes. "Why so?"

"Because the occupant of the room has now returned and you can take up the matter with him personally. Good day to you." The grains of wood shifted and relaxed; the outline of the face was gone.

There was a second or two while we stood pondering the mystery of the imp's words. Then a further second as we slowly turned to look back down the hall.

Halfway along it stood a man.

He had evidently just come in from outside, for he wore a winter coat over a dark gray suit. His head was bare and slightly windswept; a shock of brownish hair fell down across a face that was neither old nor young. It was the same man I'd seen in the park: slender, pigeon-chested, thoroughly unremarkable. He had a plastic bag of books in his left hand. Even so, something about him tugged uneasily at my memory, just as it had last time. What was it? I'd have sworn I'd not met Hopkins before.

I viewed him on the seven planes. Hard to be sure, but his aura seemed a little stronger than most humans'. Perhaps it was just the lights. He was certainly a man.

Mr. Hopkins looked at us. We looked at him.

Then he smiled, turned, and ran.

Off we went: Mwamba and Ascobol in the lead, Hodge pounding after, me next, conserving as much energy as I could, and finally poor old Cormocodran bringing up the rear.[7] Around the corner we piled, into the alcove with the lift.

"Where's he gone?"

"There! Stairs—quick—"

"Up or down?"

I saw a flash of sleeve on the turn below. "Down! Quick! Change, someone."

A shimmering. Mwamba was a bird with black-green wings, diving down the center of the stairwell. Ascobol became a vulture, a less astute choice, since he had trouble turning his bulk in the narrow space. Hodge shrank, climbed onto the balustrade in the form of an evil-looking pangolin. He curled up into a ball, so that his plates protected him, and dropped bodily down the shaft. No such speed for me or Cormocodran; we hurried after them as best we could.

---

[7] It was his wounds that slowed him mainly, but his recent meal can't have helped. He'd really bolted the manager down.

Down to the ground floor, through swing doors, out into the corridor. I halted, only to be knocked sprawling by Cormocodran charging blindly along behind.

"Which way did they go?"

"I don't know. We've lost them. No—listen!"

Sounds of shouts and screams—always a good indication of where my chums might be. It came from the direction of the dining room. As we watched, a number of humans—a pick-'n'-mix assortment of customers and kitchen staff—came bursting through the arch and fled howling up the corridor. We waited for the tubbiest to wheeze past, then hurried on. Into the dining room, along a trail of scattered chairs, cutlery, and broken glass, and through a set of swing doors into the hotel kitchen.

Ascobol looked around. "Quick!" he cried. "We've got him surrounded!"

The cyclops was standing astride a metal sink top, pointing. To his left, Mwamba blocked the space between two racks of pans, her scaly tail swishing idly to and fro, her long forked tongue flicking at the air. To his right, Hodge had hopped upon a chopping table, and was raising and lowering his poison spines with malevolent intent. All were staring fixedly at the far corner of the kitchen, where the fugitive had taken refuge. Behind him was solid wall, no doors or windows. He had no chance of escape.

Cormocodran and I took our places in the line. Ascobol glanced across at us. "The fool's refusing to come quietly," he hissed. "We need to scare him a bit. Hodge has done some pretty manic tittering, but he hasn't budged an inch. Come on, Bartimaeus—can't you manage something a *little* more fearsome? Pep up your guise."

You might argue that a man who wasn't scared of a cyclops,

a boar-headed warrior, a giant lizard, and a vicious-looking pangolin with the titters wouldn't be too fussed at one monster more or less, but I took the point. A Sheban diplomat isn't the most terrifying thing in the world. I rummaged through my inventory of guises and picked out one that used to awe the people of the plains well enough. The diplomat vanished. In his place stood a tall, sinister figure, hung about with a cape of feathers and animal bones; he had a man's body, but his head— sleek and black with eyes of yellow fire—was a savage crow's. The cruel beak opened, loosing a wicked caw upon the world. Assorted cutlery rattled across the kitchen.

I bent my head toward Ascobol. "How's that?"

"It'll have to do."

As one, the five terrible djinn stepped closer to their prey.

"You may as well put that thing down," Mwamba advised sternly. "We've got you trapped."

Ah yes. That thing. I'd noticed it too. It was a certain kind of kitchen implement that Mr. Hopkins had picked up in self-defense. But far from holding it fearfully in front of him, as you might expect, he was toying with it in a manner unbefitting a scholar, tossing it up into the air with one hand and catching it nimbly between finger and thumb of the other. If it had been a tin-opener or a potato peeler, even a ladle or soup spoon, it wouldn't have bothered me so much. But it wasn't any of those things. It was a meat cleaver, and a large one too.

Something about the way he wielded it rang a few faint bells.

"Well, now," Mr. Hopkins said, smiling. "Here's a conundrum. Have you trapped me, or is it the other way around?"

He gave a little kick of his legs as he said this, as if he were about to start dancing some horrible Celtic jig; instead of which he rose gently off the floor and hovered over us, grinning from ear to ear.

This was unexpected. Even Hodge stopped his eager snickering. The others glanced at each other in astonishment. Not me, though. I was silent, frozen where I stood, an uncomfortable finger of ice traveling at leisure down my spine.

I'd known the voice, you see. It wasn't that of any Mr. Hopkins. It wasn't even human.

It was Faquarl's.

20

"Er, chaps," I ventured. "I think we should go carefully here."

From his position in midair Mr. Hopkins tossed the cleaver high; flashing as it spun, it arced around a ceiling light and landed handle-first back upon his outstretched finger. He caught my eye and winked.

Ascobol was rattled, but he talked big to cover it. "So he can levitate," he snarled. "And do juggling tricks. So can half the starving fakirs of India, and I never ran from them. Come on. Remember, we've got to take him alive."

With an unearthly cry, he leaped down from his sink top. The crow-headed man held out a hand of caution. "Wait!" I said. "Something's wrong here. His voice——"

"You coward, Bartimaeus!" The pangolin loosed a volley of darts that pattered into the floor beside my feet. "You fear for what remains of your essence. Well, hop on the nearest chair and squeal. Four *proper* djinn can handle this man."

"But that's just it," I protested. "I'm not sure this *is* a man. He's——"

"Of *course* I am." Up on high, Mr. Hopkins tapped his chest proudly. "Planes one to seven, flesh and blood. Can't you see?" It was true. He was human whichever way you looked at it. But it was Faquarl who spoke.

The giant lizard swung her tail in agitation; it caught against a cooker and sent it crashing on its side. "Hold on," Mwamba said. "What language are we speaking?"[1]

268

"Erm . . . Aramaic, why?"

"Because he can speak it too."

"So what? He's a scholar, ain't he?" In times of stress Ascobol could pulverize Semitic tongues.

"Yes, but it seems a little odd . . ."

Mr. Hopkins inspected his watch ostentatiously. "Look, I'm sorry to butt in," he called, "but I'm a busy man. I have some important business this evening, which concerns us all. If you lot clear off now, I'll spare you. Even Bartimaeus."

Cormocodran had been resting his poorly essence against an eight-hob oven, but at these words he erupted into life. "You'll spare *us*?" he roared. "For that piece of impudence I shall gore you, and not gently!" He pawed the ground with a hoof and started forward. The other djinn followed his example; there was a general rattling of horns, spines, scales, and other armored bits. Mr. Hopkins chucked the cleaver casually to his right hand and spun it around his fingers.

"Wait, you idiots!" the crow-man shouted. "Didn't you *hear*? He knows me! He knows my name! This is—"

"It's not like *you* to hold back on the edge of a battle, Bartimaeus," Mr. Hopkins called cheerily, dropping down toward the advancing djinn. "You're normally *much* farther away, cowering in a disused catacomb or something."

"That catacomb incident has been grossly misrepresented!" I roared. "As I've explained *countless* times, I was guarding it against Rome's enemies, who might well have chosen—" I stopped right there. That was the proof. No human knew

---

[1] In the heat of the moment we djinn sometimes lose track of which lingo we're using. When working together in this world, we tend to speak languages familiar to us all and not necessarily the one used by the civilization *du jour*. (There you go, you see.)

where I'd loitered during the barbarian invasion, and precious few spirits either.[2] In fact, I could only think of one djinni that still brought it up with metronomic regularity, whenever our paths crossed over the centuries. And sure enough, that one was—

"Stop!" I cried, hopping from side to side in agitation. "It's not Hopkins at all! I don't know *how*, but it's Faquarl, and he—"

It was too late, of course. My companions were making far too many roars and rumbles for them to hear. Mind, I doubt they'd have stopped even if they *had* heard. Certainly Ascobol and Hodge, who had no respect for their elders or betters, would have carried on regardless. Maybe Mwamba might have hesitated.

But they didn't hear, and they all piled in.

Well, it was four against one. Faquarl, armed only with a kitchen knife, versus four of the most ferocious djinn then at large in London. It was a hideous mismatch.

I'd have helped my companions out if I'd thought it would make any difference.

Instead, I stole carefully toward the door. Thing was, I *knew* Faquarl. He had a certain breezy confidence that came from being very good at what he did.[3]

---

[2] The foliots Frisp and Pollux had been present when I was discovered; they'd amused themselves afterward recounting the tale to imps of their acquaintance. Sadly, both foliots and imps were all soon killed in a variety of ways during the course of a single night: a bizarre coincidence, which quite wore me out.

[3] He wasn't like old Jabor had been, i.e. moronically strong to the point of indestructible. He wasn't like grim Tchue, who rarely needed to lift a finger to his enemies, so frightful and inventive were his words. No, Faquarl was an all-rounder—he had a practical take on survival that respected power and cunning equally. As of this moment, this was my view also: it was by cunningly respecting Faquarl's power that I intended to avoid being killed.

Very good, and very quick. Crow-head had just negotiated a rack of omelette pans and was slipping past the pastry cases when a shower of plates fell around his ears. *Armor* plates, that is, lately of the pangolin.

They were followed a second or so later by one or two other things—some of which, I'm sorry to say, were recognizable.

It was only when I reached the kitchen door that I risked a quick look back. At the far end of the room was a whirl of movement, flashes of light, sounds, and screams. Occasionally hands reached out from the vortex, grasped tables or small fridges and plunged with them back out of sight. Fragments of metal, wood, and essence hurtled outward periodically.

Time to depart. Some djinn of my acquaintance let loose a billowing Fog to cover their tracks; others prefer to leave a noxious inky vapor or a few Illusions in their wake. Me, I hit the lights. Kitchen and dining room were plunged into darkness. Weird glints of a dozen colors emitted by the fighting djinn slid and spun across the walls. Ahead, a solitary wedge of light marked the way out to the corridor. I wrapped my cape of feathers close about me and was swallowed by the shadows.[4]

I hadn't got halfway across the dining room when all sounds of combat behind me ceased.

I halted, hoping against hope to hear my colleagues' cries of triumph.

No luck. The silence beat against my feathered head.

---

[4] My crow-headed guise was the totem of the tribe that lived between plain and forest. They valued the bird's stealth and secrecy, his intelligence and guile. The cape included feathers of every bird living in those parts: with their power absorbed into mine, I could walk unnoticed over grass and stone and also converse respectfully with the tribe's shaman, who wore a similar costume, complete with mask.

I concentrated and *really* strained for a scrap of sound. . . . Perhaps I strained too hard. I thought to imagine a soft noise, as of someone floating through the dark.

I hastened on. No point trying to run—stealth was the key. I was in no state to contest with Faquarl, however eccentric his guise. I kept to the margins of the dining room, keeping well clear of the tables, chairs, and discarded cutlery. My cloak of shadows covered my bowed head; a yellow eye peeped out anxiously below a fringe of feathers. It checked behind.

Through the arch leading to the kitchen came a patch of moving blackness; light glinted on something in its hand. I picked up the pace a little, and in so doing kicked against a teaspoon, which clinked against the wall.

"Dear me, Bartimaeus," a familiar voice called. "You really *are* addled tonight. A human might be foiled by the dark, but *I* can see you as clear as noonday, skulking over there beneath those rags. Stop a while and talk with me. I've missed our little chats."

Crow-head made no response, but hurried for the door.

"Aren't you just a little curious?" The voice was nearer now. "I'd have thought you'd be *dying* to know about my choice of form."

Sure, I was curious, but "dying to know" was exactly what I wasn't. I'm happy to indulge in snappy banter with the best of them, but chats are out when the alternative is escaping with my life. Mid-stride, the crow-headed man leaped forward, hands outstretched, as if diving into a swimming pool; his feathered cape swirled round him, flapped, became dark wings. The man was gone; a desperate crow darted forth, a feathered bolt making for the door—

A sigh, a thud, a cawk of pain. The crow's progress was

halted in a manner that brooked no argument, pierced through a wingtip and suspended beneath a shimmering flash that shuddered, vibrated, stilled—and became a meat cleaver embedded in the wall.

With nonchalant leisure, the thing with the body of Mr. Hopkins drifted across the empty room. The crow awaited it, swinging gently, an indignant expression on its beak.

Mr. Hopkins drew close. One shoulder of his suit was a little scorched, and he had a slight cut upon one cheek. Other than that he appeared uninjured. He hovered in the darkness a meter or so away, regarding me with a little smile. I guessed he was checking out my condition on the various planes; my weakness made me feel embarrassed, almost naked. I tapped the feathers of my free wing against the wall.

"So go on then," I snapped. "Get it over with."

A frown passed across the inexpressive face. "You want me to kill you already?"

"Not that. The rubbish joke you're thinking up. About it being good of me to *hang around*, or something like that. Go on, you know you want to. Get it out of your system."

The scholar looked pained. "As if I'd stoop so low, Bartimaeus. You judge me by your own subterranean standards of repartee, which are as regrettable as the condition of your essence. Look at you! As perforated as a sponge. If I were your master, I'd use you to mop the floor."

I gave a groan. "That's probably on the agenda. I've done everything else."

"I'm sure you have. Well, it is a sorry state of affairs to see any spirit brought so low, even one as frivolous and irritating as you. It almost moves me to pity." He scratched his nose. "Almost, but not quite."

I searched the pale gray eyes. "It *is* you, isn't it?" I said.

"Certainly it is."

"But your essence . . . Where—?"

"Right here, hidden away inside the body of our dear Mr. Hopkins. As you must have deduced, this is no mere *guise*." Faquarl's voice gave a little chuckle. "What was that pathetic birdy getup you were wearing just now? Native American totem? So messy and antiquated. Well, I've gone beyond that sort of thing."

"You're *in* his actual body?" I said. "Yeucch! That's icky. Who's done this to you, Faquarl? Who's your master?" I didn't understand this at all.

"My master?" The hovering man shook with mirth. "Why, Mr. Hopkins, of course, and very grateful I am to him. So grateful that I think he and I will be working together for some little time to come." He burst into another rich and hearty laugh.[5] "Much has happened since last we met, Bartimaeus," he went on. "Do you remember how we parted?"

"No." I did.

"You set light to me, old friend. Struck a match and left me burning in a copse."

The crow shifted uneasily beneath the cleaver. "That's a gesture of endearment in some cultures. Some hug, some kiss,

---

[5] Coming from a fairly senior djinni like Faquarl, this laughter was curiously unnerving. We higher spirits have our humor, of course, which we employ as a corrective to our endless years of servitude on Earth. Normally it falls into a certain category—dry, sardonic, and observational, perpetually amazed by the foibles of the magicians. We don't tend to fall about in hysterics—that's just not done. (I'm not talking about imps, of course, who seldom rise above recreational slapstick.) This being so, there was something oddly *unrestrained* about Faquarl's mirth here, something a little too *involved*.

some set each other on fire in small patches of woodland. . . ."

"Mmm. Well, you've been a slave to more humans than me, Bartimaeus. You'd know their ways if anyone would. Even so, it *was* a little painful. . . ." He drifted closer.

"You weren't too badly off," I protested. "I caught sight of you again a couple of days later, playing cook again in the Heddleham kitchen. Didn't seem *too* singed. What is it with you and kitchens, anyway? You're always hanging about in them."[6]

Hopkins—or Faquarl—gave a nod. "Lots of nice sharp weapons in kitchens." He flicked the cleaver with a fingertip; blade and the crow quivered and pulsed. "Which is why I came down here just now. Also it's more roomy than that corridor upstairs. I needed space to swing my arms a little. . . . Space is at a premium in this hotel. Mind you, my room *does* have a Jacuzzi."

My head spun. "Wait a second," I said. "*I* know you as Faquarl of Sparta, scourge of the Aegean. I've seen you as a slate-black giant crushing hoplite armies beneath your heels. Now what are you? A pigeon-chested human who likes his bath. What's going on? How long have you been trapped like this?"

"Just a couple of months. But I'm hardly *trapped*. The Ambassador is a very plush and exclusive establishment.

---

[6] This was true. Ever since the royal kitchens at Nineveh, circa 700 B.C., I'd been sent there by Babylonian magicians on a diplomatic mission, e.g. to slip arsenic into Sennacherib's food during a banquet. Unfortunately, Faquarl was employed by the Assyrian king to seek assassins: he took exception to my tasty calves'-fat trifle and chased me about the hall. After the mother of all food fights I felled him with a well-aimed ham bone and made good my escape. Our relationship had generally deteriorated from here.

Hopkins liked the good things in life, you see. Also it's out of reach of government spies, so I can come and go as I please. I saw no reason to change the arrangements."

The crow rolled its eyes. "*Not* the hotel. I was talking about the body."

A chuckle. "The answer's the same, Bartimaeus. It's only a few weeks since the good Mr. Hopkins—how shall I put it?—invited me in. It took a while to acclimatize, but I am now *extremely* comfortable. And despite appearances, my power is in no way reduced. As your friends have just found out." He grinned. "Haven't fed so heavily for a long time."

"Yes, well." I coughed uncomfortably. "I hope you weren't thinking of doing the same with me. We go back a long way, you and I. A wonderful association; lots of shared experiences."

Mr. Hopkins's eyes gleamed with merriment. "That's better, Bartimaeus. Your sense of humor is perking up. But in truth, I do *not* intend to devour you."

The crow had been hanging from the cleaver in rather a woebegone manner. Now, with this unexpected news, it rallied. "You don't? Faquarl, you are a generous friend! I apologize for that incident in the copse, and for our fights over the Amulet, and for that Convulsion from behind I got you with, back in Heidelberg in 'thirty-two"—I hesitated—"which I see you didn't know was me. Um, and all the rest. So—many thanks, and if you could just remove this cleaver, I'll be on my way."

The bland-faced man did not remove the cleaver. Instead he bent close to the crow. "I didn't say I was *sparing* you, Bartimaeus. Just that I'm not going to *eat* you. The idea of it! Simply looking at your essence gives me indigestion. But nor am I going to let you go. This very night you shall die horribly—"

"Oh. Great."

"In as painful and long-drawn-out a fashion as I can contrive."

"Look, you needn't put yourself out over this—"

"But first I want to tell you something." Hopkins's grinning face came close. "I want to tell you that you were wrong."

I pride myself on my swift wit and keen intelligence, but this one had me stumped. "Eh?"

"Countless times," Faquarl continued, "I have held out to you the hope that djinn would one day be free. Djinn like you and me. Why do we fight? Because we are set against each other by our cursed human masters. Why do we obey them? Because we have no choice. Countless times I have speculated that these rules might be challenged; countless times you have told me I was mistaken."

"I didn't put it *quite* like that. I said you were a complete—"

"You said that we had no chance of ever breaking free of the twin problems, Bartimaeus. The problems of free will and pain. And I see that certainty in your squinty little eyes again! But you are mistaken. Look at me now—what do you see?"

I considered. "A murderous maniac in human form? A hideous amalgam of the worst of man and djinn? Erm—I'm going out on a limb here—a former foe looking at me with unexpected pity and good fellowship?"

"No, Bartimaeus. No. I'll tell you. You see a djinni without pain. You see a djinni with free will. I'm not surprised you don't understand: in five thousand years there has never been a marvel like it!" He held out a very human hand and gently ruffled my head feathers. "Can you imagine it, you poor wounded creature? No pain! No *pain*, Bartimaeus! Ah," he sighed, "you can't *think* how clearheaded that makes me."

No pain . . . In the back of my tired, befuddled mind, I saw a sudden image: Gladstone's skeleton, leaping, prancing . . . "I met an afrit once," I said. "He said something like that too. But his essence was trapped in human bones and he went mad. In the end he embraced extinction rather than live on."

Faquarl shaped Hopkins's face into the approximation of a smile. "Ah, you speak of Honorius? Yes, I have heard of him. The poor fellow has been *most* influential! My essence is protected, just as his was, and like him I have free will. But mark *this*, Bartimaeus—*I* shall not go mad."

"But to be in this world, you must have been summoned," I persisted. "So you must be doing someone's bidding. . . ."

"*Hopkins* summoned me, and I have *done* his bidding. Now I am free." For the first time I thought I saw something of the djinni hidden within the man: deep inside the eyes a little flash of triumph, almost like a flame. "You may recall, Bartimaeus, that in our last conversation I spoke with optimism about the recklessness of certain London magicians, men who might one day give us our chance."

"I remember," I said. "You were talking about Lovelace."

"True, but not only he. Well, it so happens that I was right. Our chance has come. First, Lovelace overreached himself. His coup failed, he died, and I was—"

"Freed!" I cried. "Yes! Thanks to *me*, that was. You owe me one there, surely."

"—submerged in an offshore safe, thanks to a stringent after-death clause in my summoning. I spent my time cursing whoever killed Lovelace."

"Ah, that would be my master. I *told* him it was a hasty act, but *did* he listen—?"

"Luckily I was released soon afterward by one of Lovelace's

friends, who knew of me and my talents. I have since been working with him."

"This would be Hopkins," I said.

"Well, as a matter of fact, *no*. Which reminds me"—Faquarl looked at his watch—"I cannot stand gossiping with you all evening. Tonight the revolution begins, and I must be there to witness it. You and your idiot friends have delayed me far too long."

The crow looked hopeful. "Does this mean you won't have time for that painful long-drawn-out death you promised me?"

"*I* won't, Bartimaeus, but *you'll* have all the time in the world." His hands reached out, grasped me around the neck and plucked the cleaver from my wing. Hopkins's form rose into the air and turned to face the darkened dining room. "Let's see," Faquarl murmured. "Yes . . . that looks promising." We drifted out above the tables, toward the opposite wall. A trolley stood there, just as the waiters had left it. On the center of the trolley was a large tureen with a domed lid. It was made of silver.

The crow wriggled and fidgeted desperately in its captor's grip. "Come *on*, Faquarl," I implored. "Don't do anything you might regret."

"I most certainly won't." He descended beside the trolley, held me above the tureen; the cold radiation of the fatal metal tickled against my ragged essence. "A healthy djinni might linger for weeks in a silver tomb like this," Faquarl said. "The state you're in, I don't think you'll survive longer than a couple of hours. Now then, I wonder what we've got in here. . . ." With a hasty flick of the fingers he flipped open the lid. "Hmm. Fish soup. Delightful. Well, good-bye, Bartimaeus. While you die, take consolation from the knowledge that the enslavement of the djinn is almost over. As of tonight, we take revenge." The fingers parted; with a delicate plop, the crow fell into the soup. Faquarl waved good-bye and closed the lid. I floated in darkness. Silver all around me: my essence shrank and blistered.

I had one chance—one chance only: wait a little for Faquarl to depart, then summon up my last gasps of energy and try to burst open the lid. It would be tough, but feasible—provided he didn't wedge it shut with a block or anything.

Faquarl didn't bother with a block. He went for the whole wall. There was a great roar and crash, a fearsome impact; the tureen collapsed around me, smashed into a crumpled mess by the weight of masonry above. Silver pressed on all sides; the crow writhed, wriggled, but had no space to move. My head swam, my essence began to boil; almost gratefully I fell into unconsciousness.

Burned and squashed to death in a silver vat of soup. There must be worse ways to go. But not many.

21

Nathaniel looked out of the window of the limousine at the night, the lights, the houses, and the people. They went by in a kind of blur, a mass of color and movement that changed endlessly, beguilingly, and yet meant nothing. For a while he let his tired gaze drift among the shifting forms, then—as the car slowed to approach a junction—he focused on the glass itself and on the reflection in it. He saw himself again.

It was not a wholly reassuring sight. His face was etched with weariness, his hair damp, his collar limply sagging. But in his eyes a spark still burned.

Earlier that day it had not been so. Successive crises—his humiliation at Richmond, the threats to his career, and the discovery of his earlier betrayal by Bartimaeus—had hit him hard. His carefully constructed persona of John Mandrake, Information Minister and blithely assured member of the Council, had begun to crack around him. But it had been his rejection by Ms. Lutyens that morning that had dealt the decisive blow. In a few moments of sustained contempt she had shattered the armor of his status and laid bare the boy beneath. The shock had been almost too much for Nathaniel; with the loss of self-esteem came chaos—he had spent the rest of the day locked in his rooms, alternately raging and subsiding into silence.

But two things had combined to draw him back, to prevent him drowning in self-pity. First, on a practical level, Bartimaeus's delayed report had given him a lifeline. News of Hopkins's whereabouts offered Nathaniel a final chance to act before the next day's trial. By capturing the traitor he might yet outmaneuver Farrar, Mortensen, and the rest of his enemies: Devereaux would forget his displeasure and restore Nathaniel to a position of prestige.

Such success was not guaranteed, but he was confident in the power of the djinn that he had sent to the hotel. And already he felt revived by the mere act of sending them. A warm feeling ran across his back, making him shudder a little in the confines of the car. At *last* he was being decisive once again, playing for the highest stakes, shrugging off the inertia of the last few years. He felt almost as he had done as a child, thrilling in the audacity of his actions. That was how it had often been, before politics and the stultifying role of John Mandrake had closed in on him.

And he no longer wished to play that part. True, if fate were kind, he would first ensure his political survival. But he had long been tired of the other ministers, and sickened by their moral corruption, by their self-preserving greed. It had taken until today, with the disdain in the eyes of Ms. Lutyens and of Kitty Jones, to recognize that sickness in himself. Well, he would not sink back into the routines of the Council! Decisive action was needed to save the country from their mismanagement. He peered through the window at the smudged outlines of people on the streets. The commoners needed to be led; they needed a new leader. Someone who could impose a little peace and security. He thought of the Staff of Gladstone lying redundant in the vaults of Whitehall.

Not that he should use *force*, of course—at least, not on the commoners. Kitty Jones had been right about that. He glanced across to where—agreeably close to him—the girl sat, gazing with remarkable serenity out into the night.

She had been the second reason that his energies had revived, his spark rekindled, and he was very glad that he had found her. Her hair was shorter than he remembered, but her tongue was as sharp as ever. In their argument outside the inn she had cut through his pretensions like a knife, shaming him repeatedly with her passionate assurance. Yet—and this was the strange part—he found he eagerly wanted to continue their talk.

Not least—his brow darkened—because of that suggestion that she knew more about Bartimaeus's earlier career than he would have thought possible. It was very odd . . . but that could be explored at leisure, after the play, and after—with luck—his djinn had returned triumphant. Bartimaeus might throw some light on it himself. What he would do with her then he honestly didn't know.

The chauffeur's voice roused Nathaniel from his reverie. "Almost at the theater, sir."

"Good. How long's it taken?"

"Twelve minutes, sir. I had to come the long way around. The center of town's still barricaded off. There are demonstrations in the parks. A lot of police activity."

"Well, with luck we'll miss the beginning of the performance."

Kitty Jones spoke for the first time on the journey. As before, he was impressed by her poise. "So what *is* this play I must endure?"

Nathaniel sighed. "A Makepeace premiere."

"Not the one who did *Swans of Araby*?"

"I'm afraid so. The Prime Minister is a fan, therefore every magician in the government, from Council down to third secretary, must attend the show on pain of his absolute displeasure. It is of the first importance."

She scowled. "What, with a war going on, and people rioting in the street?"

"Even so. I have vital work of my own tonight, but I must put it aside until the curtain falls. I just hope it's got a lot of intervals." He felt the shape of his scrying glass inside his coat—between acts, he would check on the progress of his djinn.

They entered Shaftesbury Avenue—a cluttered curve of restaurants, bars, and theaters, many recently rebuilt in finest concrete under the government's slum clearance measures. Glowing neon lights, a new invention from Japan, spelled out the names of each establishment in pinks, yellows, mauve, vermilion; throngs of lesser magicians and high-caste commoners milled upon the streets, accompanied by watchful Night Police. Nathaniel looked for evidence of social disorder, but the crowds seemed calm.

The limousine slowed, pulled into a roped-off area beneath a golden awning. Police and black-coated Security magicians stood behind the barricades; a few photographers knelt below them, cameras set on tripods. The front of the theater was a blaze of light; a smart red carpet ran between the street and its open doors.

A short, round gentleman stood upon the carpet, hands frantically waving. As the car drew to a halt, Quentin Makepeace bobbed forward and thrust open the nearest side door.

"Mandrake! At last you're here! We haven't a moment to lose."

"I'm sorry, Quentin. Trouble on the streets . . ." Since witnessing the playwright's unsavory experiment with the commoner, Nathaniel regarded him with extreme dislike. The man was a pestilence and needed to be removed. All in good time.

"I know, I know. Come on, out with you! In three minutes I must be on stage! The hall doors are shut, but I have space for you in my personal box. Yes, yes—your girlfriend too. She is far prettier than you or I; we can bask in her radiance! Come on, chop-chop! Two minutes and counting!"

With a series of prods, tugs, and encouraging gestures, Mr. Makepeace ushered Nathaniel and Kitty out of the car, along the carpet and through the theater doors. The harsh light of the foyer made them blink; they fended off bowing attendants, proffered cushions, trays of sparkling wine. The walls were covered with posters advertising the play: most featured Quentin Makepeace, grinning, winking or looking profound from a variety of angles. The man himself stopped at a narrow staircase.

"Up there! My private box. I will join you presently. Wish me luck!" Then he was gone, a diminutive whirlwind of oiled hair, gleaming teeth, bright and sparkling eyes.

Nathaniel and Kitty ascended the stairs. At the top was a drawn curtain. They pushed it aside and ducked through into a small enclosure hung with satin drapes. Three ornamental chairs faced a low balustrade; beyond and below lay the stage— half concealed behind thick curtains—the orchestra pit and a sea of stalls, filled with minutely moving heads. The lights had been turned low; the crowd murmured like the wind in a forest; in the depths the orchestra emitted discordant sounds.

They sat, Kitty in the farthest chair, Nathaniel beside her. He leaned over, whispered in her ear. "This is quite an honor for you, Ms. Jones. You are without doubt the only commoner present. See in that box opposite? That fellow leaning forward with the uncouth eagerness of a schoolboy? That is our Prime Minister. Beside him sits Mr. Mortensen, the beloved War Minister. The one with the paunch is Collins, of the Home Office. In the box below, with a scowl upon his face, sits Sholto Pinn, the famous retailer. To the left, yawning like a cat, is Whitwell, of Security. Ms. Farrar, of the Police, is in the box beyond—"

He broke off—as if sensing his scrutiny, Jane Farrar had glanced at him across the great dark gulf. Nathaniel gave her an ironic salute, a little wave. His feeling of reckless excitement had grown with the passing minutes—if all went well, Ascobol and the others would soon have Hopkins under guard. He would see how dear Ms. Farrar handled *that* tomorrow. With a certain ostentation, he bent his head close to Kitty Jones's again. "What a pity your Resistance is no longer active," he whispered. "A well-directed bomb here would decapitate the government."

It was true. The stalls below were filled with all the second-ary ministers, their wives, their assistants, deputies, and special advisers. He saw the obsessive craning of heads as each person compared their position with those of their rivals; he saw the flash of binoculars, heard the rustling of sweetmeat wrappers, sensed the excitement radiating from the crowd. On the second and third planes a number of small imps were visible hopping and jigging upon the shoulders of their masters, busily inflating their chests and biceps to improbable sizes and exchanging insults with their neighbors.

The noises from the orchestra dwindled. A violin shrieked once; all was still.

Lights faded in the auditorium. A spotlight illuminated the curtains at the center of the stage.

Silence.

A drumroll; an ecstatic fanfare from the trumpet section. The curtain twitched and was flung aside.

Out strode Makepeace, resplendent in a frock coat of crushed green velvet. He spread his arms like a mother to her babes and welcomed the audience's applause. Two bows to the balconies, one to the stalls. He raised his hands.

"Ladies and gentlemen, you are too kind, too kind. Please!" The cheering died away. "Thank you. Before the show begins, a special announcement. It is a privilege—nay, an honor!—to present my latest little trifle to such a distinguished audience. I see we have a full complement of the great, led by our wonderful arbiter of good taste, Mr. Rupert Devereaux." A judicious pause for enthusiastic cheering. "Quite so. And it is because of the affection that we all feel for dear Rupert that I have penned *From Wapping to Westminster*, a small diversion based on his inspiring life. As you will see from the program notes, only the scene in the nuns' dormitory is fictitious; the rest of the marvels, sensations, wonderments, and prodigies are firmly based on fact. I hope you are educated and entertained!" A brief bow, a broad smile. "As usual with my productions, may I request that no flash photography takes place. It can put off the performers. In addition, several of the special effects used onstage tonight are magical in origin, created by a crew of willing demons. These illusions will be most satisfactory if you watch without your lenses in. There is nothing more likely to ruin the enjoyment of a wedding scene than seeing a couple of round-bottomed imps emitting the fireworks in the background." Laughter. "Thank you. Can I also request that all personal demons are dismissed for the duration of the show lest they prove distracting. Enjoy the evening. May it be one you never forget!"

A step backward; a swish of the curtain. The spotlight went out. All across the auditorium came a faint rustling and pop-ping—the sounds of lens cases being removed from bags and jacket pockets, opened, filled, shut fast again. The magicians uttered terse commands: their imps shimmered, dwindled, and vanished.

As he removed his lenses, Nathaniel glanced at Kitty Jones, who sat impassively watching the stage. She didn't *seem* likely to try anything foolish; nevertheless, he knew he was taking a risk. Fritang had been dismissed and all his other active demons were off pursuing Hopkins. He had no servants readily at hand. What if she reverted to her former type?

A roll of drums, a rush of violins in the darkness below. Horns blared in the distance: a militaristic fanfare, which swiftly became a jaunty music-hall theme. The curtains swept aside, revealing a beautifully painted depiction of a London street scene forty years before. Tall town houses, market stalls, a flat blue sky behind, Nelson's Column in the background, fluffy pigeons on strings flying to and fro. A procession of barrow boys wheeled carts on stage from either side; as they met in the middle they exchanged loud Cockney pleasantries and began slapping their thighs to the music-hall beat. With a sinking heart, Nathaniel knew that the first song was already upon them. He sat back in his chair, think-ing despairingly of the scrying glass in his pocket. Perhaps he could just slip off and check what was going on—

"Not a bad beginning, eh, John?" As if he had sprung up from a hidden trapdoor, Mr. Makepeace was at his side, settling into his seat, wiping perspiration from his forehead. "A nice lit-tle number. Sets the scene admirably." He chuckled. "Already Mr. Devereaux is transfixed. See how he laughs and claps his hands together!"

Nathaniel peered into the darkness. "You have better eyesight than I. I cannot make him out."

"That is because you have taken out your lenses, like a good obedient boy. Put them back in again and see."

"But—"

"Put them back in again, my boy. Here in my box different rules apply. You're exempt from the general direction."

"But what about the illusions?"

"Oh, you'll see enough to keep you entertained. Trust me." A hearty chuckle.

The man was a capricious fool! With a mixture of annoyance and bemusement, Nathaniel returned his lenses to his eyes. By viewing the second and third planes, he was instantly able to reduce the darkness in the auditorium and make out the magicians on the far side. As Makepeace had said, Devereaux was craning forward, eyes riveted on the stage; his head nodded to the music. The other ministers, in various attitudes of dejection and dismay, had given themselves up to the inevitable.

On stage the Cockney barrow boys skipped off, leaving the way clear for the appearance of the young Prime Minister-to-be. The pale thin youth that Nathaniel had met at Richmond now dawdled from the wings. He wore a school blazer, shirt and tie, and a pair of short trousers from which his hairy legs plunged a disconcerting distance. His cheeks had been heavily rouged to give him the appearance of childish vigor, but his movements were oddly listless. He flopped to a standstill beside a cardboard postbox and began a quavering oration. In the darkness at Nathaniel's side Makepeace gave a cluck of dissatisfaction.

"Bobby has proved *such* a trial," he breathed. "During rehearsals he developed a most dreary cough, and became quite wan. It is my belief he is consumptive. I had to give him a mighty slug of brandy just to get him on."

Nathaniel nodded. "Do you think he has enough energy to last the night?"

"I think so. It is not a long production. Tell me, how does Ms. Jones enjoy the show?"

In the secrecy of the half-dark Nathaniel's eyes flitted toward the girl sitting beside him. He made out her elegant profile, the pleasant gleam of her hair, her face contorted into a grimace of fathomless boredom. Despite himself, the expression made him grin. He—

The grin froze, and faded. After a pause he leaned back toward Makepeace. "Tell me, Quentin," he said. "How *exactly* did you know this lady was Ms. Jones?"

He looked; Makepeace's small eyes gleamed in the darkness. A whisper: "I know *many* things, my boy. But hush! Hush now! We are coming to the climax of the performance!"

Nathaniel started, frowned. "*Already?* This is admirab— remarkably short."

"I had to bring it forward, thanks to Bobby's indisposition. He would have murdered the main soliloquy; not enough breath. But—silence now. Are your lenses in? Good. Then watch."

Nathaniel's eyes returned to the stage, where he found nothing to excite him. The orchestra had struck up again. Propped against the postbox, the youth attempted a solo, his nasal whine periodically interrupted by hacking coughs. Other than him, the stage was bare; one or two of the house fronts wobbled in a breeze from somewhere in the wings. Mandrake looked in vain for some evidence of a climactic magical illusion. Nothing—on second *or* third planes. What did Makepeace mean?

A ripple of movement caught his eye on the second plane—
not from the stage, but from far off at the very back of the theater, down behind the farthest stall. At the same instant
Makepeace nudged him with an elbow, pointed. Nathaniel
looked, and looked again, his eyes wide in stupefaction. In the
darkest shadows he could just make out three exit doors leading
to the lobby, and through these doors came creeping a multitude
of tiny demons. Most were imps (though one or two—slightly
larger, with more ostentatious crests or plumage—were possibly
types of foliot), but all were small and all were silent. Their feet
and hooves, claws and stumps, tentacles and sucker-tips passed
across the theater carpet without a sound, their eyes and teeth
glittering like glass. Their clever hands held loops of rope and
cloth; their owners hopped and sprang, skittered and dodged,
darted forth with eager speed toward the back row of the stalls.
The leaders leaped onto the seats and without delay fell upon the
persons sitting there—two or three imps to each. Rags were
stuffed in mouths, hands seized and bound together with rope;
heads were wrenched back, blindfolds applied; in seconds the
magicians of that row were captives. Meanwhile the tide of imps
surged on, leaping across to the row in front, and to the next; and
still through the doors replacements came in an endless stream.
So sudden was the onslaught that most of the audience was
secured without a noise: a few managed the briefest squeals, only
to be drowned out by the thrumming violins, the swell and sob
of the clarinets and cellos. On across the stalls the demons swept
in a thin black wave, horns flashing, eyes blazing; while ahead of
them the magicians stared fixedly at the stage.

Nathaniel wore his lenses: through them the darkness of the
auditorium was moderated—he saw it all. He made to spring
to his feet; cold steel pressed against his neck. Makepeace's

urgent whisper: "Do nothing foolish, my boy. You observe my finest hour! Is this not art of the highest order? Sit, relax, enjoy! If you move a hairsbreadth, your head will bounce into the stalls."

More than half the auditorium had been engulfed, and still the imps poured on. Nathaniel's eyes rose to the boxes opposite; the senior magicians had removed their lenses, but they had vantage points similar to his own. Surely they would see, surely they would act . . . His jaw sagged in horror. In every box four or five demons, much larger than the ones below—great foliots and djinn with slim white bodies of knotted sinew—had slipped through the curtains at the magicians' backs. Up they stole behind the greatest figures of the Empire—Devereaux smiling and waving his hands to the music, Mortensen and Collins slouched, arms folded, heads nodding in their seats; Whitwell looking at her watch; Ms. Malbindi scribbling work notes in a clip-file—up they stole, ropes rising in clawed fists, gags and nets silently adjusted, until they stood motionless, like a row of towering gravestones at their backs. Then, as if at a single inaudible command, they fell upon them.

Ms. Malbindi managed a shriek that merged harmonically with the wail of violins. Ms. Whitwell, writhing in a bony embrace, succeeded in igniting an Inferno from her fingertips: it lasted an instant, then her mouth was closed and bound, her command cut short—the flame withered and died; she subsided in a mass of netting.

Mr. Mortensen struggled manfully in the grip of three fat foliots; above the orchestra Mandrake heard him call out for his demon. But as with the rest of the audience, he had obediently dismissed his slave, and the call went unheeded. Beside him, Mr. Collins went down without a sound.

The song was over. Mr. Devereaux, the Prime Minister of Great Britain and the Empire, rose to his feet: eyes glistening with tears, he busily applauded the finale. Behind him in his box, three of his personal bodyguards were overwhelmed and slain. He plucked a rose from his lapel, tossed it down to the youth on stage. A demon stepped up close; Devereaux was insensible—he cried out for an encore. The youth on stage stooped, picked up the rose, and with a sudden spurt of energy, flourished it at the imperial box. At that moment the creature looming at the Prime Minister's shoulder stepped out from the shadows; the youth gave a squeal, fainted on his feet, swayed, toppled, and crashed off stage into the mouth of the euphonium. Devereaux stepped back in shock and collided with the demon. He turned and whimpered once; black wings enveloped him.

To Nathaniel, all this happened in the blink of an eye. Down below, the tidal wave of imps had progressed to the front of the stalls. Every human head was bound and gagged; a triumphant demon pranced on every shoulder.

His panicked eyes swiveled up to Farrar's box. In her seat a grinning demon sat; over its shoulder was something trussed and wriggling. He looked elsewhere—and caught a glimpse of the only magician to mount any true resistance.

Mr. Sholto Pinn, brooding in his box, had not removed his lenses for the simple reason he did not wear any. He had ignored Makepeace's injunction and kept his monocle firmly lodged in his left eye. Occasionally he removed it and polished it with his handkerchief. It was while he was so occupied that the wave of imps burst in upon the stalls; nevertheless, he returned his monocle to his eye in time to catch them in mid-flow.

He uttered an oath, caught up his walking stick, and turned to see three hulking shadows tiptoeing into his box. Without preamble, Sholto raised his stick and fired a plasm—a shadow mewled and crumbled into dust; the others darted aside, one to the ceiling, one pressed against the floor. The stick fired again: the shadow on the ceiling was caught a glancing blow; maimed and whimpering, it fell to sprawl across a chair. But even as it did so, the shadow on the floor leaped forward. It seized the old man's stick and, using it as a cudgel, bludgeoned him to the ground.

In the box opposite, Makepeace had watched this with a furrow of discontent. "It is ever thus," he mused. "No work of art can be quite perfect—it must always have a flaw. Still, Pinn aside, I think we can consider this a job well done."

Keeping his knife pressed against Nathaniel's throat, the playwright rose from his chair and stepped forward to better survey the scene. With agonizing caution, Nathaniel turned his head a fraction; his eyes met Kitty's. Lacking lenses, the girl had only become aware of the activity at the very end, as Pinn's plasms had burst out upon the darkness, and one by one the victorious demons became visible on the ordinary plane. Eyes wide, she glanced at Nathaniel—and at last saw Makepeace and the knife. Her face showed confusion, doubt, and disbelief. Nathaniel held her gaze—his mouth worked frantically, uttering silent pleas; his eyebrows attempted complicated supplications. If the knife could just be knocked away, just for an instant, he might leap on Makepeace, tear it from his grip. *Quick*—if she could only act now, while the madman was distracted. . . .

Kitty looked across at Makepeace, then back at Nathaniel once again. Her brow furrowed. Sweat ran down the side of

Nathaniel's face. It was no good—she wasn't going to help him. Why should she? She held him in contempt.

Makepeace was half leaning on the balustrade, erupting into little private chuckles as he caught sight of new humiliations below. With each spasm, the knife pressed deeper into Nathaniel's neck.

Then Nathaniel saw Kitty give the slightest of nods. He saw her tense, prepare to spring. He licked his lips, readying himself. . . .

Kitty Jones leaped forward. Instantly a bolt of green energy smashed into her, knocking her back against the balustrade, which cracked and split under the impact. Emerald fire played over her body; her limbs jerked, her hair steamed. The fire died away. Kitty slumped to the floor, her head and arm dangling out over the auditorium. Her eyes were half open, sightless.

Green flames rose smoking, steaming from Mr. Makepeace's left hand, but the other kept the knife at Nathaniel's throat. His eyes had shrunk as small as raisins; his teeth were bared. "Silly girl," he said. He gestured with the knife; it nicked the skin on Nathaniel's chin, drew blood. "Stand up."

Dumbly, Nathaniel stood. Around the hall the command had been repeated a hundred times. With a vast rustling, all the captives rose to their feet, blind and bound and helpless, encouraged by sundry slaps and pinches from their imps. In several cases, where the experience had been too much and the victim was unconscious, one or more demons set to work to lift the body. Up in the boxes, where the djinn worked on the greater magicians, nothing was left to chance: all were swathed in thick, black nets and wrapped like sausage meat.

Nathaniel found his voice. "You have brought ruin on us all."

Quentin Makepeace's face split into the broadest grin. "Hardly that, John. We stand at the dawn of a new age! But the curtain has come down and I must attend to the logistics. Here is someone who will ensure you retain your common sense while we are apart." He nodded toward the back of the box. The curtain shifted. A tall figure in a black cloak stepped through; the mercenary's presence filled the space.

"I believe you know each other well," Mr. Makepeace said, sheathing his knife beneath his frock coat. "No doubt you will have much to discuss. I will not demean you, John, by uttering petty threats, but I do have one word of advice." He looked back from the top of the stairs. "Do not choose to die like poor young Kitty there—I still have much to show you."

He was gone. Nathaniel stood staring at the body on the floor. Below, in a terrible silence, broken only by the shuffling of feet and the twittering of demons, the British government was speedily removed.

Part Four

Alexandria: 124 B.C.

It was a dangerous time in Egypt. Raiders from the south had crept up past the Cataracts and put border towns to the sword. Bedouin tribes wreaked havoc on the merchant trains negotiating the desert fringes. At sea, Barbary pirates preyed on shipping. The king's advisers urged him to seek aid from abroad, but he was old, proud, and wary, and refused.

In a belated effort to appease his enemies at court, Ptolemy put his talents at their service. This, as he was happy to admit, meant me.

"You must forgive this indignity," he said, as we sat on the roof the night before I departed. "With due respect to Affa and Penrenutet, you, my dear Rekhyt, are the most vigorous of my servants. I feel sure you will carry out wonders on the nation's behalf. Follow the orders of the army captains, and improvise where necessary. I apologize for any hardships you may undergo, but in the long run you shall benefit too. With luck, your efforts will get my cousin's agents off my back and allow me to finish my researches."

I was wearing the semblance of a noble desert lion, and my growl was suitably low and deep. "You know nothing of the baseness of men's hearts. Your cousin will not rest until you are dead. Spies watch our every movement: I caught two priests' imps skulking in your bathhouse this morning. I had a word. In a manner of speaking, they now serve you."

The boy gave a nod. "That is gratifying to hear."

The lion gave a belch. "Yes, they kindly donated their essences to strengthen mine. Don't look so shocked. In our world we are all one anyway, as I have told you."

As usual, the merest mention of the Other Place was enough: my master's eyes sparkled with a far-off light; his face became dreamy and reflective. "Rekhyt, my friend," he said, "you have told me much, but there is more that I wish to learn. I believe that a few more weeks' work will suffice. Affa has had some experience with the shamans of a distant land; he is advising me on their methods of departing their body. When you return—well, let us wait and see."

The lion's tail struck rhythmically upon the stones of the roof. "You should concentrate on the dangers of *this* world. Your cousin—"

"Penrenutet will protect me while you are gone, have no fear. Now—see, they are lighting the watch fire on the tower. The fleet is massing below. You must depart."

There followed a spate of much activity for me, during which time I had no contact with my master. I sailed with the Egyptian fleet against the pirates, and fought in a pitched battle off the Barbary Coast.[1] Next I marched with troops to the Theban desert and ambushed the Bedouin, carrying off a number of hostages. During our return march we were set upon by a group of jackal-headed djinn, who were only narrowly defeated.[2]

Without pause for rest, I headed south to join the main body of the king's army in search of vengeance against the hill peoples of the lower Nile. The campaigns here lasted two months, ending with the infamous Battle of the Cataracts, during which I fought twenty foliots on a lip of stone high above the frothing waters. Losses were grave, but the day was won, and peace was restored to the region.[3]

I had been put through considerable trials, but my essence was strong, and I did not resent it. In truth, my master's researches—his desire to establish parity between djinni and human—had touched me, despite my skepticism. I dared to hope that something might come of it. Even so, I feared for him. He was altogether unworldly, insensible to perils all around.

One night, during our occupation of the hill country, a bubble materialized inside my tent. Ptolemy's face showed in the glassy surface, faint and far away.

"Greetings, Rekhyt. I hear congratulations are in order. Word of your successes has reached the city."

I bowed. "Is your cousin chuffed?"

---

[1] During which we successfully destroyed the principal pirate fort and released a hundred captives. The scrap was memorable mainly for me fighting single combat with a fiery afrit above two sinking ships. We chased back and forth along the burning oars, and fenced among the rigging using portions of the broken mast. In the end I brained him with a lucky blow and watched him sink, still smoldering, into the pea-green depths.

[2] A certain red-skinned individual was prominent among them. After causing general havoc, Jabor was finally put out of action when I lured him into a system of sandstone caves and caused the tunnel roof to collapse upon him.

[3] An *Egyptian* peace, that is. Still plenty of rape, pillage, and murder, but now carried out *by* us, rather than against us. So that's all right.

My master seemed to sigh. "Unfortunately the people proclaim this as *my* victory. Despite my protestations, they cheer my name to the rooftops. My cousin is not pleased."

"This is unsurprising. You must—What's that on your chin? Is that a scar?"

"It is nothing. An archer fired on me in the street. Penrenutet flung me aside and all is well."

"I'm coming back."

"Not yet. I need another week to complete the work. Return in seven days. In the meantime, go where you wish."

I stared at the face. "Really?"

"You're always moaning about the limitations of free will. Now's your chance to experience it. I'm sure you can tolerate the pain of this Earth for a little longer. Do what you want. See you in seven days." The bubble became a vapor and was gone.

This invitation was so unexpected that for some minutes I could only wander aimlessly around the tent, rearranging the cushions and looking at my reflection in the polished brasses. Then the full import of his words struck me. I stepped outside, took a last look around the camp and, with a cry, launched myself into the air.

Seven days passed. I returned to Alexandria. My master stood in his workroom, wearing a white tunic without sandals. His face was thinner than before, his eye sockets gray with tiredness, but he greeted me with his old enthusiasm.

"Right on time!" he said. "How was the world?"

"It is broad and beautiful, though there is too much water in it. In the east mountains rise to the stars, to the south forests swallow the land. The architecture of the Earth is infinitely varied; it has given me much to think about."

"Some day I shall see it too. And humans? What of them?"

"They erupt in isolated patches, like pimples on a bottom. Most do without magic, I believe."

Ptolemy grinned. "Your insights are profound. Now it is my turn." He led me to a door and showed me into a quiet inner chamber. The floor was covered with a circle—larger than average—decorated with hieroglyphs and runes. Beside it, on the floor, were herbs, charms, piles of papyrus and wax tablets, all covered in my master's scrawl. He gave me a tired smile. "What do you think?"

I was busy scanning the pentacle's barriers and word chains. "Nothing special here. Fairly standard issue."

"I know. I tried all kinds of complex reinforcements and hexes, Rekhyt, but it just felt wrong. Then it occurred to me: all our normal safeguards are there to *restrict* movement—you know, keep the djinni out, keep us secure. I want the opposite effect; I want to be able to move freely. So if I do *this*"—with a deliberate toe, he smudged the cochineal line that marked the perimeter of the circle—"that should allow my spirit to depart. Through that little hole. My body shall remain here."

I frowned. "Why use the pentacle at all?"

"Aha. Good point. According to our friend Affa, the shamans of distant regions, who converse with djinn on the borders of our realms, speak certain words and leave their bodies at will. They do not use circles. But *they* are not trying to pass through the boundaries between our worlds—those elemental walls you have told me so much about. And I *am*. I think that, just as the circle's power pulls you directly to me when I summon you, so the same circle can propel me in the opposite direction, through the walls, when the words are reversed. It is a focusing mechanism. You understand?"

I scratched my chin. "Erm . . . Sorry, what did Affa say again?"

My master raised his eyes to the heavens. "It doesn't matter. But *this* bit does. I think I can reverse the normal summons easily enough, but if a gate *does* open up, I need something on the other side to guide me safely through. Something that provides a destination."

"That's a problem," I said. "There are no 'destinations' in the Other Place. No mountains, no forests. I've told you that countless times."

"I know. That's where you come in." The boy was crouching on the floor, rummaging through a pile of the usual magical paraphernalia that every Egyptian magician accumulated: scarabs, mummified rodents, novelty pyramids, the lot. He held up a small ankh[4] and thrust it in my direction. "Think this is iron?"

A waft of essence-stinging cold; I leaned back irritably. "Yep. Stop waving it about."

"Good. I'll keep this on my body for protection. Just in case any imps come calling while I'm gone. Now, back to you. Rekhyt, I thank you for all the services you have done me; I am in your debt. In a moment I shall dismiss you. Your obligation to me, such as it is, will be at an end."

I bowed in the customary way. "My thanks, master."

He waved his hand. "Forget that master business now. When you are in the Other Place, listen out for your name—your *true*

---

[4] *Ankh*: a kind of amulet, T-shaped, with a loop at the top. Symbol of life. In pharaonic Egypt, when magic was commonplace, many ankhs contained trapped entities and were powerful protectors. By Ptolemy's time they were usually symbolic only. But iron, like silver, always repels the djinn.

one, I mean.[5] When I have finished my incantation, I shall call your name three times. If you wish, you may answer me: I believe that will be enough to provide the destination that I need. I shall pass through the gate to you."

I looked dubious in that way I have. "You reckon?"

"I do." The boy smiled at me. "Rekhyt, if you are sick of the sight of me after all this time, the solution is simple. Do not respond to my call."

"It's up to me?"

"Of course. The Other Place is your domain. If you *do* see fit to call me over, I shall be most honored." His face was flushed with excitement, his pupils dilated like a cat's; in his mind he was already tasting the wonders of the other side. I watched his movements as he went over to a bowl beside the window. It contained water. He washed his face and neck.

"Your theories are all very well," I ventured, "but have they told you what will happen to your body if you pass across? You are not a creature of essence."

He dried himself on a cloth, looking out over the rooftops, where the commotion and bustle of midday hung like an invisible pall upon the city. "Sometimes," he murmured, "I feel I am not a creature of Earth, either. All my life has been shut away in libraries, never experiencing the sensations of the world. When I come back, Rekhyt, I shall wander afar like you have done. . . ." He turned and stretched his thin brown arms. "You are right, of course: I don't know what will happen. Perhaps I will suffer for it. But it is worth the risk, I think, to see what no other man has seen!" He stepped across and closed

---

[5] Bartimaeus, this was. Thought you might have forgotten. Ptolemy never used it, for politeness' sake.

the shutters on the window, shrouding us both in dim, pale light. Next he locked the chamber door.

"Perhaps," I said, "you will find yourself in my power, when we meet again."

"Very likely."

"Yet you trust me?"

Ptolemy laughed. "What else have I been doing all this time? When did I last bind you within a pentacle? Look at you now—you're as free as I am. You could throttle me in a blink and be gone."

"Oh. Yeah." I hadn't thought of that.

The boy clapped his hands. "Well, the time has come. Penrenutet and Affa are already dismissed; I have no obligations left. So—it is your turn. If you want to hop into the pentacle, I'll set you free."

"What of your own security?" I glanced around the darkened room. Slats of light from the shutters ran like claw marks across wall and floor. "With us departed, you're helpless if your enemies find you."

"Penrenutet's last task was to take my guise and ride south along the old highway. He let himself be seen. The spies will be following his caravan. So you see, dear Rekhyt, I have thought of everything." He motioned to me. I stepped into the circle.

"You know, you don't *need* to risk yourself in this experiment," I said. I was looking at his narrow shoulders, his scrawny neck, the skinny legs sticking out beneath his tunic.

"It's not an experiment," he said. "It's a gesture. It's redress."

"For what? Three thousand years of slavery? Why take the burden of so many crimes? No other magicians have ever thought this way."

He smiled. "That's just it. I'm the first. And if my venture goes well, and I return to record it, many others will follow after me. There will be a new era between djinn and men. I've made some of the notes already, Rekhyt—my book will take pride of place in every library on the Earth. I won't be there to see it—but who knows, perhaps *you* will."

His passion won me over. I nodded. "Let's hope you're right."

He didn't answer, only snapped his fingers and spoke the Dismissal. The last thing I saw as I departed was his face gazing after me, confident, serene.

22

Kitty woke to a light that blinded her and a sharp pain in her side. As the seconds passed, and she lay quite still, she became aware of the blood pounding in her head and the dryness of her open mouth. Her wrists ached. There was a terrible smell of burned cloth and a tight pressure around one hand.

Panic swelled inside her chest; she wrenched at her limbs, opened her eyes, sought to lift her head. She was rewarded with scattershot pain and certain insights into her situation: her wrists were tied, she sat against something hard, someone was crouched beside her, looking into her face. The pressure on one hand was suddenly released.

A voice. "Can you hear me? Are you all right?"

Kitty opened one eye a fraction. A dark shape swam into focus. The magician, Mandrake, bent close; he wore a look of concern mixed with relief. "Can you speak?" he said. "How do you feel?"

Kitty's voice was weak. "Were you holding my hand?"

"No."

"Good." She was acclimatizing to the light now; both eyes opened steadily and she looked about her. She sat on the floor at the edge of a great stone room, older and grander than anything she had experienced. Thick pillars supported a vaulted ceiling; on the floor, beautiful rugs were spread upon the flagstones. Around the walls, in many recesses, stood statues of regal men and women dressed in bygone costumes. Magical globes drifted against the vaulting, creating an ever-changing pattern of light and shadow. In the center of the room sat a brightly polished table and seven chairs.

On the near side of the table a man was walking up and down.

Kitty struggled to shift her position, an operation made difficult by the cords binding her wrists. Something dug into her back. She cursed. "Ah! Can you—?"

Mandrake held up his hands, bound tightly together with the fingers swathed in thin white cord. "Try wriggling to the left. You're leaning against a stone shoe at the moment. Careful—you've been badly knocked about."

Kitty shifted her bottom sideways and became marginally more comfortable. She looked down at herself. One side of her coat was blackened and burned away; she could see tattered fragments of her shirt beneath and, hanging loose in an inner pocket, a singed corner of Mr. Button's book. Her brow furrowed. How had—?

The theater! In a rush, she remembered: the explosions in the box opposite, the raising of the lights, the sea of demons in the stalls below. Yes, and Mandrake next to her, pale and frightened, with the fat little man holding the knife to his throat. She had tried—

"I'm glad you're alive," the magician said. His face was gray, but his voice was calm. There was dried blood on his neck. "That's impressive resilience you've got there. Can you see through illusions too?"

She shook her head irritably. "Where are we? What's—?"

"The Hall of Statues at Westminster. This is the room where the Council meets."

"But what's happened? Why are we here?" Panic engulfed her; she pulled frantically at her bonds.

"Calm down . . . we're being watched." He jerked his head toward the figure by the table. It was someone Kitty didn't know, a young man with long, bandy legs, still pacing back and forth.

"*Calm down?*" Kitty gave a strangled cry of fury. "How *dare* you? If I was free—"

"Yes, but you're not. And nor am I. So shut up for a minute and let me tell you what's happened." He leaned in close. "The whole government was taken captive in that theater. Everyone. Makepeace used a host of demons to subdue them."

"I've got eyes, haven't I? I saw all that."

"All right, fine. Well, some might have been killed, but most, I think, are alive, but gagged and tied so they can't summon anything. We all got rounded up and taken out the back of the theater, where a group of vans was waiting. Everyone got bundled in; they threw the ministers in one on top of the other, like sacks of beef. The vans left the theater and drove here. No one outside the theater is any the wiser yet. I don't know where the prisoners have been taken. They must be locked in somewhere close. That's what Makepeace is seeing to now, I think."

Kitty's head ached. She struggled to grasp the implications. "Was it him who"—she looked down at her side—"did this to me?"

"He did. An Inferno. Close range. When you tried to"—his pale face flushed a little—"when you tried to help me. You ought to be dead; in fact, we thought you *were* dead, but just as the mercenary was taking me off, you groaned and dribbled, so he scooped you up, too."

"The mercenary?"

"Don't ask."

Kitty was silent for a time. "So Makepeace is taking over?"

"It seems he thinks he is." The magician scowled. "The man's quite mad. How he plans to rule the Empire without a governing class, I can't imagine."

Kitty gave a snort. "Your governing class wasn't doing so well, let's face it. He might be an improvement."

"Don't be a fool!" Mandrake's face darkened. "You haven't the slightest idea what—" He controlled himself with difficulty. "I'm sorry. You're not to blame. I shouldn't have brought you to the theater in the first place."

"True." Kitty looked around the chamber. "But what gets me is I don't understand why either of us has been brought *here*."

"Nor me. We've been singled out for some reason."

Kitty regarded the man walking to and fro beside the Council table. There was an air of nervousness about him; he frequently consulted his watch and looked over toward a set of double doors. "He doesn't look that hot," she whispered. "Can't you whip up a demon and get us out of here?"

Mandrake groaned. "All my slaves are on a mission. If I could get to a pentacle I could summon them here easily, but without one, and with my fingers tied like this, I'm stuck. I haven't got so much as an imp on tap."

"Useless," Kitty snapped. "Call yourself a magician."

A scowl. "Give me time. My demons are powerful, especially Cormocodran. With luck, I'll get a chance to—"

The doors at the end of the hall burst open. The man by the table swiveled around. Kitty and Mandrake craned their heads.

A small procession walked in.

The first few persons were unknown to Kitty. A diminutive man with round, moist eyes, built like a winter twig; a dull-faced, somewhat slatternly woman; a middle-aged gentleman with pale, shiny skin and protruding lips. Behind them came a young man, slender, sprightly of step, with oiled ginger hair and glasses perched on a little nose. About these four an air of suppressed excitement seemed to hang: they tittered, grinned, and looked about them with quick, nervous movements.

The bandy-legged man beside the table hurried to join them. "At last!" he said. "Where's Quentin?"

"Here, my friends!" In through the doors strode Quentin Makepeace, emerald frock coat flapping, chest puffed out like a bantam cock's. His shoulders rolled, his arms swung with an insolent swagger. He passed his companions, clapping the ginger-haired man soundly on the back, ruffling the hair of the woman and winking at the rest. On toward the table he went, glancing up and down the room with proprietorial ease. On noticing Kitty and Mandrake sitting by the wall, he gave a plump-fingered wave.

At the Council table Makepeace selected the largest of the chairs, a golden throne, ornately carved. He sat himself, legs crossed; with a flourish, he drew from a pocket an enormous cigar. A snap of the fingers: the cigar tip burst into smoldering life. Quentin Makepeace placed it between his lips and inhaled with satisfaction.

Kitty heard Mandrake beside her give a gasp of rage. She herself saw little but the ostentatious theatricality of the performance. If she hadn't been a prisoner, she might have been amused.

Makepeace made an expansive gesture with the cigar. "Clive, Rufus—would you be so kind as to bring our friends over?"

The ginger-haired man approached, followed by his thick-lipped companion. Roughly, without ceremony, Kitty and Mandrake were hauled to their feet. Kitty noticed that both conspirators were regarding Mandrake with malevolent dislike. As she watched, the older man, lips moistly parted, stepped forward and struck their prisoner hard across the face.

The man rubbed his hand. "*That's* for what you did to Lovelace."

Mandrake smiled thinly. "Never been slapped by a wet fish before."

"I hear you were *looking* for me, Mandrake," the ginger-haired man said. "Well, what are you going to do to me now?"

From the golden chair a mellifluous voice projected: "Steady, boys, steady! John is our guest. I have affection for him! Bring them over, I say."

A grip on Kitty's shoulder; she was propelled forward to stand with Mandrake on a rug before the table.

The other conspirators had seated themselves. Their eyes were hostile. The sullen-faced woman spoke. "What are they *doing* here, Quentin? This is a crucial time."

"You should kill Mandrake and have done," the fish-faced magician said.

Makepeace took a puff on his cigar; his little eyes sparkled with merriment. "Rufus, you are far too hasty. You too, Bess. True, John is not yet part of our company, but I have high hopes that he might become so. We have long been allies, he and I."

Kitty took a sharp side-glance at the young magician. One cheek was scarlet where the blow had struck. He did not reply.

"We haven't got time to play games." This was the little man with wide, wet eyes; his voice was nasal, whiny. "We need to give ourselves the power you promised." He looked down at the table, ran his fingers over it in a gesture at once covetous and fearful. To Kitty he seemed weak and cowardly, and angrily conscious of this cowardice. From what she could see, none of the conspirators was any different, save for Makepeace, radiating self-satisfaction from his golden throne.

The playwright tapped a dollop of ash from his cigar onto the Persian carpet. "No *games*, my dear Withers," he said, smiling. "I can assure you I am perfectly serious. Devereaux's spies have long reported that—among commoners—John here is the most popular of the magicians. He could give our new Council a fresh, attractive face—well, certainly more attractive than any of *you*." He grinned at the displeasure he had caused. "Besides, he has talent and ambition to spare. I have a feeling he's long desired the chance to kick Devereaux out and start again. . . . Isn't that right, John?"

Again Kitty looked at Mandrake. Again his pale face gave no inkling of his thoughts.

"We must give John a little time," Quentin Makepeace said. "All will become clear to him. And you will shortly get all the power you can handle, Mr. Withers. If only the good Hopkins would hurry along, we can proceed." He chuckled to himself—and with that noise, with that name, Kitty knew him.

It was as if a thick veil had fallen from her eyes. She was back in the Resistance again, three years before. On the advice of the mousy clerk, Clem Hopkins, she had gone to a rendezvous in a disused theater. And once there . . . a dagger held to the back of her neck, a whispered conversation with an unseen man—whose words of guidance led them to the abbey and to the dreadful guardian of the crypt. . . .

"You!" she cried out. "*You!*"

All eyes turned to her. She stood stock-still, staring at the man on the golden throne.

"*You* were the benefactor," she whispered. "You were the one who betrayed us."

Mr. Makepeace winked at her. "Ah! You recognize me at last? I *wondered* if you'd ever recall. . . . Of course, *I* knew you as soon as I saw you with Mandrake. That's why it amused me to invite you to my little show tonight."

At Kitty's side John Mandrake stirred at last. "What's this? You've met before?"

"Don't look so shocked, John! It was all in a good cause. Through my associate Mr. Hopkins—whom you will meet shortly; he is currently tending to our captives—I had long followed the activities of the Resistance. It amused me to watch their efforts, to see the outrage on the faces of the fools in Council as they failed to track them down. Present company excepted, John!" Another chuckle.

Kitty's voice was expressionless. "You knew about the monster in Gladstone's tomb, but you and Hopkins still sent us there to get the Staff. My friends *died* because of you." She took a small step in his direction.

"Oh *tush.*" Quentin Makepeace rolled his eyes. "You were traitorous commoners. I was a magician. Did you expect me to *care*? And don't come any closer, young lady. Next time I won't bother with a spell. I'll cut your throat." He smiled. "In truth, though, I was on *your* side. I hoped you would destroy the demon. Then I'd have taken the Staff from you for my own use. In fact"—he tapped his cigar, refolded his legs, and looked around at his audience—"in fact the outcome was mixed: you ran off with the Staff, and let Honorius the afrit escape the tomb. *What* an impact Honorius made! Gladstone's bones,

315

hopping around the rooftops with a demon encased inside! A marvelous spectacle. But it set Hopkins and me thinking . . ."

"Tell me, Quentin." Mandrake spoke again; his voice was soft. "This Mr. Hopkins was supposed to have been involved with the golem too. Was it so?"

Makepeace smiled, and paused a while before answering. He's *performing* the whole time, Kitty thought. He's an incorrigible show-off, treating this like one of his plays.

"Of course!" Makepeace cried. "Under my direction! I have my fingers in many pies. I am an *artist*, John, a man of restless creativity. For years the Empire has been going to rack and ruin; Devereaux and the others have mismanaged it disgracefully. Did you know that several of my plays have actually had to close in Boston, Calcutta, and Baghdad, thanks to local poverty, unrest, and violence? And this endless war! . . . Things have got to change! Well, for years I have watched on the sidelines, experimenting here and there. First, I encouraged my good friend Lovelace in his attempt at rebellion. Remember that decidedly *large* pentacle, John? That was my idea!" He chuckled. "Then came poor Duvall. He wanted power, but he hadn't a creative bone in his body. All he could do was follow advice. Through Hopkins I encouraged him to use the golem to spread unrest. And while the government was distracted"—he beamed at Kitty once again—"I nearly acquired the Staff. Which, by the way, I fully intend to take into my possession this very night."

To Kitty, most of this meant nothing; she gazed at the hateful little man in the great gold chair, almost quivering with fury. She saw, as if from far off, the faces of her dead companions—with every word, Makepeace defiled their memory. She could not have spoken.

By contrast, John Mandrake seemed to be becoming almost

talkative. "This is all very interesting, Quentin," he said. "The Staff will certainly be useful. But how will the government be run? You have emptied all the departments. That is bound to cause problems, even with such titanic figures as these in your team." He smiled around at the sullen conspirators.

Makepeace made an easy gesture. "Some of the prisoners will be freed in due course, once they have sworn loyalty."

"And the others?"

"Will be executed."

Mandrake shrugged. "It seems a risky prospect for you, even with the Staff."

"Not so!" For the first time Makepeace seemed annoyed. He rose from his chair, tossed the remnants of the cigar aside. "We are about to augment our power with the first creative act in two thousand years of magic. In fact, here is the very man who will show you. Ladies and gentlemen, I give you—Mr. Clem Hopkins!"

A meek and diffident figure stepped into the room. Three years had passed since Kitty had last set eyes on him, sitting at a café table in the pleasant summer air. She had been little more than a girl; she'd drunk a milk shake and eaten an iced bun while he'd asked her questions about the stolen Staff. Then, when she'd failed to supply the information he required, Mr. Hopkins had gently betrayed her once again—sending her to the house where Mandrake waited to entrap her.

So it had been. As the years had passed, and the scholar's features had faded from her memory, his shadow had grown inside her, spread like a contagion at the back of her mind. He sometimes taunted her within her dreams.

And now here he was, stepping quietly across the rugs of the Hall of Statues, a little smile on his face. His appearance seemed to awake a great excitement in the conspirators; there was a stirring of anticipation. Mr. Hopkins came to stand beside the table, directly opposite Kitty. He looked at Mandrake first, then at Kitty. His pale gray eyes surveyed her, his face expressionless.

"You traitor," Kitty growled. Mr. Hopkins frowned a little as if in some perplexity. He showed not the slightest hint of recognition.

"Now then, Clem"—Makepeace clapped him on the back—"do not be put off by the presence of young Kitty here. It is just my little joke to remind you of your Resistance days. Don't let her get close, mind. She is quite the little vixen! How are the prisoners?"

The scholar nodded eagerly. "Quite safe, sir. They cannot go anywhere."

"And what about outside? Is all quiet?"

"There is still unrest in the central parks. The police go about their business. No one knows we have left the theater."

"Good. Then it is time to act. My friends, Hopkins here is a *marvel*, an absolute gem. He breathes ideas like you and I gulp air; he dreams 'em in his sleep, digests 'em with his dinner. It was *he* who first noticed the unique properties of the afrit Honorius. Isn't that right, Clem?"

Hopkins gave a little smile. "If you say so, sir."

"Hopkins and I immediately observed that the demon *inhabited* Gladstone's bones. It was not a mere guise, an illusion of essence: the skeleton was *real*. The demon had mingled with the actual bones. An ambitious idea occurred to us: why not summon a demon into a *living* body—specifically, the living body of a magician? If the magician could control the demon, and use its power—what wonders he might perform! There would be no more need for pentacles, for fiddling about with runes and chalks, no more risk of fatal errors! Indeed, summoning itself would soon become unnecessary!"

Kitty had learned enough from Mr. Button to realize the radical nature of this proposal; she knew enough to share Mandrake's utter disbelief. "But the risks are far too great!" he was saying. "That commoner in your workroom—he heard the demon talking in his head! It would have driven him mad!"

"Only because he did not have the *will* to suppress the demon." Makepeace was impatient now; he spoke quickly. "With individuals of intelligence and strong personality such as *us*, the effect will be harmonious."

"You don't mean you're *all* going to take this risk?" Mandrake protested. "Surely not! The effects might be catastrophic! You don't know what might happen."

"Oh, but we do, we do. Hopkins summoned a demon into himself two months ago, John. He has suffered no ill effects. Isn't that right, Clem? Tell them."

"That's right, sir." The scholar seemed embarrassed to be the focus of attention. "I summoned quite a powerful djinni. When it entered, I felt a certain struggling, like a living worm inside my head. But I merely had to concentrate and the demon accepted the inevitable. He is thoroughly quiet now. I hardly know he's there."

"But you are able to call on his power and knowledge, aren't you, Hopkins?" Makepeace said. "It is really quite remarkable."

"Show us!" the female conspirator whispered.

"Yes, show us! Show us!" Around the table the plea was taken up, over and over. Each face shone with furious, avid hunger. To Kitty they seemed wicked, but also helpless, like nestlings waiting to be fed. She was filled with a sudden repulsion; she longed to get away.

Makepeace's eyes were glittering slits; he nudged the scholar's arm. "What do you think, Hopkins? Show them a little, just to whet the appetite?"

"If you think it appropriate, sir." The scholar took a step back, bent his head in concentration. Then, without apparent effort, he rose into the air. Several of the conspirators gasped. Kitty glanced at Mandrake; he was watching openmouthed.

Hopkins rose six feet above the floor, then drifted off, away from the table. When he was some way distant, he raised a hand, pointing it at an alabaster statue on the far side of the hall. It showed a bald, stocky magician smoking a cigar. There was a flash of blue light—the statue exploded in a shower of sparks. The ginger-haired magician whooped with excitement; the others stood and clapped, or banged the table in wild joy. Mr. Hopkins rose higher, toward the ceiling.

"Show them something else, Hopkins!" Makepeace called. "Put on a show!"

Everyone's eyes were craning upward. Kitty took her chance. Slowly, slowly, she backed away from the table. One step, two . . . No one had noticed; all were watching the scholar perform acrobatic feats high against the ceiling, trailing gouts of flame from his fingertips. . . .

Kitty turned and ran. At the end of the hall the double doors were open. Her feet were noiseless on the thick, soft rugs. Her hands were tied, which made the running awkward, but in seconds she was through—out into a corridor of stone, with oil paintings on the wall and glass cases with ornaments of gold. . . . She headed right; the corridor ended at an open door. Kitty plunged through. She halted, cursed. An empty room, perhaps an official's study: a desk, a case of books, a pentacle on the floor. It was a dead end.

With a gasp of frustration, she turned, ran back the way she had come—along the corridor, past the double doors, around another corner—

—and collided full pelt with something hard and heavy. Thrown to the side, she instinctively tried to break her fall with an outstretched hand—but her arms were bound, she could not do so; she landed heavily on the flagstones.

Kitty looked up and caught her breath. A man stood over her, framed against the ceiling globes; a tall man, bearded, dressed in black. Bright blue eyes considered her, black brows runkled in a frown.

"Please!" Kitty gasped. "Please, help me!"

The bearded man smiled. A gloved hand reached down.

In the Hall of Statues Mr. Hopkins had returned to earth. The faces of the conspirators were filled with wonder; two of the men were pulling rugs away from the center of the room. As Kitty was brought in, half choked, hanging suspended by her collar from the bearded man's upraised grip, they stopped and dropped the rugs again. One by one, everyone turned to look at her.

A deep voice spoke at Kitty's shoulder. "What about this girl? I caught her making for the street."

The ginger-haired man shook his head. "Blimey. Didn't even notice she had gone."

Mr. Makepeace stepped forward, a petulant frown upon his face. "Ms. Jones, we really have *no* time for such distractions. . . ." He scowled, shrugged and turned away. "At first her presence amused me, but to be frank she interests me no longer. You may kill her."

23

Nathaniel saw the mercenary dump Kitty on the rug; he saw him fling back his cape, reach into his belt, and draw forth a long knife, curved like a scimitar. He saw him reach out to clutch her hair, lift up her head, expose her throat . . .

"Wait!" Nathaniel stepped forward; he spoke with as much authority as he could muster. "Don't touch her! I want her alive."

The mercenary's hands paused. He looked up at Nathaniel with his steady pale blue eyes. Then, slowly and very deliberately, he continued to pull Kitty's head back and bring the knife around.

Nathaniel cursed. "*Wait*, I said."

The conspirators were watching with some amusement. Rufus Lime's pale, damp face grimaced. "You're hardly in a position to be so lordly, Mandrake."

"On the contrary, Rufus. Quentin has invited me to join your company. And after seeing Mr. Hopkins's remarkable demonstration, I'm delighted to agree to that proposal. The results are most impressive. That means I'm one of you now."

Quentin Makepeace had been busy unbuttoning his emerald frock coat. His eyes were narrowed, calculating; he looked at Nathaniel askance. "You have decided to fall in with our little scheme?"

Nathaniel met his gaze as calmly as he could. "I have indeed," he said. "Your plan is an act of genius, a masterstroke. I only wish I'd paid more attention to you when you showed me that commoner the other day. But I intend to rectify that now. In the meantime, strictly speaking, the girl is still *my* prisoner, Quentin. I have . . . plans for her. No one touches her, save me."

Makepeace rubbed his chin; he did not answer. The mercenary adjusted the knife a little in his hand. Kitty gazed sightlessly at the floor. Nathaniel felt his heart thudding against his chest.

"Very well." Makepeace moved suddenly. "The girl is yours. Put her down, Verroq. John, you have spoken well and have confirmed my good opinion of you. But take heed: words are easy—actions are better! In a moment we shall free you and watch as you bond with a demon of your choice. But first I shall prepare for my own summoning! Burke! Withers! Clear those rugs away! The pentacles must be readied!"

He turned to issue further orders. Without expression, the mercenary loosened his grip on Kitty's hair. Nathaniel, conscious of hostile eyes upon him—Jenkins and Lime in particular were watching with undisguised suspicion—did not hasten to her side. She remained where she was, slumped on her knees, head lowered, hair hanging over her face. The sight pierced him.

Twice now that evening Kitty Jones had nearly died, and all because of what he'd done. Because *he'd* found her, because *he'd* wrenched her out of her quiet new life and brought her with him, just to satisfy his selfish curiosity.

When, in the theater, the Inferno struck her, Nathaniel had thought her dead. Sorrow had overwhelmed him; he had been almost unmanned with guilt. Despite the mercenary's harsh warning, he had flung himself beside her, and only *then* realized that she breathed. For the next hour, while she remained unconscious, his sense of shame had slowly grown. Little by little he began to recognize his folly.

Already, in the last few days, he had begun to detach himself from the name of Mandrake, from the role that for years had become a second skin. But only with the events in the theater did that detachment become a true separation. The two key certainties that governed him—his belief in the invulnerability of the government and in the essential virtue of his motives—were dashed from him in a matter of moments. The magicians were overpowered. Kitty was struck down. Both came at the hand of Makepeace, and it was with horror that Nathaniel recognized, in that callous, indifferent hand, a reflection of his own.

At first the enormity of Makepeace's crime almost blinded him to its nature: the theatrical panache of the coup, the bizarre perversion of the demons within the body, all the silly talk of genius and creativity helped divert attention from the banal reality of the truth. It was nothing but another cold, ambitious little man playing for power. No different from Lovelace, or Duvall or—and at this thought Nathaniel felt a chill upon his spine—from Nathaniel's *own* musings that very evening, as he sat in the car and dreamed of seizing the Staff and putting an end to the war. Oh, yes, he'd *told* himself it was for the right reasons, to help the commoners and save the Empire, but where did such idealism end? With bodies like Kitty's lying on the floor.

How naked and obvious Nathaniel's ambition must have been! Makepeace had seen it. Farrar, too. Ms. Lutyens had understood it and walked away.

No *wonder* Kitty had treated him with such disdain. . . . As he had watched over her body in the Hall of Statues, he had come to share her contempt.

But then she had woken, and with his relief came new determination.

The conspirators were busy. Back and forth across the room they scampered, bringing out the paraphernalia of summoning: candles, bowls, herbs, and flowers. In the center of the hall the heavy rugs had been pulled clear and unceremoniously dumped to one side. Several pentacles were revealed beneath, beautifully inlaid in mother-of-pearl and lapis lazuli. Makepeace stood within one, stripped down to his shirttails, pointing, pouting, issuing shrill commands.

Kitty Jones still crouched as before.

Nathaniel strolled forward, bent at her side, and spoke softly. "Kitty, get up." He extended his bound hands. "Come on. That's it. Sit over here." He pushed aside a heavy chair of redwood, and helped lower her down. "Rest there. Are you all right?"

"Yes."

"Then wait. I'll get you out of this."

"How's that exactly?"

"Trust me." He leaned against the table, appraising the situation. By the door the mercenary stood, arms folded, gazing implacably toward them. No possibility of escape there. The conspirators themselves were feeble; it was easy to see now why Makepeace had recruited them. He had chosen the weak, the unpreferred, those eaten away with jealousy and malice, who would seize the opportunity but never be a threat to him. The playwright was a different matter, a formidable magician. Without his demons, Nathaniel was helpless.

Makepeace . . . He cursed again his own stupidity. For *years* he had suspected the presence of a traitor high in government, someone connected to both the Lovelace and the Duvall plots. Four magicians had been needed to summon the great demon Ramuthra back at Heddleham Hall—the fourth had never been seen, save for a fleeting glimpse in an open-topped car—a flash of goggles, a red beard . . . gone. Makepeace in disguise? Easy to imagine now.

During the golem affair Nathaniel had been surprised how easily the playwright had discovered the location of the fugitive Kitty: that must have been Hopkins, then—Makepeace's contact with the Resistance. Nathaniel ground his teeth. How *swiftly* Makepeace had won him over, used him as an ally, played him for a fool. Well, the matter wasn't over yet.

Stony faced, Nathaniel watched Mr. Hopkins hurrying past to obey his leader's orders. So *this* was the mysterious scholar he had sought so long! A demon's power coursed through the villain's body—of that there was no doubt. But the meek little man would hardly be a match for Cormocodran, Ascobol, and the others if Nathaniel could only bring them to his side. Yet while Hopkins worked his mischief here, the incompetent djinn were a mile away, waiting vainly for him at the Ambassador Hotel!

Nathaniel's brows knotted with frustration. He fidgeted with the cords that bound his hands. All he could do was wait until Makepeace freed him and let him step within a pentacle. *Then* he could act. In an instant his servants would be summoned and the traitors brought to account.

"My friends, I am ready! Come, Mandrake, Ms. Jones—you must join the audience!" Makepeace was standing in the nearest circle, shirtsleeves rolled up, collar undone; he had adopted a heroic pose: hands on hips, pelvis thrust forward, legs wide enough to straddle a horse. The conspirators congregated at a respectful distance; even the mercenary showed sufficient interest to stalk a little closer. Together, Nathaniel and Kitty approached the pentacle.

"The time has come!" Makepeace cried. "The moment toward which I have worked for so many years. Only the thrill of anticipation, my friends, keeps me from bursting with my pent emotions!" With a dynamic flourish, he removed a lacy handkerchief from a pocket and dabbed at his eyes. "How much sweat, how many tears have I shed to get so far?" he cried. "Who can tell? How much blood—?"

"Secretions aside," Rufus Lime interjected sourly, "hadn't you better get on with it? Some of those candles are burning low."

Makepeace glared at him, but returned his hanky to his pocket. "Very well. My friends, following the success of Hopkins here in subduing a demon of moderate power"— Hopkins gave a little smile, which might have meant anything—"I have decided to apply my more considerable ability to the taming of a greater entity." He paused. "This very evening Hopkins located in the London Library a volume listing the names of spirits from ancient Persia. I have decided to make use of a name he found there. My friends, here and now, before your very eyes, I shall summon into myself the greater demon known as . . . Nouda!"

Nathaniel uttered a small exclamation. *Nouda?* The man was mad. "Makepeace," he said. "Surely you're joking. This procedure is risky enough without trying something so powerful."

The playwright pursed his lips fretfully. "I'm not joking, John, just ambitious. Mr. Hopkins has assured me that control is simplicity itself—and I am *very* strong-willed. I hope you don't mean to imply that I'm not up to this."

"Oh no," Nathaniel said hastily. "Not at all." He leaned close to Kitty. "The man's a fool," he whispered. "Nouda is a *terrible* entity; one of the most fearsome recorded. It left Persepolis in ruins. . . ."

Kitty leaned over, whispered back. "I know. Destroyed Darius's own army."

"Yes." Nathaniel nodded. Then he blinked. "What? How did *you* know?"

"John!" Makepeace's voice was tetchy. "Enough canoodling! I need silence now. Hopkins—if you see anything go amiss, reverse the process; use Asprey's Overrule. Right. Quiet, all."

Quentin Makepeace closed his eyes, bent his head toward his chest. He flourished his arms and flexed his fingers. He breathed deeply. Then he lifted his chin, opened his eyes, and began to declaim the incantation in a loud, clear voice. Nathaniel listened hard: as before, it was a simple enough Latin summons, but the strength of the oncoming spirit meant that it had to be reinforced with multiple word-locks and tortuous subclauses doubling back on themselves to shore up the binding. He had to admit that Makepeace spoke it well. Minutes passed—his larynx never faltered, he ignored the perspiration running down his face. There was a hush in the chamber: Nathaniel, Kitty, the conspirators—all watched, transfixed. Most avid of all was Mr. Hopkins—he was leaning forward with his mouth open; he had a slightly hungry look.

On the seventh minute the room grew cold. Not slowly, but in an instant, as if a switch had suddenly been pressed. Everyone began to shiver. On the eighth minute came the sweetest of fragrances, that of meadow flax and celandine. On the ninth minute Nathaniel detected something in the pentacle with Makepeace. It was there on the third plane—something hazy,

328

fluctuating, sucking in the light—a dark, horned mass, now tall, now broad, with arms that spread out and pressed against the pentacle. Nathaniel looked down; he thought he saw the inlaid boundaries of the circle bulge out a little in the floor. The features of the newcomer could not be seen. It towered over Makepeace, who spoke on, quite oblivious to his new companion.

Makepeace came to the climax of his command, the moment when he bound the demon inside himself. With a cry, he spoke the final words: the dark figure vanished, like blinking.

Makepeace stopped. He was quite still. His eyes looked out beyond his audience, as if at something far away.

Everyone watched, frozen to the spot. Makepeace did nothing; his face was blank.

"Hopkins," Rufus Lime said hoarsely. "Dismiss it . . . Quick!"

With a great cry, Makepeace sprang into life. It was quite without warning. Nathaniel cried out, everyone jumped; even the mercenary stepped back.

"Success!" Makepeace leaped from the circle. He clapped his hands, capered, hopped, skipped, and twirled. "Success! Such triumph! I cannot begin to tell you . . ."

The conspirators inched closer. Jenkins peered out above his glasses. "Quentin . . . is it true? How does it feel . . . ?"

"Yes! Nouda is here! I feel it within! Ah—for a moment or two, my friends, there was a struggle—I admit it. The effect was disconcerting. But I commanded it most strictly, with all my power. And I felt that demon shrink back and obey. It is subservient within me. It knows its master! What is it like? Hard to describe. . . . It is not painful exactly. . . . I sense it like a hard, hot coal within my head. But when it obeyed—I felt such a surge of energy! Oh, it cannot be imagined!"

With this, the conspirators erupted into raucous celebration; they squealed and jumped for joy.

"The demon's power, Quentin!" Lime shouted. "Use it!"

"Not yet, my friends." Makepeace held up his hands for calm; the room fell silent. "I could destroy this room," he said, "turn all of it to powder if I chose. But there shall be time enough for fun once you have followed me. Go to your pentacles! Summon your demons! Then we shall set about our destiny! We shall seize the Staff of Gladstone and take a stroll through London. I believe some commoners are busy demonstrating. Our first task will be to put them in their place."

Like eager children, the conspirators scampered to their circles. Nathaniel grasped Kitty by the arm, drew her to one side. "In a moment," he hissed, "I will be called upon to join this madness. I will pretend to do so. Do not be alarmed. At the last minute I shall use the pentacle to summon a troupe of the strongest djinn. With luck they will destroy Makepeace and these other fools. At the very least we shall have the opportunity to escape!" He paused triumphantly. "You don't seem overly impressed."

Kitty's eyes were tired, red-rimmed. Had she been crying? He hadn't noticed. She shrugged. "I hope you're right."

Nathaniel swallowed his irritation; in truth, he was nervous too. "You'll see."

Across the hall the summonings began: Rufus Lime, eyes tight shut, fish-mouth open, intoning his words in a muttered croak; Clive Jenkins, glasses removed from his little nose and held anxiously between his hands as he spoke in a rapid monotone. The others, whose names Nathaniel could not remember, stood in solitary postures, hunched, erect, shaking, stammering out their incantations, making the necessary gestures. Hopkins and Makepeace walked approvingly among them.

"John!" That was Makepeace; with a trill of delight, he bounded over. "Ah! Such energy! I could leap to the stars!" His face went serious. "Not holding back on us, are you, boy? Why aren't you in a circle?"

Nathaniel raised his hands. "Perhaps if I was untied?"

"Ah, yes. How discourteous of me. There!" A snap of the fingers; the cords burst into lilac flames. Nathaniel shook himself free. "There is an empty pentacle in that corner, John," Makepeace said. "What demon have you chosen for yourself?"

Nathaniel chose two at random. "I was debating between two djinn from Ethiopian texts: Zosa and Karloum."

"An interesting, if modest, choice. I suggest Karloum. Well, off you go."

Nathaniel nodded. He took a quick sidelong glance at Kitty, who was watching him intently, then strode toward the nearest vacant pentacle. He hadn't much time: through the corner of his eye he saw strange, contorted shadows flittering above Jenkins and Lime. Heaven knew what the idiots had summoned, but with luck it would take a while for them to control their internal slaves. Before that happened, Cormocodran and Hodge would make short work of them.

He stepped inside his circle, cleared his throat and looked around. Makepeace was watching him intently. Doubtless he was suspicious. Nathaniel grinned bleakly to himself; well, those suspicions were about to be confirmed in the most dramatic possible way.

A final moment of preparation—he would need to work

swiftly when his djinn arrived, give precise and urgent orders—then Nathaniel acted. He made an ornate gesture, cried out the names of his five strong demons and pointed at the neighboring circle. He steeled himself for the explosions, the smoke and hellfire, the sudden appearance of straining, hideous forms.

With a miserable squelch, something small and insubstantial struck the center of the circle, spattering outward like a fruit dropped from on high. It had no discernible shape, but gave off a strong smell of fish.

A bulge rose in its center. A small voice sounded. "Saved!" The bulge rotated, appeared to notice Mr. Hopkins. "Oh."

Nathaniel gazed at it wordlessly.

Quentin Makepeace had seen it also. He stepped close, inspected it. "How peculiar! It seems to be some kind of uncooked meal. With added sentience. What do you think, Hopkins?"

Mr. Hopkins approached; his eyes glittered as they glanced at Nathaniel. "Nothing so innocent, I am afraid, sir. It is the remains of a pernicious djinni, which earlier this evening attempted my capture. Several other demons, who accompanied him, I have already slain. I fear that Master Mandrake was hoping to catch us unawares."

"Is that so?" Quentin Makepeace straightened sadly. "Oh dear. That rather changes things. I always had such high hopes for you, John. I really thought we might work well together. Still, never mind—I have Hopkins and my five *loyal* friends to count on." He glanced round at the conspirators who, having finished their summonings, stood quietly in their circles. "That is enough. Our first pleasure will be to watch you and your creature die—*Ulp!*" He put his hand to his mouth. "Excuse me. I fear I—*hic!*—have indigestion. Now then—" Another gulp, a gasp; his eyes bulged. "This is most curious. I—" His tongue protruded. His limbs shook, his knees sagged; he seemed about to fall.

Nathaniel stepped back in shock. Makepeace's body gave a sudden wriggle; it writhed, somewhat like a snake, as if all his bones were newly fluid. Then it steadied, stiffened. The playwright seemed to rally. For the briefest of instants a panicked look erupted in the eyes; the tongue managed to gabble out the words: "It is . . ."

A furious writhing drowned out the rest. Makepeace moved like a puppet on twisted strings.

The head jerked up. The eyes were staring, lifeless.

And the mouth laughed.

Standing all around him in their circles, Lime, Jenkins, and the rest of the conspirators joined in the laughter. Their bodies seemed to ape their leader's; they twitched and wriggled too.

Nathaniel stood transfixed as the noise erupted around him. It was not kind or pleasant laughter, nor was it particularly malicious, greedy, triumphant, or cruel. It would have been less distressing if it had been. Instead the sound was hollow, discordant and utterly alien. It contained no recognizable human emotion.

In fact, it wasn't human at all.

24

It was the soup that saved me. Fish soup, it was, thick and creamy, filling the space of the silver tureen. At first, when I was pressed hard up against the silver walls, my essence dissolved rapidly away. But unexpectedly, things got better. Almost as soon as Faquarl left me, I lapsed into silver-induced unconsciousness, and that meant my crow guise fell apart. I subsided into an oily, fluid mass, not unlike dishwater, which floated within the soup, insulated from the silver by the liquid all around. I wouldn't say I was well off exactly, but my essence was now disintegrating a good deal slower than Faquarl would have expected.

Flickers of awareness came and went. One moment I thought I was far away in Egypt, talking with Ptolemy for the last time; the next I was watching fragments of cod and halibut drift by. Occasionally Faquarl's declaration echoed in my mind: *From tonight, we take revenge.* Sounded ominous for somebody. Well, they were welcome to it. I was tired. I'd had enough. I was glad to be somewhere quiet, dying on my own.

And then, all of a sudden, the soup was gone; the freezing taint of silver likewise. I was freed from the tureen.

Good news, unquestionably. Trouble was, I was no longer alone.

My master—yes, that was predictable, I could just about cope with him. But then, when I rotated gloopily to check out the scene, who did I see next? Let's just say that when your archenemy's trapped you in a place of certain death, and you've survived heroically against all the odds, the last thing you want to see, when you escape at last, is that same archenemy glaring down at you with an expression of annoyed distaste.[1] Not only that—you're weak, look like a jellyfish, and smell of clam chowder. In such circumstances the wind kind of goes out of your sense of triumph.

But that wasn't the half of it. As well as Mandrake and Faquarl, there were others in that room, and I arrived just in time to see exactly what they were.

Five gates to the Other Place were open and my essence trembled with the onrush of activity. Humans stood in five pentacles. On the first plane they seemed to stand alone. On the second and third, they were accompanied by billowing shadows of uncertain proportions; on the higher planes these shadows resolved themselves into hideous writhing masses, in which numerous tentacles, limbs, eyes, spines, and prongs kept uncomfortable proximity. As I watched, each mass compressed itself down and merged inside the waiting human. Soon even the most awkward leg or feeler was withdrawn from sight.

For the first few seconds the humans seemed to be in charge. They blinked, stirred, scratched their heads and, in the case of my old chum Jenkins, placed his glasses carefully on his nose. Only the fact that their auras now glowed with extraordinary strength indicated that anything odd had happened. I wasn't fooled, of course. From what I'd seen of Faquarl and his treatment of Mr. Hopkins, I didn't think the humans would be on top for long.

And sure enough, they weren't.

---

[1] Even a *different* archenemy would have been marginally better.

A vibration in the planes behind me: I swiveled like an amoeba on a turntable and saw another human, a short, round man wearing an excessively frilly shirt. And this is when I got *really* worried: his aura was *huge*—it radiated out like a sunburst, vibrating with otherworldly colors and a malevolent vitality. I didn't need to be told that *something* had already taken residence in him.

He spoke; I wasn't listening. All of a sudden, his aura pulsed, just once, as if a door to a furnace deep inside him had been opened wide. And the short, round man lost his mind.

For all Faquarl's protestations to the contrary, the notion of bonding with a human is a pretty obnoxious one. For one thing you don't know where it's been. For another, mixing your essence with horrid heavy earthy flesh is an aesthetic no-no; it makes you queasy just thinking about it. And then there's the small matter of control, of learning how to operate the human body. Faquarl had had some practice at this with Hopkins. But the newcomers had not.

As one, the six magicians—the short, round man and the others in the circles—laughed, twitched, shook, stumbled, jerked their arms every which way, and fell over.

I looked up at Faquarl. "Oooh, scary. The revenge of the djinn begins."

He scowled, bent to assist his leader and was distracted by a movement near the door. It was another old friend—the mercenary. His face, which normally showed all the weakness and soft emotion of a granite slab, was wide-eyed with shock. Perhaps it was the sight of the magicians lying on their backs like upturned wood lice, arms and legs wriggling helplessly. Perhaps it was the realization that he was unlikely to get a fee. Whichever it was, he decided to depart. He moved to the door—

Faquarl sprang through the air; he landed by the mercenary. A single shrug of the spindly arms—the mercenary was flung across the room to land heavily against a statue. He struggled to his feet and drew a knife; Faquarl was on him in a flash. There was a blur of movement, the sound of multiple blows being struck; it sounded like a brawl in a saucepan factory. The scimitar spun across the floor. The mercenary slumped against the flagstones, gasping for breath. Faquarl straightened, adjusting Mr. Hopkins's tie, and strode back to the center of the room.

I'd watched with grudging approval. "Nice one. I've been trying to do that for years."

Faquarl shrugged. "The secret is to avoid magic, Bartimaeus. The fellow's resilience is excessive; it almost seems to feed off our energies. It helps to be encased in a mortal body. And don't think *you're* going anywhere either. I'll tend to you shortly." He trotted after the body of the short, round man, which was now rolling across the floor, uttering odd barks and cries.

Maybe it was a vanity thing, but I was a bit tired of remaining as a pool of glop. With a tremendous effort, I drew myself up into a pyramid of slime. Was that any better? No. But I was too far gone to try anything sophisticated. The slime looked about for Mandrake. If things were bad for me, they weren't too sunny for him either.

To my astonishment I saw him standing at a table with Kitty Jones.[2]

Now *that* took me by surprise. I couldn't fit her into the equation at all. What was more, Mandrake was busily trying to untie some cords binding her hands. Weird! If anything, this was

---

[2] It was the Kitty Jones bit that was astonishing. Not the table. Though it was very nicely polished.

odder than the Faquarl/Hopkins combo thing. Neither looked in very good nick, but they were talking avidly, peering toward the door. The mercenary's misadventure had not been lost upon them—they made no hasty move.

Slowly, as slime will, I set off across the floor toward them. But I hadn't gone far when the whole floor shook, flagstones cracked, and statues toppled against the wall. It was as if an earthquake had struck, or a mother roc had landed overhead. In fact, the culprit was the short, round man, who still lay upon the ground. He had managed to roll onto his side, but was now attempting to rise using his legs alone—an effort that made him rotate slowly in a clockwise direction. Whatever was inside him was growing frustrated; a hand slapped petulantly against the stones—with every slap, it shook the room.

Faquarl had hastened over and was seeking to haul him upright. "Press the feet flat against the ground, Lord Nouda. There! Let me take your weight. That's it. Steady yourself. Now you can rise. Success! We are vertical!"

Nouda . . . The pyramid of slime tilted its apex. Had it heard correctly? Surely not. Surely not even the stupidest magician would have been so vain, so foolhardy, so plain *ignorant* as to invite a being like Nouda within them. Surely *everyone* knew his track record.[3]

It seemed not. Faquarl was ushering the twitching body forward like an invalid, encouraging it with soothing words. "Just a little farther, Lord Nouda. A chair awaits. Try moving the feet instead of the hands. That's it—you are doing splendidly."

From the man's sagging mouth came a great voice. "Who speaks?"

"It is I, Faquarl."

"Ah, Faquarl!" the great voice cried. "You did not lie. It is exactly as you said! What joy I feel! No pain! No compulsion! I smell the human world and all the juicy bodies waiting. Oh, but my coordination vexes me. *This* you did not prepare me for."

"It takes a little time, a little time," Faquarl crooned. "You will soon acclimatize."

"So many peculiar muscles—I cannot make out their use! Joints that swivel so far and no more, tendons running every which way! The dull sloshing of the blood—how strange for it to be my own! I wish to tear the flesh apart and drink it down."

"I would curb that impulse, sir," Faquarl said crisply. "You might find it inexpedient. There will be plenty of other flesh to enjoy, fear not. Now, here: sit on this throne. Rest awhile." He stood back; the short, round body of Makepeace sank upon the golden chair. Its head lolled sideways, its limbs twitched. On the other side of the table Kitty and Mandrake shrank away.

"Where are my troops, dear Faquarl?" the great voice said. "Where is my army that you promised?"

Faquarl cleared his throat. "Right in this room, sir. They, like

---

[3] Oh. Right. Well, it's like this. As I may have mentioned once or twice, there are five basic levels of spirit: imps (reprehensible), foliots (negligible), djinn (a fascinating class, with one or two absolute gems), afrits (overrated), and marids (dreadfully full of themselves). Above these levels exist more powerful entities, shadowy by nature, who are only occasionally summoned or even defined. Nouda was one such, and his rare appearances on Earth left a trail of blood and misery. Only the most unpleasant regimes employed him: the Assyrians (during the battle of Nineveh, when Nouda devoured a thousand Medes), Timur the Cruel (at the sack of Delhi, during which Nouda stacked the heads of prisoners to a height of 50 feet), the Aztecs (a regular engagement for Nouda this; in the end he discovered an ambiguity in Montezuma's summons—as a reward, Nouda ravaged Tenochtitlán and left it defenseless against the Spanish). He was a formidable customer, in other words, hungry and not sympathetically inclined.

you, are just . . . coming to terms with their new status." He looked over his shoulder. Of the five magicians, three were still lying on the floor, one was sitting up and grinning inanely, while the fifth had actually risen and was stumbling randomly about the hall, with arms rotating like a windmill and feet tripping on the rugs.

"Looking good," I said. "One day they may even manage to conquer this room."

Faquarl turned purposefully. "Ah, yes. I'd *forgotten* about you."

Eyes rotated blindly in the limp round head. "To whom do you speak, Faquarl?"

"A djinni. Pay no attention. He will not be with us long."

"What djinni is this? Is he a supporter of our plan?"

"It is Bartimaeus, a skeptic."

One arm rose, made a spasmodic movement that was probably meant to beckon. The great voice boomed. "Come here, djinni."

The pyramid of slime hesitated, but there was no help for it. I did not have the power to resist or flee. With all the verve of a wounded slug I squelched my way toward the golden chair, leaving an unpleasant trail behind. I bowed as best I could.

"It is an honor to meet a spirit of such strength and renown," I said. "I am but a wisp upon the wind; nevertheless, my power is yours."[4]

The limp head gave a jerk; with a wild swivel, the eyes discerned me. "Greater or less, we are all children of the Other Place. May your essence prosper."

---

[4] Note the absence of any jokes, sneers, or satirical content in these sentences. Despite Nouda's current indisposition, I didn't doubt that he could atomize me with a single glance. Best to be polite, I felt.

Faquarl stepped forward. "Well, I wouldn't go too far," he said. "Bartimaeus is as fickle as a moonbeam and as flighty as a colt. And sarky with it. I was about to—"

The great spirit waved a plump little hand in what was probably intended to be a mild gesture; it swung out wildly and cracked the tabletop in two. "Be gentle, Faquarl. After centuries of slavery *all* our personalities distort a little."

"I don't know," Faquarl said doubtfully. "He's pretty distorted."

"Even so. We do not fight among ourselves."

The pyramid of slime nodded eagerly. "That's right. Hear that, Faquarl? Listen and learn."

"Especially," the great voice continued, "when the djinni is as pitiable as this. Look at him! A baby's burp could disperse his essence. You have been poorly treated, Bartimaeus. Together we shall locate your oppressor and devour his flesh."

I glanced surreptitiously at my master, who was steadily backing away toward the door, shepherding Kitty with him.[5] "That's a generous offer, Lord Nouda."

Faquarl looked a little peeved. "The problem," he said, "is that Bartimaeus does not approve of our scheme. He has already referred to my occupation of this vessel"—he pointed to Hopkins's chest and paused dramatically—"as 'icky.'"

"Well, *look* at you," I snapped. "Trapped inside a horrid—" I controlled myself, conscious again of Nouda's fearsome aura. "To be honest, Lord Nouda, I am not sure exactly what your scheme *is*. Faquarl has not explained fully."

---

[5] His treatment of her seemed . . . well, let's put it this way: it was hard to tell exactly *how* it was self-serving. No doubt there were ulterior motives aplenty, if you only knew where to look for them.

"That is easily remedied, little djinni." Nouda seemed aware that his jaw muscles were somehow associated with speaking. As he spoke, the mouth opened and closed at random, sometimes wide, sometimes not; in any event, it was entirely out of sync with his words. "For centuries we have suffered pain at human hands. Now it is our turn to impose that pain on them. Thanks to Faquarl, and to the foolish magician whose body I now wear, our chance has come. We have entered the world on our own terms—and it is for us to decide what to do with it." His teeth clacked together twice in a hungry sort of way. *This* spasm looked quite intentional.

"But with all due respect," I ventured, "there are only seven of you, and—"

"The hard part has already been *done*, Bartimaeus." Faquarl smoothed down his coat. "By me. It has taken years to lure Makepeace to his doom. His ambition was always unwieldy, but it wasn't until the appearance of Honorius in Gladstone's bones that I saw how best to use it. Makepeace's weakness was his vainglorious desire for innovation, for the reckless creative act. After Honorius, he and Hopkins became interested in summoning a spirit into a living body. By subtle insinuations, I encouraged them. In due course Hopkins volunteered for the experiment, and *I* was the djinni summoned. After that, things were easy. I destroyed Hopkins's mind but concealed this from Makepeace. Now he has also sacrificed himself and several of his friends."

"There are seven of us now," Nouda said, "but we can soon get reinforcements. All we need are more human vessels."

"And thanks to Makepeace we have plenty," Faquarl added.

The great entity seemed surprised. "How so?"

"The entire government lies in a nearby chamber, gagged

and bound and ready. You have devoured the magician's memory, Lord Nouda. You would not recall."

Nouda gave a wild laugh that knocked over a nearby chair. "True—there is no point sharing these brains . . . So—all is well! Our essences are protected! We have no bonds! Soon we shall roam in hundreds about the world and feed, feed, feed upon its people!"

Well, I suppose I didn't think it was going to be simple tourism. I was watching Mandrake and Kitty; they were almost at the door. "One question," I said. "When all the killing's done, how will you get back?"

"Back?" Nouda said.

Faquarl echoed him. "What do you mean, *back*?"

"Well . . ." The pyramid of slime attempted a shrug, with scant success. "Back to the Other Place. When you've had enough of it here."

"That is not part of the plan, little djinni." Nouda's head rotated toward me in a sudden rush. "The world is big. It is varied. It is ours now."

"But—"

"Our hatred has grown so long, it cannot be healed even in the Other Place. Think of your own experiences. For you too it must be so." A sudden outcry. Nouda jerked confusedly in his chair, splitting the back panel down its center. "What disturbance is this?"

Faquarl grinned. "Bartimaeus's master, I believe."

Shouts, screams . . . Sure enough, with the incompetence that was his trademark, Mandrake hadn't reached the door. Instead he and Kitty had been apprehended by the body of Jenkins, which was beginning to move with some coordination. Evidently the spirit inside it was a fast learner.

Nouda's voice held interest. "Bring him here."

It took a while; Jenkins's legs were not yet bending at the knees. But finally two disheveled humans stood before the golden chair, Jenkins's hands around their necks. Both Mandrake and Kitty looked haggard and defeated. Their shoulders slumped, their clothes were ripped; Kitty's coat had been burned right through. Unnoticed, the pyramid of slime gave a small, short sigh.

Nouda experimented with a ghastly, half-baked smile; he twitched and wriggled excitedly where he sat. "Meat! I smell it! What a blissful flavor."

A light of defiance glimmered in Mandrake's eyes. "Bartimaeus," he croaked, "I am still your master. I order you to help us now."

Faquarl and Nouda laughed heartily at this; I did not. "That time is past," I said. "You would do well to keep silent."

"I order you—"

A deep feminine voice emerged from Jenkins's mouth. "Is that *you*, Bartimaeus?"

The slime gave a start. "Naeryan! Haven't seen you since Constantinople!"

"*Listen* to me! I order—"

"What's with the slime, Bartimaeus? You're looking peaky."

"Yeah, been better. How about you, though? Ginger hair, glasses, just two legs . . . bit of a comedown, isn't it?"[6]

"I order you to . . . to . . ." Mandrake's head dropped. He said no more.

---

[6] This was true: Naeryan's normal form involved an inky blue-black torso, three piercing eyes placed at random intervals, and a multitude of spiderlike limbs. Okay, that guise was an acquired taste, but it was a lot more dignified than *Jenkins*.

"It's worth it, Bartimaeus!" Naeryan said. "You can't imagine what it's like. The body is dreary, but it gives such freedom! Will you join us?"

"Yes!" Nouda's great voice put in. "Join us! We shall find you an appropriate magician. We will force him to summon you forthwith."

The slime drew itself as tall as it could. "My thanks to you both. The offer is courteous and kind. But I fear I must decline. I have had enough of this world, and everything in it. My essence hurts me; my only wish is to return to the peace of the Other Place as fast as I can."

Nouda seemed a little put out. "This is an odd decision."

Faquarl spoke eagerly. "It is as I said—Bartimaeus is both fickle and perverse! He should be destroyed with a Spasm!"

A great growl came from Makepeace's throat; the air quivered with heat haze. The clothes on Faquarl's body crackled into flame. Nouda sucked the air back in. The flames went out. Makepeace's eyes glittered.[7] "Beware, Faquarl," the great voice said, "lest your good advice becomes officious. The djinni is free to go."

The slime bowed. "My gratitude is undying, Lord Nouda. If it pleases you to hear me further, I have one last request to make."

"On this triumphant day," Nouda said, "when my earthly reign begins, I shall grant the wishes of even the weakest, most insignificant of my fellow spirits. And that's you, without a

---

[7] Somewhere deep inside those eyes I glimpsed the fearful energies of the Other Place, swirling, swirling. I couldn't help but wonder how long the mortal body would survive the strain of such an inhabitant.

doubt. I shall permit your request, if it lies within my power. Speak on."

The slime bowed lower still. "Spare the lives of these two humans, Lord Nouda. The world, as you say, is big. There are many others to devour. Spare these."

That got a bit of a reaction. Faquarl gave a snort of disgust, Naeryan tutted with surprise. As for Nouda, he clashed his teeth together with such force that several cherubs fell off his chair. His eyes flashed fire, his fingers gouged the tabletop like butter. I'd say he wasn't overly pleased. "I have given my word, djinni, and I cannot break it," the great voice said. "But this is ill done. I need some ballast in my belly. I was looking forward to these two, particularly the girl. The boy looks sour and sinewy—I believe his flesh would taste like candle wax—but she is edible beyond doubt. And you would have me spare them! It seems that Faquarl was right. You *are* perverse."

That was pretty rich coming from someone who had purposefully trapped himself within the human world, but I didn't argue. I just bowed lower.

"Tcha!" Nouda was working himself into a strop; with sudden rough coordination, Makepeace's body half rose from his seat. "To have a bond with a human . . . Ah, you are a corruption! A traitor! I itch to destroy you. . . . But no, I cannot break my promise. Go from here! Be gone from my sight!"

I did not show my anger. "We *do* have a bond of sorts," I said quietly, "but for the present there are limits to it. Which is why I take my leave." The pyramid of slime rotated to face Mandrake, who had been listening, white-faced. "Dismiss me."

It took him several seconds to respond, and only then when Kitty nudged him sharply. When he spoke, he stumbled three times and had to begin again. His voice never rose above a whisper; he did not look in my direction. By contrast—as I rose, flickered, faded, vanished—Kitty never took her eyes off me.

My last sight was of them cowering together, two hunched and fragile forms, alone among the djinn. What did I feel? Nothing. I'd done what I could. Nouda's word was his bond; he would spare their lives. Beyond that, it wasn't my business what happened to them. I was getting out, and about time too. I was lucky to escape with my life.

Yes, I'd done what I could. I didn't need to think about it any more. I was free.

Free.

Look, even at full strength I'd *still* have been a speck of insignificance compared to Nouda. What else could I have done?

25

For Kitty, the moments following Bartimaeus's departure were the bleakest and most terrible of all. The last fragment of hope departed, and with it, the focus of her captors immediately changed. Hopkins's head turned; in the golden chair, the glassy eyes of Makepeace rolled around to stare at her. She felt the ferocity of the demons' gazes, of the cold intelligences hidden behind the waxy faces. She knew what it was to be a lump of meat upon a butcher's slab.

The great demon seemed to be gaining control of his human body—its twitches and shaking had diminished; it sprawled quietly across the chair. Elsewhere in the room, by a similar gradual process, the bodies of the conspirators had risen to their feet, and in a spirit of experimentation were hobbling about the room in little jerks and scampers. Their arms swung, they jumped, crouched, spun on the spot. Their mouths were open: the room was full of the gabble of languages, of triumphant laughter, and animal cries. Kitty shuddered; it was a parody both of everything that was human *and* of the dignity she had previously observed in spirits—even the most grotesque.

At her back the demon in Jenkins's body spoke. She did not understand the words. Hopkins nodded, replied, turned to the great demon sitting in the chair. A long conversation ensued. Kitty and Mandrake stood dead still, waiting.

Then Hopkins's body moved; the suddenness made Kitty jolt with fear. It turned to them and beckoned. With stiff movements and rigid limbs they followed it across the hall, among the gamboling demons, past the bearded man crouching silently in a corner, and out into the corridor. They took the passage to the left, around numerous twists and turns, above a broad stone staircase leading underground, into an area of many doors. Kitty thought to hear moaning coming from behind the first they passed. The demon continued on; in due course he halted, flung open a door, and gestured for them to enter. It was an empty, windowless room, lit by a single electric light.

The demon's voice was harsh. "Thanks to Lord Nouda's unbreakable oath, we are obliged to be merciful. You"—it indicated Kitty—"are not a magician, so you shall become an ordinary servant. However, *you*"—this to Mandrake—"are due a greater honor. You shall become a host to one of our number before dawn. Do not look so glum. Think of all the spirits you have enslaved! This judgment upon you has a pleasant symmetry. Until then you shall remain here. It is not seemly for you to observe us in our current state." The door closed, a key turned. Footsteps receded.

Kitty could feel her body shaking with suppressed shock and fear. She bit her lip, forced the feeling down. No good— they hadn't time for that. She looked at Mandrake, and to her surprise saw flecks of tears in the corners of his eyes. Perhaps, like her, he was almost overwhelmed. He was speaking quietly, as if to himself: "Demons have entered the world . . . without restraint. It is a catastrophe. . . ."

No. They hadn't *time* for that. "A catastrophe?" she said. "Funny, the way *I* see it, things are looking up."

"How can you say—?"

"The demons plan to use me as a slave. Not good, true. But half an hour ago your friend the fat magician was going to have me *killed*. I look on that as a marked improvement."

John Mandrake blew out his cheeks. "Makepeace was *not* my friend. He was insane, a reckless, arrogant madman. And I wouldn't get too optimistic," he went on dully. "*Nouda* may have promised not to kill you, but that doesn't mean one of the others won't. I'm surprised they haven't spotted that. It's the kind of ambiguity they normally pounce on. Yes, they'll eat you soon enough, take it from me."

Icy fury surged through Kitty; she stepped forward and slapped Mandrake hard. He reeled back in shock, clutching his face. "What was *that* for?"

"What *for*?" Kitty shouted. "For everything! For abducting me, for getting me into this mess! For being a member of the stupid government! For the war! For being a magician! For enslaving demons and spurring them to invade our world! For being a complete and utter idiot!" She took a breath. "*And* for what you just said. For being defeatist now. Especially that. I *don't intend* to die."

She halted, but kept him speared squarely on her gaze. He blinked, ran a hand through his stubbled hair, looked away, looked back at her. She stared at him.

"All right," he said. "I'm sorry. Sorry for what I've done to you—for what I did before, and now. I should have left you alone. I regret I've got you into this. But what's the point of saying it? It's all irrelevant. The demons are loosed upon the world and we're powerless to stop them, so whether you're here or back in that pub won't make much difference in the long run."

Kitty shook her head. "You're wrong. Your apology isn't irrelevant and you're a fool if you can't see it. I'm grateful that you stopped Makepeace from having me killed. Now stop being such a wet blanket and try to think of something to do."

He looked at her. "Hold on—was there a thanks buried in that pile of invective?"

She pursed her lips. "If so, it was a very small one. Now— you're a magician. But you've not got any slaves to hand? Not even any imps?"

"No. All my slaves are dead. Except Bartimaeus. And *he* left us."

"*He* saved our lives."

Mandrake sighed. "Yes." He looked at Kitty intently. "And I don't think he did it for *me*. Why—?" His eyes widened suddenly. "Hold on, I *do* have this." He fished in his jacket and produced a metal disc. "You might recall it."

Kitty's heart, having leaped with hope, descended leadenly. "Oh. Your scrying glass."

"Yes. The imp within can observe and speak to third parties, but it cannot act. It cannot free us, or the other magicians—" He broke off, thinking hard.

"Observation might be useful . . ." Kitty couldn't hide her doubt. "Providing you can trust what it says. It's a slave. Why should it speak truthfully after all its ill treatment?"

"Compared to most, I am a kind and sensitive master. I never—" He made an impatient noise. "Oh, this is ridiculous. Bickering will get us nowhere. Let's see what the demons are doing."

He raised the disc and waved a hand across its surface. Kitty moved closer, fascinated despite herself. The polished bronze surface seemed to ripple; a round shape formed, hazy and remote, as if deep down underwater. It swelled, drew close, became a sweet little baby's face, contorted into an expression of the purest woe.

"Not again, master!" the baby whimpered. "I beg you! Do

not punish me again with the cruel Stipples or the Infernal Coals! I will do my best, I swear! Ah, but I must accept your harsh justice, your stern discipline. What choice have I, alas . . . ?" It finished with a pathetic, lingering sniffle.

Mandrake glanced furtively at Kitty. "So . . ." she said grimly. "'A kind and sensitive master . . .'"

"Ah! No! He exaggerates! He excels in melodrama!"

"That poor, innocent little babe—"

"Do not be misled. He is a hellish, vile—oh, what's the use? Imp! In a hall close to here you will find several potent entities, masquerading in the bodies of men and women. What are they doing? Observe and do not linger, or they will seize you and place you on a griddle. Next, and still within this building, locate the government magicians. Are they alive or dead? What condition are they in? Could we communicate with them? Finally observe the situation on the Whitehall streets. Are government forces anywhere to be seen? That is enough. Be off with you."

A plaintive cry; the disc went blank. Kitty shook her head sourly. "How can you claim *any* moral authority, when you keep such a thing imprisoned? It's pure hypocrisy."

Mandrake scowled. "Never mind that now. You wanted me to act. I'm acting." There was a new urgency about him; he paced the room. "The demons are formidable, particularly Nouda . . . it is a marid, or stronger. Once it learns to control the body, its power will be terrible. How can we oppose it? If the government were freed, we might summon enough djinn to destroy it But the government is captive. So what remains?" He glanced at the scrying glass; all was still within it. "There *is* one possibility," he went on, "but the odds against it are excessive."

"What?"

"Gladstone's Staff is in this building. It would be a match for Nouda. But it is magically guarded. I'd have to find a way to get to it."

"And evade Nouda first," Kitty said.

"And then there's the little question of whether I'd have the strength to use it."

"Yes. You didn't last time."

"All *right*. I know. I *am* stronger than then. But I'm also tired." He took up the disc again. "Where *is* that imp?"

"Probably dead in a ditch from ill treatment. Mandrake," Kitty said, "do you know of the magician Ptolemaeus?"

He frowned. "Of course. But how have you—?"

"And his *Apocrypha*? You have heard of that?"

"Yes, yes. It is on my shelf. So—"

"What is Ptolemy's Gate?"

He regarded her blankly. "Ptolemy's Gate? Kitty, that is a question for scholars and magicians, hardly for commoners. Why do you ask?"

"Simple," she said. "Because I can't read ancient Greek." She put her hand in her tattered coat and drew out Mr. Button's book. "If I could, I'd have found out for myself. You, I assume, with all your privileges, can and have. What is this Gate? How does one get to the Other Place? And stop asking *me* questions; we haven't time."

Mandrake reached out and took the small, slim volume, slightly scorched where the Inferno had struck. Handing her the blank broze disc, he opened the book with gentle fingers and flipped the pages slowly at random, eyes scanning the columns. He shrugged. "A work of fiction; charmingly idealistic in some of its conceits, if not wrongheaded. Some of its statements . . . well, Ptolemy's Gate is a supposed method of reversing the normal summoning process, whereby the magician, or some element, spirit or sentience thereof, withdraws for a time to the particular remoteness where demons reside; the author—by reputation this was the Alexandrine, Ptolemaeus—claims to have done it himself, though *why* he should risk such a terrifying ordeal is far from clear. Good enough for you? Oh, sorry—that's a question."

"No. It's not good enough. What's the exact formula? Does he give it?"

Mandrake clapped his head in irritation. "Kitty! Have you gone quite mad? We have more important things to—"

"Just *tell* me!" She started toward him, fists clenched.

Mandrake veered back; as he did so, the scrying glass throbbed and hummed in Kitty's hands. The baby's face returned, looking frightened and out of breath. For a few seconds it did not speak, but only wheezed and puffed immoderately. Kitty shook her head in pity. "Your slave's back. He's practically dead, poor little mite."

The baby belched loudly, then spoke in a hoarse whisper. "Who's this trollop?"

With pointed gallantry, Mandrake took the disc from her hands. "Just tell us what you saw."

"It wasn't a pretty sight, boss." The baby picked its nose with an agitated finger. "Am I right in thinking this will be the last job you give me? On account of the fact that you're locked in a cell and surrounded by rampant demons preparing to take the vengeance that they've craved for thousands of years? Just wondering."

Kitty ground her teeth with impatience. Mandrake glanced at her. "What do you think? The Infernal Coals?"

354

"Anything."

The baby gave an anxious croak and spoke at speed: "I followed your orders to the letter; you can have no complaint. First, the great spirits. Ah—they are powerful; the planes warp with their passing. There are seven; all wear actual human bodies, concealing their true forms. At their center sits Nouda; he issues rapid commands. The others scutter to do his bidding. In neighboring chambers the corpses of Whitehall bureaucrats lie like skittles. From a side room—"

Mandrake interrupted the desperate flow. "Wait. How do the demons move? Are they comfortable in their hosts?"

"For the most part, no. They move as if with broken limbs. But yet they sing with the joy of freedom. Would that I could join them," the baby said wistfully. "I would set your bones upon a metal platter and make percussive music. You want more?"

"Descriptions, yes. Empty threats, no."

"From a side room comes a steady herd of bedraggled humans. Their arms are bound, their mouths stopped with wax and linen. The great spirits herd them like goats toward a precipice. One by one, in the center of the hall, their mouths are freed and they stand before Lord Nouda's chair. He gives them an ultimatum."

"These humans," Mandrake said. "Describe them."

The baby sniffed. "Tricky . . . Could you individuate a tribe of rabbits?" It considered. "Several lacked chins, while others boasted several."

Kitty and Mandrake exchanged a glance. "It is the government."

"Nouda gives each a choice. Following a certain formula, they must summon a spirit into themselves. The djinni Faquarl stands by Nouda's chair, holding a weighty tome: he gives them the name to call. If they agree, the procedure is carried out. If not, they are to be destroyed."

Mandrake bit his lip. "What is the general consensus?"

"So far, each politician has agreed to surrender his or her mind. They prefer to accept the vilest humiliation rather than a more honorable way out."

Kitty kicked out at the wall. "Nouda isn't wasting time. He's creating his army."

"And by doing so, removing the only people capable of resisting him," Mandrake said. "Imp, what is the situation elsewhere?"

The baby shrugged. "It depends on your point of view. From my perspective the outlook is rosy. Few humans remain alive within this building. Beyond, in central London, great gatherings of commoners assemble, emboldened by the lack of response from the government. In Whitehall, two battalions of werewolves maintain ragged defense of the Parliament zone. A few magicians try frantically to communicate with their leaders, but to no avail."

"Ha! Some magicians are still in action!" Mandrake nodded eagerly. "The lower orders did not attend the play. Perhaps they can aid us. . . . What demons do they use?"

"A hotchpotch of foliots that cower behind the dustbins as the commoners march by."

Mandrake groaned. "Hopeless. Imp, your news is poor, but you have done well." He made a magnanimous gesture. "If I survive, you shall have your freedom."

"That's me here for all eternity then." The disc went blank.

"So, there will be no outside help," the magician said slowly. "It will have to be the Staff, if I can reach it. *If* I can get it to work . . ."

Kitty touched his arm. "You were telling me about Ptolemy's Gate. What's the exact method? Can it be easily done?"

He tore himself away, eyes angry and bewildered. "*Why* do you persist in this?"

"Ptolemy used the Gate to reach out to the djinn—it was a gesture of reconciliation, of good faith. We need to do this, and fast, if we're to get some help."

"Get some——? Oh dear." Mandrake spoke as if to a simple child. "Kitty, the demons are our *enemies*. They have been for millennia. True, their powers are useful, but they are wicked things, and will hurt us if they can. As proved this very night! Given half a chance, they are invading!"

"*Some* are invading," Kitty said. "But not all. Bartimaeus did not agree to stay."

"So what? Bartimaeus is nothing! Nothing but a middling djinni, frayed to a thread, whom I kept here too long."

"Even so, he has loyalty to us. Certainly to me. Maybe even you."

The magician shook his head. "Rubbish. His loyalty changes with every summoning. Just days ago he served another master, doubtless one of my rivals. But this is beside the point. To get the Staff—"

"I summoned him."

"—I will need to get away. You must cause a distract—hold on. What?"

"*I* summoned him."

Mandrake's eyes seemed to glaze; he swayed where he stood. His mouth made odd popping noises like a stranded fish. "But . . . but you're a—"

"Yes," Kitty cried. "I'm a commoner. Well done. But that

doesn't mean much anymore, does it? Look around you. Everything's turning upside down: magicians have destroyed the government; demons are willingly being summoned by their own kind; commoners are taking control of the streets. The old certainties are falling apart, Mandrake, and only those who adapt are going to prevail. *I* intend to. What about you?" She indicated the door. "Any moment now Faquarl's going to walk back in and lead you before Nouda. Do you want to keep quibbling until then? Yes, I learned a little of your art. I summoned Bartimaeus. I wanted an alliance with him, but he rejected it because I couldn't trust him. He's skeptical about us, you see. Only one person in his past has treated him with absolute trust, and that was Ptolemaeus."

Mandrake's eyes bulged. "What? Not the same Ptolemy that—"

"The very same. He used the Gate, he made the gesture. Why do you think Bartimaeus still wears his form? Oh, you hadn't realized? All those years of training and you can't see what's right in front of your eyes." She shook her head sadly. "When I summoned him," she went on, "Bartimaeus told me that he would have done anything for Ptolemy because of the gesture he made. '*There was no limit to our bond.*' That's how he put it. And you heard what he said just now, when he left?"

A dozen emotions had washed across the magician's face, leaving it smooth, blank, chastened. He shook his head. "I didn't hear."

"He said he had a bond with *us* too, but that there were 'limits' to it. That's what he told Nouda. And he was looking at me as he went. Don't you see? If I can follow him . . ." She was gazing beyond Mandrake now, eyes sparkling. "I know that I need to call Bartimaeus's name as part of the incantation, but beyond that I haven't a clue. Until you tell me what's in the book." She smiled at him.

The magician took a slow, deep breath. Then he opened the book and skimmed to a certain page. For a moment he read in silence. When he spoke, his voice was flat. "The procedure is simplicity itself. The magician reclines in a pentacle—he must sit, or lie, since his body will collapse at the moment of transfer. No candles or specific runes are required; indeed such barriers are kept to a minimum to speed the return of the magician to his body. Ptolemy suggests breaking the circle symbolically to help this process. . . . He also recommends holding something iron—such as an ankh—to keep out evil influences; that, or one of the normal herbs—rosemary or suchlike. Okay, well, the magician closes his eyes and shuts his mind to all outside stimuli; then he inverts the basic summoning. His own true name is substituted for the demon's one, and all directions are reversed: 'to go' instead of 'to come' and so forth. Finally the name of a 'benevolent' demon—Ptolemy calls it the 'sponsor'—is called three times. The attention of this demon is necessary for an opening to be made. If all goes well, the magician separates from himself, the Gate opens, and he passes through. Ptolemy does not give details of how or where." He looked up. "Satisfied?"

Kitty sniffed. "I like your assumption that the magician must be male."

"Look, I've told you the method. Listen, Kitty"—Mandrake cleared his throat—"I'm impressed with your initiative and bravery, really I am, but this is just impossible. Why do you suppose no one has followed in Ptolemy's footsteps? The Other Place is alien and terrible, a region removed from normal physical laws. It would harm you, maybe kill you. And

Bartimaeus—even if you survived, even if you found him, even if he agreed to somehow help you—is just a djinni. His power is negligible compared to Nouda's. Your idea is noble, but the chances of success are absolutely minute." He coughed, and looked away. "Sorry."

"That's all right." Kitty considered. "Your plan—the Staff. What are the chances of success there, would you say?"

"Oh, I'd say they were . . ." He caught her eye, hesitated. "Absolutely minute."

She grinned. "Exactly. And we probably won't get away from Nouda in the first place. But if we do . . ."

"We both do what we can." He smiled at her then, for the first time. "Well, if you *do* try, I wish you luck."

"Good luck to you too, Mr. Mandrake."

A rattle of a key, a metal screeching: the bolt beyond the door being drawn.

"You don't need to call me that," he said.

"It's your name."

"No. My name is Nathaniel."

Without ceremony, the door was flung aside. Kitty and the magician stepped back; a figure stepped through, black-coated, implacable. The mercenary gave a flinty smile.

"Your turn," he said.

26

Curiously, Nathaniel's immediate sensation was one of relief. The mercenary, at least, was human. He spoke quickly. "You are alone?"

The bearded man stood in the doorway and regarded him steadily with his pale blue eyes. He did not reply. Nathaniel took this as a yes. "Good," he said. "Then we have a chance. We must forget our differences and escape together."

The mercenary remained silent. Nathaniel plowed on. "The demons are still slow and awkward. We will be able to slip out and organize defenses. I am a notable magician; somewhere near here other ministers lie bound—if we can release them we will be able to fight the invaders. Your, er, skills will be invaluable in the battles to come. Past murders and other atrocities will be discounted, I'm sure. There may even be a reward for your service. Come, sir—what do you say?"

The mercenary gave a little smile. Nathaniel beamed back. "Lord Nouda," the mercenary said, "is waiting for you. We would do well not to be late." He stepped into the room; grasping Nathaniel and Kitty by the arms, he led them to the door.

"Are you mad?" Kitty cried. "The demons threaten us all, and you *willingly* serve them?"

At the doorway the mercenary paused. "Not willingly," he said in his deep, soft voice. "But I must be realistic. The demons' power waxes every moment. Before dawn all London will be in flames and those who oppose them will be dead. *I* wish to survive."

Nathaniel squirmed in the iron grip. "The odds are against us, but we *can* prevail. Reconsider, before it is too late!"

The bearded face bent close; the teeth were bared. "*You* have not seen what I have seen. Quentin Makepeace's body sits on the golden chair, hands clasped upon the plumpness of his belly. His face is smiling, smiling. One by one the magicians of your precious government are brought before him. Some he allows to pass—they go to the pentacle to receive a demon. To others he takes a liking. He beckons them. They approach his chair, helpless as rabbits; he leans forward . . ." The mercenary's jaw closed with a snap; Kitty and Nathaniel flinched. "Afterward he wipes his waistcoat and sits back smiling. And the demons around him howl like wolves."

Nathaniel swallowed. "Not pleasant. Even so, with those boots of yours, surely you could—"

"I see all seven planes," the mercenary said. "I see the power in that room. It would be suicidal to resist it. Besides, with power comes profit. The demons require human helpers; there is much here they do not understand. They have offered me wealth if I serve them, and this girl has that option too. Who knows, by cooperating with Lord Nouda, she and I may flourish. . . ." He reached out his gloved hand and touched Kitty's neck. She recoiled from him with an oath. Blind anger surged inside Nathaniel, but he fought it down.

The mercenary spoke no more. Gloved hands grasped their collars; firmly, but without undue roughness, they were guided out of the door and up the corridor. In the distance they heard a great gabbling and babbling, a cacophony of shrieks and yells—the gathering sound of pandemonium.

Nathaniel was quite calm. So black was the outlook now that fear had become redundant. The worst was upon them, death was all but inevitable, yet he faced it without anxiety. His final conversation with Kitty had lit a fire within him—to Nathaniel it seemed she had burned away all his weaker emotions. His head still spun with her revelations of Bartimaeus's past, but it was her own example that inspired him as the crisis approached. It scarcely mattered that she had pinned her hopes on Ptolemy's Gate—a mirage, a phantom, a fairy tale that all sensible magicians had long ignored—it was the look in her eyes as she talked of it that fascinated him. Excitement had shone there, and wonder, and belief—sensations that Nathaniel had almost forgotten. Now, at the last, she had reminded him, and he was grateful. He felt cleansed, almost eager for what was to come. He glanced across; her face was pale, but set. He hoped he would not weaken in front of her.

His eyes flickered from side to side as they went, taking in the familiar surroundings of the Whitehall passages, the oil paintings, the plaster busts sitting in their niches, the paneled walls and imp-light. They passed the stairs that led to the vaults and, distantly, the Staff; instinctively, Nathaniel flinched toward it. The grip on his collar tightened. They rounded the final corner.

"Here," the mercenary whispered. "Let this sight put an end to your dreams."

During their absence the demons had been busy. The Hall of Statues, for a hundred years the sedate meeting place of the Council, had been transformed by its new rulers. Everywhere was movement, noise, uncoordinated hubbub. Nathaniel's senses were briefly overwhelmed.

The round table and its chairs had been swept from the center of the room. The table now rested against the far wall; upon it sat the golden chair. Here lolled Nouda, the great demon, in an attitude of temporary repletion. One leg dangled over a chair arm, the other extended before him. Makepeace's shirt had been untucked—it hung loose about the swollen stomach. The eyes were glazed; the mouth unnaturally stretched—it wore a tired smile, as of one who has lately completed a pleasant meal. A few odd rags and clothes lay on the tabletop around him.

Below the table, upon a redwood chair, the demon Faquarl stood cloaked in Mr. Hopkins's body. It was he who orchestrated events: he held a book open in his hands and uttered crisp orders to the company below.

The bodies of the five original conspirators—Nathaniel recognized Lime, Jenkins, and the scrawny Withers—were now operated by their demons with some efficiency. True, there were still plenty of trips and stumbles, the legs and arms swinging with abrupt staccato movements, but they no longer fell or collided with the wall. This had enabled them to venture out of the room and—as the scrying-glass imp had reported—bring forth selected members of the government from their cells. Batch by batch, great and small, the magicians were being transformed.

To the left, Lime and Withers stood watchful guard over a huddle of waiting prisoners, perhaps twenty in number, their hands still bound. Not far away, in a pentacle close to Nouda's throne, one of these prisoners had been untied; now she stood free, uttering the fatal summons in a quavering voice. She was a woman unknown to Nathaniel, presumably from another department. As he watched, she stiffened and shook. The air about her shimmered as the arriving demon took possession. Faquarl made a gesture; the demon Naeryan, dressed in

Jenkins's body, led her gently to the far corner of the hall, to join—

The hairs prickled on Nathaniel's head. There they were— more than two dozen magicians from every level of the government, rolling, twitching, laughing, falling, as their masters explored their limitations. Occasional bursts of magical energy exploded against the walls; the air was full of the murmuring of alien tongues, strange cries of joy and pain. And what was that among them, head twitching, hands rising and falling like a puppet's, florid face gleaming and vacuous? Nathaniel recoiled.

Rupert Devereaux, the Prime Minister . . .

Despite everything that had occurred, despite his awakening abhorrence of what the man had been and represented, Nathaniel felt tears pricking at his eyes. For an instant he was twelve years old again, caught up in the swirl of Westminster Hall, seeing Devereaux for the first time—dazzling, charming, everything *he* aspired to be. . . .

Devereaux's body gave a caper, collided with another, and collapsed in a writhing heap. Nathaniel was sick with horror; he felt his knees sag.

"Up with you!" The mercenary gave him a cursory shove. "Join the line."

"Wait!" Nathaniel half turned. "Kitty—"

"She does not share your destiny, for which you may be thankful."

Nathaniel stared across at Kitty, who for a single moment caught his gaze; then he was propeled savagely toward the crowd of prisoners. Lime's body turned, caught sight of him; he saw green lights far off behind the eyes. A harsh voice, like the snapping of twigs, emerged from the loose mouth: "Faquarl! Here is Bartimaeus's friend! You want him next?"

"Certainly I do, Gaspar. He can jump the queue. He shall come after *this* sour creature. Lord Nouda, I assume you have no wish to taste this one."

The great voice rumbled from on high. "I have seen better flesh on a pharaoh's corpse. When she turns sideways, she all but disappears. Process her and be done."

Nathaniel's eyes were fixed on the figure in the pentacle. Stick-thin, white hair disheveled, his old master Jessica Whitwell stood staring up toward the throne. The demon in Withers's body had just removed her bonds; her hands were knotted fists.

"Very well." Faquarl consulted his book. "Number twenty-eight. Let me see. I have chosen the afrit Mormel for you. You should be honored. He is a noble spirit."

Ms. Whitwell stared up at the figure on the throne. "What is your plan for us?"

"Do not think to address the great Nouda!" Faquarl cried. "You and your kind have enslaved us for centuries, showing no consideration. What do you *think* we plan? This revenge has been incubated for five thousand years! No portion of the world will be safe from us."

Ms. Whitwell laughed contemptuously. "I think you are overoptimistic. Look at you all, trapped in awkward bodies, barely able to walk in a straight line."

"Our inconveniences are only temporary," Faquarl said. "Yours shall be permanent. Begin the summons."

Jessica Whitwell spoke quietly. "To all the others you have given a choice. You have not asked me for mine."

Faquarl lowered his book; his eyes were narrowed. "Well, I assume, like all the other wretches, you prefer life to death, even if it is life worked through another."

"You assume wrongly."

Ms. Whitwell raised her hands and made an ornate sign; she shouted out two words. A burst of yellow light, a cloud of brimstone—her afrit, wearing the form of an uneasy-looking grizzly bear—appeared above her head. Whitwell screamed an order; a shimmering blue Shield rose up around her body. The afrit sent a Detonation at the startled Faquarl: it struck him head-on, knocking him off his chair and halfway through the wall.

The demons in the bodies of the conspirators set up a clamor. Naeryan raised a finger: from Jenkins's hand a lance of emerald light stabbed at Whitwell. The Shield absorbed it; Whitwell was already turning, running for the exit. The demon Gaspar, encased in the body of Lime, leaped forward to intercept her; Nathaniel stretched out a boot; the demon tripped, was unable to right itself, fell crashing to the ground.

Nathaniel turned and ran; above his head the bear afrit sent successive Detonations toward the golden throne.

Where was Kitty? There! But the mercenary held her by the arm. She struggled, kicked, could not break free.

Nathaniel sped toward her—

The floor shook; he stumbled, fell—and, for a moment, looked behind him.

The body in the golden chair had moved. It was surrounded by a nimbus of pale fire. Energies crackled from its fingers; its eyes were silver notches in the darkened face. One hand was outstretched. The power that came from it—arcing out in five looping bolts, one from each finger—made statues fall and mortar tumble from the ceiling. The bolts were randomly directed: two plunged harmlessly into the floor; one leaped among the crowd of newly summoned demons, destroying several human bodies. The fourth struck Whitwell's Shield, broke it into shards and cut straight through her back, killing her instantly. The bear afrit vanished. She fell midstride, facedown upon the flagstones.

The fifth bolt burst the floor at the mercenary's feet: he was blown one way, Kitty Jones the other.

Nathaniel was on his feet. "Kitty!"

His voice was drowned out by assorted howls, roars, bays, and trumpetings from the demons in the hall. Confused and panic-stricken, they willed their human carriers in every direction, legs working oddly, knees too high, elbows out. They collided with each other, let fly random Detonations and Infernos. Among them stumbled a few magicians who had yet to be processed, arms still tied, mouths gagged, eyes wide and staring. The room was filled with smoke, lights, and rushing forms.

Amid the tumult Nathaniel came to the place where Kitty Jones had fallen. She was nowhere to be seen. He flinched as a magical pulse passed above his head, and looked round a final time. No, she had gone.

Without further hesitation he ducked between two flailing demons and made for the double doors. As he left the Hall of Statues, he could hear Faquarl's voice rising above the commotion. "Friends, calm down! Calm down! The crisis is over! We must resume the summonings. Calm down. . . ."

It took Nathaniel less than a minute to negotiate the corridors and arrive at the stairs to the Whitehall vaults. Abandoning all caution, he leaped over the balustrade and careered down the staircase two steps at a time. Down, down . . . the air grew colder, all sound from above faded clean away; Nathaniel heard nothing now but the gasping of his breath.

At the end of the third flight the steps opened out into the entrance vault. Two days before—or was it three?—he had come here as Information Minister and been shown the treasure room by a supercilious clerk. It seemed another life. Now the clerk's desk was empty. It gave signs of being abandoned in a hurry; papers were scattered upon it, a pen lay on the floor.

At the end of the chamber a passage led away into the earth. A line of red tiles marked the beginning of the security zone. Nathaniel stepped toward them; as his shoe rose to cross the line, he cursed, stopped dead, and felt inside his pocket. Careful! He had almost triggered the trap. Nothing magical was permitted beyond the line! He deposited the scrying glass upon the desk, smoothed down his hair, and stepped across the tiles.

If only the Pestilence guarding the Staff could be so easily bypassed. He hadn't a clue how to—

A little noise behind him, a scraping of metal.

Nathaniel stopped, looked back . . . Across the chamber, at the bottom of the stairs, the mercenary was standing. A curved knife glinted in his hand.

27

Kitty shut the door.

Noises from the Hall of Statues echoed in her ears; she could hear the commotion even down the corridor and through the heavy wood. She remained still for a time, pressing her ear against the door. More than anything else she feared being followed by the terrible bearded man. Something in him filled her with more dread than the massing hordes of demons.

She listened. . . . As far as she could tell, nothing stirred in the corridor outside.

A heavy key protruded beside her hand. With some difficulty, and fully conscious of the only moderate security it represented, Kitty locked the door. Then she turned to face the room.

It was just as she remembered it from her failed escape attempt: someone's office, sparsely furnished. A bookcase ran along one wall; opposite was a desk piled high with papers. And, crucially, in the near corner, scuffed and scoured with many years of bureaucratic use—two circles, two pentacles.

Kitty only needed one.

The pentacle design was simple, of the kind she had frequently prepared with Mr. Button: conventional star, double circle, normal Latin hex-locks. It had been painted on a raised dais and, owing to the dimensions of the room, was not particularly large. Elsewhere—she made a quick inspection—she found the usual magician's accessories, gathered in the drawers of the desk. Chalks, pens, paper, candle stubs, lighters, jars of assorted herbs. The herbs were what she needed. She extracted them with calm efficiency and set them on the floor beside the outermost circle.

From somewhere not so very distant came a loud explosion. Kitty started nervously, heart pounding in her chest; she looked toward the door. . . .

Concentrate. What did she have to do?

Mandrake's—no, *Nathaniel's* summary of the instructions in the *Apocrypha* had been rapid and hard to digest, but Kitty had grown used to such things during her time with Mr. Button. Her memory was suitably elastic.

So . . . a conventional pentacle. No candles required. Yep, this one was fine.

But her body should be protected—and that meant herbs and iron. She emptied out the rosemary, Saint-John's-wort, and sticks of rowan wood, mixed them together, and separated the result into several rough piles, which she placed at intervals within the pentacle. As for the iron, *that* was more tricky. For a moment she cast her eyes about the room in vain. Perhaps she would have to do without it. . . .

The key. Was it iron? Kitty had no idea. If it was, it might protect her. If not, it would do no harm. She pulled it from the door.

What else? Yes . . . Nathaniel had said something about breaking the circle, a symbolic act to allow the magician to return to his body. Very well, that could be done. She bent down, and with the key's edge scored a gash in the painted circle. It was useless now for any ordinary summons. But this was not what Kitty planned.

She stood upright. Finished. No other physical preparations were necessary.

Except . . . the small matter of her comfort. On the chair

behind the desk she discovered a dirty old cushion, much used and battered, and this she placed in the pentacle as a pillow.

A mirror hung on the wall behind the desk; as she returned from the door, she caught sight of herself in passing. Only then did Kitty pause.

It had been a while since she had looked at her face; she could not remember the last time. There she was: the thick dark hair, dark eyes (complete with outstanding bags), the quizzical lips, a purple bruise swelling becomingly above one eye. No doubt about it, she was a little shopworn. But still young, still well.

And if she succeeded in what she planned? Terrible things had happened to those magicians who had tried to follow Ptolemy's course. Mr. Button had been unspecific in the details, but given dark hints of madness and deformity. As for Ptolemy himself, she knew he had not survived for long after creating his Gate. And Bartimaeus had said his face had—

With a curse, Kitty turned from the mirror. In truth, whatever risk she ran was immaterial compared with what was going on nearby. She had resolved to try and that was an end to it. There was nothing more she could do. Getting teary would achieve nothing. So.

So there was nothing left for her but to lie within the pentacle.

The floor was hard, but the cushion felt pleasant against the back of her head. Herb smells filled her nostrils. She took the key and closed it in her fist. A deep breath—

An afterthought struck her. She raised her head, looked along her body, and to her annoyance discovered an awkward fact. She was too long for the circle—her feet stuck out over the inner lines. Perhaps it wouldn't matter, but perhaps it would. Kitty rolled onto her side, drew her knees to her chest, and assumed a curled-up position, as if she were in bed. A quick squint along . . . fine, she was nice and tidy now. Nice and ready.

But ready for what? A sudden burst of skepticism exploded in her. This was nothing but another of her dreams, one of the ridiculous fancies Bartimaeus had derided. It was the height of arrogance to think she could succeed where no one else had in two thousand years or more. What was she thinking? She was no magician.

But perhaps this was an advantage. Bartimaeus had prompted her to try it, she *knew* he had. His last words as he left them had echoed his description of Ptolemy: "We do have a bond . . . but for the present there are limits to it." *For the present . . .* What was that if not an implicit invitation to her and her alone? Ptolemy had known no limits: he had come to the Other Place by rejecting all the established magical conventions—by turning them on their head. And you didn't need more than the basic knowledge of summoning to do what he had done—the instructions in the *Apocrypha* were entirely straightforward. The crucial part was calling to the demon at the end. Kitty could do all this. The question was: would it work?

There was only one way to find out.

She closed her eyes and tried to relax her muscles. The room was very quiet—no sound came through the door. Time to begin the summons? No, something was still not right. . . . What was it? After a moment she realized her hand was clenched so tightly upon the key that it dug hard into her skin. That was a symbol of her fear. She concentrated for a few moments, allowing her finger-grip to slacken. . . . Now she cupped the metal gently. Better . . .

Remembered fragments came into her head, words written

by past authorities about the Other Place: *a region of chaos, a whirl of endless abominations, a sump of madness* . . . cheerful pronouncements all. Then there was Mr. Button's pithy edict: *to venture there risks body and soul.* Oh, God, so what would happen to her? Would she melt or burn? Would she see—? Yes, but whatever she saw could hardly be worse or more abhorrent than Nouda and his crippled hybrids—his demons cloaked in human flesh. And none of Mr. Button's authorities had even visited the Other Place! It was all pure speculation. Besides, Ptolemy *had* returned alive.

She ran through the words of the reverse summons in her head, then—since to delay was merely to invite further fears—she spoke them out loud. As far as she could tell, it was all correct—she used her own name rather than a demon's and swapped the normal verbs. She finished by calling Bartimaeus's name, three times.

Done.

She lay there in the quiet room.

Seconds passed. Kitty quelled her mounting frustration. No good being impatient. Conventional summonings needed time for the words to travel to the Other Place. She listened, though for what she did not know. Her eyes were closed. She saw nothing but darkness and flickering brain-echoes of light.

Still nothing. Evidently the process was not going to work. Kitty's hopes passed away; she felt hollow and a little sad. She toyed with getting up, but the room was warm, she was comfortable on her pillow and after the privations of the night, was happy to rest a little. Her mind drifted on currents of its own devising: she wondered about her parents, what they were doing, how these events would touch them; how Jakob, far away in Europe, might respond; whether Nathaniel had survived the conflagration in the hall. She found herself hoping so.

A distant sound came to her ears, a clear bell ringing. The demons, perhaps, or survivors trying to alert the city . . .

Nathaniel had saved her from the mercenary's knife. She had enjoyed sparring with him, forcing him to face the truth about many things, Bartimaeus most of all. He had taken it surprisingly well. As for Bartimaeus . . . she remembered how she'd last seen him, a forlorn shapeless mass of slime, worn down by weariness of the world. Was it wrong to be pursuing him? Like anyone else, the djinni needed rest.

The bell continued to ring. It was an odd sound, now she thought about it—high and pure, as if struck on crystal, not low and booming as most bells in the city were. Also, rather than repeatedly ringing, it was a single continuous vibration that remained slightly out of reach, right on the edge of her hearing. She strained to catch it. . . . First it faded, then grew louder— but though alluring, its character was still impossible to pin down; it was lost somewhere amid the pulsing of her blood, her quiet breathing, the little rasps of her clothing as her chest went up and down. She tried again, suddenly fascinated. The ringing seemed somewhere above her, far away. She strove to listen, wishing she could draw closer to the source. She tried to block out all other sounds. Her efforts paid off—little by little, then with a sudden rush, the ringing clarified, became unmuffled. She was alone with it. It rang perpetually, like something precious on the verge of breaking. She felt that it was very close.

Was it visible too? Kitty opened her eyes.

And saw many things at once. A complex grid of stonework all around, little walls and floors running off in three dimensions, separating, joining, arching, ending. Among them were stairs, windows, and open doors; she was passing among them at speed, both very close and somehow far away. Glancing down, she saw a girl's body curled up at a distance—it reminded her of a sleeping cat. Other figures were frozen, doll-like, all about the grid of stone—groups of men and women clustered closely, many lying prone, as if asleep or dead. Around them stood strange blurry things with uncertain outlines—neither human nor completely otherwise. She could not distinguish their nature—each one seemed almost to cancel itself out. Below it all, in some remote corridor, she saw a youth fixed in a running posture, face turned over his shoulder; behind him was a figurine that *moved*—a man with a knife, legs going slowly, boots covering ground. And about them both, different shapes, remote and indistinct . . .

Kitty felt a certain detached curiosity about all this, but her real interest lay elsewhere. The ringing sound was louder than before; somewhere very close. She concentrated still harder, and slightly to her surprise the pretty little latticework of stones and figures distorted and twisted out of focus, as if pulled in four directions all at once. First it was quite clear, next it had blurred into a smudge; then even the smudge had gone.

Kitty felt a rushing on all sides; not a physical sensation, for she was not aware of having an actual body, but a conceptual one. Dimly she glimpsed four barriers all around her: they towered above, plummeted below, stretched to infinity on either side. One was dark and solid, and threatened to crush her with remorseless weight; the next was a raging fluid, which surged avidly to carry her away. The third barrier tore at her with the unseen tumult of a hurricane; the fourth was an implacable wall of unquenchable fire. All four beat upon her for an instant only, then they recoiled. With reluctance, they gave her up and Kitty passed through the Gate to the other side.

28

It was as well for Kitty that she experienced what followed with the detachment of an observer, rather than as a helpless participant—if it had been otherwise, she would immediately have gone mad. As it was, the lack of bodily sensation gave what she saw a certain dreamlike quality. Curiosity was her main emotion.

She found herself in—well, *in* did not seem quite appropriate: she found herself *part of* a ceaseless swirl of movement, neither ending nor beginning, in which nothing was fixed or static. It was an infinite ocean of lights, colors, and textures, perpetually forming, racing, and dissolving in upon themselves, though the effect was neither as thick or solid as a liquid nor as traceless as a gas; if anything it was a combination of the two, in which fleeting wisps of substance endlessly parted and converged.

Scale and direction were impossible to determine, as was the passing of time—since nothing remained still and no patterns were ever repeated, the concept itself seemed blank and meaningless. This mattered little to Kitty, and it was only when she attempted to locate *herself*, with a view to establishing her position in her surroundings, that she grew a little disconcerted. She had no fixed point, no singularity to call her own; indeed, she seemed often to be in several places at once, watching the whirling traces from multiple angles. The effect was most disorientating.

She tried to fix upon a particular fleck of color and follow it, but found it no easier than following the motion of a single leaf in a distant windblown tree. As soon as it formed, each color split, melted, merged with others, shrugged off the responsibility of being itself. Kitty grew dizzy with the looking.

To make matters worse she began to notice something else too, flicking in and out of existence within the general swirl—random images, so fleeting she could not pin them down—like photographs turned on and off by crackling electric light. She tried to work out what they were, but the movement was too fast. This filled her with frustration. She sensed they might have told her something.

After an unknown duration Kitty remembered that she had come here for a purpose, although what that purpose was she could not recall. She had no inclination to *do* anything particularly; her main impulse was to remain exactly as she was, moving among the rushing lights. . . . Nevertheless something about the ceaseless change irritated her and kept her separate from it. She wanted to impose a little order, some solidity. But how could she do this when she lacked solidity herself?

Halfheartedly she willed herself to move toward a particular patch of orange and maroon swirling at an unknown distance. To her surprise, she moved all right, but in several discordant directions; when her vision stabilized, the patch of color was no closer than before. She tried several times with the same result: her movements were veering and haphazard; it was impossible to predict the outcome.

For the first time Kitty felt a faint anxiety. She noted several patches of boiling darkness curling and uncurling among the lights; they stirred echoes of old earthbound fears—of nothingness and solitude, of being alone amid infinity.

This is no good, Kitty thought. *I need a body*.

With mounting disquiet, she watched the remorseless movement flowing all around, the images flickering near and far, the crackles of light and senseless trails of color. One merry dancing blue-green coil caught her attention.

Stand STILL! she thought furiously.

Was it her imagination, or had a little portion of the flowing coil deviated from its course, slowing for an instant? The motion was so quick, she could not be sure.

Kitty spied another random wisp and willed it to halt and attend to her. The results were immediate and satisfactory: a sizable tendril of matter solidified into something resembling the rolled tip of a fern frond, colorless and glassy. When she relaxed her attention, the coil unfurled and vanished back into the general swirl.

Kitty tried again, this time willing a patch of matter to form a thicker, more compact object. Once more she had success, and by concentrating further was able to mold the glassy lump into something approaching a block, unevenly squared. Again, when she desisted, the block dissolved to nothing.

The malleability of the substance all around reminded Kitty of something she had seen before. What was it? With difficulty, her mind grasped at a memory—that of the djinni Bartimaeus, changing form. He needed to occupy a shape of some kind when he came to Earth, though his choices were always fluid. Perhaps, now that the positions were reversed, she should try the same.

She could make herself a shape. . . . And with this inspiration, the object of her visit came back to her. Yes, it was Bartimaeus she had come to find.

Kitty's anxiety faded; she was enthused. She set to work straightaway, building herself a body.

Unfortunately this was easier thought than done. She had no difficulty, by applying her will once more, in forming a patch of the flowing energies into something approximating a human shape. It had a bulbous head of sorts, a stumpy torso, and four uneven limbs, all dully see-through, so that the rushing colors and lights behind were distorted on its surfaces. But when Kitty tried to improve this rough marionette into something more refined and accurate, she discovered she was unable to concentrate on it all at once. While she shaped and evened out the legs, the head slumped like melted butter; when she hastened to repair this and add a token face, the bottom half dripped and sagged. So it went, until her series of rushed improvements had entirely ruined the figurine, and it had stabilized as a pinheaded blob with enormous buttocks. Kitty regarded it with dissatisfaction.

It also proved overly complex to maneuver. Although she was able to direct it back and forth—it floated among the raging energies like a bird amid a storm—Kitty found she could not individually direct its limbs. While she struggled to do so, the body's substance dribbled away from its extremities, like thread unraveling from a spindle. After a time Kitty gave up in disgust and allowed the figure to dissolve into nothing.

Despite this setback she felt pleased with her idea in principle, and immediately began work again. In quick succession she tried a variety of other surrogate bodies, testing each for ease of control. The first, a stick figure—rather like a child's drawing—contained less substance than its predecessor; Kitty was able to prevent it from unraveling, but found the savage energies all around made it crumple like a cranefly. The second, a snaking sausage with a questing tendril at its front, was more stable, but aesthetically unsound. The third, a simple ball of swirling matter, was far stronger and easier to maintain, and with it she progressed a considerable distance, floating serenely through the chaos.

Lack of limbs is the key, Kitty thought. *A sphere is good. It imposes order.*

The shape certainly had *some* effect on her surroundings, since it was not long before Kitty began to notice a slight change in the fabric through which her ball was passing. Up until then the coils of color, the shimmering lights, the inter- mittent images had all been entirely neutral and unresponsive, flowing randomly where they would. But now—perhaps because of the new decisiveness with which she maintained the sphere—they seemed to become aware of her presence. She sensed it in the movement of the swirls, which suddenly became more definite, intentional. They began to change direc- tion slightly—darting in close to the ball, then veering away as if in doubt. Time and again this happened, with the coils and flickers growing steadily in strength and number. They seemed merely inquisitive, but it was an ominous kind of attention, like sharks gathering about a swimmer, and Kitty didn't like it. She slowed the progress of her ball, and with a careful exertion of will—she was now gaining in confidence—imposed herself upon the whirling substance. Taking the static sphere as her center, she drove outward, pushing back the nearest intrepid coils, which dissolved and scattered.

The remission this provided was short-lived. Just as Kitty was congratulating herself on her strength of purpose, a sudden glassy coil extended out from the main mass like an amoeba's pseudopodium and bit into the edge of her sphere, carrying off a chunk. As she strove to make good the damage, another coil darted in from the opposite side and took another slice.

Furiously she beat the coils back. The main mass all about her pulsed and quivered. Lights flickered intently in random clusters. For the first time Kitty felt true fear.

Bartimaeus, she thought. *Where are you?*

The word seemed to conjure a reaction in the substance; a sudden burst of static images fired and faded, stronger and more lingering than before. One or two lasted long enough for her to catch details: figures, faces, random snatches of sky, once a definite building—a roof with columns. The figures were human, but wore unfamiliar styles of clothes. The fleeting pictures reminded Kitty of past occasions, when long-forgotten memories rose unbidden into her mind. But these were not *her* memories.

As if in response to this thought, a sudden burst of activity far out in the whirling confusion ended with an image that *did* linger. It was fractured, as if seen through the lens of a broken camera, but what it showed was clear enough: her parents, standing together hand in hand. As Kitty watched, her mother raised a distorted hand and waved.

Kitty! Come back to us.

Go away . . . Kitty reacted with confusion and dismay. It was a trick, obviously it was, but that didn't make it any less upsetting. Her concentration wavered; her hold over her sphere and her single area of cleared order lurched and trembled. The sphere slumped and sagged; coils of matter came creeping in from every side.

Kitty, we love you.

Get lost! She drove the coils back again. The image of her mom and dad winked out. With grim determination, Kitty returned her sphere to its proper shape. She was increasingly dependent on it for any semblance of control, for any semblance of being *herself*. More than anything she feared being adrift again without it.

Other pictures flashed on and off, each one different, most too fast to fathom. Some, though barely perceptible, must have been familiar to her—they awoke inarticulate feelings of agitation and loss. A flurry of lights; another picture, very far away. An old man leaning on a stick. Behind his back was a rushing slab of blackness.

Kitty, help! It's coming!

Mr. Pennyfeather . . .

Don't leave me! The figure looked over its shoulder, cried out in terror. . . . The vision was gone. Almost immediately another appeared—a woman running between columns with something dark and agile skittering in pursuit. A flash of white among shadows. Kitty concentrated her energies on the sphere. Ignore them. They were nothing but phantasms, blank and empty. They meant nothing.

Bartimaeus! Again she thought the name, beseechingly this time. Again it awoke activity among the floating lights and drifting spurs of color. Close up, with crystal clarity, came Jakob Hyrnek, smiling sadly.

You always did try to be too independent, Kitty. Why not just give up? Come and join us here. It's best not to go back to Earth. You won't like it if you do.

Why? She couldn't help but ask the question.

Poor child. You'll see. You are not as you were.

Another image appeared alongside, a tall man with dark skin, standing on a grassy hill. His face was grave.

Why do you come here and molest us?

A woman wearing a high white headdress, gathering water at a well.

You were a fool to come here. You are not welcome.

I come for help.

You will not get it. The woman's image scowled and vanished. The man with dark skin turned to walk away up his hill.

Why do you molest us? he asked again, over his shoulder. *You wound us with your presence.* A flicker of lights; he too was gone.

Jakob Hyrnek gave a rueful smile.

Give up, magician. Forget yourself. You cannot get home in any case.

I am not a magician.

True. You are nothing now. A dozen coils enveloped him; he crackled and fizzed into a multitude of whirling shards that floated far away.

Nothing . . . Kitty regarded her ball, which during her recent inattention had melted away like snow. Little flakes were fluttering off what remained of its surface; as if blown by a wind, they skipped and danced across to join the endless whirl about her. Well, it was true, of course—she *was* nothing: a being without substance, without anchorage. There wasn't any point in pretending otherwise.

And they were right about another thing too: she didn't know how to get home.

Her will faded. She allowed the sphere to dwindle; it spun like a top, streaming into nothing. She began to drift. . . .

Another image flickered into view at an indeterminate distance.

Hello, Kitty.

Get lost.

And there I was thinking you were asking after me.

29

For almost thirty seconds Nathaniel and the mercenary regarded each other silently across the chamber floor. Neither of them moved. The knife in the mercenary's hand was still; his empty hand hovered close beside his belt. Nathaniel watched intently, but without hope. He had seen how fast those hands could move. And he was quite defenseless. At their other meetings he had had Bartimaeus on his side.

The mercenary spoke first. "I have come to take you back," he said. "The demon wishes to have you alive."

Nathaniel said nothing. He didn't move. He was trying to think of a strategy, but his brain was stiff with fear; every thought moved with the creaking sluggishness of ice.

"I believe several of the prospective hosts have been killed," the mercenary went on. "Nouda is keen to save as many young bodies as he can. Well? Or would you prefer a more honorable death? I can oblige."

"We don't"—Nathaniel's voice was thick; his tongue felt too large for his mouth—"we don't *have* to fight at all."

A rumbling laugh. "*Fight?* That implies some parity between us."

"I have one slave left at my command," Nathaniel lied. "Think quickly, before he strikes. We can still work together against the enemy. It is in your interests too, you must see that; I will pay you well from the nation's treasury. I shall give you gold uncounted! I can make you a lord, give you lands, territories, whatever your black heart desires. Only you must fight alongside me. Here—in these vaults—are weapons we can use—"

For answer the mercenary spat upon the chamber floor. "I want no lands or titles! My sect forbids such fripperies. Gold—yes! But *that* the demons will give me, if I serve them. And—Do not speak! I know your argument! So *what* if Nouda destroys all London—or all Europe, for that matter? He can burn the world for all I care! I have no faith in empires, ministers, or kings. Let chaos come! I shall flourish. So, what is your answer? Will you die here?"

Nathaniel's eyes narrowed. "My answer comes behind you on tiptoed feet. Kill him, Belazael! Strike him down!"

As he shouted, he pointed back up the stairs. The mercenary ducked, whirled around in readiness, saw the stairs empty. Breathing a curse, he spun again, a silver disc now cupped in his hand, only to glimpse Nathaniel also turning, heading up the passage, into the vaults. His arm moved; the disc was gone—

Nathaniel had twisted and tried to run in a single desperate movement. He lost his balance, tripped on a flagstone's edge and fell—

The silver disc flashed through the air, struck the wall above Nathaniel's falling head, ricocheted against the opposite side of the passage, and clattered to the floor.

Nathaniel landed on hands and knees; he scrambled to his feet and, scooping up the silver disc, ran on. He snatched a glance behind him.

In the distance the mercenary strode across the chamber floor toward the passage, his face heavy with irritation. He went unhurriedly; about his boots hung pulsing lights and smudges. His first step was three times an ordinary man's; with his second he was right at Nathaniel's back. He raised his knife. Nathaniel cried out, lurched to one side—

From the stonework of the passage a gray shadow emerged, silent as smoke. A coiling limb entwined itself around the mercenary's waist; an arm looped upon his throat. The man's head jerked back. He raised his knife, slashed out. The shadow moaned, but clung on tighter. A sickly blue radiance emerged from the shadow and enveloped the mercenary; he coughed and spat. Other shadows drifted from the walls and floor, wound themselves around the boots and trousers, grasped the flapping cloak. The mercenary slashed left and right; he tapped a heel—the seven-league boots took wing. In a single step he was away along the corridor, halting at a junction far ahead. But the blue glow hung about his head, the shadows clung to him like leeches, and still more came hurrying from the stones.

Nathaniel leaned against the wall for support. It was the *boots*, of course: their aura had triggered the trap as soon as the mercenary entered the corridor. The shadows had immediately set upon their owner. Trouble was, it was a magical attack, and—as he knew from bitter experience—the mercenary's resilience to magic was huge.

But their intervention had given him respite. The treasure vault was somewhere up ahead, past where the mercenary thrashed and struggled. There was no help for it. Clutching the silver disc gingerly (the edges were very sharp), Nathaniel stole along the corridor, past numerous doors, and side turnings, nearer and nearer to the junction.

By now, so many of the shadows had poured themselves upon his enemy that Nathaniel could scarcely make him out. He was hidden amid a pile of writhing bodies. Their weight alone had forced him to his knees; occasionally his face, purple behind the beard and the choking radiance, came in sight. He seemed half throttled, but his knife still flashed about him. Curls of melting essence littered the floor like wood shavings.

It's silver too, Nathaniel thought. *The knife—they can't withstand it. Sooner or later he'll be free.*

This unpleasant knowledge spurred him on. He reached the junction; keeping the disc raised and his back to the wall, he rounded it, watching the combatants the whole time. Even as he did so, one shadow fell away, cut clean in two by a single blow. Nathaniel lingered no longer; he didn't have much time.

Down the corridor, dead straight into the earth. There at the end: the steel door with the little grille—the entrance to the treasure vault.

Nathaniel reached it at a run. He looked back the way he had come. Distant scuffles, gasps, unearthly moans. *Forget the mercenary now.* What was he to do?

He inspected the door. It was ordinary enough: the hatch with the viewing grille, a simple handle, no other marks or indentations. Might it contain a trap? It was possible; then again, the clerk had not mentioned one. A Pestilence guarded the treasures inside, he knew that much, but how was this triggered? Perhaps simply opening the door would set it going. . . .

Nathaniel's hand hovered over the handle. Should he?

He looked back over his shoulder. It was no good, he *had* to get the Staff. He was dead otherwise. He grasped the handle, turned, and pulled—

Nothing happened. The door remained fast.

Nathaniel cursed and let go. Locked somehow . . . He racked his brains. There seemed no obvious keyhole. Some magical hex-lock? If so, he'd never find the Charm.

A foolish thought struck him. He turned the handle again. This time he *pushed*.

Ah. The door swung open. Nathaniel let it swing. He held his breath. . . .

No Pestilence bubbled forth. Automatic lights, perhaps from some captive imp imprisoned in the ceiling of the treasure vault, switched on. Everything was as he had seen it two days before: the plinth of marble in the center, piled high with treasures; the otherwise empty room; the wide ring of olive-green floor tiles all around the plinth, stretching almost to the door.

Nathaniel rubbed his chin. In all probability, if he stepped upon those green floor tiles, the Pestilence would rise up, and in seconds he would perish horribly. The idea was unappealing. But how could he bypass it? The ring of tiles was far too wide to jump, he had no means of climbing above them, and he could not fly. . . .

Indecision gripped him. He could not go back—the situation was too desperate, and Kitty was relying on him to succeed. But to enter the room was death. He had no means of defense; no Shield or Charm. . . .

His eyes fixed upon an object lying in the center of the distant plinth. A jade stone set in a delicate oval of pressed gold; it hung by a chain from a wooden stand. The Amulet of Samarkand . . . Nathaniel knew very well what it could do. He had seen it repel the power of the demon Ramuthra; it could cope with a little Pestilence all right. What if he *ran* as hard as he could . . . ?

He bit his lip. No—the distance to the plinth was much too great. He'd *never* be able to get to the Amulet before—

It was not a *sound* that alerted him; the corridor behind his back was utterly silent. But an intuition, a sudden sharp foreboding that sent prickles along his spine, made him turn. The sight along the corridor knotted his stomach, made his knees weaken.

With knife and fist, the mercenary had succeeded in dislodging all but one of the shadows; fragments of the others lay flopping on the floor around him. New shadows were still emerging from the stonework—one of them fired a blue pulse at the mercenary that knocked him momentarily against the wall, but he did not falter. Ignoring the shadow on his back that sought to throttle him, the mercenary stooped and kicked off first one boot, then the other. They struck the stones, lay on their side.

The mercenary stepped away from the boots; instantly the shadows' interest in him receded. They flitted about the boots, sniffing and prodding with long fingers. The shadow on his back was distracted, it loosened its grip. A shrug of the back, a swing of the silver knife—where was the shadow now? Two pieces clawing for each other on the floor.

As Nathaniel watched, the mercenary set off up the corridor toward him. He came implacably, but slowly; his cape was tattered, he walked in his socks. The ferocity of the shadows' assault seemed to have weakened him—his face was mauve with exertion; he limped, and coughed with each step.

Nathaniel stood in the doorway, half in, half out of the treasure room. His head made frantic movements—side to side, green tiles to mercenary. He was sick with panic; he had nothing to decide but the method of his death.

He steeled himself. One way, death *was* inevitable. The expression on the mercenary's face promised him pain. As for the other way . . .

The cool glint of the Amulet shone on the plinth across the

room, beckoning him over. It was so *far* . . . but the Pestilence would at least be quick.

Nathaniel made his decision. He walked out of the door, away from the treasure room, toward the oncoming mercenary.

The blue eyes bored into him. The man smiled. The knife rose.

Nathaniel spun on his heels and sprinted back toward the door. He ignored the snarl of rage behind him, focused only straight ahead. It was crucial to pick up speed, hit the green tiles at maximum velocity. . . .

An explosion of pain in his shoulder; he cried out like an animal, stumbled, but ran on. Through the door, into the room; green tiles stretched out ahead—

Limping footsteps right behind. A muttered cough.

The tiles' edge. He sprang, leaped through the air as far as he could—

Landed. Ran on.

All about him, the hiss of a thousand serpents; yellow-green vapor rose from the tiles.

Ahead was the plinth; treasures gleamed upon it. Gladstone's Staff, a jeweled glove, an ancient violin, stained with blood; goblets, swords, caskets, and tapestries. Nathaniel's eyes were fixed on the Amulet of Samarkand, juddering and jerking with the impact of each stride.

Green vapor covered everything in a sallow veil. Nathaniel felt his skin sting—the stinging intensified, became a sudden desperate pain. He smelled a burning—

A cough behind him. Something brushed his back.

The plinth. His hand reached out, snatched up the necklace; tore it from its stand. He jumped, twisted, fell sprawling upon the plinth, sent jewels and wonders scattering, rolled across, dropped to the tiles on the other side. His eyes burned; he screwed them shut. His skin was afire; at a distance he heard a voice give a scream of agony—it was his own.

Blindly he pulled the necklace over his neck, felt the Amulet of Samarkand brush against his chest—

The pain was gone. His skin still burned, but it was a residual stinging, not an escalating torment, save in his shoulder, where it throbbed with sick intensity. He heard a whispering, opened one eye—saw the vapor coiling all about him, swirling, seeking out his flesh, but being drawn inexorably around and down, into the jade stone at the center of the Amulet.

Nathaniel raised his head from where he lay. He could see the ceiling, the side of the plinth beside him, the vapor that filled the room. The view beyond was hidden.

So where—?

A cough. Just behind the plinth.

Nathaniel moved; not fast, but as fast as he could. The pain in his shoulder prevented him putting weight on his right arm. With the left he levered himself into a crouching position, then slowly rose.

On the other side of the plinth the mercenary was standing, surrounded by the billowing cloud of yellow-green vapor. He still held the knife; his eyes were fixed on Nathaniel. But he leaned heavily on the plinth top, and coughed with every breath.

Slowly he drew himself up. Slowly he started to walk around the plinth to Nathaniel.

Nathaniel backed away.

The bearded man moved with the utmost care, as if his limbs pained him. He ignored the boiling Pestilence, which ate away his cloak, which bit into his black clothes, into the thick black socks upon his limping feet. He stepped away from the plinth.

Nathaniel's back bumped against the wall at the far end of the chamber. He could go no farther. His hands were empty. He had dropped the silver disc somewhere as he ran. There was no defense now.

The Pestilence swirled ever darker around the oncoming form. Nathaniel saw a grimace flicker across the mercenary's face, perhaps of doubt or pain. Was his resilience waning? It had already been forced to cope with the shadows' long assault, and now the Pestilence beat against it too.... Had the skin changed color? Was it perhaps a little yellowed, a little blotchy ... ?

The remorseless steps continued; the pale blue eyes pierced him.

Nathaniel pressed back against the stones. Instinctively his hand closed around the Amulet; the metal was cold to the touch.

The cloud of Pestilence gave a sudden flurry, billowed around the mercenary like a cloak. It was as if it had suddenly found a puncture, a weakness in his armor. It swirled like a storm of hornets enveloping a foe, stinging, stinging. The mercenary kept walking. The skin on his face cracked like old paper. The flesh below fell inward, as if being sucked dry. Color drained from the jet-black beard. The pale blue eyes stayed fixed upon Nathaniel with consuming hatred.

Closer, closer. The hand that held the knife was shriveled, nothing but a knot of bones beneath a rind of skin. Now the beard was gray, now it was white; cheekbones protruded through the hair like jags of slate. To Nathaniel, it seemed the mercenary smiled. The smile broadened, displayed impossible extents of teeth.... The skin on the face fell away entirely, to leave a gleaming skull with clipped white beard and pale blue eyes, which gave a burst of brightness and suddenly went out.

Bones in black clothes. Its step became wholesale collapse; it dropped, splintered, crashed down upon itself, scattering a mess of rags and scraps about Nathaniel's feet.

The malignity of the Pestilence diminished; what remained of it was sucked away into the Amulet as Nathaniel hobbled back across the room. He came to the plinth. Viewed through his lenses, the collective aura of the treasures hurt his eyes. Brightest of all was the Staff. He reached out his hand (noting subconsciously the patina of little wounds upon his skin) and picked it up. He recalled at once the smoothness, the lightness of the aged wood.

Nathaniel felt no triumph. He was too weak. The Staff was in his hand, but the mere notion of activating it daunted him. The pain in his shoulder made him nauseous. He caught sight of the culprit—a bloodied silver disc lying on the tiles. Beside it was a second disc—the one he'd dropped. Stiffly he stooped and placed it in his pocket.

The Staff, the Amulet . . . Anything more? He considered the array of objects on the plinth. Some—the ones he had heard of—were of no immediate use; others were gloweringly mysterious, and best left well alone. Without further delay, he departed the room of treasures.

On his way back through the passages the guardian shadows, attracted by the pulsing auras of the Staff and Amulet, attempted to waylay him. Their freezing blue radiance was absorbed by the Amulet; any individuals that flung themselves upon Nathaniel were, in short order, sucked into the piece of jade. Nathaniel was unmolested. As he went, he retrieved the seven-league boots; a few minutes later he crossed the line of tiles and came out into the entrance room.

His scrying glass lay on the desk.

"Imp, you have three tasks, then you are free."

"You've got to be kidding. One of them's impossible, right? Making a rope of sand? Building a bridge to the Other Place? Hit me with it. Give me the worst."

During the imp's absence the magician sat slumped upon the desk, supporting himself with the Staff. His shoulder throbbed; the skin about his face and hands still burned. His breathing came in fitful gasps.

The imp was back. Its face was newly scrubbed and gleaming; it could barely contain its eagerness to be off. "First question. The great spirits are at this very moment leaving the building. Observe." A picture in the depths: Nathaniel recognized the aged front of Westminster Hall. A hole had been blown in the wall. From this issued a cavorting throng—men and women of the government, bounding with awkward, inhuman movements. Detonations flashed, Infernos sparked, random bolts of magic plumed and faded. At their heart stalked the short, round figure of Quentin Makepeace.

"Off they go," the imp remarked. "About forty-odd, I'd say. Some of them are still a bit uncertain on their feet, like newborn calves. They'll get used to it, I'm sure."

Nathaniel sighed. "Very well."

"Second question, boss. You'll find a cache of weapons up the stairs, third door on the left. Third question—"

"Yes? Where is she?"

"Upstairs, take a right, past the Hall of Statues. Door straight ahead. Here, I can show you if you like." A picture formed:

a Whitehall administrator's study. On the floor, in a pentacle, a girl lay very still.

"Closer in," Nathaniel ordered. "Can you get closer in to her?"

"Yep. But it's not pretty. It *is* the same girl, mind. Don't think it's not. *There*. See what I mean? I couldn't be sure at first, but I recognized the clothes. . . ."

"Oh, *Kitty*," Nathaniel said.

30

*Y*ou *took your time* Kitty thought.

What do you mean? You've only just arrived.

Rubbish! I've been floating here forever. They've been all around me, telling me to go, and that I was nothing and shouldn't bother looking, and I began to believe them, Bartimaeus. I was just giving up completely when you came to me just now.

Giving up? You've not been here more than a few seconds. Earth time, that is. It doesn't work the same way on this side. More looped. I would try to explain it, but hey. The important thing is—you're here. I didn't think you'd come.

It wasn't so difficult. I suppose it was because you helped me through.

It's harder than you know. You're the first since Ptolemy to succeed. It requires the ability to separate from yourself, which is an impossibility for magicians, being what they are. Those who fail go mad.

That's my problem now, that separation. Not being me.

Why don't you try making yourself a guise? Something to focus on. You might feel better.

I've already made some! The only one that worked was a ball, and that seemed to get the—to get them angry.

We're not angry. Do I seem angry to you?

Kitty considered the distant, flickering image. It was a stately woman, dark-skinned, long-necked, wearing a tall headdress and a long white gown; she sat on a marbled throne. Her face was beautiful and serene.

No, she thought, *not at all. But you're* different.

I don't mean her. That isn't me—it's a memory. I'm all around you. We're all around you. It's not the same as on your side of the Gate. There's no difference between the spirits here. We're all one. And that includes you now.

Coils of multiple shades and textures swirled all around, as if in confirmation. The image of the woman vanished; others reappeared. Kitty could see each one a dozen times, as if refracted in an insect's eye, but she knew it was not the images that were multiplied, but herself.

I don't like this much, she thought.

The pictures are memories; some of them might even be yours. It is a bit hard to get your head around, I know. Ptolemy found it tricky too, but he perked up when he made himself a shape. Quite artistic it was, a good approximation of himself. Why don't you have another go?

I can do a ball.

I'm not conversing with a ball. Have a bit of confidence.

Kitty steeled herself and applied her will to the surging substances; as before, she managed to create something that approximated a human form. It featured a big wobbly head, a long thin body ending in a triangular mass that might have been a skirt, two stick arms, and a pair of rather trunklike legs. It had an ungainly look.

Several tendrils of matter inspected it tentatively.

What's that bit?

That's an arm.

Oh, right. That's a relief. Hmm . . . Is this how you see yourself, Kitty? There's serious self-esteem issues going on here. Here's a tip: your real legs aren't quite that thick. Not around the ankles, anyway.

Tough, Kitty thought. *It's the best I can do.*

Give yourself a face, at least, and for heaven's sake make it a nice one.

Kitty strove hard and succeeded in forming a couple of piggy eyes, a long witchlike nose, and a mouth crooked in a wonky smile.

Well, you're no Leonardo.

A brief image flickered on and off close by—a bearded man staring at a wall.

It would help, Kitty thought savagely, *if I had something to look at other than all this mess.* With an extreme effort, she made her surrogate body jerk an arm out at the swirling matter all around.

Some of the curling tendrils recoiled in mock horror.

You humans are so inconsistent. You claim to love stability and order, but what's Earth if not one big mess? Chaos, violence, dissent, and strife whichever way you look. It's far more peaceful here. But maybe I can help you out. Make things a little easier. Keep control of that lovely body of yours, now. I wouldn't want those arm things to fall off—that would ruin its perfection.

As Kitty watched, nearby regions of the flowing matter underwent a transformation. Flickering wisps of light elongated, broadened, solidified into planes; coils and spirals grew straight and tall, branching out at right angles, joining others and redividing. In moments the semblance of a room had formed around her body: a glassy floor; squared pillars on all sides; beyond them, steps leading down to a lip, then nothingness. Above was a simple flat roof, also translucent. Beyond the roof, between the pillars, below the floor, the relentless movement of the Other Place continued unabated.

The illusion of a physical space made Kitty suddenly fearful of the void around; her mannequin cowered in the center of the room, as far from the verges as possible.

How's that?

It's . . . okay. But what about you?

I am here. You do not need to see me.

But I would prefer it.

Oh, very well. I suppose I am the host.

From between the pillars at the end of the little hall a figure stepped—the boy with the ageless face. Where he had been attractive on Earth, here he was resplendently beautiful; his face radiated joy and calm, his skin shone with light and color. He stepped silently across the floor and came to a halt facing Kitty's wobble-headed, stick-chested, trunk-thighed form.

Thanks, Kitty thought bitterly. *That's made me feel a lot better.*

It's not actually me, any more than that's *you. In fact, you're as much part of this form as I am. There aren't any divisions in the Other Place.*

It didn't feel that way before you came. They told me I wasn't wanted, said I was a wound.

*Only because you keep trying to impose order on us—and order means limitations. There should be no limitations here: nothing definite, nothing defined. Whether it's a clumsy stick figure or a floating ball—or a "house" like this—*the boy waved a careless arm—*it's alien, and cannot last long. It pains us to be restricted in any fashion.*

The boy stepped away from her and looked out between two pillars and the rushing lights. Kitty's surrogate tottered after him.

Bartimaeus—

Names, names, names! Now they're the ultimate restriction. They're the worst curse of all. Each one is a sentence of slavery. Here *we are one—we have no names. But what do the magicians do? They reach in with their summons; their words draw us out, piece by screaming piece. As each piece passes through, it is defined: it gains a name and powers of its own, but is separated from the rest. What happens then?*

Like performing monkeys, we do tricks to please our masters, lest they hurt our fragile essence. Even when we return here we are never safe. Once a name has been bestowed we can be called again, and yet again, until our essence is worn away.

He turned and patted Kitty's semblance on the back of its bulbous head.

You're so disturbed by the connectedness *of things here that you prefer to cling to something as unappetizing as this monstrosity—no offense I'm sure—rather than float freely with us at will. For us, on Earth, it is the reverse. Suddenly we are cut off from this fluidity, left alone and vulnerable in a world of vicious definition. By changing shape we get a little solace, but it never keeps the pain away for long. No wonder some of us become resentful.*

Kitty had ignored the monologue. She so disliked the crudeness of her creature that she had been stealthily adjusting the size of the head, channeling some of the matter down to plump up her spindly torso. She'd reduced the nose a little too, and made the mouth smaller and less lopsided. Yes . . . it was markedly better.

The boy rolled his eyes.

This is exactly *what I mean! You can't get your mind away from the notion that this thing is in some way you. It's nothing but a puppet. Leave it alone.*

Kitty gave up her attempt to draw out some hair from the back of the creature's head. She turned her full attention on the radiant boy, whose face was suddenly grave.

Why have you come here, Kitty?

Because that's what Ptolemy did. I wanted to prove myself, show that I trusted you. You said that after he managed it, you'd have been happy to be his slave. Well, I don't want slaves, but I do need your help. Which is why I've come.

The boy's eyes were black crystals full of stars.

In what way do you wish my help?

You know why. Those de—those spirits that have broken free. They plan to fall on London, kill its people.

Haven't they yet? the boy remarked casually. *They are being slow about it.*

Don't be cruel! In her agitation, Kitty's creature swung its stick arms above its head and lurched forward across the hall. The boy stepped back in surprise. *Most of the people in London are innocent! They don't want the magicians any more than you do. I'm asking you on their account, Bartimaeus. It's they who are going to suffer when Nouda's army gets loose.*

The boy nodded sadly.

Faquarl and Nouda are sick. It's what happens to some of us when we're summoned many times. Slavery corrupts us. Our personalities become brutalized, dull, vindictive; we dwell far more on trivial indignities suffered in your world than on the wonders and pleasures of this place. Hard to believe, but true.

Kitty looked out at the flashes of light and the infinity of moving essence.

What do you actually do *here?* she asked.

It's not about doing. It's about being. Don't expect to understand it: you're a human—you can only see surfaces, and then you want to impose yourself upon them. And Faquarl and Nouda and the rest have been twisted in your image. They define themselves now by their hatred—it's so strong, they actually want *to be apart from this, providing they can take revenge. In a way it's a final capitulation to the values of your world. Hey—you're getting better at manipulating that thing. . . .*

Shielded from the full energies of the Other Place, Kitty was finding it easier to make her mannequin move about. It strutted to and fro about the little hall, swinging its arms and moving its balloon head jerkily from side to side as if acknowledging an audience. The boy nodded with approval.

You know, it's almost an improvement on your real self.

Kitty ignored this. The mannequin stopped at the boy's side.

I've done what Ptolemy did, she thought. *I've proved myself to you. And you answered my call—you've acknowledged it. Now I need your help to stop what the de—what Faquarl and Nouda are doing.*

The boy smiled.

Your sacrifice is indeed great, and in Ptolemy's memory I would be pleased to return the gesture. But there are two problems that prevent it. First you'd have to summon me back to Earth, and that may be beyond you now.

Why? Kitty asked. The boy was looking at her with a gentle, almost kindly expression. It unnerved her. *Why?* she asked again.

The second problem, the boy went on, *is my unfortunate weakness. I haven't been here long enough to rebuild my energies fully, and Faquarl—let alone Nouda—has more power in one of his big toes than I do right at this moment. I'm disinclined to enter into slavery that is guaranteed to be fatal. I'm sorry, but there it is.*

It won't be slavery. I told you that before. The mannequin stretched out an arm toward the boy in a hesitant gesture.

But it would *be fatal.*

Kitty's mannequin lowered its arm. *Okay. What if we had the Staff?*

Gladstone's? How? Who'd use it? You couldn't.

Nathaniel's trying to get hold of it right now.

All very well, but could he use—Wait a minute! The radiant features of the boy contorted, slipped out of true, as if the controling intelligence had drawn back in shock; an instant later

403

they were as perfect as before. *Let's get this straight. He told you his name?*

Yes. Now—

I like that . . . I like that! He's been giving me gyp for years, simply because I could have spilled the beans, and now he's telling any old broad he meets, free of charge! Who else knows? Faquarl? Nouda? Did he deck his name out in neon lights and parade it round the town? I ask you! And I never told anyone!

You let it slip last time I summoned you.

Well, apart from that.

But you could have told his enemies, couldn't you, Bartimaeus? You'd have found a way to harm him if you'd really wished it. And Nathaniel knows that too, I think. I had a talk with him.

The boy looked thoughtful. *Hmm. I know all about those talks of yours.*

Anyway, he's gone for the Staff; I went to find you. Together—

The long and the short of it is that none of us are up to a fight. Not anymore. You won't be, for starters. As for Mandrake, last time he tried to use the Staff he knocked himself out. What makes you think he'll have the strength to do it now? He was exhausted last time I saw him. . . . Meanwhile, my essence is so shot I couldn't maintain a simple form on Earth, let alone be useful. I probably couldn't even withstand the pain of materializing in the first place. Faquarl's got one thing right. He doesn't have to worry about the pain. No, let's face facts, Kitty— A pause. *What? What's the matter?*

The mannequin had tilted its bulbous head and was regarding the boy with an air of quiet intentness. The boy became uneasy.

What? What are you—? Oh. No. Absolutely no way.

But, Bartimaeus, it would protect your essence. You wouldn't feel any pain.

Uh-uh. No.

And if you combined your power with his, maybe the Staff—

No.

What would Ptolemy *have done?*

The boy turned away. He crossed to the nearest pillar and sat down on the steps, looking out over the swirling void.

Ptolemy showed me the way it might *have been,* he remarked at last. *He thought he would be the first of many—but in two thousand years you, Kitty, are the only one who's followed him. The only one. He and I conversed as equals for two years. I helped him out from time to time; in return he let me explore your world a little. I wandered as far as the Fezzan oasis and the pillared halls of Axum. I floated over the white crests of the Zagros Mountains and the dry stone gulches of the Hejaz deserts. I flew with the hawks and the cirrus clouds, high, high over earth and sea, and took with me memories of those places when I returned home.*

As he spoke, little flickering images danced beyond the pillars of the hall. Kitty could not make them out, but she had little doubt they showed fragments of the wonders he had seen. She sent her mannequin to sit beside him on the step; their legs dangled out over nothingness.

The experience, the boy continued, *was exhilarating. My freedom echoed that of my home, while my interest was roused by what I saw. The pain I felt was never too pressing, since I was able to return here when I wished. How I danced between the worlds! It was a great gift that Ptolemy gave me, and I have never forgotten it. I knew him for two years. And then he died.*

How? Kitty asked. *How did he die?*

At first no answer came. Then:

Ptolemy had a cousin, the heir to the throne of Egypt. He feared my master's power. Several times he attempted to get rid of him, but we—the other djinn and I—stood in his way. Out among the swirling matter Kitty glimpsed recurring images of more than usual clarity: figures crouching on a window ledge, holding long curved swords; demons flitting over nighttime roofs; soldiers at a door. *I would have taken him from Alexandria, particularly after his journey here had rendered him more vulnerable. But he was stubborn; he refused to go, even when Roman magicians arrived in the city and were housed by his cousin in the palace citadel.* Brief flashes in the void: sharp triangular sails, ships below a lighthouse tower; six pale men in coarse brown cloaks standing on a quay.

It pleased my master, the boy went on, *to be carried about the city most mornings, to let the scents of the markets drift over him—the spices, flowers, resins, hides, and skins. All the world was present in Alexandria, and he knew it. Besides, the people loved him. My fellow djinn and I carried him in his palanquin.* Here Kitty caught the suggestion of a curtained chair, suspended on poles. Dark slaves supported it. Behind were stalls and people, bright things, blue sky.

The images winked out; the boy sat silent on the step.

One day, he continued, *we took him to the spice market—his favorite place, where the scents were most intoxicating. We were foolish to do so; the streets were narrow, clogged with people. Progress was slow.* Kitty saw a long, low stall studded with racks of wooden boxes, each filled with colored spice. A barrel maker sat cross-legged before an open door, fixing struts into a metal ring. Other images came and went: houses, painted white; goats milling among crowds; children fixed midrun; the chair again, its curtains shut.

In the center of the market I spotted something moving on a roof up ahead. I gave my pole to Penrenutet, became a bird, rose up to check. Above the roofs I saw—

He broke off. The fabric of the Other Place was black as syrup; it swirled angrily, slowly, lit by lightning flashes. An image lingered—rooftops stretching away, bleached bone-white by a dazzling sun. Across the sky dark figures hung in silhouette— great wings spread, long tails outstretched; here and there light glinted on armored scales. Now Kitty saw horrors: a snake's head, a wolf's snout, a skinless face with bared teeth grinning. The picture vanished.

The Roman magicians had summoned many djinn. Afrits too. They came at us from all sides. We were four djinn. What could we do? We stood and fought. There in the street, among the people, we stood and fought for him. A final confusion of images, rapidly changing and out of focus—smoke, explosions, blue-green energies crackling up and down a narrow lane; humans screaming; the demon with the skinless face falling from the sky, clawing at a hole in the center of its torso. Other djinn too—one had a hippo's head, one an ibis's bill—standing close beside the curtained chair.

Affa died first, the boy continued. *Then Penrenutet and Teti. I threw up a Shield, snatched Ptolemy away. I broke through the wall, killed those who pursued me, fled across the sky. They came after us, like a swarm of bees.*

What happened? Kitty asked. The boy had fallen silent once again. No images appeared in the void.

I was caught by a Detonation. Wounded. Couldn't fly. Broke into a little temple; barricaded us in. Ptolemy was in bad shape—worse, I mean, than he had been before. I think it was the smoke, or something. The enemy surrounded the temple. There was no way out.

And then?

I cannot speak of it. He gave me a final gift. That is the essence of the matter.

The boy shrugged then. He looked across at Kitty's mannequin for the first time.

Poor Ptolemy! He thought his example might help to reconcile our kinds. He was convinced the account of his journey would be read and followed down the centuries, and lead to a union of worlds. He told me so, right here! Well, for all his light and clarity, he was completely wrong. He died, and his ideas have been forgotten.

Kitty's creature frowned. *How can you say that, when I'm here too? And Nathaniel's read his book, and Mr. Button, and—*

The Apocrypha's *only fragments. He never survived to write the rest. Besides, people like Nathaniel read, but they don't believe.*

I believed.

Yes. You did.

If you come back, and help save London, you will be continuing Ptolemy's work. Humans and djinn working together. That's what he wanted, isn't it?

The boy looked out at the void. *Ptolemy made no demands on me.*

I'm not making any demands either. You can do what you wish. I'm asking for your help. If you don't want to respond, that's fine.

Well . . . The boy stretched out his thin brown arms. *It's against my better judgement, but it would be nice to settle scores with Faquarl. We'd need the Staff, mind. Useless without the Staff. And I'm not staying long, especially if I'm cooped up in—*

Thank you, Bartimaeus! In a swell of gratitude, Kitty's mannequin leaned across and flopped its stick arms out around the boy's neck. The bulbous head rested briefly against his slim, dark one.

All right, all right. Don't get soppy. You've made your sacrifice. Now I suppose it's my turn.

Firmly, but with restraint, the boy extricated himself from the mess of limbs and stood upon the step.

You'd better get back, he said. *Before it's too late.*

The mannequin looked up, head twisted accusingly, then sprang to its feet in a fury.

What do you mean, exactly? You keep *saying this. What sacrifice?*

I thought you knew. I'm sorry.

What? I'm going to thump you in a minute.

How? You haven't any hands.

Or—or—I'll push you off the edge. Just tell *me.*

The truth is, Kitty, the Other Place is not conducive to humans. In the same way that my essence suffers on Earth, so your *essence suffers here.*

Meaning?

Meaning you have wilfully separated yourself from your body. Not for too long, which is to your advantage. Ptolemy stayed far longer, asking questions, always asking questions. He was here twice the time that you have been. But . . .

But? Come on.

The mannequin leaped forward, arms outstretched, head thrust out aggressively. The boy stepped back to the final step, teetering on the edge of the void.

Don't you see how good you're becoming at maneuvering that thing? You were hopeless at first. Already you're forgetting your earthly ties. When Ptolemy got back, he'd forgotten almost everything. He couldn't walk, could barely use his limbs. . . . Took him all his strength even to summon me again. And that's not all. While you're here, back on Earth your body's busy dying. Can't really blame it, can you? It's been abandoned. Better get back fast, Kitty. Better get back fast.

—But how? she whispered. *I don't know how.*

Fear flooded her; her mannequin, her bubble-headed creature, stood disconsolate on the step. The boy smiled, stepped forward and kissed it on the forehead.

That's easy, Bartimaeus said. *The Gate's still open. I can dismiss you. Relax. Work's over. You've done your bit.*

He stepped away. The mannequin, the boy, and the pillared hall exploded into wisps and trails. Kitty burst across the maelstrom of the Other Place, among the lights and whirling colors. She drifted, drifted. All around her was the weightlessness of death.

Part Five

Alexandria: 124 B.C.

A hop, a limp—we fell up the steps between the columns. Ahead of us, a door of bronze, green with age. I shoved it open, pitched forward into the sanctuary of the god. Cool, dank air, no windows. I pushed the door shut and slammed fast an ancient bolt. Even as I did so, something collided against the other side.

I put a Seal upon the door for neatness' sake, then sent a Wisp-light flaring against the ceiling, where it hummed and flickered with a pinkish glow. At the end of the room a metal statue of a bearded cove looked at us with grave disapproval. Beyond the door, and all around the sanctuary, came the thwack of leather wings.

I laid my master beneath the Wisp-light and bent my muzzle close. His breathing came erratically. Blood seeped against his clothes. His ravaged face, all weals and wrinkles like an ancient fruit, was bleached of color.

His eyes opened; he raised himself on one arm. "Steady," I said. "Save your strength."

"I don't need to, Bartimaeus," he said, using my true name. "Not anymore."

The lion gave a growl. "None of that talk," I said. "This is called tactics. We're having a rest. I'll break us out of here in a minute."

He coughed. Blood came up. "To be honest, I don't think I could take another of your flights."

"Oh, go on. It'll be even more interesting with just one wing. Think you could flap an arm?"

"No. What happened?"

"It was this stupid mane! I didn't see that djinni coming from the side. He ambushed us; got me with a Detonation! That's the last time I wear one as bushy as this."

There was a small grating up near the top of the old smooth wall. Several shadows wheeled across its strips of light. Something heavy landed on the roof above.

Ptolemy cursed softly under his breath. The lion frowned. "What?"

"Back at the market. I dropped the parchment. My notes on the Other Place."

I sighed. I could sense the movement all around, the click-clack of claw on stone, the small skitterings of scales across the roof tiles; I could hear the whisperings in Latin. I visualized them, clinging to every surface of the building like giant flies. "That's unfortunate," I said, "but it's not our main concern."

"I've not finished my account," he whispered. "Nothing's left in my rooms but fragments."

"Ptolemy, it doesn't matter."

"But it does! This was going to make things different. It was going to change the way magicians worked. It was going to end your slavery."

The lion looked down at him. "Let's be frank," I said. "My slavery—and my life—are going to end in . . . oh, approximately two minutes."

He frowned. "Not so, Bartimaeus."

The walls echoed to the muffled sound of blows. "Yes so."

"I can't get out, but *you* can."

"With *this* wing? You must be—Ah . . . I see." The lion shook its head. "Not a chance."

"I'm technically your master, don't forget. I say you can go. I say you *will* go."

By way of reply, I rose, stood in the center of the little temple, and let out a roar of defiance. The building shook; for a couple of seconds afterward all activity outside was stilled. Then it industriously resumed again.

I snapped my teeth together nastily. "In a few moments," I said, "they're going to break through, and when they do, they'll learn to fear the power of Bartimaeus of Uruk! Anyhow—who knows? I've taken out six djinn at once before now."

"And how many are out there?"

"Oh, about twenty."

"Right. That settles it." With shaking arms, the boy rose to a sitting position. "Help me lean back against that wall. Come on! Come on! Do you want me to die lying down?"

The lion did as he was bid, then straightened. I took up my post facing the door, which, in the center, was glowing red with an intense heat and beginning to bulge a little. "Don't ask again," I said. "I'm not shifting."

"Oh, I won't *ask*, Bartimaeus."

Something in his tone made me swivel round. I saw Ptolemy grinning lopsidedly at me, one hand raised.

I reached toward him. "Don't—"

He snapped his fingers, spoke the Dismissal words. Even as he did so, the door exploded in a shower of molten metal; three tall figures sprang into the room. Ptolemy gave me a small salute, then his head fell back gently against the wall. I rotated toward the enemy and raised a paw to smite them, but my substance had become diffuse like smoke. Despite my most desperate urgings, I could do nothing to hold it firm. All light around me vanished, my consciousness departed; the Other Place pulled me away. Furiously, against my will, I accepted Ptolemy's last gift.

31

The first feeling was that of terrible constriction. With the sudden act of waking, her infinite dimensions were all at once reduced to a single point. She was compressed back down to the margins of her body, tangled up within its lumpen weight. A moment of suffocation, the hideous sensation of being buried alive—then she remembered how to breathe. She lay in darkness, hearing the rhythms within her: the blood moving, the air wheezing back and forth, the bubbles shifting and gurgling in stomach and bowels. She'd never realized before quite how *noisy* she was, how heavy, how densely packed. It seemed an appalling complexity, and one that would be quite impossible to operate. The idea of *moving* it mystified her.

Gradually the confusion resolved itself into vague recognition of the contours of her limbs—the knees drawn up almost to her waist, the feet gently overlapping each other, the hands clasped close against her breast. She visualized it in her head, and with this, a sensation of affection and gratitude for her body came flooding through her. It warmed her: awareness grew. She sensed the hardness of the surface on which she lay; the softness of the cushion pillowing her head. She remembered where she was—and where she had been.

Kitty opened her eyes. Everything was blurred. For a second the swimming lines of light and shadow beguiled her; she thought she was drifting in the Other Place again. . . . Then she steadied herself and concentrated, and slowly, grudgingly, the lines snagged and stopped and yielded up a picture of a person sitting in a chair.

He sat in a posture of extreme exhaustion. His head had slumped sideways; his legs lolled left and right. She heard the rasping of his breath. His eyes were closed.

A chain hung about his neck; at its end was an oval piece of gold, centered with a green-black stone. It rose and fell with the rhythmic movement of his chest. Between his knees a long wooden staff rested at an acute diagonal. One hand was cupped loosely to support it; the other hung limply over the chair arm.

After a while she remembered his name. "Nathaniel?"

Her voice was so faint she could not be sure whether she had actually made a noise, or only sounded the word in her head. Nevertheless, it seemed to work. A grunt, a splutter—the magician's legs and arms jerked as if electrically charged. The staff fell to the floor; with something midway between a leap and a plunge, he was crouching at her side.

She tried to smile. It was hard. Her face hurt. "Hello," she said.

The magician didn't answer. He just stared.

"You got the Staff then," she said, and: "My throat's dry. Got any water?"

Still no reply. His skin, she noticed, was red and chafed, as if he had been out in a high wind. He was gazing at her with extreme attention, yet still contriving to ignore her words completely. Kitty became irritated.

"Move out the way," she snapped. "I'm getting up."

She tensed her stomach muscles, moved an arm, and pressed her fingers to the floor to push herself up. An object fell from her grasp with a dull clang. A wave of nausea filled her; her muscles felt like water.

Kitty's head fell back upon the cushion. Something about her weakness scared her. "Nathaniel . . ." she began. "What . . . ?"

He spoke for the first time. "It's all right. Just rest there."

"I want to get up."

"I really don't think you should."

"*Help me up!*" The fury was fueled by anxiety blossoming into sudden terror. The weakness was all wrong. "I'm not lying here. What is it? What's happened to me?"

"You'll be fine if you just stay put. . . ." His tone was unconvincing. She tried again, pushed herself up a little, collapsed with a curse. The magician swore in tandem. "All right! Here. I'll try to support your back. *Don't* try and take your weight. Your legs will—There! What did I tell you? Do what I *say* for once." He grasped her beneath her arms, lifted her up and swung her round, hauling her toward the chair. Her legs trailed behind her; her feet scraped across the lines of the pentacle. With scant ceremony, Kitty found herself dumped in a sitting position. The magician stood facing her, breathing hard.

"Happy now?" he said.

"Not really. What's happened to me? Why can't I walk?"

"They're not questions I can answer." He stared at his boots—large scuffed leather ones—then across at the empty circle. "When I broke in, Kitty," he said, "the room was icy cold. I couldn't find a pulse on you, and you weren't breathing, just lying there. I thought you were—I *really* thought you were dead this time. Instead . . ." He raised his eyes. "So. Tell me. Did you really—?"

She looked at him for a time without speaking.

The tension in the magician's face loosened into blank astonishment. He exhaled slowly, and half sat, half slumped against the desk. "I see," he said. "I see."

Kitty cleared her throat. "I'll tell you in a minute. First, pass me that mirror, would you?"

"I don't think—"

"I'd rather look," she said crisply, "than use my imagination. So hurry it up. We've got things to do."

No amount of argument could dissuade her.

"After all," she said at last, "it's nothing very different to what happened to Jakob with the Black Tumbler. . . . And *he* was fine."

"That's true." The magician's hands were growing tired. He adjusted the position of the mirror.

"I can dye the hair."

"Yes."

"And as for the rest—I'll kind of grow into it."

"Yes."

"In about fifty years."

"It's just lines, Kitty. Just lines. Lots of people have them. Besides, they might fade."

"You think?"

"Yes. They look a lot less bad already than when I first found you."

"Really?"

"*Definitely*. Anyway, look at me. Check out these blisters."

"I was meaning to ask about them."

"Pestilence did it. When I got the Staff."

"Oh . . . But it's the *weakness* that really scares me, Nathaniel. What if I never—?"

"You will. Look at you waving your hands about. You weren't doing that five minutes ago."

"Wasn't I? Oh. Good. Now you mention it, I *do* feel a little stronger."

"There you go, you see."

"But it's just so difficult," she said, "to look in the mirror and see . . . a different face. To see that everything's *changed*."

"Not everything," he said.

"No?"

"No. Your eyes. They haven't changed at all."

"Oh." She peered dubiously at the glass. "You think?"

"Well, they were fine before you started squinting. Take my word for it." He lowered the mirror, placed it on the table. "Kitty," he said. "I have to tell you something. The demons have broken out across London. After I found you, I tried to set the Staff of Gladstone going, but"—he sighed—"I couldn't make it. It's not the incantations. I've got the knowledge that I didn't have before. It's just . . . I haven't got the physical strength to force my will upon it. And without the Staff, we can't face up to Nouda."

"Nathaniel—"

"There *may* be other magicians left alive and unpossessed. I haven't gone looking yet. But even if we can round up some allies and get their djinn on our side, Nouda's much too strong. The Staff was our only hope."

"That's not so." Kitty leaned forward in the chair. (It was true what he'd said—she was moving a little more easily now. To begin with, everything had felt uncomfortable and misaligned, as if she were out of sync with her bones and sinew.) "I didn't go to the Other Place just for fun," she said primly. "You got the Staff, I found Bartimaeus. Now all we need to do is put them together." She grinned at him.

The magician shook his head in vexation. "Meaning what?"

"Ah. Now, you're not going to like this part."

32

The sulphur cloud contracted into an ailing column of smoke that slouched in the middle of the pentacle. It dribbled up toward the ceiling with the awesome force of water spurting from a drinking fountain. Two timorous yellow eyes materialized in the heart of the smoke. They blinked anxiously.

I was having second thoughts.

The dark-haired youth stood in the pentacle opposite, leaning heavily on the Staff. I recognized it straightaway. Difficult not to: the aura of the talisman beat upon my circle with the intensity of a solar flare. My essence quailed at the proximity.

Bad. I was too weak. I should not have agreed to this.

Mind you, it looked to me as if the magician was of similar mind. His face was the delightful color of off milk.

He drew himself up as best he could and tried to look imposing. "Bartimaeus."

"Nathaniel."[1]

He cleared his throat, gazed at the floor, scratched his head, hummed a few odd notes . . . did everything in fact but look me straight in the eye like a man should. Not that I was *much* better. Instead of billowing ominously, the column of smoke seemed intent on winding its rising threads into pretty braidy patterns. If we'd been left to ourselves, I'd probably have ended

---

[1] We each strove to make the sounds curt, assertive, growling. Neither of us quite succeeded. His voice had the kind of pitch usually reserved for bats and dog whistles, while mine warbled like that of an elderly spinster requesting a cucumber sandwich with her cup of tea.

up knitting a virtual cardigan or something, but after a few seconds of high-quality dithering, a rude interruption came.

"Get *on* with it!"

No prizes for guessing who *that* was. Magician and smoke swiveled in their circles, coughing and muttering. Both wore expressions of wounded aggravation.

"I know, I know," Kitty said. "I don't envy either of you. Just *do* it. We haven't time to waste."

I must say she was looking rather more spry than I expected. Okay, she was a bit frail looking, and she had gray hair and her skin was lined and aged, but she was nothing *like* Ptolemy had been. And her eyes were as bright as a bird's; they shone with the light of what they'd seen. I regarded her with mingled reverence and compassion.

"Keep your knickers on," I said. "We're getting to it."

"That's right," Nathaniel agreed. "Can't rush these things."

"Like you'd *know*," she snorted. "What's the holdup?"

"Well," he began. "It's just—"

"For *my* part," I said, in tones of quiet dignity, "I agreed to this proposal on the assumption that my host would be of moderate physical quality. Now, having viewed him, I'm having doubts."

The magician glared at me. "What's that supposed to mean?"

"Well, you wouldn't buy a horse without seeing it, would you? I'm allowed an inspection. Let's see your teeth."

"Get lost!"

"I'm sorry," I said. "He's rubbish. Can barely stand. Skin's been burned by a Pestilence. And his shoulder's bleeding. I bet he's got worms and all."

The girl frowned. "What's that about his shoulder? Where?"

Nathaniel made a dismissive gesture, and winced. "It's nothing. Not a problem."

"Why didn't you tell me?"

"*Because*," he snarled, "as you keep saying, we haven't got time."

"Fair point," I said.

"In fact, I'm not sure *I* want to go ahead with it either," the magician continued, rewarding me with an unpleasant look. "I don't see how it could possibly work. He's far too weak to help with the Staff, as well as being utterly vile in a thousand ways. Heaven knows what damage he'd do to me! It's like inviting a herd of hogs to come and live in your bedroom."

"Is that so? Well, *I'm* not too enamored of being encased inside your earthly gunge," I cried. "There's a darn sight too much drippy stuff going on in there. All that phlegm and congealing wax and—"

"Shut up!" Kitty shouted. It has to be said, her journey hadn't affected her lungs. "Both of you—*shut up*! My city is being destroyed out there, and we need that Staff to work. The only way we can think of to do that is by combining *your* knowledge, Nathaniel, with *your* energies, Bartimaeus. All right, both of you might be a little inconvenienced, but—"

I looked at Nathaniel. "Hear that? A *little*, she says."

He shook his head in deep disgust. "Tell me about it."

"—but it won't last long. Hours at the most. Then, Nathaniel, you can dismiss Bartimaeus for good."

"Wait," he said, "I want a guarantee that this creature won't try to destroy my mind. It'd be just like him."

"Yeah *right*," I cried, "and burn my only ticket out of there? I'm not hanging out in *your* head for all eternity, pal. Don't worry. I need that Dismissal. I won't touch nothing."

"You'd better not."

We glared at each other for a spell.

The girl clapped her hands. "Ohhh-kay. Posturing over?

Good. I didn't ruin my health just to sit here and watch you two idiots fight. Can we *please* get on with it?"

The magician sniffed. "All right."

The smoke coiled sullenly skyward. "All right."

"That's better."

I would never have done it had it not been for the girl. But she had been quite correct, back there in the Other Place, to appeal to me in Ptolemy's name. As she'd instantly perceived, that was my weak spot, my open wound. And two thousand years of accumulated cynicism hadn't managed to heal it up, try as I might. For all that long and weary time I'd carried round the memory of his hope—that djinn and humans might one day act together, without malice, without treachery, without slaughter. Let's face it, it was a stupid idea and I didn't believe it for an instant—there was simply too much evidence to the contrary. But *Ptolemy* had believed it and that was enough. Just the echo of his faith was powerful enough to win me over when Kitty repeated his great gesture, and came across to meet me.

She'd renewed his bond. And once *that* was done, my fate was sealed. No matter what the groans and cussing of my better judgement, I'd have thrown myself into a pit of fire for Ptolemy, and the same was true for Kitty now.

Mind you . . . pit of fire? Vat of acid? Bed of nails? Any of them would've been preferable to what I was about to do.

In one circle the magician was busy psyching himself up. He was getting his lines straight, readying the incantation. In the other, the column of smoke drifted back and forth like a caged tiger. I noticed that both pentacles had had holes scratched in their perimeters to allow me immediate transit from one side to the other. Boy, they were trusting . . . I could have nipped out there and then, and gobbled them both up before departing with a smile and a song. Part of me *itched* to do it as well, just to see the expression on my old master's face. It had been *ages* since I'd devoured a magician.[2] But of course, unscheduled devouring was off Kitty's agenda for the day. Regretfully, I resisted the temptation.

There was also the small matter of my condition. Even so simple a form as the smoke was proving hard to maintain. I needed protection, and I needed it fast.

"Sometime today," I said. "*If* you don't mind."

The magician ran nervous fingers through his hair and turned to Kitty. "Any snide comments when he's in there and I'll dismiss him right off, Staff or no Staff. You tell him."

She tapped a foot. "I'm *waiting*, Nathaniel."

A curse, a rub of the face, then he was off. The incantation was a tad improvised, I felt—didn't have the elegance and refinement I was used to. The clause "snare this cursed demon Bartimaeus and compress him with unmerciful precision" was a little crude, for instance, and could have been misinterpreted. But it seemed to do the trick. One moment the column of smoke was rising innocently in its circle, the next it had been sucked up and outward, over the break in my pentacle, over the break in his, and drawn down, down, down toward my master's head. . . .

---

[2] A couple of hundred years, in fact. A Czech master of mine had been inclined to plumpness. I used to criticize him for his lack of condition, gradually building up in him a sense of annoyed defiance. One night I challenged him to touch his toes while in his pentacle. He succeeded valiantly, but in so doing stuck his backside over the edge of the circle, allowing me to break my bonds. And sure enough, he *was* a bit fatty, but he still tasted pretty good.

I braced myself. I glimpsed him squeeze his eyes tight shut. . . .
Plunk.

Gone. The pain was gone. That was my first sensation. That was
all that mattered. It was like a curtain had suddenly been flung
open and everything had gone from dark to light. It was like
being plunged into an ice-cold spring. It was a *little* like returning to the Other Place after months of slavery—the crisscross
lattices of hurt that ran throughout my essence just fell away
like scabs, left me suddenly feeling whole. It was like being
refreshed and rebuilt and reborn, all at the same time.

My essence surged with a terrible joy, the kind I hadn't
felt on Earth since my first few summonings back in Sumer,
back when I thought my energies could cope with *anything*.[3] I
hadn't realized how much of my recent weakness had simply
been down to the accumulated pain; the moment it was gone
I was ten times the djinni that I'd been before. No wonder
Faquarl and the others had recommended it so.

I let out a cry of triumph.

Which echoed curiously, as if I were trapped in a bottle.[4]

An instant later came *another* cry, curiously loud and all

---

[3] *That* didn't last long, of course. "Oh, Bartimaeus, could you just irrigate the Fertile
Crescent?" "Could you just divert the Euphrates *here* and *here*?" "Look, while you're
at it, do you mind just planting a few million wheat seeds up and down the flood-
plain? Thanks." Didn't even give me a dibble. By the time I got to Ur I wasn't surging with any of that terrible joy, oh no. My back was *killing* me.

[4] Believe me, I know all about bottle acoustics. I spent much of the sixth century in
an old sesame oil jar, corked with wax, bobbing about in the Red Sea. No one heard
my hollers. In the end an old fisherman set me free, by which time I was desperate
enough to grant him several wishes. I erupted out in the form of a smoking giant,
did a few lightning bolts, and bent to ask him his desire. Poor old boy had dropped
dead of a heart attack. There should be a moral there, but for the life of me I can't
see one.

around. It deafened me. With this distraction, I awoke to my surroundings. To what cloaked me and shielded me from the world. Not to put too fine a point on it, it was human flesh.

Nathaniel's, to be precise.

Where the soup in Faquarl's tureen had given me a *modicum* of protection from the deathly silver on all sides, Nathaniel's body made a much better job of it. My essence was immersed—in bone and blood and little thready things that I suppose might have been sinew; I'd spread throughout him from hair to toe. I felt the pulsing of his heart, the endless flow across the veins, the whispery wheeze-box of his lungs. I saw the flitting drifts of electricity moving back and forth across the brain; I saw (less certainly) the thoughts they signified. And for a moment there I marveled—it was like stepping into a great building—some holy mosque or shrine—and glimpsing its perfection; something airy built of clay. Then came the secondary wonder: that such a ropey thing could actually work at all, so fragile was it, so weak and cumbrous, so tied to earth.

How *easy* it would have been to take control, to treat the body like a cart or chariot—a humble vehicle to be ridden where I pleased! The faintest of temptations ran through me . . . Without a second's pause, I could have closed in upon the brain and damped down its little energies, set myself to pull the levers to keep the mechanism going. . . . No doubt Nouda and Faquarl and Naeryan and all the rest had been pleased to do this. It was their revenge in microcosm, their triumph over humanity carried out in miniature.

But that was not for me.

Not that it wasn't tempting, mind.

I've never been the biggest fan of Nathaniel's voice. It was just about bearable at a distance, but now it was as if I were tied up inside a loudspeaker on full volume. When he spoke, the reverberations hummed and quivered through my essence.

"Kitty!" that great galumphing elephant of a voice cried. "I feel such energy!"

Her voice came to me slightly muffled, refracted through his ears. "Tell me! What does it feel like?"

"It ripples through me! I feel so light! I could leap to the stars!"[5] He hesitated, as if embarrassed at his unmagicianish enthusiasm. "Kitty," he said, "do I look any different?"

"No ... Except you're less stooped. Can you open your eyes?"

He opened them for the first time and I looked out. It was an odd double vision to begin with; for a moment it was all blurred and vague. I suppose that was his human vision—so weak and halting! Then I shifted my essence into alignment and things got clearer. I ratcheted through the seven planes and heard Nathaniel gasp.

"You'd never believe it!" he bellowed in my ear. "Kitty! It's like everything's got more colors, more dimensions. And around you there's such a *glow*!"

That was her aura. Always stronger than average, since her visit to the Other Place it had waxed into noonday splendor. Just as Ptolemy's had done. I never saw another human one like it. Ripples of wonder ran through Nathaniel's body; his brain fizzed with it. "You're so *beautiful*!" he said.

"Oh, only now?" He'd really fallen into that one. It was the tone of stupefied amazement that had sunk him.[6]

---

[5] A logical sensation from his point of view. He had absorbed *me*: a being of fire and air.

[6] Nothing changes. Nefertiti was *always* doing that to Akhenaton, sidling over while he was doing the crop accounts, asking him how she looked in her nice new head-dress. He never learned.

"No! I only meant—"

I thought it was time to assert myself. The poor sap wasn't doing so well on his own. I took control of his larynx. "Do you mind keeping your voice down?" I said. "I can't hear yourself think."

He went very quiet then. They both did. I felt him raise a hand to his mouth, as if he'd just hiccuped in company.

"That's right," I said. "Me. What, did you think I'd be all nice and quiet for you? Think again, sonny. There are two of us in this body now. Check this out."

To prove my point I lifted one of his fingers and methodically picked his nose. He uttered a squawk of protest. "Stop that!"

I lowered the arm. "That's not all I can do if I put your mind to it. Sheesh . . . it's a strange little world in here . . . Like being dunked in chocolate mousse, except without the nice flavor. Some of your thoughts, Nathaniel . . . *Well!* If Kitty only knew. . . ."

He wrested control of his mouth again. "Enough! *I'm* in charge. We agreed that. We must act in harmony, or risk destruction."

Kitty spoke from her chair. "He's right, Bartimaeus. We've wasted too much time already. You've got to work together."

"Fine," I said, "but he needs to listen to *me*. I know more about Faquarl and Nouda than he does. I'll be able to preempt their actions. And I can move his body around all right. Watch this. . . ."

I'd figured out the leg muscles nicely; I bent them, stretched them—my essence did the rest. From a standing start we leaped over the desk to the far side of the room.

"Not bad, eh?" I chuckled. "Smooth as silk." I bent the legs again, gave a stretch . . . At exactly the same time the magician attempted to walk in the opposite direction. Our body floundered, one leg up in the air, the other about 170 degrees akimbo from it. We did the splits, uttered harmonic cries of mild discomfort, and crashed upon the carpet.

"Yeah," Kitty said. "*Really* smooth."

I allowed Nathaniel to organize the business of getting to his feet again. "I *knew* that would happen," he snarled. "This is hopeless."

"You just don't like taking orders," I snapped back. "Don't like your slave calling the shots. Once a magician, always a—"

"Quiet," Kitty said. Whether it was her aura or not, something about her nowadays brooked no argument. We stood quiet and let her speak. "If you took a moment to stop squabbling," she went on, "you'd see that you're acting together far better than Nouda and the others are managing in their stolen bodies. Faquarl was at home in Hopkins, but *he'd* had practice. The others were almost helpless."

"She's right. . . ." Nathaniel said. "Nouda couldn't walk."

It took a djinni to get to the nub of the matter. "There are two crucial differences," I said. "*I* haven't destroyed your mind. That's *got* to help. Also, I know your birth name. I'll bet that gives me deeper access to you than the other spirits can hope to gain. There you go, you see. I *knew* it would come in useful one day."

The magician scratched his chin. "Maybe . . ."

Our philosophical speculations were curtailed by an impatient cry. "Whatever," Kitty said. "Just tell each other what you plan and you should avoid stupid pratfalls. Now—how about the *Staff*?"

How *about* the Staff? All this time we had held it in our fist, and even through Nathaniel's insulating bones and flesh I could feel its immanence. I sensed the restless writhing of the great beings trapped inside it, dimly heard their pleading to be free. The locks and binding seals that Gladstone had wrought upon the wood were still as strong as the day he fixed them. Fortunate, that—since, if released all at once, the pent-up energies would have leveled a city block.[7]

Kitty was watching us narrowly. "Do you think you can activate it?"

"Yes," we said.

Nathaniel held the Staff with both hands. (I allowed him to manipulate our limbs here. This was his moment—we needed *his* formula to start the process, his direction. I was just providing the extra energies, the strength behind his will.) We stood with legs slightly apart, body braced for the impact. He began to speak. While he did so, I looked through his eyes around the little room. There was Kitty, sitting in the chair. Her aura more than matched the Staff's. Beyond was a doorway, broken in by some small blast. Piled up on the floor were several Inferno sticks and elemental spheres. Nathaniel had brought them; he'd used a Detonation cube to destroy the door. He'd been so anxious about Kitty, he'd forgotten the pain in his shoulder, forgotten his weariness for a time. . . .

---

[7] Using an item like this is a bit like unscrewing the top of a cola bottle. No. Perhaps it *is* moderately more exciting: imagine shaking the bottle first. Then you slowly, slowly turn the top. . . . The secret is to turn it enough to get just a *little* fizz. Then the magician can direct that power where he wants. Too much turning or doing it too fast, and your hands get sticky. In a manner of speaking. Notable buildings destroyed by careless use of talismans include: Alexandria's Library and the Pharos Lighthouse, Babylon's Hanging Gardens, the citadel of Great Zimbabwe, and the Underwater Palace of Kos.

A curious thing, feeling a man's mind move. It shifted like a sleeper in the dark, while elsewhere his conscious thoughts churned out the incantation. Faces floated past me: Kitty's; an older woman's; others that I didn't recognize at all. And then (a shock this)—Ptolemy's too, clear as a bell. So *long* since I had seen it. . . . two thousand years . . . But of course, *this* image was nothing but a memory of me.

Time to concentrate. I felt my energies being drawn upon—sucked out through Nathaniel's words and converted into bonds around the Staff. The incantation was coming to its close. Gladstone's Staff shuddered. Pale streams of light ran up its length and congregated by the carved pentacle at the end. We felt the beings within pressing against the crack we had created in their prison; we felt Gladstone's locking mechanisms struggling to seal themselves. We denied them both.

Nathaniel's chant came to an end. The Staff pulsed once—a brilliant white light filled the room on every plane. We stumbled where we stood: Nathaniel shut our eyes. Then the light fell back. Equilibrium was reached. All was still. The room was quiet. Almost too faintly to be heard, the Staff of Gladstone hummed in our grasp.

As one, we turned to where Kitty sat watching in her chair.

"Ready now," we said.

33

Just for a moment, when the Staff had been activated and the djinni's energies had flowed through him to keep its power in check, Nathaniel remembered the wound in his shoulder. He got an indignant stab of pain, a sudden wooziness in his head . . . then his new strength waxed in him once again, and the frailty vanished. He felt better than he had ever done.

His body still echoed with the sensation of that first instant, when Bartimaeus's powers had fused within him. It was like an electric shock, a surge that threatened to carry him off the floor, to deny gravity altogether—all his weight and weariness fell away. He burned with life. With sudden clarity (his mind seemed sharper, newly whetted), he perceived the djinni's nature—understood its ceaseless urge for movement, change, and transformation. He sensed how harsh a fate it was for this nature to be forcibly restricted, to be pent up among earthly, solid things. He glimpsed (only blearily at first) an endless succession of images, memories, imprints, stretching back into a terrible abyss of time. It gave him a feeling not unlike vertigo.

All his senses were afire. His fingers felt each whorl and grain upon the Staff, his ears caught its minute hum. Best of all he saw and understood each plane—all seven of them. The room was bathed in the colors of a dozen auras—from the Staff, from himself and, most extraordinary of all, from Kitty. Through its glow her face seemed smooth and young again, her hair shone like flames. He could have gazed at her forever—

Stop that nonsense right now. I feel quite sick.

If a wretched djinni hadn't been gabbling in his head.

I wasn't doing anything, he thought.

Not much you weren't. Staff's up and running. We need to go.

Yes. Warily, in case the djinni had other plans for his legs, Nathaniel turned to Kitty. "You should stay here."

"I'm feeling stronger." To Nathaniel's alarm, she inched forward in the chair and, supporting her weight with shaking hands, got to her feet. "I can walk," she said.

"Even so, you're not coming with us."

He felt the djinni stir within his mind; its voice echoed from his mouth. As before, the effect was disconcerting. Also, it rather tickled. "Nathaniel's right," Bartimaeus said. "You're far too weak. If his memory's up to scratch, which I doubt, there may still be prisoners in the building—if Nouda hasn't killed them all. Why not try to find them?"

She nodded. "Okay. What's your plan? Why don't you use the scrying glass to see where Nouda is?"

Nathaniel shifted. "Well—"

"He's bust it," the djinni said. "Set the imp free. Big mistake, in my opinion."

"I can answer for myself," Nathaniel growled. He found it particularly annoying to be interrupted by his own larynx.

Kitty smiled at him. "Good for you. Well, see you later then."

"Yes . . . Sure you'll be all right?"

He felt a burst of impatience from the djinni. His limbs quivered; he longed to give a leap, surge through the air. . . . "I'll be fine. Here—you'd better take this." He ducked his head, lifted the Amulet of Samarkand from around his neck and held it out to her. "Wear it," he said. "It'll protect you."

"Just against *magic*, mind," the djinni added. "Not against physical attack, or tripping up, or banging your head, or stubbing your toe, or anything like that. But within its strictly limited parameters, it works pretty well."

Kitty hesitated. "I do have *some* resilience," she began. "Maybe I shouldn't—"

"Not enough to cope with Nouda," Nathaniel said. "Especially after what you've been through. Please . . ."

She put the necklace over her head. "Thanks," she said. "Good luck."

"You too." There was nothing more to say. The moment had come. Nathaniel strode to the doorway, chin foremost, eyes somber and purposeful. He did not look back. A mound of debris from the broken door littered the floor; he stepped carefully over it at the very moment that the djinni forced his legs into a skip and a jump. His feet collided; he tripped, sprawled, dropped the Staff, and rolled head across heels over the debris and out through the door.

Suavely done, Bartimaeus said.

Nathaniel made no audible response. Scooping up the Staff of Gladstone, he trudged off down the corridor.

A scene of inventive devastation unfolded at the Hall of Statues, where the marble heads of every deceased Prime Minister had been ripped from their torsos and apparently used to play a game of bowls. The broken Council table sat near the wall; around it, on the seven chairs, the bodies of various magicians had been placed in comical positions, as if in ghastly conclave. The room had suffered every kind of magical assault, sporadic and at random: areas of floor, wall, and ceiling were broken, pierced, blackened, melted, and cut away. Smoking fragments showed where the rugs had been. Corpses lay higgeldy-piggeldy, forlorn, broken, like discarded toys. At the far end of the hall a giant hole had been blasted in the stonework. Cold air came gusting through it.

"Look at the pentacles," Nathaniel said suddenly.

I am looking. I've got your eyes, haven't I? And I agree with you.

"What?"

What you're thinking. They've destroyed them systematically. They want to make it harder for any magicians who've survived.

Every pentacle had been somehow defaced or ruined: the mosaic circles torn up and scattered, the careful lines shot to fragments by casual bursts of fire. It was just like the scenes in the Forum at Rome, when the barbarians came knocking at the gate and the citizens rose up against the ruling magicians. *They'd* begun by destroying the pentacles too. . . .

Nathaniel shook his head. "That's irrelevant," he said. "Stick to the job in hand."

I am. Can I help it if you raid my memories?

Nathaniel didn't answer. He had caught sight of faces he recognized lying amid the rubble. The corners of his mouth clamped down. "Let's go," he said.

What's with the retrospective grief? You didn't like them anyway.

"We need to speed up."

All right. Leave the movement to me.

This was the most peculiar sensation of all: to relax your muscles, to deliberately cut off all command from them, yet feel them tense and spring, move with great harmonious sweeps and bounds, feel them surging with an exuberance that was not human. Nathaniel kept tight hold of the Staff; other than this, he allowed the djinni free rein. With a single bound, he had crossed the hall, landed on a fallen block. A pause; his head moved left and right, then he was away again—a giant stride, then another; he ducked down through the hole in the wall, soared up into another room, dark, ravaged, filled with debris. He did not get a chance to focus on it; he was too busy trying to cope with his lurching stomach, with the thrill of the energies awoken within him. Up into the air and down again—out of this room and through another—past a staircase blown to matchwood, across a mess of masonry, boulder-sized. Through a gaping arch of ruptured stone—

Out onto the streets of Whitehall.

They landed, knees bent, ready to spring again. Nathaniel's head was cocked, his eyes swiveled; they saw all planes.

"Oh no . . ." he whispered.

Oh YES, the djinni said.

Whitehall was aflame. Above the rooftops the lowest clouds glowed pink and orange; fiery light drained between them into chasms of blackness, pricked with stars. The great ministries of government, where imperial business never ceased, stood dark and empty. All lights were off, the street lamps too. A building to the north—was it the Education Ministry? Nathaniel could not tell—had a fire burning on an upper floor. Little flickering darts of redness waved from the windows like autumn leaves. Smoke rose to mingle with the clouds. Other blazes crackled in buildings opposite. It all had an unreal quality, like illusions in one of Makepeace's plays.

The street was empty save for debris, toppled lamps and statues, and—lying dark and small like scalded ants—scattered human bodies. Here a limousine had been hurled through the glass front of the Ministry of Transport; there one of the vast sculptures "Respect for Authority" lay in ruins—its monolithic feet all that remained upon its pedestal. The war memorials had been likewise shattered, the road half blocked with granite. From up the slow curve of Whitehall, from the direction of Trafalgar Square, a dull explosion sounded.

"That way," Nathaniel said. His legs sprang, he soared high, dived low. At his height he was level with the second story of the buildings; each time he dropped to earth he gave it only the lightest glancing touch before springing on. His boots rattled loosely on his feet.

"You know I'm wearing the seven-league boots," he gasped. The wind took his breath away.

Of course I know. I am you for the moment, like it or not. We don't need them yet. Are you ready with the Staff? There's something up ahead.

Past the war memorials, past abandoned cars. The body of a wolf lay in the middle of the road, along with tatters of barbed wire, warning signs, the remnants of a police cordon. Ahead was Trafalgar Square. Nelson's Column rose into the night, bathed in a mustard-yellow glow. Small explosions echoed back and forth beneath it. Among the stalls and booths of the tourist market, little shadows fled and scattered. Something bounded at their heels.

Nathaniel came to rest at the edge of the square. He bit his lip. "It's chasing the people."

Bit of sport. Probably thinks she's back at the Colosseum . . .[1] *Look! That man survived a Detonation. Some of these guys have resilience.*

---

[1] Slaves and prisoners of war were given iron knives and sent into Rome's great arena to combat captive djinn. The Roman elite used to just *love* the comedy chases and all the hilarious methods of death.

Nathaniel placed a hand over his eyes. "Your thoughts went in different directions there. Keep it simple. I can't cope."

Okay. Staff ready? Well then, here we go-o-o-!

Before Nathaniel could prepare himself, his legs had given a bound: he was across the road, in among the burning stalls. Down through the smoke—past a cowering woman and a small child. A hop, a leap . . . Straight ahead, standing by a fountain, bent like a beast—the body of Clive Jenkins. Pale green fires burned behind his eyes; his mouth hung slack, distended. Yellow vapor curled from his hands.

Nathaniel stared in shock, with difficulty regained control. He raised the Staff—

His legs leaped once more. He found himself flying through the air. At his back, an explosion; tiny pieces of concrete struck the side of his face. He landed on the head of a lion statue, directly beneath the column.

"What did you move us for?" he shouted. "I was just getting ready—"

Another second and we'd have been blown apart. Got to be faster. Naeryan's an afrit; she doesn't waste time.[2]

"Will you *stop* doing that? I'm trying to concentrate." Nathaniel focused the Staff, readied himself . . .

Well, hurry it up. She's getting closer. If we had the Amulet we'd be laughing. Why'd you have to give it to Kitty anyhow? . . . Mmm, yeah, I know. Fair point. Isn't it hard to maintain an argument when you can read each other's mind? Uh-oh—Detonation coming. I'm going to jump.

"Go on then."

---

[2] I first encountered Naeryan in Africa during the Scipio campaigns. Her favorite manifestation was as a lissom belly dancer, who would lure—

Sure? You don't mind?

"Just do it!"

Out from the smoke came a horribly hopping figure. The afrit within had mastered the limbs, yet chose to move on tiptoe rather than with human tread. A flash of golden light blew the lion statue apart, but Bartimaeus had already pulled the correct tendons, engaged the muscles—Nathaniel found himself somersaulting directly over the monster's head, landing at its back.

Now, Bartimaeus said.

Nathaniel spoke a single word. The Staff was triggered. A shaft of white light, diamond hard, narrow as a hand's breadth, shot from the center of the carved pentacle at its head. The ground shuddered; Nathaniel's teeth rattled in his jaw. The light missed Clive Jenkins's body by several feet and struck Nelson's Column, snapping it like a bread stick. The white light vanished. Nathaniel looked up. The afrit looked up. In utter silence the column teetered, shifted, and slowly, slowly seemed to grow. . . . Then it was collapsing on them with a whistling almost like a scream, and Bartimaeus was launching them sideways, through the fabric of a burning stall, down onto the paving, hard upon the wounded shoulder, as the column fell to earth and sliced the square in two.

Nathaniel was on his feet in an instant. Pain flared in his collarbone. A voice of fury was shouting in his mind. *You've got to direct it properly! I'll* do *it next time!*

"No, you won't. The demon—where is it?"

Long gone by now, no doubt. You really messed that up big time.

"Now listen—" A movement a few meters away attracted his notice. Four white faces—a woman and her children crouching between the stalls. Nathaniel held out his hand. "It's all right," he said. "I'm a magician—"

The woman gave a little scream; the children started and clustered close to her. A sardonic voice sounded in his head. *Oh, nice one. Very reassuring. Why not offer to cut their throats too, while you're about it?*

Nathaniel cursed inwardly. Outwardly, he tried to smile. "I'm on your side," he said. "Stay here. I'll—"

He looked up suddenly. The voice in his head: *See it?* Through the burning tatters of the stall, amid the clouds of dust that rose from the shattered pieces of the fallen column, he caught the glint of green. He refocused: on the higher planes he glimpsed the narrowed eyes more easily, the furtive lolloping movement in the dark. Nearer and nearer Clive Jenkins's body came, tiptoeing from stall to stall, hoping to catch him unawares.

Bartimaeus spoke quickly: *It'll be a Flux this time. . . . Because I'm a djinni—that's how I know these things. Fluxes cover a wide area. She'll hope to disable you. I can put a Shield over us, but that'll deflect the stream from the Staff.*

"Can you put the Shield over those people? . . . Do that, then. *We* won't need one."

Nathaniel allowed his hand to lift. Energies coursed through the outstretched fingers. A blue sphere extended over the huddled commoners, sealing them in. He turned back toward the square. Dust rose; black fragments drifted from the burning fabric of the stalls. No tiptoeing demon to be seen.

"Where is it?"

How should I know? You've not got eyes in the back of your head. I can only look where you do.

"All right, all right, calm down."

I'm calm. It's you who isn't. All these weird chemicals shooting through your system, pepping you up. It's no wonder humans don't think straight. There! No—just the wind flapping that canvas. Ooh. Made me jump, that did.

Nathaniel scanned the square. The Staff hummed in his hand. He tried to tune out the constant flitter of the djinni's voice, its flood of memories; at times they almost swamped him. Where was the demon hiding? Behind the column's splintered base? Doubtful . . . too far away . . . *Where*, then?

It's beyond me, Bartimaeus said. *Maybe she's run off.*

Nathaniel took a few tentative steps forward. His skin crawled; he felt the imminence of danger. Far away across the square he saw a railing, a set of steps leading below the pavement. It was the subway, the Underground. . . . Below the square stretched a network of tunnels, connecting with the trains, carrying pedestrians beneath the roads. And those tunnels came up . . .

At different points about the square. . . .

Turn! He thought the order, relaxed his muscles, allowed the djinni to do the rest. As he spun, he spoke the word, directed the Staff. A bolt of white light beamed out—cut through the air, atomized the body of Clive Jenkins that came creeping up behind him. One minute the demon was there, clammy hand outstretched to deal a Flux, the next it had vanished, along with the subway entrance beyond it. Foul ash blew upon the molten pavement.

Good thinking, that was, the djinni said. *Didn't remember Naeryan being that sneaky.*

Nathaniel took a slow breath. He crossed to where the little group crouched beneath their Shield and waved a hand. Bartimaeus removed the sphere. The woman stood up quickly, clutching the children close. "Whitehall's the safest way," Nathaniel began. "The demons are gone from there, I think.

Go that way, but do not fear, madam. I'll—" He halted; the woman had turned from him; face blank, eyes sullen and remote, she ushered the children away between the stalls.

What do you expect? The djinni's voice cut in on his surprise. *You and your kind got her into this mess in the first place. She won't be thanking you in a hurry, whatever you do. Don't worry, though, Nat. You're not totally alone. You've always got me.* Laughter bubbled unbidden through his mind.

For a few seconds Nathaniel stood where he was, head a little bent, looking out upon the desolation of the square. Then he set his shoulders, firmed his grip upon the Staff, rapped the heel of his boot once upon the ground—and was gone.

34

Kitty located the prisoners far faster than she had expected. The slowest part was at the outset—as she geared herself up to leave the little room. When she first stood, every muscle in her body protested to the skies; she shuddered as if from extreme cold; her head felt light and watery. But she did not capsize.

I've just got to relearn it, she thought. Remind my body what it can do.

And it was true that with each shuffling step, her confidence grew. She made it to the cache of weapons piled beside the door. She grimaced, bent her knees, crouched, and held that position, wobbling and cursing, as she rummaged through the pile. Jolt-sticks, Inferno sticks, elemental spheres . . . familiar objects from the Resistance years. She had no bag, but tucked an Inferno and a jolt-stick in her belt. Two spheres, with difficulty, fitted in the tattered pockets of her jacket. (She removed Ptolemy's *Apocrypha* and set it, not without a certain reverence, on the floor. It had served its purpose well.) Among the magical objects lay a silver disc, smooth and razor-edged. Subduing a slight, unaccountable, aversion, she added it to a pocket. Then, supporting herself against the wall, she clawed herself back to her feet.

Carefully, little by little, she set off out of the room, over the shattered fragments of the door, down the corridor, past the bleak expanse of the ruined Hall of Statues. She had a memory in her mind—of plaintive sounds coming from behind a door close to where Nathaniel and she had been imprisoned.

As she went, Kitty was conscious of a strange division within her. Never had she felt so appallingly weak, so tentatively tied to earthly strength. Yet, by the same token, neither had she ever felt so wholly sure of herself as she did now. Often in the past she had been filled with reckless certainty, with joyful confidence in her youth and vigor. This was not like that. It was a calmer feeling, quieter, entirely unconnected with physical things, and lacking the edginess they tended to involve. It was a kind of implacable assurance; she felt it radiate from her as she shuffled along.

Her first test did not dent this feeling in the slightest. At the point where the corridor broadened out, close to a set of stairs, Kitty encountered one of the demons. Probably it was the last to take possession of a body; certainly it had not mastered it with any great success. Its host had been a tall, thin man with blond and lanky hair, dressed in dark clothes of obvious expense. Now the clothes were ripped and torn, the hair disordered, the eyes opaque like sea glass. The legs stumbled from one side of the corridor to the other, the arms thrashing blindly. A feral growling issued from his throat, with—every now and then—angry words in an unknown language.

The head turned; it caught sight of Kitty. A yellow gleam burned behind the eyes. Kitty halted, waiting. The demon's interest showed itself in a sudden wild ululation that set the glass rattling in the cabinets along the corridor. It decided to attack, but seemed in doubt exactly *how* to issue a magical bombardment. First it raised a leg, pointed a foot, and blew its own shoe off. Next it tried an elbow, with comparable success. Lastly, with painful hesitation, a hand was raised, a trembling finger extended, and a bolt of lilac light was delivered forth, to strike the Amulet of Samarkand and be at once absorbed.

The demon inspected its finger in annoyance. Kitty took the jolt-stick from her belt, stepped quietly forward, and sent a burst of shimmering blue current rattling through its body. Swathed in black smoke, the demon jittered, jigged, flung itself backward, crashed through the balustrade, and fell four meters to the steps below.

Kitty went her way.

Minutes later she came to the door she had remembered. Listening closely, Kitty detected muffled groans. She tried the door, found it locked and blew it open with the first of her elemental spheres. Once the final winds had died away, she stepped inside.

The room was not large, and what space it had was blotted out by recumbent bodies. At first sight Kitty feared the worst; then she saw that all were neatly tied and gagged, just as they had been left by Makepeace's imps so many hours before. Most were secured by the minimum of ropes and cords, but one or two were swathed in sheets or thick wads of black netting. There were perhaps twenty individuals in the room, sardine-packed, head to toe. To Kitty's great relief, she saw that many of them were moving with sad little wriggles, like maggots in a jar.

One or two pairs of staring eyes caught sight of her; their owners writhed and uttered pleading moans. She took a moment to gather herself; her legs shook with the effort of her stroll thus far. Then she spoke as clearly as she could.

"I'm here to help you," she said. "Wait as patiently as you can. I'll try to cut you free."

This pronouncement induced a remarkable flurry of squirms and wails. Legs thrashed, heads bucked and twisted.

Kitty was nearly knocked over by the flailing of the bodies next to her. "If you don't lie quiet," she said severely, "I'll *leave* you." Instant quietness among the prone magicians. "*That's* better. Now then . . ."

With clumsy fingers, she took the silver disc from her pocket and, holding it carefully so as not to slice her fingers, set to upon the nearest bonds. The cords parted like butter to a hot knife. Cramped hands and feet moved tentatively, their owner emitting cries of pain. Without ceremony, Kitty removed the gag. "When you can stand," she said, "find something sharp and help me untie the others." She moved on to the next magician.

Within ten minutes the room was filled with limping, stretching men and women; some sitting, others standing first on one foot, then on the other, trying to wring the pins and needles from their numb and swollen limbs. There was no conversation; the bodies had been freed, but the minds remained wrapped in shock and disbelief. Kitty worked silently on the penultimate captive, a large gentleman swathed in netting. He seemed inert; blood had seeped through the cloth around his head. Beside her, the first person she had freed, a young woman with mousy hair, struggled with the cords of the last magician. This one, covered in a coarse gray blanket, was very much alive; her legs kicked back and forth with furious impatience.

Kitty passed the silver disc across. "Here."

"Thanks."

In moments the swathes of net and blanket had been removed and the two captives lay revealed. One, a woman with long dark hair hanging over a red and puffy face, sprang instantly to her feet and shrieked with agony as her cramp kicked in. The other, an immense old man with a badly beaten face, lay still. His eyes were closed; his breathing came in ragged gasps.

The dark-haired woman leaned back against a wall and massaged a leg. She gave a snarl of pain and fury. "Who? *Who* is responsible for this? I'll kill them. I'll kill them, I swear it."

Kitty was busy talking to the woman with mousy hair. "He's in a bad way. Someone needs to get him to a hospital."

"I'll fix it," the woman said. She looked around the room, picked out a spotty youth. "George. Can you oblige?"

"All right, Miss Piper."

"Wait." This was Kitty. Wearily she tried to rise, extended a shaking hand. "Can you help me up, please? Thanks." She turned to face the room. "You all need to know what's happened. The situation outside may be . . . difficult. Demons have broken loose in London."

Gasps, oaths; the assembled faces registered sagging dismay. Young and old, they gaped at her, vulnerable and uncomprehending. Gone was any vestige of magicianly assurance—now they were nothing but humans, panic-stricken, leaderless, stripped bare. Kitty held up a hand. "Listen," she said, "and I'll tell you."

"One moment." The black-haired woman reached out and clutched at Kitty's arm. "First, who the hell are *you*? I don't recognize your face, or"—she curled a lip—"your dirty little clothes. I don't think you're even a magician."

"Correct," Kitty snapped. "I'm a commoner. But you'd do well to shut up and hear me out if you want to avoid being killed."

The woman's eyes widened. "How *dare* you—?"

"Yes, shut your trap, Farrar," a man said.

The woman seemed to choke; she looked around wildly, but let go of Kitty's arm.

This one exception apart, everyone in the room seemed

449

eager, grateful even, to listen to what Kitty had to say. Whether it was their residual shock that kept them quiet, or whether they glimpsed, in the gray-haired girl with the lined and weary face, something that commanded unequivocal respect was hard to say. But they listened with complete attention as Kitty told them what had happened.

"What about the *rest* of us?" one of the older men said plaintively. "There were a hundred at least sitting in that theater. Surely they haven't all—"

"I'm not sure," Kitty said. "Perhaps there are other rooms of prisoners that the demons forgot, or decided to ignore. You'll have to see. But many of you are dead."

"What about Mr. Devereaux?" a woman whispered.

"Or Jessica Whitwell, or—?"

Kitty held up her hand. "I'm sorry, but I don't know. I think it likely that many of the most senior magicians have been possessed or killed."

"*This* one hasn't." The dark-haired woman spoke savagely. "Until they are found, *I* am the sole Council member remaining. So *I* am now in charge. We must get to our pentacles and conjure our slaves. I shall contact my police wolves forthwith. The renegade demons will be found and destroyed."

"Two things," Kitty said quietly. "No, three. This man must be seen to first. Can anyone provide transport?"

"I can." The spotty youth bent beside the limp body. "Going to need three of us for this. Mr. Johnson, Mr. Vole, can you lend a hand, help me get him to a limo?" Assistance came; the men departed, supporting the invalid between them.

A clap of the hands; the dark-haired woman was by the door. "To the pentacles!" she commanded. "No time to waste!"

Nobody moved. "I think this lady had something more to

say," an older man said, nodding toward Kitty. "We should hear her out, don't you think, Ms. Farrar? Out of courtesy, if nothing else."

Ms. Farrar's lips twisted. "But she's nothing but a—"

"I had *two* further points to make," Kitty said. She felt very tired now, light-headed; she needed to sit down. *No*—get a grip; get the job done. "The chief demon, Nouda, is very terrible. It would be suicide for you to approach him without the greatest possible weapon. And that is already being done." She looked around the silent group. "A magician, *another* surviving Council member"—Kitty could not resist a sly glance at Ms. Farrar here—"has gone to meet it. He uses Gladstone's Staff."

She was only half surprised by the stifled exclamations of astonishment. Ms. Farrar in particular seemed incensed. "But Mr. Devereaux has forbidden it!" she cried. "Who would dare to—?"

Kitty smiled. "It is Nath—John Mandrake. You had better hope he is successful."

"*Mandrake!*" Farrar's face was pale with fury. "He doesn't have the talent!"

"The final thing I would like to say," Kitty went on remorselessly, "is that with this being so, the most important thing for us—for *you*, I should say; *you* are the magicians, *you* have the power—is to provide protection and guidance for the people. Since Makepeace imprisoned you all, there has been no leadership, no one to evacuate areas where the demons are at large. We risk mass casualties here, mass casualties. If we do not act, many commoners will die."

"Never bothered us before," a young man muttered at the back, but general opinion was against him.

"What we need is a crystal," Piper said. "See where the demons are."

"Or a scrying bowl. Where do they keep them in this place?"

"*Must* be one. Come on."

"Let's get to the pentacles. I could summon an imp, send him off."

"We'll need more cars. Who here can drive?"

"I can't. My man does that."

"Nor me—"

At the door, a harsh, forced cough. Ms. Farrar's face was haggard, her hair tangled and disheveled, her mouth a thin-lipped slash. White hands pressed hard against the door frame on either side. Her arms were bent, her shoulders slightly hunched—the posture gave her a faint resemblance to an inverted bat. Her gaze spat venom. "Not one of you," she said, "is anything better than a junior minister. Most of you are scarcely even *that*—just secretaries and desk-hands. Your knowledge of magic is painfully limited; your judgement, it seems, is even worse. The commoners will look after themselves. Some have resilience—no doubt they can repel a few Detonations. There are, in any case, many of them. We can afford to lose a few. What we *cannot* do is stand around dithering while our capital is under attack. What, we're going to leave it up to Mandrake? How good a magician do you think he *is*? I'm going for my wolves. Anyone with any remaining ambition will follow me."

She pushed herself back from the door frame, and without a backward glance, set off down the corridor. Uneasy silence. After a pause three of the young men, heads lowered, brows scowling, pushed their way past Kitty and departed. Several others wavered, but remained.

The young woman with mousy hair shrugged; she turned

to Kitty. "We're following you, miss . . . um, sorry, what *is* your name?"

Clara Bell? Lizzie Temple? "Kitty Jones," she said. Then, more faintly: "Can anyone get me something to drink?"

While Kitty rested, while she sipped cool mineral water from the Council's own supply of bottles, the junior magicians set about their work. Some ventured around the Whitehall chambers: they returned trembling and wan, with reports of bodies piled in side rooms, of pentacles slashed and ruptured, of such devastation as none had ever dreamed. Carnage like this was generally visited on enemies at a distance. It was troubling for the magicians to experience it first hand. Others crept to the front of the building and peered forth into Whitehall. Buildings were on fire; corpses lay in full view—what was most unsettling was the utter absence of the people. Ordinarily, even in the small hours, buses and taxis continued to pass that way, together with the comings and goings of night staff in the ministries, and patrols of police and soldiers. The machinery of government, beheaded by the treachery of Makepeace and surprised by the appearance of Nouda, had for the moment ceased altogether.

The destruction of the pentacles was a setback, but it soon became clear that the ferocity of the demons exceeded their efficiency, and here and there circles were found that had been overlooked and spared. A few small imps set forth on reconnaissance; meanwhile, in a chamber close to the Hall of Statues, a giant crystal ball, formerly employed by the Council, was located and brought to the room where Kitty sat. The magicians congregated, hushed and somber. Without preamble, the strongest individual present—a junior minister from the

Fisheries—summoned the djinni trapped within the ball. In ringing tones it was directed to its task: to reveal the position of the renegade demons.

The ball went smoky, dark. . . . Everyone leaned closer.

Lights within the crystal! Red and orange. Leaping flames.

The focus cleared. Raging fires, near and far; lanterns among dark trees. In the distance, a giant humpbacked glow of light . . .

"The Glass Palace," someone said. "That's St. James's Park."

"The commoners were demonstrating there."

"Look!" In the foreground, hundreds of running forms, wheeling, scattering like fish shoals through the trees.

"Why don't they get out?"

"Surrounded." Here and there, bursts of magic, corralling the panic-stricken crowds, redirecting them back upon themselves. Glimpses of unnatural movement on the margins—great bounds and leaps, sudden rushes. Hopping, prancing figures, human in their shape, inhuman in their gleeful capering, active on all sides. One loped into clear view beneath a lantern; it spied a cluster of men and women fleeing in its direction. It bent its back, prepared to spring—

A shaft of white light—a tremendous explosion. The loping creature vanished—in its place a smoking crater. A figure passed beneath the lantern out of sight, going with steady strides; it held a long staff in its hand.

Kitty placed her mineral water carefully on the floor. "Summon whatever demons you can," she said. "If we're going to do any good at all, *that's* where we have to be."

35

It has to be said, we worked well together. Better than either of us expected.

Okay, maybe it took a *little* while to get the system sorted—we had a couple of embarrassing moments when our body did two things at once, but we always rectified it sharpish, so no harm done.[1] And once we got into our seven-leagued stride, we really began to motor, and to enjoy the advantages of our irregular condition.

It was our first success against poor old Naeryan that really fired us up: it showed us what we had to do; how to combine to best effect. We stopped trying to second-guess each other and did a bit of *delegation*.

Here's how it went. Nathaniel worked the boots: if we had a long straight distance to travel, he did the strides. Once at our destination (one or two seconds later, generally—those boots were pretty snappy), I took over the legs, imbued them with a little of my trademarked vim, and sent us bounding like an impala, back, forth, up, down, left, and right, until any enemy, and occasionally even myself, was hopelessly confused.

---

[1] Well, not to *me*, anyway, safely encased as I was inside. Nathaniel maybe got a few unnecessary bruises, like the time he went right when I was pointing left, and the Staff bashed him on the nose; or when he fired the Staff during the middle of an extra-fancy leap, and we were blown sideways into a gorse bush. Or that little incident down at the lake when he got so angry (we were only under water for a measly four or five seconds, and let's face it a little bindweed never hurt anyone). But by and large we managed to avoid self-inflicted wounds.

Meanwhile, Nathaniel retained full control of his arms and of Gladstone's Staff; he fired it whenever we came within range, and since I could anticipate his intentions, I usually stayed put long enough for him to do so. The only exception (justified, I feel) was when I was hurrying us out of the path of a Detonation, a Flux, or a Spiraling Dismemberment. Always best to avoid such things if you wish to retain momentum.[2]

We communicated with pithy, rather monosyllabic thoughts: viz. *Run, Jump, Where? Left, Up, Duck,* etc.[3] We didn't ever quite say *Ug*, but it was a close-run thing. It was all a bit butch and male, and left little room for introspection or emotional analysis, a factor that fitted in nicely with the business of staying alive, and also with a certain subdued detachment that now flooded Nathaniel's mind. It hadn't been so noticeable at first, when we were back with Kitty (his head was full of softer things, then—half-formed, eager, outward-looking), but after that moment in Trafalgar Square, when the woman had turned away from him with a face of fear and scorn, it rose up swiftly and closed him off. His softer emotions were new and hesitant—they didn't like rejection. Now they were sealed away; in their stead returned the old familiar qualities: pride, remoteness, and steely determination. He was still committed to his task, but he undertook it in an attitude of vague self-disgust. Not healthy, maybe, but it helped him fight well.

And fighting, now, was what we had to do.

Naeryan, dawdling at the square, had been the most tardy of the spirits; the others had hurried on, drawn by the sound and

---

[2] Or indeed your vital organs.

[3] This latter was an observation I made on the edge of the lake. Nathaniel unfortunately took it as a command, which resulted in our temporary immersion.

smell of human bodies, under the Churchill Arch and out into the dark acres of St. James's Park. Perhaps, if the commoners had not been congregated here in considerable numbers, Nouda's army would have immediately dispersed across the capital and so been far harder to discover and waylay. As it was, the people's protest had been gathering through the night, emboldened by the government's inertia; now, for the avid spirits, their teeming masses provided an unmissable temptation.

When we arrived, the entertainment was well underway. Far across the park the spirits wandered, chasing herds of fleeing humans as the whim took them. Some used magical attacks; others preferred to move for the sake of moving, trying out the unfamiliar stiffness of their limbs, racing around to cut off scurrying prey. Many of the distant trees were aflame with colored lights; the air was a montage of flashes, spinning cords of smoke, shrill screams, and general outcry. Behind it all, the great Glass Palace cast illumination down upon the hectic lawns: across its projected slabs of light the people ran, the spirits bounded, the bodies fell, the breathless hunt went on.

We paused under the arch, at the gateway to the park, taking it all in.

Chaos, Nathaniel thought. *It's CHAOS.*

It's nothing to a real battle, I said. *You ought to have been at al-Arish, where for two square miles the sand clogged red.* I gave him a mental picture.

Lovely. Thanks for that. See Nouda?

No. How many demons are there?

Enough.[4] *Let's go.*

---

[4] There were probably forty or so. But when entering battle, a wise warrior deals with his enemies one by one.

He tapped his heel; the boots took wing. We launched ourselves into the fray.

Strategy dictated that the spirits did not *collectively* notice our presence. One by one, we could fell them; facing them en masse would be a mite more tricky. Hence rapid-fire attacks and continual movement. Our first objective, close by on the lawns, was an afrit cloaked in the body of an elderly woman; uttering shrill whoops, it sent Spasms ricocheting among the crowds. In two strides we were behind it. The Staff pulsed. The afrit was a memory, sighing on the wind. We turned, moved . . . and were far off among the fairground stalls, where three strong djinn, plumply dressed in human skin, industriously toppled the Sultan's Castle. Nathaniel pointed the Staff and claimed them in a single greedy flash of light. We looked, saw: up by some trees, a rickety hybrid stalking a child—in three strides we had him in our sights. White fire consumed him. The child fled into the dark.

We need help, Nathaniel thought, *for the people. They're running round in circles.*

That's not our con—Yep; I see them. Go.

A stride, a leap—we landed on a bandstand roof, spun round the central pole, fired the Staff four times. Three hybrids perished; the fourth, alerted by the others' deaths, dodged, jumped back. It spied us, sent a Spasm. The bandstand shook itself to splinters, but we had somersaulted clear, slid down a tent awning and, before our boots touched ground, reduced the culprit's essence to a twirl of dwindling sparks.

A prickle of regret, a slackening of desire. Nathaniel hesitated. *That . . . that was Helen Malbindi! I know it was. She's . . .*

She's been dead long since. You killed her killer. Shake a leg! There—by the lake! Those children. Quick—be swift!

Best to keep moving. Best not to think of it. Fight on.[5]

Ten minutes passed; we stood beneath an oak tree in the center of the park. The remains of two djinn rose smoking from the earth.

Notice anything about the spirits? I thought. *I mean, what you can see of them.*

The eyes? I catch a glow sometimes.

Yes, but also the auras. They seem bigger somehow.

Meaning what?

I don't know. It's like the human bodies aren't containing them so well.

You think—

The spirits Faquarl summoned are strong. Perhaps their feeding makes them stronger. If—

Wait. By the lake . . . And we were gone.

Back and forth across the park we went, among the pavilions and pleasure grounds, the bowers and the walkways, wherever we saw the flash of predatory movement. Sometimes the djinn perceived us and fought back; more often we slew them unawares. The power of the Staff was irresistible, the seven-league boots carried us more swiftly than the enemy could see. Nathaniel was cold and resolute; with every minute he

---

[5] Had the boy been there alone, without my prompting presence, would he have acted with such speed against the bodies of his fellow ministers? Despite their deformities, their slack faces and oddly angled limbs, I doubt it. He was a human; always, always humans gravitate to surfaces.

controlled the Staff with greater skill. As for me, whether or not it was the adrenaline we shared, I began to enjoy myself hugely. I slowly awoke again to the old bloodlust, to the fierce joy of combat that I'd known in early Egypt's wars, when the utukku of Assyria marched from the deserts and the gathering vultures blotted out the sky. It was the love of speed and cleverness, of defying death and dealing it; it was the love of carrying out new exploits that would be told and sung around the campfires till the sun went out. It was the love of energy and power.

It was part of Earth's corruption. Ptolemy wouldn't have been pleased.

But it was a good deal better than being a pyramid of slime.

I noticed something and gave a mental prod. Nathaniel stopped where he was in the middle of the field to get a better look. We stood awhile, considering. As we stood, we held the Staff out horizontally, clasped in casual fingers. It glowed and crackled; white smoke drifted from the end. The ground beneath our boots was blackened, charred. All around us bodies lay, and shoes and coats and placards; beyond *them* were burning trees and the deep abyss of night.

Away across the park, the gleaming lights of the great Glass Palace. Within it, silhouetted upon the grass, distant figures seemed to move. We were too far away to make out any details.

Nouda? Faquarl?

Could be . . .

Watch out. Away to our left, something coming. We raised the Staff. Paused. Out from the dark a man came—human, with negligible aura. He was shoeless, shirt half torn away. He stumbled past on bloodied feet. He never looked at us.

What a mess, Nathaniel thought.

Give the poor bloke a chance! He's just been chased by forty demons.

Not him. This. Everything.

Oh. Yes. Yes, it is.

So you reckon there were forty, total?

I didn't say that. A wise warrior—

How many have we killed?

I don't know. Wasn't counting. There aren't so many here now, though.

The central vistas of the park were largely empty. It was as if an invisible skin or barrier had been punctured, and the mass of frantic movement had suddenly poured, then ebbed, away.

Nathaniel sniffed and wiped his nose upon a sleeve. *The Glass Palace it is, then. We're just about finished here.*

One step, two . . . up across the lawns and in among some ornamental hedges, flower beds, ponds, and tinkling fountains. Nathaniel slowed the boots; we took stock of our surroundings.

The Glass Palace rose like a breaching whale from the center of the park, two hundred meters long and a hundred wide. It was constructed almost entirely of glass panes, set among a web of iron girders. The main walls were gently soaring curves; here and there protruded secondary domes, crests, minarets, and gables. It was nothing but a giant conservatory, really, but instead of containing a few moldering tomato plants and a sack of compost, it boasted lines of full-grown palm trees, a man-made stream, aerial walkways, gift shops, and refreshment booths, as well as all manner of ramshackle entertainments.[6] Thousands of electric lights hanging from the girders illuminated the area night and day. In ordinary times it was a favorite place for commoners to whittle away their lives.

In the past I had rarely ventured near the palace, since its iron skeleton made my essence squeamish. Now, however, protected within Nathaniel, I had no such worries. We climbed some steps toward the eastern entrance. Here, tropical ferns and palm trees pressed thickly against the inside of the glass; it was hard to see beyond them.

Faint noises echoed from the building. We did not pause, but strode to the wooden doors. We pushed; the doors opened. Holding the Staff before us, we stepped within.

An instant mugginess: out of the night's cold, under the roof of glass, the air was warm. An instant stench of magic too—the after-plumes of sulphurous Detonations. Somewhere to our right, beyond a knot of trees and a Japanese style sushi bar, came sounds of lamentation.

Commoners, Nathaniel thought. *Need to get close. See who's got them.*

Try the walkway?

To our left, a spiral stair of iron led by rapid revolutions to a walkway high above. An elevated vantage point would give us

---

[6] These included: bumper cars, roller-skating arenas, "Ride-an-imp" merry-go-rounds, Madame Houri's Mystic Tent of Prophecy, a hall of distorting mirrors, Bumpo the Bear's Grotto of Taxidermy, and the central "One World Exhibition"—a series of pathetic stands displaying the "cultural riches" of each country of the Empire (mainly involving squash, yams, and crudely painted wooden love spoons). The billboards outside proclaimed the palace as the "Tenth Wonder of the World," which, speaking as someone who had a hand in constructing five of the other nine, I found a little rich.

immediate advantage. We crossed swiftly and scaled the steps without a sound. We rose above the spreading palm fronds, up tight against the curve of the great glass wall, and came out upon the narrow gantry, which extended like an iron thread to the opposite side. Nathaniel crouched low; he held the Staff horizontal against the floor. With slow and careful movements, we shuffled out across the void.

It did not take long before we could see beyond the trees to the center of the palace, directly below the highest domes of soaring glass. Here, in an open space, wedged between a gaudily painted merry-go-round and an area of picnic tables, we saw a throng of humans, perhaps a hundred strong, huddled together like penguins in a winter storm. They were marshaled by seven or eight of Nouda's spirits, who stood on every side. Rufus Lime's body was among their vehicles, as was—I knew this from an agitation within Nathaniel's mind— that of the Prime Minister Rupert Devereaux. From the authority of their movements, the spirits seemed comfortable in their hosts. Their auras had spread far around the outlines of the bodies. It was not they, however, who attracted our attention.

Look at Nouda, Nathaniel thought. *What's* happened *to him?*

I had no answer. Up on the roof of the merry-go-round, perhaps twenty meters ahead and as many below us, the old body of Quentin Makepeace was standing. When we'd last set eyes on it, Nouda had been having a little trouble getting to grips with the limitations of his host. Now, belatedly, he seemed to have got the hang of it. The legs were firmly planted, the arms loosely folded, the chin high—he had the exact posture of a successful general, mid-campaign.

He also had horns.

Three black ones, to be exact, poking from his forehead at irregular angles. One was long, the other two mere stubs. And that wasn't all. Some kind of dorsal spine had split the back of his shirt; a gray-green flange protruded from his left arm. The face was waxy and irregular, swollen with internal pressure. The eyes seemed living flames.

That's unexpected, I thought.

His essence is breaking out of the body. It was Nathaniel's boundless capacity for stating the obvious that made him so charmingly human.

As we watched, the horns, spine, and flanges shrank back into the skin, as if by a stern effort of will. A quivering, a shaking: a moment later they sprang back, bigger than ever. From the open mouth the great voice came roaring. "Ah! The discomfort! I feel the old burning! Faquarl! *Where* is Faquarl?"

He's not happy, Nathaniel thought. *His power must simply be too great. The fabric of his host is breaking apart and he's lost its protection.*

Can't help that he's been wolfing down humans since he got here. That must have swelled his essence. . . . I surveyed the commoners cowering below him. *Looks as if he's still hungry too.*

This ends now. All Nathaniel's unhappiness and dissatisfaction had coalesced into cold, hard fury. His mind was a piece of flint. *Think we can pick him off from here?*

Yes. Aim carefully. We'll have one chance only. Better make it a strong one.

Now *who's stating the obvious?*

We were still crouched, peering through the ornate iron railings that bounded the gantry. As Nathaniel composed himself to stand, I erected a precautionary Shield. When the strike was done, the other spirits would no doubt seek revenge. I

464

scanned the possibilities. . . . First an evasive leap, either to the palm tree, or backward onto the sushi bar roof. Then down to the floor. Then—

That was enough forward planning.

Nathaniel stood. We pointed the Staff at Nouda, spoke the words—

A tremendous explosion, as expected.

Only, not around Nouda, but all around *us*. My Shield just about held firm. Even so, we were blown sideways down the gantry and through the glass wall of the palace in a shower of crystal fragments, to go spinning out over the entrance steps and down to the darkness of the ornamental gardens far below. We landed heavily, our fall only partially buffered by the Shield. The Staff, torn from our grip, clattered distantly on the path.

Our dual consciousness was shaken apart by the impact; for a few seconds we vibrated separately in a single head. As we lay there, groaning independently, the body of Hopkins came drifting out through the shattered aperture high above. It floated down to the steps and approached on foot, at a calm and steady pace.

"It's Mandrake, isn't it?" Faquarl said, in conversational tones. "I must say, you're a persistent little fellow. If you'd had any sense you'd have been a hundred miles away by now. What on earth's got into you?"

If he only knew. We lay on the soil, trying hard to focus. Slowly our vision steadied, our intelligence realigned.

"The Lord Nouda," Faquarl continued, "is a little fractious at the moment and needs careful handling. His temper would not be improved by being stung by your toy."

"*Stung?*" Nathaniel croaked. "It'll wipe him out."

"Do you really think so?" The voice was tired and amused.

"Nouda is greater than you can guess. He is ravenous for energy; he absorbs it like a sponge. See how he grows already! He would welcome your attack and feed off it. I *would* have let you try it, but I am tired of unnecessary disruptions. However, in a moment I shall take the Staff for my own use." He raised a languid hand. "So then, farewell."

Nathaniel opened his mouth to scream. I hijacked it for a better purpose. "Hello, Faquarl."

The hand started; its baleful energies remained unreleased. Behind Hopkins's eyes, twin points of bright blue light flared in wonder and confusion. "Bartimaeus . . . ?"

"Little me."

"How—how . . . ?" Here was a thing. For the first time in three dozen centuries Faquarl's impregnable assurance was shaken by my arrival. He was at a loss for words. "How can this be? Is this a trick . . . some voice projection . . . an illusion . . . ?"

"Nope. It's me in here."

"It *can't* be."

"Who else would know the truth about the death of Genghis? Those little poisoned grapes we slipped into his tent under the noses of his djinn . . . ?"[7]

Faquarl blinked; he hesitated. "So . . . It *is* you."

"My turn to deal out the surprise, old friend. And I might just mention that while you and Nouda play around in there, most of your army has already been killed. By me."

As I spoke, I felt Nathaniel squirming. He didn't like lying helpless on the ground—a natural instinct of self-preservation made him desperate to get up. I quelled him with a single thought: *Wait.*

---

[7] I won't go into this. It was just a little Asian job, a long while back.

"Ah, you *traitor* . . ." Faquarl had been in Hopkins's body for a long time; he licked his lips just as a human might. "I care nothing for that loss—the world is crammed with humans, and there are spirits enough to fill them all. But as for *you* . . . To murder your own kind, to defend your old oppressors . . . No, it sickens my essence to think of it!" His hands were clenched; his voice was high with emotion. "We have fought each other many times, Bartimaeus, but always because of chance, because of our masters' whims. And now, when *we* are the masters at last, and should celebrate together, now you choose to carry out this rank betrayal! *You*, Sakhr al-Jinni himself! How can you justify your actions?"

"*Me*, the traitor?" To begin with, I had just been keeping him talking, waiting till our strength recovered from our fall, but now I was too incensed to think. My voice rose to the old wendigo roar that echoed through the pinewoods and kept the tribes cowering in their teepees. "*You're* the one who's turned his back forever on the Other Place! How much more of a traitor can you be—to desert your home, to encourage fellow spirits to abandon it forever by becoming squatters in these bags of bones? And for what? What do you get from this benighted wasteland?"

"Vengeance," Faquarl whispered. "Vengeance is our master here. It keeps us in this world. It gives us purpose."

"'Purpose' is a *human* concept," I said quietly. "We never needed that before. This body of yours isn't just a disguise anymore, is it? It isn't just a barrier against pain. It's what you're busily becoming."

The fire behind the eyes flared indignantly, then dwindled suddenly, grew dull. "Perhaps so, Bartimaeus, perhaps so . . ." The voice was soft and wistful; the hands patted the front of the rumpled suit. "Between ourselves, I will admit to feeling a certain *discomfort* in this body that I had not anticipated. It is not like the old sharp pain we have long withstood; rather, it's a dull itch that nags at me, a hollowness inside that no amount of slaughter can quite ease. *So far*, at any rate." He gave a rueful grin. "I intend to keep trying."

"That hollowness," I said. "It's what you've lost. The tie to the Other Place."

Faquarl gazed at me. For a moment he did not speak. "If that is true," he said heavily, "then you have lost it too. You are just as much a squatter as I, Bartimaeus, cooped up in that young magician of yours. Why did you do it, if you despise the notion as you claim?"

"Because *I* have a way out," I said. "I haven't burned my bridges."

The blazing eyes narrowed in puzzlement. "How so?"

"The magician summoned me in. The magician can dismiss me."

"But his brain—"

"Is whole. I share it with him. Which is tough, admittedly. There's not much to go round."

Nathaniel spoke then: "It is true. We work together."

If Faquarl had been surprised when I first spoke, he was now dumbfounded. The possibility simply hadn't occurred to him.

"The human retains his intelligence?" he muttered. "Who then is the master? Which of you has dominance?"

"Neither of us," I said.

Nathaniel concurred. "It is an equal balance."

Faquarl shook his head, almost as if in admiration. "Remarkable," he said. "As a perversity it is unique. Or almost so: that brat from Alexandria you were always going on about at one time, Bartimaeus. He'd have approved, wouldn't he?" His lip curled a little. "Tell me, do you not feel soiled by such an *intimate* association?"

"Not particularly," I said. "It's no more intimate than yours, and it's a lot less permanent. I'm going home."

"Oh, dear. What makes you think that?" Faquarl moved his hand; but I'd anticipated him. Our long discussion had given us a chance to recover from the fall; our energies were rekindled. Nathaniel's fingers were already pointed in his direction. The green-gray Spasm hit Faquarl's Shield directly; though uninjured, he spun round—his Detonation struck the earth well clear. Meanwhile, I exercised our limbs. With a scattering of soil, we launched from the ground, soared above the path, landed right beside the Staff. Nathaniel scooped it up; we turned, quick as a striking krait.

Faquarl stood on the path, not distant, hand half raised. Light from the Glass Palace cut across him, blending with the shadow. Fast as we'd been, he was still faster. I sometimes wonder if he could have got us in the back, as we bent beside the Staff, before we'd got it in our hand. But maybe our Spasm had shaken him, put him off his stride. It's difficult to say. For a second we gazed at each other.

"Your discovery is remarkable," Faquarl said. "But it comes too late for me."

He made some movement or other with his fleshy body; I don't remember what. I did nothing, but I was conscious of the boy's immediate command. A stab of pure white light—it faded, vanished, scoured Faquarl from the Earth.

We stood alone on the path beneath the palace.

Shake a leg, the boy thought. *People are coming, and we've got a final bit of work to do.*

36

Kitty

It was fortunate for Kitty that most of the magicians in her company were from the very lowest ranks, since this meant that several of them could drive. Limousines were located in the lot beneath Westminster Hall; the Chauffeurs' Mess provided a choice of keys. By the time six vehicles arrived, revving, in the deserted street outside, Kitty and the others had retrieved what weapons they could, negotiated the summoning of a number of imps, and were waiting at the door. Without ceremony, they bundled in, four to a car, and with the demons hovering in their wake, proceeded in procession up the road.

They did not get far. Halfway up Whitehall, they found the way blocked by rubble from a toppled war memorial. Progress was impeded; laboriously the convoy turned, retreated to Parliament Square, and turned right toward St. James's Park.

If Whitehall had been empty, the streets to the south of the park were anything but. Not far ahead came explosions, reflected lights, and the sound of howling wolves. Closer still, as if a human dam had burst, hundreds of people surged from the side roads, swamping the thoroughfare and pouring down toward the limousines.

Kitty was sitting in the lead car, beside the driver. Sudden fear lurched in her. "Get out!" she snapped. "It isn't safe!"

He saw the danger, switched off the engine, fumbled with the door. As one, they left the cars and ran for shelter; seconds later the crowd engulfed the limousines, eyes wild, faces set in expressions of terror and despair. Many ran straight past; others, seeing in the sleek black vehicles stark symbols of the magicians' rule, lashed out at them, kicking, screaming. A brick appeared from nowhere: a windscreen smashed; the crowd's voice roared.

Ms. Piper supported Kitty, who was shaking with the effort of their escape. "The commoners . . ." she whispered. "They've gone insane. . . ."

"They're scared, they're angry." Kitty struggled to gather her strength. "Look at their injuries. They've escaped from the park. Now, are we all present?" As she looked down the straggling line of magicians, a thought struck her. "Those of you with imps, get them under your jackets!" she hissed. "If anyone with resilience spots them, you'll be torn apart! Ready? Right—come on, we've no time to waste."

Without delay they continued up the street on foot, keeping to the margins as the flow of human traffic swept by. The first few side roads were choked with rushing bodies and proved impassable. Little by little they drew near to the sounds of fighting.

A flash of light in the darkness. Silhouetted on a building, the outline of a man. Green fires billowed all about him. The light went out. In the street below, a small number of wolves were massing; they heard a high voice shouting orders, glimpsed a dark-haired form—

"That's Farrar," one of the magicians said. "She's got some wolves together. But what . . . what was that shape?"

"One of the demons . . ." Kitty was leaning wearily against a wall and looking down a narrow alley. "This way's clear. It'll get us to the park."

"But shouldn't we—?"

"No. That's just a sideshow. Besides, I don't think dear Ms. Farrar would really *want* our help, do you?"

The alley led, by circuitous twists and turns, to a quiet road running along the edge of the park. This they crossed, and from a small eminence, looked down upon the black expanse. A few fires burned here and there—in trees, in pavilions, in the pagoda down by the lake—but little movement could be seen. At Kitty's suggestion, a number of imps were sent ahead to spy out the land. They returned in moments.

"Terrible battle has been waged here," said the first, wringing its webbed hands. "At intervals the ground is crisp and charred. Magical effusions hang over the ground like fog. But the battle has ceased everywhere, save in one place."

"Many humans have perished," said the second, goggle-eyes blinking on their stalks. "Their bodies lie like fallen leaves. Some lie wounded; they cry for help. A few others wander without purpose. But most have fled. The park is empty of crowds, save in one place."

"The great spirits are likewise gone," said the third, flapping its gauzy wings. "Their spilled essence hangs amid the echoes of their screams. A few survivors have fled across the city. But none remain in the park, save in one place."

"And what," Kitty asked, tapping her foot gently, "*is* that place?"

Wordlessly the three imps turned and pointed up at the lights of the great Glass Palace.

Kitty nodded. "Why didn't you say so? All right, let's go."

★ ★ ★

For ten hard and silent minutes they walked across the blackened ground. Kitty went slowly, forcibly completing each step against the shrill protests of her body. In the hours since her return, her strength had dripped back steadily. Even so, she longed to rest. She knew she was reaching the end of her endurance.

The imps' reports had been pithy, but the implication of them was clear, and fitted in with the glimpse in the crystal. Nathaniel and Bartimaeus had been here: it was they who had cleared the park and enabled many of the people to escape. Perhaps—the hope swelled inside her with each step—perhaps they would soon complete the process: perhaps she would see them coming toward her in triumph, with a group of grateful commoners in their train. Surely, with the Staff, it was only a matter of time. . . .

But while there was *any* doubt, she could not hold back. She could not leave them. At her neck the Amulet of Samarkand bounced gently with each faltering step.

Five minutes passed. Kitty's eyes grew heavy. Suddenly they blinked alert.

"What was that?"

"Magical blast," Ms. Piper whispered. "By the eastern entrance."

They kept walking.

Four minutes later, with the palace looming over them, they entered the ornamental gardens. As they did so, the ground shook; a piercing white light flashed upon the path before the building. The company stopped dead, waited. The light was not repeated. Nervousness crackled between them like an electric charge.

Kitty's eyes strained in the dark. The glow from the palace cast the night into even greater shadow. It was hard to be sure. . . . But—yes—there upon the path, a figure standing. As she watched, it moved and was silhouetted against the glass.

Kitty hesitated just a moment. Then she stumbled forward, calling.

Nathaniel

At the sound of the voice Nathaniel stopped dead. It barely even carried to his brain, what with his ears buzzing from a hundred Detonations and with the vibrations of the thirsty Staff humming near at hand, but the little call did what all the demons across the park had failed to do: it set his heart racing.

Throughout the battle he had moved with demonic speed and efficiency, avoiding death without much effort and exerting, through the Staff, destructive energies greater than many djinn possessed. It was an experience that had been desired by most magicians through the centuries, and certainly by Nathaniel himself in idle daydreams. It was the feeling of consummate superiority, the delight of power wielded without peril. He danced beneath the dark night sky, smiting down his enemies. And yet, with all his nimbleness and guile, with all the adrenaline pumping through him, deep inside he was curiously inert. He felt aloof, disconnected, and alone. If his hatred for the demons that he had killed was dull and almost matter-of-fact, so was his sympathy for the people whose lives he saved. The woman in Trafalgar Square had shown what he could expect from them. They would regard him with fear and distaste, and rightly so. He was a magician. It was thanks to him and his kind that London was in flames.

Pride spurred him on—that, and the djinni talking inside his head. Yes, he would seek to end the destruction. But after that . . . Actions were one thing, expectations another. He had no idea what he would do.

And then, on the path outside the great Glass Palace—

The djinni's thought drifted through his mind. *That's Kitty's voice, that is.*

I know. *You think I don't know?*

It's just, you've gone all limp and heavy. Like wet cardboard. Thought you'd had a seizure out of fear.

It's not fear.

So you say. Your heart's going like the clappers. Eeuch, and you've gone a bit sweaty. Sure it isn't a fever?

Quite sure. Now will you shut up?

Nathaniel watched her coming slowly through the garden. Across the seven planes her aura lit the ground like day. A group of people straggled close behind.

"Kitty."

"Nathaniel."

They looked at each other. Then his mouth opened with a wrenching noise something like a belch. "And me! Don't forget me!" Nathaniel swore and clamped his mouth tight shut.

Kitty grinned. "Hello, Bartimaeus."

An entirely unconnected anger suddenly rose within Nathaniel. He frowned at her. "I thought I told you not to come with us. You're too weak. It's too dangerous."

"Since when have I ever listened to you? What's the situation?"

Nathaniel's mouth opened of its own accord; Bartimaeus

spoke. "We've destroyed most of Nouda's army, but he himself is still at large. In there"—Nathaniel's thumb jerked back over his shoulder—"with seven other spirits and maybe a hundred commoners. And we're—"

"About to deal with him," Nathaniel finished.

"—in serious trouble," the djinni said.

Kitty blinked. "Sorry, which . . . ?"

Nathaniel shifted the Staff; thin bands of energy pulsed and crackled around his hand. He felt a surge of joyful impatience—he would destroy Nouda, rescue the commoners, and return to Kitty. Beyond that, everything could wait.

But the djinni was cutting across his thoughts, speaking urgently to Kitty. "Nouda is growing in strength all the time. He's not reacting like the others. He may not be as susceptible to the Staff as we thought."

Nathaniel interrupted angrily. "What do you mean? It'll be fine."

"That's not what Faquarl said."

"Oh, and you believed him."

"Faquarl didn't tend to lie. That wasn't his style."

"No, his style was trying to kill us dead—" Nathaniel broke off. He had caught sight of a ring of silent listeners, watching him seemingly argue with himself. Among several magicians that he recognized was his personal assistant.

He cleared his throat. "Hello, Piper."

"Hello, sir."

Kitty held up a hand. "Bartimaeus—there are many prisoners in there and we have little time. Do we have any alternative to the Staff?"

"No. Unless this crowd is all magicians of the thirteenth level."

"Right. Then we've got to go for it, better or worse. Nathaniel," Kitty said, "you'll have to do what you can. If you deal with the demons, we'll evacuate the commoners. Where are they?"

"Close by. In the center of the palace." In the past her presence disconcerted him; now it filled him with renewed purpose and self-belief. He spoke swiftly, with his old authority. "Piper, when you get inside, you'll see a path running to the right between the palms. It leads behind the carousel to an open area. That's where the demons and the captives are. If you wait down that path, in cover, I'll attack from the opposite side. When the demons follow me, try to lead the prisoners out and as far away as possible. Anyone with imps, use them to help you. Is that clear?"

"Yes, sir."

"Good. Kitty—you should wait outside."

"I should, but I won't. I've got the Amulet, remember?"

Nathaniel knew better than to argue. He turned toward the entrance to the palace. "Absolute silence when we're in. I'll give you a minute to get into positions."

He held open the door. One by one, with wide eyes and pale, strained faces, the company of magicians trooped past and disappeared up the path. Several were accompanied by their imps, who wore identical expressions of unease. Last to go through was Kitty. She paused for a moment on the step.

"Well done," she whispered, gesturing back toward the empty park. "You and Bartimaeus. I should have said."

Nathaniel grinned at her. Impatience tugged within him. The Staff sang. "It's almost over," he said softly. "Go on. After you."

The door shut quietly behind them.

Bartimaeus

There are times when even a near omnipotent djinni knows to keep his mouth shut, and this was one of them. I wouldn't have got anywhere.

Trouble was, neither of them was in a mood to listen to my doubts. For one thing they smelled success too strongly: him with the Staff held casually in his hand; her with the Amulet warm against her breast. Such trinkets breed confidence. And besides, they'd done too much already to imagine any stumbles now.

But the main problem was the way they played off each other. Simply put, their mutual presence spurred each other on. Trapped as I was inside Nathaniel, I could certainly see how the girl inspired him.[1] Perhaps I can't vouch for Kitty so much, but in my vast experience, strong characters of their sort tend to gravitate together. Pride has a part to play in it, and other emotions too. Neither wishes to fail; each redoubles their efforts to impress. Things get done—but not always the right things, or not always the things expected.[2] And there's not much you can do to stop it.

It has to be said, however, that in the present instance there really *wasn't* any viable alternative to Nathaniel's plan. Nouda

---

[1] Too right I could. It was as if she'd triggered an internal one-man band, all Klaxons, bells, and pennywhistles, with enthusiastic cymbals strapped between his knees. The noise was *deafening*.

[2] That's how it was with Nefertiti and Akhenaton, of course. One moment it was lingering looks and assignations by the crocodile enclosure; next it was tearing up the state religion and moving Egypt's capital 60 miles into the desert. One thing just led to another.

was far too powerful for the (rather lackluster) remnants of the government to destroy. So the Staff *was* the only option. But Faquarl's phrase rang uneasily in my mind: *He would welcome your attack and feed off it.* And call me pessimistic, but that struck me as a mite ominous.[3]

But it was too late to worry about that now. The Staff had flattened cities. With luck, it would stand us in good stead.

Kitty and her ragtag company went one way through the palms; Nathaniel and I went the other. We ignored the stairs this time, kept to ground level. Away to our right we heard roars and screams. So that was all right: Nouda hadn't gone anywhere.

What's the plan? My thought flitted through Nathaniel's mind.

We need to draw Nouda off, get him away from the commoners before we attack. How can we do that?

I recommend goading. Goading usually works.

I'll leave that up to you.

The other spirits need to be dealt with too, I thought. *Before or after?*

Before. Or they'll kill the commoners.

You control the Staff. I'll keep us moving. I warn you, we're going to have to be pretty mobile for this.

He made a dismissive gesture. *I can cope with a few leaps and bounds.*

Ready, then?

---

[3] Faquarl wasn't a sly old equivocator like Tchue; he prided himself on blunt speaking. Mind you, he *did* have a weakness for boasting. If you believed all his stories, you'd have thought him responsible for most of the world's major landmarks as well as being adviser and confidant to all the notable magicians. This, as I once remarked to Solomon, was a quite ridiculous claim.

The others will be in position. Yes, let's g—Oooooh—

I hadn't tried flying up to now, since it took a lot of energy, but this was the big one, this was where everything counted. And Faquarl had seemed to manage it well enough. So without further ado, I lifted us off the path, up beside the palms. For a nasty moment I thought the boy was going to drop the Staff. For an even nastier moment I thought he was going to be sick. But he held on to one and held in the other.

What's the matter with you?

Never . . . never flown before.

This is nothing. You should try looping the loop on a carpet. That would really make you green.[4] Okay, enemy's coming in sight. Staff at the ready . . .

We soared up over the palm trees. Electric lights shone down upon us. All around stretched the great glass dome; beyond it was the greater dome of night. And there ahead—the open space, with huddled prisoners and spirit guards much as before. Perhaps there were slightly *fewer* prisoners this time; it was hard to tell. But surprisingly little had changed. The reason for this stood writhing on the roof of the carousel.

Poor Nouda was having a *terrible* time with his host. Makepeace's body just wasn't up to scratch. From almost every surface, protuberances of one sort or another were zealously poking, carving the clothes to ribbons. There were horns, spines, wedges, flanges, wings, tentacles, and polyps of a dozen hues. Other bulges remained beneath the skin, deforming it

---

[4] It was an odd historical fact that the British magicians had no interest in magical flying, being inclined (wisely, it must be said) to trust to mechanical means instead. But other cultures had no qualms about fusing djinn with inanimate objects: the Persians went in for carpets; certain down-at-heel Europeans went by mortar and pestle. Venturesome Chinese magicians even tried their hand at riding *clouds*.

into rippling crests and valleys, so that the human contours were almost entirely blurred. The old legs had been joined by three others, of varying stages of development. One arm seemed to have gained a second elbow joint—it swung to and fro in complex agitation. The face was contorted like a puffer fish's. Small barbs extended from the cheeks.[5] The eyes had disappeared in gouts of flame.

The mouth, which now swept round from ear to ear, let out a piteous roaring. "The pain of it! All around me is the pinch of iron! Bring Faquarl here! Bring him here before me. His advice has been most—ah!—*most* unsatisfactory. I wish to reprimand him."

The spirit in the body of Rupert Devereaux spoke cringingly from below. "We do not know where Faquarl is, Lord Nouda. He appears to have departed."

"But I gave the strictest instructions—he is—ah!—to attend me while I feed! Oh—there is such an ache inside my belly— a void that must be quenched. Bolib, Gaspar—bring me another brace of humans, that I might distract myself."

It was at this moment that Nathaniel and I, flying down from on high, with the air buffeting against us and our coat billowing in our wake, shot three spirits with a triple blast. We did it so fast, so precisely, that the humans trembling nearby scarcely noticed they had gone.

The other spirits looked up. The ceiling lights dazzled them: their retorts went wide, arcing out harmlessly beneath the glass. We swooped low. The Staff flared, once, twice—another two hybrids vanished. A turn—so sharp that Nathaniel was, for an instant, horizontal in the air; a sudden gut-churning drop as a

---

[5] N.B. I'm still talking about the face here.

Disembowelment flittered overhead. Another shot—this one missed the target. Gaspar, the spirit with the unenviable fate of occupying Rufus Lime, had himself taken to the air. He climbed toward us, firing Detonations. We banked, flew behind a knot of trees; as we emerged above them, their canopy burst into livid flames. Below us, the humans were suddenly possessed by panic; they split in myriad directions. Out of the corner of our eye we saw Kitty and the magicians breaking from the trees.

Up on the roof of the carousel Nouda was swaying from side to side in some annoyance. "What is this intrusion? Who besets us?"

We flew past at a cheeky distance. "Bartimaeus here!" I called. "Remember me?"

A sudden twist high toward the dome; Rupert Devereaux's body had risen to meet us—blue fire gusted from his hands. Nathaniel's thought protruded. *THAT was your goading?* "Remember me?" *I could do better than that.*

I can't goad properly when I'm . . . concentrating on something else. We had risen almost to the ceiling glass; we saw stars glinting peacefully, far away. Then I dropped us vertically, like a stone. Devereaux's Spasm shattered the pane above; it arced out into the night. Nathaniel fired the Staff: it caught Devereaux a glancing blow upon the legs, setting them aflame. Tumbling and flailing, he spiraled down in a trail of smoke, plunged into the Mystic Tent of Prophecy and exploded in a burst of iridescent light.

Where's Lime? Nathaniel thought. *Can't see him.*

Don't know. Look at Nouda. He's our problem now.

Whether or not spurred to action by my coruscating wit, or simply through displeasure at seeing the remnants of his army slain, Nouda had suddenly exerted himself. Great green wings erupted from his back. Slowly at first, laboring under the disadvantages of his grotesque asymmetry, he stumbled to the lip of the carousel roof, hesitated like a fledgling on its maiden flight, then stepped off. The mighty wings beat once—too late. He'd already landed spread-eagled on the ground.

Get him, I said. *Get him NOW.*

We dropped down as fast as I could manage it, Nathaniel's jaw clamped tight shut with the speed of the descent. As we plummeted, Nathaniel lessened the constraints upon the entities of the Staff, opened it up as much as he dared. Their energies erupted, lanced down upon the wriggling body in a flower of light.

Keep it going, I said. *Keep it going. Don't leave anything to chance.*

I know. I'm doing it.

Our descent slowed, slowed. We hovered in midair. Below, a milky-white inferno raged: Nouda and the carousel were deep within it. Heat plumed outward, cracked the glass on nearby panes, burned the air around us. I erected a small Shield to deflect the full ferocity. The vibrations of the Staff grew greater, ran up our arm and shook within our skull.

What do you think? the boy thought. *Enough?*

Must be . . . No, play safe. A little longer.

I can't hold it for much—Ah!

I'd seen the shadow rising, sensed the movement in the air. I'd flung us aside. But the Detonation caught us, broke my Shield apart, struck us on the side even as we spun away. The boy cried out and I cried with him—for the first and only time I shared a human's pain. Something in the feeling—perhaps it was the dull immobility of the flesh, the way it just sat there, accepting the wound—made panic ripple through my essence.

The boy's mind teetered on the edge of consciousness. His fingers loosened on the Staff; its energies died back. I gripped it harder, spun it round, sent white fire lashing beneath the dome, to cut straight through the pursuing body of Rufus Lime. The halves dropped separately to earth. I sealed the Staff securely. We landed awkwardly amid a clump of palms and pot plants.

The boy was busy fainting. Our eyes were closing. I forced them open, and set my essence tingling through his system. *WAKE UP.*

He stirred. "My side . . ."

Don't look at it. We're all right.

And Nouda?

Well . . . that's not so good. Across the open space, beyond a number of scattered picnic tables and litter bins, the earth was broken, blistered. Where once the kiddies rode the carousel, a smoking crater split the earth. And in that smoke, something big and shapeless roared and stumbled, calling out my name.

"Bartimaeus! I order you, come here! I must chastise you for your impudence!"

It no longer looked anything much like a man.

"See how my strength grows, Bartimaeus, despite my pain! See how I shrug off this pathetic coat of flesh!"

Bartimaeus . . . my side . . . I can't feel it.

It's fine. *Don't worry about it.*

You're concealing something . . . That thought—what was it?

Nothing. I was thinking we have to get up; get away.

"Where *are* you, Bartimaeus?" the great voice called. "I shall add you to myself. It is an honor!"

My side feels numb . . . I can't—

Relax. I'll see if I can fly us out.

No, wait. What about . . . Nouda?

He's a big boy; he can fly himself if he wants to. Now—

We can't go, Bartimaeus. Not if he's—

He'll keep. We're going.

NO.

I tried to exert my energies to fly, but the boy was actively resisting—the muscles tensed, his will wrestled with my own. We half rose, crashed back down among the ferns, ended up leaning against a tree. One advantage of this: it concealed us from the many eyes of Nouda, now a squatting blackness that scuttled on the crater's lip.

You idiot, Nathaniel. Let me take over.

There isn't any point.

What do you—?

Is there? I read your mind. Just now.

Oh . . . that. Look, I'm no medic. Forget it. I could be wrong.

But you're not, are you? Tell me the truth for once.

A surreptitious rustling in the leaves. I turned our head, grateful for the opportunity to change the subject. "This'll cheer us up," I said heartily. "Here's Kitty."

Nathaniel

Her hair was matted and disordered. One side of her face was scratched. But Nathaniel was relieved to see that she seemed otherwise unharmed. Once again his relief revealed itself as anger. "What are *you* doing back?" he hissed. "Get away."

A scowl. "We've got the commoners clear," she whispered.

"And it was no small task. Check out what one of them did to me." She pointed at the scratch. "Nice bit of thanks that is. Anyway, I had to come back to see how you were ... doing. ..." Her eyes dropped to rest on Nathaniel's side; they widened. "What the hell?"

"According to Bartimaeus," Nathaniel said blandly, "it's nothing to worry about."

She bent close. "Oh, God. Can you walk? We've got to get you out."

"Not yet." After the first pain, the numbness had spread fast. Nathaniel felt a little light-headed, but provided he remained still, leaning against the tree, his discomfort was minimal. His mind was clear, or at least it would have been had the djinni not been messing with his thoughts, trying to block out knowledge of his injury, trying to influence his decisions. He spoke quickly. "Kitty—the attack with the Staff failed. The thing's too strong. I tried it at maximum controllable power, but it wasn't enough. Nouda absorbed the energy."

"Well, then." She bit her lip. "We get you out. Then we think again."

"Bartimaeus," he said. "What will happen if we leave Nouda now? Speak honestly."

The djinni's answer was delayed by a colossal crashing and rending sound from somewhere behind them. "In time," Bartimaeus said, speaking through Nathaniel's mouth, "Nouda will become bored with the manifold delights of the 'One World Exhibition.' He will turn his attention to the rest of London. He will feed on its people, and so swell in size and power; this growth will further stimulate his hunger until either the city lies barren, or he bursts. That honest enough for you?"

"Kitty," Nathaniel said. "I have to stop the demon now."

"But you can't. You just said so. Even at full power, the Staff failed."

"Maximum *controllable* power, I said. There's one way of getting more energy from it, and that's by removing Gladstone's safeguards—the spells that bind the Staff. All—no, wait, let me finish—*all* its power would be unleashed in one fell swoop." He smiled at her. "I think *that* might give Nouda pause."

The girl shook her head. "I don't buy it. Who's to say it won't just make him even stronger? Now, Bartimaeus; can't you—?"

"There is *one* other factor to be taken into the equation," Nathaniel said. With some difficulty, he lifted the Staff and gestured toward the roof. "What's this building made of?"

"Glass."

"And . . ."

"Ah," the djinni's voice cut in at once. "You know, reluctant as I am to say it, he might actually have a point there."

"Iron," Nathaniel said. "Iron. And Nouda, being a spirit, is not protected against it. If the Staff is broken, and it all comes crashing down on him . . . What do you think, Bartimaeus?"

"It might work. But there's one small flaw."

Kitty made a face. "Exactly. How do you break the Staff without being harmed? And what about the roof-fall?"

Nathaniel stretched; his neck felt cold and stiff. "Leave that to me. We'll be all right."

She looked at him. "Okay . . . Fine. I'll do this with you."

"No, you won't. Bartimaeus's protective Shields won't extend to you as well. *Will* they, Bartimaeus?"

"Um . . . no."

"We'll be all right," Nathaniel said again. His mind drifted a little; he felt the djinni prompting him. "Look," he said, "I've got seven-league boots on. We'll catch you up. Just get out now and keep on running."

"Nathaniel . . ."

"Better go, Kitty. Nouda will leave the palace soon, and the chance will be gone."

Kitty stamped her foot. "No way. I'm not going to allow this."

Her defiance warmed him. He grinned at her. "Listen—I'm the magician. You're the commoner. *I'm* the one who orders *you* about, remember?"

She scowled. "Sure you'll be able to use the boots?"

"Of course. No problem."

"So I'll see you both outside? Promise?"

"Yes."

"Yes. Now—*go*."

She turned slowly, with reluctance; then spun back to him, grasping at her neck. "The Amulet! It'll keep you safe!" She held it out, spinning on its chain. The jade stone glinted softly.

Nathaniel felt a great weariness. "No. That won't be any good for me."

Tiny glints of light shone in the corners of her eyes. "Why—why not?"

"Because," Bartimaeus's voice broke in, "it's so powerful a charm. It might absorb too much of the Staff's energy and enable Nouda to escape. The best thing you can do is take it, and wear it, and go now." His voice echoed silently in Nathaniel's head. *How's that?*

Not bad.

He looked at Kitty. She had halted with the Amulet outstretched; her eyes searched Nathaniel's face. He saw her aura shining all about them, picking out everything in clear, unblemished detail—the tree bark, the veins upon the leaves, the stones and grass about their feet. He felt himself bathed within it. His weariness departed.

He pushed himself away from the tree, tapped the Staff upon the ground. It flared into life. "See you later, Kitty," he said.

She lowered the Amulet around her neck and smiled. "See you. You too, Bartimaeus."

"Good-bye."

Then she was gone among the trees, away toward the eastern entrance, and Nathaniel was turning away from her, feeling the djinni's energy supporting his, turning to look across the great expanse at where the monstrosity shambled in its loneliness, tearing and sundering and crying out for food.

What do you think, Bartimaeus? he thought. *Do we go for it? I suppose we might as well. Got nothing better to do. Exactly.*

Kitty

Kitty was almost at the entrance when she heard the sound of a voice raised loud behind her, in a tone of imperious command. The answering roar the demon gave made the gravel rattle across the path and set the glass panes shivering in the dome. Then she was shoving open the door and falling out into the cold night air.

Her legs shook with the effort; her arms were as weak and ineffectual as in a dream. Down the steps she went and away through the ornamental garden, stumbling through tilled soil, veering wildly round low hedges, until she reached the open expanse of park.

The light from the great Glass Palace shone on her back; she saw her shadow stretching out ahead of her upon the illuminated grass. Away, away . . . if she could get beyond the lights, into the darkness, perhaps then she would rest. She drove herself on, slowing all the while, as her breathing became ever shallower and her muscles ever more labored, until finally, despite her fury and desperation, she came to a limping halt.

At that same moment she was conscious of a noise, of a dull bulb of sound that seemed almost to swallow itself, flaring and subsiding on the instant. The grass she stood on rose and fell in a little tremor that passed away into the dark. Kitty turned toward the Glass Palace, sinking to her knees; she was just in time to see its orange glow eaten from within by a dazzling swell of whiteness, which rose up and outward, through the margins of the dome, shattering each and every pane of glass so that the shards exploded into the night. The whiteness hid the palace; it streamed on across the ornamental gardens, ate away the remaining distance and engulfed Kitty, knocking her backward with its force. The Amulet of Samarkand fell hard against her face; dimly she saw it glowing, drawing in the raging energies. All about her was a fearful rushing. All about her, grass burned.

Then, with equal suddenness, the buffeting ceased, the air was raw and still.

Kitty opened her eyes; with some difficulty, she propped herself upon her elbows.

It was very dark. Somewhere, at an unknown distance, a great fire was burning, orange red. Outlined against it was a complex mess of metal, twisting, bending, fragile as a net of wire. As she watched, it crumpled in upon itself, growing dense and darkly packed. With the faintest of sighs, it subsided into the flames, which rose up to meet it, licked against the sky and gradually fell back.

Kitty lay there, watching. By and by tiny flecks of glass came tumbling silently out of the night. Within minutes the earth was glittering like frost.

37

At nine-thirty in the morning, precisely two days and five hours after the explosion in St. James's Park, the Interim Council of the British government gathered for an emergency meeting. They occupied a pleasant committee room in the Ministry of Employment, which had been largely undamaged by the Whitehall fires. Pale sunlight filtered through the windows; tea, coffee, and sweet biscuits were in substantial supply. Ms. Rebecca Piper, who presided, directed proceedings with crisp efficiency. Certain matters were immediately attended to: the provision of funds for the care and treatment of the injured, and the annexation of two military hospitals for the same purpose. A subsidiary committee, with direct access to the Treasury, was then established to begin restoration work on the city center.

Next came issues of Security. A junior minister gave his report. Four demon hybrids were known to be still at large; all had been driven from the urban areas into rural zones beyond. Imps kept track of their wandering and went ahead to organize evacuations where necessary. Soon expeditionary forces would be assembled to remove the threat. This response was complicated by the near total destruction of the Night Police and the disappearance, presumed death, of its leader, Ms. Farrar. The junior minister hoped that a new, fully human, police force might presently be established, and requested authority to begin recruitment, ideally from among the commoners.

At this the commoners' representatives interrupted the

discussion to demand resolution of an equally important issue—the return of the troops from America. They cited, as support for their position, the imminent likelihood of rebellions among the occupied states of Europe, and the strong possibility of renewed attacks on London. They hinted that failure to accede to their request would result in widespread strikes and rioting, which would hit the interim government hard. Their air of grim truculence aroused the passions of several magicians, who had to be physically restrained. Ms. Piper, banging her gavel repeatedly upon the table, restored order only with the help of the acting Secretary, Mr. Harold Button. He added his voice to the commoners' cause, giving, at length, several historical examples where faltering empires had been saved by their loyal troops.

After heated debate Ms. Piper put the issue to a vote. By a tight margin, authority was given to order the withdrawal of troops from America. At this the commoners' representatives asked for a recess, that they might give the news to the people waiting in the street outside. Permission was given; the Interim Council disbanded, and Mr. Button ordered himself more tea.

Kitty, who had watched all this from a chair beside the window, stirred and escaped into the corridor. The heat of variant opinions had given her a headache.

She had declined Ms. Piper's offer, the previous morning, of a seat among the Council. Quite apart from the strangeness of the notion, of sitting with magicians as an equal, she knew she did not have the energy required. If the endless debates she'd witnessed back at the Frog Inn were anything to go by, anyone wishing to take part in a more open system of government would need qualities of supreme patience and endurance.

Kitty, for the present, had neither of these in great supply. But she did put forward Mr. Button's name, as a surviving magician with a broader view of things than many. Through her contacts at The Frog she was also able to suggest several prominent commoners whose presence might give the Interim Council more validity. After that she had requested a private room, and retired for sleep.

Late in the afternoon she had woken and made her way back to St. James's Park. She pushed through the temporary barricades and entered the dead zone, where purple threads of residual magic hung above a vast circle of hard, black ground, crisp as burned carpet. Glass crunched beneath her shoes. The air was foul. Only with the Amulet held tightly in her hand could Kitty feel entirely safe.

At the center of the zone the remnants of the palace hulked dark and tangled against the autumn light. A few spurs of iron protruded; most were molded together in a complex weft, like giant brambles—choked and impassable. Magical vapors clung low about them, motionless, as if fused to earth. Their acrid taint made Kitty cough.

She stood there quietly for a time.

"So much for your promises," she said at last.

No answers sounded from the ruins. Nothing stirred. Kitty did not linger. With slow steps, she returned to the living world.

At one o'clock, when the Council broke for its lunchtime recess, Ms. Piper went in search of Kitty. She discovered her sitting alone in the ministry library, intermittently flicking through an atlas and staring into space.

The magician flopped down opposite, her face heavy with

vexation. "Those delegates are being quite *impossible*," she cried. "Impossible! Not content with forcing through the American motion, by tactics tantamount to blackmail, they have just informed me that they now object to us using imps for surveillance of the ports. Though it is manifestly in the national interest! They say it 'contravenes the rights of the workers there,' whatever *that* might mean." She gave a little pout. "It is blatant posturing! Mr. Button has just thrown a bun at them."

Kitty shrugged. "Security's important, but so's the trust of the people. Spies, vigilance spheres—all that's going to have to change. As far as the ports go, you'll just have to argue it out with them, I suppose."

"Are you *sure* we can't persuade you to take part?" Ms. Piper said. "You would be a perfect intermediary between us and the more . . . extreme factions."

"Sorry," Kitty said. "I'm tired. I'd just get stroppy. You'd be packing me off to the Tower by nightfall."

"I hardly think so!" Ms. Piper seemed suddenly thoughtful. "Mind you, some of those delegates . . . The idea *is* tempting . . ." She shook her head. "What am I saying? So then, Ms. Jones, I see you have an atlas out. Does this indicate your plans?"

"I don't know," Kitty said slowly. "I think, maybe, when things calm down a little on the Continent, I'll go abroad for a while. I've got a friend to visit in Bruges, and after that I'd like to travel a bit, see the world. I hope it will help me regain my health." She pursed her lips; looked toward the window. "Perhaps I'll go to Egypt. I've heard a lot about it. I don't know. It all depends."

"You wouldn't care to continue your magical studies here? Mr. Button speaks highly of your aptitude, and we have a conspicuous lack of talent in the government. We could recommend some tutors."

Kitty shut the atlas cover; spirals of dust rose up and drifted in the light. "You are very kind, but that door's closed to me now. My studies were always directed toward summoning one particular . . ." She paused. "I had one particular objective in mind. And two nights ago Nathaniel accomplished it for me. In all honesty, I wouldn't know how to follow on from that."

There was silence in the room. All at once Ms. Piper looked at her watch and gave a little cry. "Recess is almost over! I must go. Heaven knows whether we can make any headway this afternoon." She sighed heavily as she stood. "Ms. Jones, after a single morning I am already close to throttling the commoners' entire delegation. A single morning! And we are barely started. The outlook could hardly be worse. I really don't believe we shall be able to cooperate at all."

Kitty smiled and sat back in her chair. "Keep trying," she said. "It's possible. Not easy, but it's possible. You'll be surprised what you manage to achieve."

38

Dying was the simple part. Our main problem was catching Nouda's attention.

We stood, the two of us, in our single body, directly beneath the middlemost dome. This was the place to lure him to, the epicenter, the place of maximum iron. But Nouda was too big, too noisy, too confused and desolate to be easily lured. Back and forth he lurched on his mess of limbs, trampling stalls and kiddies' rides and stuffing trees at random into his gaping mouth. He undertook this serious work with admirable conviction, and none of his eyes were turned our way.

Flying was out for us now. Even bounding would be a stretch. It took most of my remaining energies to keep the boy upright. Left to his own devices, he'd have crumpled to the floor.

So we stopped where we were, and shouted instead. Or at least I did, with the kind of cry that triggers Tibetan avalanches.[1] "Nouda! It is I, Bartimaeus, Sakhr al-Jinni, N'gorso the Mighty and the Serpent of Silver Plumes! I have fought a thousand battles and won them all! I have destroyed far greater entities than you! Ramuthra fled before my majesty. Tchue cowered in a crack in the earth. Hoepo the Thunder Snake ingested his own tail and so swallowed himself rather than taste my fury! So then, I challenge you now. Come face me!"

---

[1] When shouted from *Nepal*. *That's* how loud it was.

No answer. Nouda was busily munching on some of the exhibits in the Grotto of Taxidermy. The boy ventured a tentative thought. *Does that count as a goad? It was essentially straightforward boasting, wasn't it?*

Listen, a goad's anything that provokes or incites an enemy, and— Oh, look, it didn't work, did it? We're running out of time. Another few steps and he'll break outside.

Let me have a go. The boy cleared his throat. "Cursed demon! You have met your end! The Shivering Fire awaits you! I shall spread your vile essence across this hall like . . . um, like margarine, a very thick layer of it. . . ." He hesitated.

Ye-es . . . I'm not sure he'll pick up on that analogy. Never mind, keep going.

"Cursed demon—*attend to me!*" The pity of it was that the boy's voice was desperately faint and growing fainter. *I* could barely hear it, let alone Nouda. But he finished up with a very effective extra, namely a bolt of force from the Staff that jabbed Nouda sharply in the rear. The great spirit responded with a roar; he rose up, limbs twitching, bulb eyes questing. All at once he saw us and sent multiple bolts crashing all around. His aim was lousy. One or two landed a few meters distant, but we stood firm. We did not budge.

The great voice: "Bartimaeus! I *see* you. . . ."

The boy whispered something in reply, too weak to hear. But I read his mind, spoke the words for him. "No! I am Nathaniel! I am your master! I am your death!"

Another burst of white energy pricked Nouda's essence. He hurled a stuffed bear aside and turned in ponderous wrath. He came crawling toward us—a colossal shadow, alien to this world, sundered from the other, blocking out the light.

Now that's what you call a proper goad, Nathaniel thought.

Yeah, it wasn't bad. Right, wait till he's on top of us, then we break the Staff.

The longer it takes, the better. Kitty—

She'll get out, don't worry.

The boy's strength was failing, but his resolution was undaunted. I felt him summon his remaining powers. Steadily, calmly, muttering under his breath, he loosed the bonds restraining Gladstone's Staff until, all at once, the hopes of the entities trapped inside were raised: they pushed, strained, pressed against the remaining loops of magic, desperate to be free. Without my assistance, Nathaniel could not have controlled them—they would have instantly broken through. But Nouda was not yet where we wanted him. I held the Staff in place. There was nothing now to do but wait.

According to some,[2] heroic deaths are admirable things. I've never been convinced by this argument, mainly because, no matter how cool, stylish, composed, unflappable, manly, or defiant you are, at the end of the day you're also dead. Which is a little too permanent for my liking. I've made a long and successful career out of running away at the decisive moment, and it was with some considerable regret, as Nouda bore down upon us, in that soaring tomb of iron and glass, that I realized I didn't actually have this fallback option. I was bound to the boy, essence to flesh. We were going out together.

The nearest I'd ever come to this dubious last-stand business before was with Ptolemy—in fact, he'd only prevented it with his final intervention. I suppose, if my old master could have seen me now, he'd probably have approved. It was right up his street, this: you know—human and djinni united, working

---

[2] Generally those who don't have to do it. Politicians and writers spring to mind.

together as one, etc, etc. Trouble was, we'd taken it all a bit too literally.

Bartimaeus . . . The thought was very faint.

Yes?

You've been a good servant. . . .

What do you *say* to something like this? I mean, with death bearing down and a 5,000-year career of incomparable accomplishment about to hit the fan? The appropriate response, frankly, is some sort of rude gesture, followed up by the loudest of raspberries, but again I was stymied—being *in* his body made the logistics too cumbersome to bother with.[3] So, wearily, wishing we had some kind of maudlin sound track, I played along. *Well, um, you've been just dandy too.*

I didn't say you were perfect . . .

What?

Far from it. Let's face it, you've generally managed to cock things up.

WHAT? The bloody cheek! Insults, at a time like this! With death bearing down, etc. I ask you. I rolled up my metaphorical sleeves. *Well, since we're doing some straight talking, let me tell you, buddy—*

Which is why I'm dismissing you right now.

Eh? But I hadn't misheard. I knew I hadn't. I could read his mind.

Don't take it the wrong way . . . His thought was fragmented, fleeting, but his mouth was already mumbling the spell. *It's just that . . . we've got to break the Staff at the right moment here. You're holding it in check. But I can't rely on you for something as important as this. You're bound to mess it up somehow. Best thing is . . . best*

---

[3] Well, try giving yourself a rude gesture. It just doesn't work, does it?

thing is to dismiss you. That'll trigger the Staff automatically. Then I know *it'll be done properly.* He drifted. He was having trouble keeping awake now—the energy was draining unhindered from his side—but with a final effort of will, he kept speaking the necessary words.

Nathaniel—

Say hello to Kitty for me.

Then Nouda was upon us. Mouths opened, tentacles slashed down. Nathaniel finished the Dismissal. I went. The Staff broke.

A typical master. Right to the end, he didn't give me a chance to get a word in edgeways. Which is a pity, because at that last moment I'd have liked to tell him what I thought of him. Mind you, since in that split second we were, to all intents and purposes, one and the same, I rather think he knew anyway.

Acknowledgments

My thanks to Laura Cecil, Delia Huddy, Alessandra Balzer, and Jonathan Burnham; to the late Rod Hall; and to everyone at Random House, Hyperion, and Miramax. And to Gina, most of all.